MW00327939

A
LITRPG NOVEL

SKY REALMS

ONLINE

SILVER PEAK

TROY OSGOOD

AETHON
BOOKS

ALSO IN THE SERIES

PROLOGUE

HE AWOKE WITH A START, IMMEDIATELY CHECKING HIS STATUS bars.

All were full, even Vitality.

A good and full night's rest. So why had he awakened so abruptly? A nightmare? There was nothing that he could recall. If there had been, it was fading fast.

Something had awoken him, but what?

Listening carefully, he heard no sounds. As it should be.

The tower was empty.

As it should be.

No one could find it, not without a key map.

He was safe and isolated.

Just how he wanted it.

For now.

It wouldn't last. He knew it. Eventually, his isolation would end. By his choice, just as he had designed it. But that didn't mean he had to like it. He'd been alone for so long, nothing but his research, that he was not looking forward to the day it ended.

But it was not today.

He glanced out the glass window and saw the familiar star-filled night sky. Dark shapes blocked out the stars, islands floating in the air. Still a couple hours until the sun would start to rise, he decided to get out of bed. He was awake now, and there was always something that needed to be done.

Walking over to the window, pulling a robe on, he looked out into the night. Dark shadows hung below the window, the tower built right on the edge of the island. Each shadow was another island so far below that even the largest was small from this height.

The shattered and fractured world of Hankarth.

————

He paused as he passed the library, a room he had not entered in weeks, looking through the open stone archway. Books lined all of the circular walls, from floor to the very high ceiling. Ladders on steel runners gave access to the highest shelves. A gaslamp hung from the high ceiling above, smaller ones attached to the shelves at intervals along the walls, sending light throughout the room. In the middle of the room was a large table with six globes positioned around it.

Something about one of the globes caught his eye. It was showing a myriad of colors, constantly shifting, where the others were all a foggy gray.

Excited, he walked into the room, coming around to the front of the table. Made of pine, incredibly large and worn, cracks ran along its length. Spread out over it and held down in the corners was a large map. Parchment, cracked with age, the lines written upon it were still as crisp and clear as the day they had been drawn.

It was a map, a map of Hankarth and all the scattered islands. Because of the nature of the world, islands floating over other islands, there were no world maps. They were impossible to make, one landmass would always obscure another. Maps were fragments, notations that gave rough directions from one island to another.

But somehow this map showed the world in detail. No island obscured another, they all lay together like a giant puzzle, space separating them. It was like the islands were all at the same elevation, pieced together how they had once been with gaps between them that indicated the land that had fallen into the abyss below. Hundreds of lines, handwritten notes, covered the map, each island having dozens of sentences in a tight and small font.

In the middle of the map, where no island existed, was a large black metal spike. It pierced the map and the table but did not rip the paper. The cracks in the table spiraled out from the spike.

He ignored the map and the spike, instead focusing on the globe. Smooth, a ball made of clear crystal, in its depths there was the image of a lone tower at the top of a flat hill. Laying his hand on top, the image changed and shifted. It zoomed in on the tower, and he saw the bodies of what looked to be Boarin, humanoid boars, picked apart by scavengers. Tilting his hand, the image shifted again and moved, following a path into the tower. Up a couple flights of stairs, the image stopped on a room and rotating around, showing a chest in the middle of the wooden floor.

An open chest.

One of the maps had been found.

He smiled.

It was coming together. The plan he had worked so hard for, the designs he had impossibly worked and somehow created. It was starting.

Quickly he searched the large world map, locating the tower shown in the crystal. Finding it on the island called Cumberland, he looked around the area, searching for signs.

He concentrated on the many small villages and ruins that dotted the island.

But there was nothing.

With a sigh, knowing it would be even longer now, he stepped back from the table and its map and the spike. He turned and started to walk away when something on another island caught his attention.

Edin. Just to the northeast of Cumberland, it would have been floating above Cumberland on any other map. There on the southeastern edge was a new marking. A town, small and ruined, the old marking had changed. Before there had been the symbol for ruins, now there was a half-built house.

A Settlement Stone had been claimed.

He tapped his fingers against the aged table. Things were in motion and he had much to do.

The Sage, known as Bastian, smiled. Things were going to get very interesting.

PART ONE
THE VILLAGE

CHAPTER ONE

HALL LOOKED DOWN AT THE TOWN SITTING ALONE IN THE WIDE-open meadow, most of it sunken down and below the ground. Grass covered the roofs, the front walls mostly rotted away, the sunken dirt street overgrown with weeds. It looked ruined, abandoned. No one had lived there for years.

And it was now his.

Only five or so days after claiming the Settlement Stone of Skara Brae and the fight with Vertoyi, the Wood Elven Custodian of the Grove, and then defending the Gnomes of Greenheight Vale against the Spriggan, he still couldn't believe it. He was the Lord of a town. A small town, it would only support around one hundred if that, but it was still a town.

Or was it a village?

From the top of the ridge, called Breakridge, that separated the meadow from the rest of Edin, Skara Brae looked small and forlorn. Lonely. Its emptiness emphasized. He had a hard time imagining it as thriving at all. Why would anyone choose to live there?

The small village, sunken into the ground, was nestled in the middle of a wide meadow surrounded by mountains on the north and south and the high ridge on the east. The west side was the edge of Edin, nothing beyond but the sky and the long fall to the nothingness below.

A harsh, sometimes cold wind came off the open sky and cut through the meadow. It pushed along, funneled by the mountains. To the north, there were two plateaus cut into the mountainside. The higher had nothing on it, a river coming out of the mountain and falling to the next level below. That plateau contained a Druid's Grove and a Branch of the World Tree.

He had fought a battle there only days before, coming close to dying.

The river continued through a small pond, the Branch on an island in the middle surrounded by standing stones, and then fell down the side of the mountain again into another small pond before continuing to the ridge and ending in a larger pond at the base.

Small brooks flowed across the meadow, small groups of trees dotted the grassland.

The south mountains extended closer to the village itself, almost curling around a dense forest of pines, oaks, and other trees that rose up from the grade of the meadow, disappearing in the shadows of the mountains. Greenheight Vale, where the Valedale Gnomes lived.

A lot of land but isolated and cut off from civilization.

Auld, the city they had arrived at was in the southern part of Edin, over a week away and no roads connecting the two. It was all overland travel through moors and highlands. Dangerous lands as they knew of a Trow village in the area. A road did come west out of Auld, heading in Skara Brae's direction for a bit before turning more south. That one led to what would be the nearest city, Silver Peak Keep.

The mountains to the south of Skara Brae were known as the Thunder Growl Mountains. The name came from the way the wind tore through the valleys and gaps between them. A deep roar like an animal growling and loud like thunder. To the north were the Frost Tip Peaks, running from Skara Brae all along Edin's western edge to the north end of the island. The meadow containing the village was called Breakridge, the same name as the ridge itself. So named, said the Gnomes, because it created a break in the mountains. Two immense mountain ranges that covered the entire western edge of Edin and only a mile or so of meadow between the two.

It had taken a couple days to start to recover from the fight with Vertoyi, the former and corrupted Custodian of the Druid's Grove, and then the fight with the Spriggans after. Hall still wasn't fully recovered. His Vitality below maximum, and it wouldn't raise any higher. He needed a good night's sleep, or twenty, and there were no facilities in Skara Brae that would currently give that. They were comfortable in the village but it was not the same as staying at an Inn or in real beds with full meals.

The others in his small party were the same. They all had small bruises and aches that magical healing could not help. Only rest could.

It was an easy decision to make. They needed supplies and Hall needed to figure out what to do with his village. Leigh, the Human Druid who was the new Custodian, needed materials so she could start cleansing the corruption. Roxhard, the Dwarf Warden, and Sabine, the Human Witch, both needed training as they had leveled up after the fight with Vertoyi.

There were supplies to get, healing to be done, gear that needed repairing. The list was long and growing longer as Hall thought about what was needed for Skara Brae. At the minimum, they needed materials to build up enough of the village to make it livable for them. Or at least for him and Leigh.

The Druid was the new Custodian; she would be tending the Grove.

It was his town, and he intended to use it as a base of operation.

He hadn't had the conversation with Roxhard and Sabine yet if they intended to stay as well or move on. The Skara Brae Settlement Stone interface currently showed the two as part of the village's population.

Skara Brae Town Stats:
Lord: Hall
Status: Ruins
Morale: N/A
Government: N/A
Appointed Officials: N/A
Population: 4
Production: N/A
Faction: None
Allies: Gnomes of Valedale
Trade Partners: N/A
Enemies: N/A

Hall had a feeling that Roxhard would stay. He was starting to think of the Dwarf, really a fourteen-year-old kid in the body of a hundred-plus-year-old Dwarf, as a younger brother. And there was Roxhard's crush on Leigh to help motivate him. Sabine was a different story. He wasn't sure what her overall motivation was. He hoped she would stay. She could be a bit harsh at times, snarky, but she was an excellent Witch, knowing her class well. And overall Hall liked her, the first Player he had met and talked to after the Glitch.

The problem as Hall saw it: they were short on funds to do all that was needed. Each of them had a tiny bit of gold but it would go quickly. There was the emerald sunstone and some other jewels that could get a lot of gold, but those were for emergencies only. They needed coins to get everything they needed. Staying in Skara Brae would not help that problem.

They needed to go to Silver Peak Keep.

And probably spend a lot of time there.

Which was time away from Skara Brae.

With a sigh, Hall turned away from the village and started down the long switchback trail that led down into Edin's highlands. He walked under the stone arch, seeing the other three not that far down the trail along with Leigh's cow companion, Angus. He looked up into the sky and saw Pike, his dragonhawk, circling.

He'd only spent a handful of nights in Skara Brae, but it already felt like home.

———

They kept close to the mountains, not going too deep into the grassy hills of the highlands. The last time they had come this way, through the hills, they had encountered Trow in the fog. There was always fog in the mornings, most of the time burning off as the sun rose, but sometimes lingering.

The Trow had surprised them, and they had gotten lucky in their response. It had been a quick but brutal fight, and Hall did not want to press their luck. He wanted to avoid another ambush if possible. They were not at full strength, bruised still from the recent fights, gear in bad need of repair, and low on potions. The plan was to avoid combat on the journey to Silver Peak Keep. Once there, repaired and healed, it would be time to head out and start making some gold.

Hall knew all plans were destined to fail.

"We need a name," Roxhard said on their second day out from Skara Brae.

It was morning, just a couple hours after sunrise and a cold meal. The fire had died out in the middle of the night, and they had all woken chilled and damp. Hall wanted to get moving so they had not taken the time to light a fire. Now, they walked with cloaks pulled tight to ward off the morning's lingering chill.

"What?" Sabine asked.

Hall could barely hear them as he was twenty feet or so ahead, scouting and trying to avoid ambushes.

"A Guild name," Roxhard explained.

His voice was deep, rough like gravel. The body of a hundred- or so year-old Dwarf from the Stonefire clan, Roxhard was, in reality, a fourteen-year-old boy. Or used to be. After the Glitch that had trapped the minds of a couple dozen Players in the Sky Realms Online game, Roxhard was now truly a Dwarf. Just with the mind of a teenager.

A fine Warden for his age, Roxhard knew his class and his abilities. But Hall was worried about how the teenager was dealing with his new reality. It had to be tougher than an adult. Not only was Roxhard dealing with being trapped in Sky Realms Online, but he was also dealing with puberty and teenage awkwardness on top of it.

The Dwarf walked at the rear of the line, behind the women and the cow with the dragonhawk riding on its back. Angus mooed at Roxhard's suggestion.

"Angus agrees," he said with a chuckle.

Angus mooed again.

"There's four of us," Sabine said. "Why do we need that?"

"Isn't that what you do when you find a group of people you want to adventure with?" Roxhard asked, a bit embarrassed.

Sabine, a Witch, didn't answer. Either she couldn't think of a reply that defeated Roxhard's dubious logic or else she just didn't care. Hall felt it was the latter. Sabine was a hard one to get a read on. She was trustworthy, he knew that, but sometimes she could be arrogant, angry, and a bit mean.

But like Roxhard, she knew her class and abilities.

Both were Players, like Hall himself. They had all been from Earth, the real world, and had been gamers playing the VRMMORPG called Sky Realms Online. The most advanced game ever. During a play session, there had been a glitch, and they all awoke to find themselves now living in the game and back at Level One. Their minds had apparently, according to Electronic Storm, the developers, been downloaded into the game itself. They were now digital consciousnesses that were living in the gameworld.

Each dealt with it in their own ways. Sabine was angry and Hall suspected scared, which was where her meanness came from. Roxhard was scared and worried about his mother and brother. Hall wasn't sure what he was. Practical. He didn't really feel anything about not being in the real world and was starting to accept and even enjoy that he was now in Sky Realms and truly living the life. He didn't miss his old one.

Leigh, the fourth member of their party, was an NPC: a non-Player character, generated from the code of the game. But she was not like any NPC Hall had ever encountered in any game before. Her AI was like that of a real person.

Which is what Hall thought of her as.

He also thought he was developing feelings for her and her for him.

"Do they even have Guilds now?" Sabine asked.

"Why wouldn't they?" Roxhard responded. "Leigh?"

The Druid, as an NPC, had become their unofficial Wikipedia. She still found their lack of common knowledge strange, and Hall was afraid it would become too strange at some point. He feared the day she would think them too crazy and leave. But she answered their questions as best she could.

"Of course," she said. "That is how Factions are created. They start out as Adventuring Guilds, align with other like-minded Guilds and soon enough, a new Faction is born."

"Like the Greencloak Rangers?" Hall asked.

"Exactly," Leigh answered.

The Greencloak Rangers had been a Faction that Hall had joined in the previous game, before the Glitch. Their headquarters was on Edin, further north, near a town called Timberhearth.

"There are not many Guilds now," Leigh continued. "It's like the Skirmisher in Land's Edge Port said, there isn't much need for Adventurers. Most are Traders Guilds or Merchants Guilds. And as we saw in Land's Edge Port, the Class Guilds are still somewhat existing."

"I can see the benefits for a Merchants Guild," Sabine said. "But what are the benefits for others?"

"Allies, shared resources," Leigh replied with a shrug.

"How is a Guild formed?" Roxhard asked.

"Visiting a Councilor of Deeds and signing a Charter."

"There's one in Silver Peak Keep, right?" Roxhard asked excitedly.

Leigh nodded. "What would we call ourselves?" she asked with a smile. He couldn't see her, but Hall could hear it in her voice.

Hall could picture Roxhard smiling as well, glad that Leigh was engaging with him. The poor kid had a severe crush on her, where Hall was pretty sure she thought of him as a kid brother. Hall was just glad that she was including herself in the Guild idea of Roxhard's.

The four of them made an odd party. Warden, Skirmisher, Witch, and Druid.

"I don't know," Roxhard said, his voice never losing the enthusiasm. "Just think we should have a name. What do you think, Hall?" he asked.

Hall stopped, hand resting on a large boulder as he looked south along the edge of the mountains. The ground was hilly, rising and dropping with the slopes of the peaks. Rocks littered the grass, small bushes here and there. No trees but there were many further out. Bare patches of gray and white stone broke through the thin grass.

The same landscape for as far as he could see.

"I don't know," he finally answered. "I agree with you," he added when he really didn't care but it obviously made Roxhard happy. "So come up with something by the time we get to Silver Peak Keep."

CHAPTER TWO

THE CAVE WAS DARK, THE LIGHT ONLY PENETRATING TEN FEET or so into the dark opening. Not large, it was about ten feet wide and tall. Almost a perfect square, it was not a natural opening. Along the edges, there were hints of symbols carved into the rough face of the cliff, worn down by age and weather.

Hall ran his fingers over some of the symbols, not able to make any of them out. They were deep, large. The edges smoothed and rounded.

"I don't remember there being a cave here," Sabine said from the other side, running her fingers over the runes.

"Me either," Hall said and looked over at Roxhard, who just shrugged.

Hall had explored every inch of Edin in the original game, but he was finding that their new version was vastly different. Skara Brae itself; along with the meadow, forest, and Grove; were all new.

"I'm from the far side of Edin," Leigh said. "I have no idea about anything on this side of the island but that one there looks like a Firbolg symbol," she added, pointing at one of the clearer symbols.

Etched on Hall's side of the opening, it was about halfway up. Three inches tall, twice wide, there were two long lines over each other. Wavy, they looked to Hall like representations of a flowing river. Two more lines ran vertically at the third points, a break in each at the top to look like a lowercase i.

"What does it mean?"

It was Leigh's turn to shrug.

"Don't even know if it is Firbolg," she said.

Hall stepped back, looking into the cave. It looked to turn about fifteen feet in, thinning down to a smaller tunnel.

Four days of hard travel out from Skara Brae had brought them to the trail that had led to the cave. They had found the trail along the base of a mountain. It had cut into the stone, leading up into the mountains and curiosity, the bane of adventurers, had led them to follow it. At the end was the cave, only a half-mile of path and a couple switchbacks later. Hall thought they had turned back around so they were facing the highlands of Edin and not out toward the island's edge.

The passage had been smooth, both floor and sides, wide and level, gently sloping to the cave. The remnants of etchings lightly carved into the surface had been visible, designs that were worn down to be unrecognizable.

Someone, or something, had gone to a lot of trouble to carve the passage and the cave itself. In the original game, Hall knew it would have meant there was a dungeon within the mountain. That would mean quests and treasure. Did the same rules still apply?

There was only one way to find out.

"Should we?" Hall asked and pointed at the cave with his spear.

Sabine walked into the cave, just past the threshold and into the shadows. Taking a couple steps to the side so she could see down the turn, trying to look ahead, she shrugged.

"We need coin and experience," she said. "And caves usually mean dungeons, which means coins and experience."

"Is this a dungeon?" Roxhard asked. "You said this wasn't here before."

"It wasn't," Hall said. "Which means a new dungeon to explore." New. Something that they had not encountered playing Sky Realms Online before. *Which is what we've been dealing with on a daily basis now*, he thought but didn't say.

He had played Sky Realms Online since the beta testing and had been over every map in the game multiple times. He knew all the quest locations, all the dungeon locations. Ever since the Glitch, the new version of the game they found themselves trapped in was turning out to be something completely new and different. New skills. New quests. New and better NPCs, he thought with a glance toward Leigh.

Post-Glitch the developers had worked hard to give the trapped Players a new and more immersive experience. This cave had to be another example of that.

"There was a new patch coming, right?" Sabine said as Hall stepped further into the cave, taking the lead. "Maybe this cave was part of it."

Pike spread his wings, the dragonhawk lifting off Hall's shoulder to settle on Angus' back. He mooed softly as the dragonhawk's talons dug into the thick highlander cow's fur. Curling his wings in tight, Pike settled down.

"Which means it'll be high level," Roxhard pointed out.

"If it looks too tough, we'll back out," Hall said.

He looked at Leigh, who was studying the runes around the opening. Hall had started to notice that whenever the three Players had a conversation about the world outside the game, or even the inner workings of the game world, Leigh's attention would focus on something else. It was like she was ignoring the conversation.

Ignoring or programmed to ignore.

Hall pushed that thought away, not liking it. She was a person, the same as him, as far as he was concerned.

———

The doors were made of bronze. They stood twice as high as Hall's height and each was as wide as Roxhard's height. The tunnel had turned and continued for a hundred feet before ending in the great pair of doors.

Fitting tightly in the carved tunnel opening, there didn't appear to be an obvious way to open them, the seam between the panels barely noticeable. Smooth shadows played across the surfaces as the torches the party carried flickered. They held them up, trying to see into the shadows at the top of the doors, moving them along the edges. Nothing. No runes, no markings, no handles. Not even any hinges that they could see.

Roxhard had tried pushing on the doors. The heavy metal had not budged or even vibrated from the pressure.

"Are they even doors?" Sabine asked, frustrated.

She had a point. With no hinges or handles, the bronze doors were just plates set into the tunnel wall. Doors wanted to open. These appeared to be just a barrier.

Hall ran his fingers along the edge where the bronze met the stone of the tunnel. There was a gap there, thin with a slight draft. The bronze was not cut into the stone, which meant it could be moved. Or removed.

Running his fingers along the seam, he crouched low, examining the floor. Up close, he could feel a slight gap at the bottom edge of the bronze-like sides, and now that he felt it, he could see it. Barely. A quarter-inch, if that, he judged. Staying crouched, he shuffled to the middle where the joint between the doors was.

He had to bend down closer to make out what he was now seeing. Four grooves, only a half-inch wide, were cut into the smooth floor of the tunnel. An inch between each pair, a couple inches between each set. They were only an inch or so past the face of the door, which was why they had not been noticed before. The grooves were smooth, the edges rounded, as was the bottom. An arc.

"Here," he said drawing the other's attention.

"What is that?" Leigh asked.

"Tracks," Hall answered standing up and looking at the door again. "They open inward," he added, sure of it.

He was positive he had guessed right. If they could have gotten to the top of the doors, used the torches to drive away the shadows, he knew they would have seen a duplicate set of grooves. Top and bottom tracks.

Knowing the doors could move still didn't open them. But now, they were more motivated. There had to be a way to open them from the outside.

Torches moved about the tunnel, up and down the length, as they looked for anything out of the ordinary. No matter how small, they examined it. A rock outcropping alone in a span of smooth wall, each tried to move it someway. Any way. They crawled on their knees, moving the torches down low. Hall, the tallest, stretched as high as he could, moving the torch at Firbolg height.

An hour stretched into two and still nothing. Each was on their second or third torch.

"Give up?" Sabine asked, leaning against the wall.

She had given up a couple minutes before. The others, except Pike and Angus, who had fallen asleep in a corner, had kept searching, but Sabine had leaned against the wall and not moved. She was frustrated, angry.

"Time to move on," she said. "Silver Peak is still days away."

Hall knew she was right. This was pointless, but he still did not want to give up. Not yet. This cave, these doors, they existed for a reason. It could be simply that they did not have the quest associated with the doors. If that was the case, they would not find the quest here in the tunnel.

"I think she's right," Leigh said a minute or two later. Sighing, she stood up, stretching her back. "We know where this place is. We can try again on the way back home to Skara Brae."

Hall smiled. Leigh had called the village *home*. He knew she would live there, like him. As the Custodian of the Grove, she would need to. He could leave for lengths of time, but could she? He didn't like the idea of adventuring without her. It had only been weeks since they had met, but he had grown fond of her. The four of them were turning into a good party.

But she had called the village home. His village. Her home.

Roxhard stood in front of the doors, his own torch out and the light from the others barely reaching, rapping on the bronze plate with an iron-mailed knuckle. The metal on metal sound echoed through the tunnel, bouncing off the stone walls. *Tap, tap, tap.* The echo came back to them. The Dwarf tapped again, harder, leaning in closer.

"What the—" he exclaimed. "Check this out."

Hall stepped forward, holding the torch close. Roxhard tapped again. Hall saw nothing.

"What am I looking at?" he asked.

"Weird," Roxhard replied. "It's not doing it now."

With a shrug, Hall stepped away from the doors. He joined Leigh and Sabine further down the tunnel. The torches were all away from the Dwarf and the doors, the light not reaching, which was not a problem for Roxhard as he possessed *Dark Vision* from his Dwarven heritage. The two women gathered their travel packs from where they had been set down. Leigh was nudging Angus with a leather boot, trying to wake the cow. The tapping started up behind them again.

Hall was about to turn back, tell Roxhard to join them as it was time to go, when the Dwarf yelled louder.

"Get over here," he said, his voice filled with excitement.

With a sigh, Hall turned back, bringing the torch with him. Roxhard kept tapping on the bronze doors. At the edge of the torchlight, the Dwarf's whole fist struck the bronze, which seemed to ripple. A trick of the light.

"Dammit," Roxhard cursed as Hall got closer, the light from the torch burning bright.

He looked from the door to the torch in Hall's hand, tapping on the bronze panel lightly. He studied the torch and the door while Hall stood there impatiently.

"Get rid of the torch," the Dwarf finally said, his voice filled with a confidence it usually lacked.

With a shrug, Hall walked back to the women and handed Sabine the torch. He turned away stepping out of the limits of the light. He paused, letting his own racial bonus acclimate to the shadows. For him, as a Half-Elf, the *Limited Night Vision* turned the world into gray and black shadows. There were no details, everything just shadows upon shadows. Lighter gray on darker gray on lighter black on darker black. The ambient light from the torches enough to activate the sight so he could walk, make out the shapes, but not enough to truly know the details of things. Inside a dark tunnel carved from rock with barely any torchlight, it was enough.

Standing next to Roxhard in the dark, he watched as the shadowed shape of the Dwarf's hand struck the black of the bronze door. He had expected nothing, just like before, but was surprised.

Ripples spread out from where Roxhard struck. The metal itself moved like a small wave. What he had thought a trick of the light before was something shifting within the bronze.

"The hell," Hall exclaimed, running his leather-gloved

hand over the area Roxhard had hit. It felt smooth, the same as before.

"See," Roxhard said proudly. "I knew it was doing something weird. It was the light," he added. "You couldn't see it with the light."

"See what?" Sabine asked, the torch coming closer.

"Stop," Hall said, holding his hand out toward the women. "Don't bring the torches closer."

He reached out and struck the bronze with a leather-clad fist. He saw the rippling effect and felt it. The door gave way from his impact. It flowed away from his fist. There was resistance but not as much as expected.

Somehow, the lack of light made the doors less solid.

It was a puzzle. The doors becoming liquidy had something to do with how they opened.

But what?

Hall moved closer to the joint where the two panels of bronze met. He ran his hands over both sides where he imagined door handles would be for a Human or an Elf. The two races were essentially the same size, Elves being the taller of the two but only by a foot. Their door handles, tables and chairs were all functionally the same height as those of the Humans. The other races of Hankarth were all noticeably taller or shorter, which affected the height of their furniture and doors.

Tapping in the general area of where a door handle would be, Hall saw the ripple effect again but it was more pronounced. Instead of the small movements like elsewhere in the door, he could see the ripples were larger than before. A half-inch or so off the edge of the door the bronze waves moved away from the spot Hall had struck, flowed away. The liquid metal spread away from the impact zone, thinning the door and revealing a handle.

Built into the door itself, the handle was an inch in diameter. Made of a dark rock, onyx or obsidian, it ran up and down about six inches. Just long enough for a man to get his hand around, the metal flowing away on the back enough for fingers to slide around the handle.

"You should have the honors," Hall said, stepping away and motioning Roxhard to take his place.

The Dwarf moved to where Hall had been. He had to stretch up but the area was not out of reach. Dwarves were shorter but not that short. He struck the area Hall had, the metal flowing away and revealing the dark rock handle. Grabbing it, his fingers barely fitting around in the armored glove, Roxhard pushed on the door.

With a groan, it started to slide, moving easily. There was no squeaking of wheels, the door moving back smoothly. Roxhard only pushed it open a foot or so, enough for them to squeeze through.

He stepped back, the room beyond in total darkness.

CHAPTER THREE

HALL LED, STEPPING PAST THE DOOR AND INTO THE ROOM beyond. Roxhard followed. They both moved in a different direction away from the door, weapons drawn and ready.

The torches were in the corridor behind the partially open door, Leigh and Sabine pulling further back with the light.

He looked around with his limited night vision, just enough light leaking through the open door to allow it to work. They were in a room, almost perfectly square. The walls were smooth, the floor and the ceiling were as well. About twenty by twenty, with a ceiling as high, there was a wagon wide opening on the far wall. Another corridor leading off from the room, lost in shadow too deep to see through. There didn't appear to be anything on the walls, no writing or decoration.

Reaching out, he didn't feel stone like he had expected. Instead, he felt metal. Bronze like the doors, or copper. He wasn't sure. Tapping on the wall, there were no ripples. A solid wall. He could hear Roxhard on the other side doing the same.

They reached the opening at the same time, standing to the side and looking down the tunnel.

"How long is it?" Roxhard asked.

Hall shrugged, realizing the Dwarf probably couldn't see the motion and answered. "No idea, but let's find out."

———

The torch's light flickered against the bronze walls, the metal reflecting it and casting odd shadows as it played across the smooth surface. Like the room, which they thought of as an entrance chamber, the corridor was sheathed in the same metal. This new corridor was only about ten feet wide and ten feet high. Smaller than the first rocky tunnel and the room.

They had gone about a hundred feet, and it showed no sign of ending. Hall felt a slight slope to the floor. They were heading down, deeper into the mountain.

"I don't recognize the design," Sabine said. "Never saw anything like this before."

Hall agreed. There were a couple dozen dungeons in Sky Realms Online but none had looked like this. Renegade Dwarven halls dug deep into the mountains, Elven halls carved out of giant trees, dragon caves and all manner of other creatures and their lairs. Each had their own unique look and designs, but there had never been anything like this. Blank, no ornamentation, sheathed in bronze.

He thought about the expansion that had been forthcoming, which was going to introduce a new kingdom, the Desmarik Republic. Sabine had thought the cave might have had something to do with that. Could this new design be reflective of that new kingdom? This cave and dungeon some kind of way to unlock access to that kingdom and their lands?

Ahead he could see the tunnel finally ending. Dark shadows filled the space beyond indicating a wider and larger room. Slowing, they stepped carefully out of the tunnel. Hall's foot slid across the threshold, and he heard a click.

They all stopped, statue still.

More clicks sounded from deeper in the room, so large that the light of the torches could not show any details, the ends lost in shadow. The clicking came from both sides, sounding along the wall, echoing through the room. Hall braced himself waiting for the trap to be sprung.

The clicking continued, the sound reminding Hall of a lighter being flicked. The two ends seemed to come together in a far wall, becoming one large click. Light bloomed, a small pinpoint over a good distance away. More light as what looked to be globes ignited along the wall. The globes were spaced every ten feet and not all bloomed with light. It seemed every other globe stayed dark, sometimes two or three in a row.

It cast weird shadows across the room, revealing the details in shadows and light. The last globes ignited on either side of the tunnel opening, and they got their first good look of the room beyond.

The globes were mounted to the wall about ten feet high, clear with a bright flame flickering in the center. They cast light in all directions, a diffused light that didn't hurt to look at but spread deep into the room. If they had all been working, the room would have been brightly lit. As it was, they were able to see good enough.

Forty or so feet long, twenty feet to the smooth metal ceiling, the side walls twenty feet away. Shelves lined the walls, more stood in rows in one corner of the room. Tables filled another corner. Large metal tables on some kind of hinge that allowed them to move so they could be lying flat or straight up. Smaller workbenches filled the rest of the space. All were made of metal, bronze, and other materials.

From where they stood, there did not appear to be any more doors. Just the room. Empty.

"What is this place?" Sabine asked.

Hall moved over to the nearest globe, examining it, craning

his neck to look up. About a foot in diameter, made of glass or similar material, it was filled with a swirling fog with a small flame on a wick suspended in the middle. Wires, or piping, or something that he couldn't identify ran from the wick and out the backside of the globe through the metal attachment that held it to the wall.

That must have been what the clicking was, Hall thought. *Some kind of power turned on when we crossed the threshold.*

"Look," Leigh exclaimed and pointed up.

Hall looked where she was pointing and saw the shadowed shape of a larger globe suspended from the ceiling, light reflecting off the metal. Now that he saw the one, there were three more, spaced evenly in the roughly square room. None of them worked.

"This looks like some kind of workshop," Roxhard said as he stepped deeper into the room.

Hall made to stop the Dwarf but didn't. They had already entered the room, activating the lights, and if there were traps, then it was too late to avoid them. If there had been, they would have been sprung by now. Roxhard was right; it did look like some kind of workshop. Which meant there would be no traps inside the space.

He hoped.

Even though he was pretty sure there were no traps, he kept Angus and Pike back at the entrance. The cow didn't know how to move carefully. He was a cow, big and clumsy, and Hall did not want Pike flying through the room until they had looked at it in more depth. The dragonhawk could fly off Angus' back quickly if needed.

As they moved about the space, they confirmed that it was empty. There were no books, no materials, on the shelves or the workbenches. The large tables had nothing laying on them. Two were lying flat while the other two were upright, thick leather straps hanging to the sides. Each was four or five feet wide and ten or so long, made of thick planks of wood sheathed and banded in the bronze metal.

Hall ran his fingers along the edges of the closest, lying flat. There were faint lines carved into the side. Swirls, straight lines, shapes.

"There are runes along the edge," he said.

He moved away from the table, toward the wall. There had to be more to the space. It was well protected. They were missing something.

"Oh no," Leigh said, her cry quiet but scared. "We need to leave. Right now."

He turned to her. The Druid was standing in the middle of the room, a clear space where there was no shelving or benches, a space framed by the rest of the room. Unlike the smoothness of the walls and floors everywhere else in the room, where she stood was covered in lines. A large circle, about ten feet in diameter, Hall realized as he moved closer. A circle within a circle, rings, still smaller ones stepping toward the middle. Between each ring were dozens of runes. Each swirl and line, different shapes, making a single character in the language of runes. There had to be hundreds written in the rings.

Runes had been one aspect of the game that Hall had never bothered to learn more of as they were a written language and every rune in the game was translated for ease of reading. Each race had a rune language, a way of communicating complex thoughts in a few symbols.

Within the game there had been other uses for runes, used by NPCs, to create a wide variety of magical effects. These were just for the Players' benefits as the runes were used to enhance the story of the game. If the developers needed a random magical effect that was not already covered in a Player or NPC Class Ability, then it was done by an NPC with some previously unknown runic magic.

Hall studied the runes in the circles, trying to count them all but quickly losing track. Some he recognized, having seen them on magical items or carved in dungeons, but most he did not. There was a mix of the different races' languages, each represented many times, along with many unknowns. Each ring was the same width, but having fewer and fewer runes as the circumference shrunk with each new ring until only a single rune remained in the last ring, dead center of the design.

"What's the matter?" Hall asked.

Leigh was staring at the single rune. There was hate in her eyes, anger and fear. Hall looked at the symbol, one he thought he knew but was not sure. It was an oval that looked cut in half, the two arcs remaining around two smaller lines laid horizontally. Above and below the oval were six lines, three at the top and three at the bottom, with two more at either side. To Hall, it looked like an eye surrounded by light.

Where had he seen it before?

Roxhard and Sabine had now come up to the giant circle, all four standing outside the largest ring. All four unwilling to step on the runes.

"Don't you recognize that symbol?" Leigh asked. She pulled her arms around herself, holding tight as if she was cold. "Everyone on Hankarth knows that symbol and who it is the mark of."

None of the three Players answered. Hall looked at the other two, blank stares and shrugs meeting his gaze.

"That's not a rune?" Hall finally asked.

"It's the Sage's mark," Leigh said, practically spitting the name out.

"Who?" Roxhard asked.

Hall knew that title. There had been only one person in the entire game that was called The Sage. The one NPC that actually seemed to age as Players leveled up and accessed new areas. The character that started many of the quest chains, that always seemed to show up at the start and end of World Events.

"Bastian," he said.

"Do not say that name," Leigh barked.

Hall stared at her, shocked. He had never heard such anger in her voice. The others looked surprised. No one spoke.

"Why?" Roxhard finally asked, drawing an angry look from the Druid.

Leigh sighed, taking a deep breath. She looked up at the ceiling and then the globes on the wall, seeing them with a new understanding. Glancing back at the large tables, she shuddered.

"No one speaks The Sage's name," she said after a minute of silence, the other three looking at each other worried. "He is not worthy of a name. This must be one of his," she added a little calmer, but still as angry. "One of his workshops. It is said that he has dozens scattered around the realms. Legends even say one on each island." Leigh was somewhat rambling, reciting stories from memory. "What atrocities did he create here?"

"Leigh," Hall started, reaching out and lightly touching her shoulder. "What—" he started to ask but she continued, ignoring him.

"It's been years," Leigh said, looking at the shelves. "There are no books, no reason for anyone to be here. We can go and forget we ever saw it."

"But we're not done exploring it," Sabine said, turning to look around. "Sure, it's empty but there has to be something here. There always is."

"We can't be here," Leigh said with some urgency.

"Why?" Sabine asked, annoyed.

"This is his workshop," Leigh replied exasperated, angry that they were not understanding.

"It's just a workshop," the Witch said, annoyed. "Why is it so vital we leave?"

"He is The Worldbreaker," Leigh said with a shudder.

CHAPTER FOUR

HALL CURSED, INVOLUNTARILY CLUTCHING HIS SPEAR AT THE mention of the name.

Roxhard stepped back, eyes darting around the room as if the person would appear. Showing up as if called.

Sabine looked at Leigh, confused.

"The Feardagh?" she asked. "What does the Dark Man need a workshop for?"

Now it was Leigh's turn to look confused. She looked from one to the other, seeing their lack of understanding. The Druid pointed down at the symbol in the center of the circle.

"No, not the demon," she said. "This is one of The Sages."

"Bast—" Hall started to say, holding up a hand and stopping as Leigh turned toward him sharply. "The Sage is not the Worldbreaker," he said. "The Feardagh caused Hankarth to fracture by pitting Surtr and Ymir against each other."

All Players knew the story of how Hankarth was turned from one world into the fractured islands it was today. There was a cutscene, the quality almost movie-like, when the game was first started. It said how the Dark Man, a demon known as the Feardagh convinced the elemental titans of fire and water to attack each other. For millennia, the elemental titans, primordial creatures of the planes each representing one of the four elements, had existed in an uneasy peace. None would use their great powers against the other, letting the lesser elementals wage war. It lasted until the Feardagh, at the command of the great demon Balor the Corruptor, somehow got the two titans to attack each other.

The resulting battle tore the world apart, fracturing Hankarth into dozens of smaller islands, all held together and floating by the magical roots of the World Tree, called the Branches.

"The Feardagh was the catalyst, his actions that caused the titans to fight. But it was The Sage that allowed the Feardagh to fracture the world."

It didn't make sense, Hall thought, looking at Sabine and Roxhard. They both looked as confused as Hall felt. For all their gaming years, Bastian the Sage had been a force for good in the world. He was a guider, directing the Players through the larger story of the world. Never participating himself, just pushing and prodding. That man would not have destroyed the world, he had always been working to keep it at peace, balanced.

Hall thought about all the quests he had done where Bastian had been involved. The more he thought about it, the more he realized now that not all of them had been what he would call good. They had all been for maintaining the fragile balance of Hankarth with the various kingdoms, islands, and monsters. Some had called for the destruction of magical artifacts used by power-mad lords. But some had been about thinning a tribe of Trow or Goblins, while others had been about sabotaging free cities or opposing kingdoms.

Was Bastian really all that good? He was mostly good, that was for sure, but there was enough evidence that the Sage's motives could not be considered completely pure or unselfish.

But to cause the fracturing? That, Hall had a hard time believing.

And the timeline didn't add up. The fracturing was almost a thousand years ago. Bastian had only been a couple hundred years old. Old, but not that old.

As much as it didn't make sense to Hall, Leigh believed it.

"I don't know," Roxhard said. "That doesn't sound..." he stopped as he bumped into one of the empty shelves behind him.

It shifted, rocking a little bit.

"Whoops," he said and moved forward away from the shelf.

Too far forward, his booted foot stepped over the first ring of the circle.

"Stop," Hall shouted, but it was too late.

Just an inch over the line was all it took. The runes started to glow, the solid lines of the ring pulsing. First the outer ring, then the runes, moving to the next ring and next set of runes before continuing all the way through. In only seconds, all the runes were flaring with a bright white light except the center one, the mark of Bastian The Sage.

They all spread out, turning and facing the walls, waiting.

"Sorry," Roxhard said, embarrassed.

"Watch it next time," Sabine snapped holding her staff out before her.

Hands clutched weapons tightly, bodies tense in anticipation.

Still nothing happened.

The runes flared and then faded, one by one, ring by ring.

"What," Roxhard exclaimed, surprised, looking over his shoulder at the circle.

The last rune died down, the light disappearing. But a new light appeared against the back wall. Thin, starting at the floor and running up the wall before turning to the side. It ran horizontal and then turned and ran back down to the floor. A rectangle of thin light. Then came the grinding of metal against metal. The panel framed by the light pushed forward, sliding along the smooth metal floor. It stopped and slid slowly to the side.

Behind the panel was a room, pitch black with no light. Shadows on darker shadows.

The panel slid fully open and a dark shape stepped from within.

It was large, twice the height of Hall and three times as wide. Humanoid shaped, but thick and lumbering. Arms as thick as Hall's body, legs like tree trunks. A head with no neck. In the limited light, the thing looked to have dark black skin, like rock. It stepped forward, each step loud against the metal. It moved slowly toward them, arms hanging down to its sides. There was a side to side shambling gait as it walked, a towering block of stone.

"A Golem," Hall said, the features of the room finally making sense.

"What kind?" Roxhard asked, stepping in front of the others.

"Let's not wait and find out," Hall replied. "Out the door."

They turned, except Roxhard who held the rear, sprinting for the opening and the long tunnel that led out into the cave and safety in the mountains. Sabine was the first, stepping from the room and into the tunnel. Her booted foot touched the floor of the tunnel, and they heard a slam that echoed down its length.

"I think that way is blocked," she said with a curse.

Hall turned to face the Golem, moving slowly closer. It was almost too close to Roxhard for him to use his *Battle Rush* ability. Hall stared at the Golem for a couple seconds, trying to *Identify* it.

Skill Gain!
Identify Rank 1 +.3

Elite Dark Stone Golem
Level 7

Hall wasn't sure why he got a level value with *Identify* this time where he hadn't gotten one before. He had just hoped the Skill would give what type of Golem it was. It had, and the level information was a bonus.

Not that it helped them any.

The others were all level three, and he had just gained level four helping the Gnomes. This would be a tough fight. Not as bad as the battle against the Corrupted Druid Vertoyi, where only luck had saved them, but they were greatly outleveled. But what choice did they have? They were trapped, and experience had taught Hall that in this situation, the only way out was to kill the Boss monster.

"Spread out," he told the others. "Hit it from a distance. Move in and move out. It's slow so we should be able to avoid those arms."

They all nodded, Sabine and Leigh stepping away from him and off to the sides. Angus and Pike walked out of the tunnel, standing near Hall who moved forward. Roxhard held his position, axe in hand.

"Let's do this," Hall said.

Roxhard took off. The Dwarf's short feet pounded on the metal, his footsteps drowned out by the Golem's. He ran hard and fast, straight at the lumbering creature.

———

The Dwarf was a speeding barrel of stone. Heavy, solid, and now with momentum behind him, Roxhard slammed into the

Golem's lower right leg. The moving mass of stone shifted, wobbled, as Roxhard was thrown backward. He tumbled across the floor and into the side of an examination table. The Golem ignored him.

Hall mentally reached out and grabbed at the Golem's health bar. Roxhard's strike had done some damage but not much. As the creature stepped into a pool of light from a globe, Hall could see faint cracks along the leg.

He glanced up at the ceiling, estimating the height. Activating *Leap*, Hall jumped into the air in a low arc. High enough that he soared over the Golem, who reached up a couple seconds too late and missed the Skirmisher. Hall reached behind him with his spear, using *Leaping Stab*, the new Class Ability he had learned.

The sharp tip of the weapon struck a glancing blow across the carved face of the Golem, small chips of stone flying.

He was surprised at how sharp the wooden tip of the spear was. He had yet to use the new spear, a gift from the Gnomes, and had been worried how it would hold up.

EXCEPTIONAL BREAKRIDGE
IRONWOOD SPEAR

Attack Power +2

Damage 1d6 +2

Agility +1

Durability 12/12

Weight 3 lbs.

On successful hit, has a 50% chance of causing Splinter. A shard of wood lodges within the wound causing 1 DMG every 3 Seconds for 15 Seconds.

Carved from a single piece of an Ironwood tree, the spear was strong and light. The Gnomes had insisted that even though it was wood, the tip would do just as much damage, more even, than a steel tip. It seemed they were right.

Hall landed and pivoted quickly, thrusting out with the spear again. More small shards of the creature were sent flying across the room. The Golem barely slowed, turning to face Hall. He backed away from the Golem and its reaching arms.

Behind the Golem, he could see Sabine raising her arms, pointing at the great stone back. She cast *Hexbolt* and a line of crackling purple energy shot out, slamming into the Golem. Streaks of purple lightning spread out, crawling over the Golem's shoulders, around its chest, and down onto its legs. The bolt would cause the Golem intense pain when it tried to concentrate or move.

Or it should have.

The Golem seemed to shrug, and the purple lightning flared and vanished. It came closer to Hall. Sabine cursed loudly and fired off a *Shadow Bolt*. The black beam, a solid bar of light extending from Sabine's palm to the Golem, took off a small bit of the creature's high health. Hall wished his *Identify* was higher, he really wanted to know what the Golem's Health and Protection values actually were.

Angus moved to the side, looking for a good angle to charge the Golem. Pike stood up, spread his wings, and the dragonhawk launched into the air. He rose to the top of the room, circling, building up speed and momentum for a strike.

Hall thrust out with the spear, making sure to land another glancing blow. He didn't want to slam the tip straight on into the stone, fearing it would break. Even with the Gnomes' assurances, he didn't want to run the risk.

A loud boom, like that of thunder, sounded in the open space, bouncing off the metal walls. The Golem shuddered, large pieces of its body falling to the ground. Hall stepped to the side, avoiding a piece.

It turned, wobbling more, as smaller pieces still fell from

the gaping wound in its side. Behind it stood Leigh, cudgel in hand. She looked down at the weapon and at the mess it had made of the Golem. She was distracted, and the Golem was reaching for her.

"Leigh," Hall shouted.

She reacted, barely in time. A heavy arm swung for her and Leigh ducked out of the way, taking a glancing blow that sent her rolling across the floor. She slammed into a table and struggled to get up.

Sabine fired another *Shadow Bolt*, turning the Golem's attention to her. Hall stabbed at it again. They were having an effect, but it was barely harming the Golem. Leigh's cudgel had done the most damage with its secondary ability, but that was only activated twenty-five percent of the time. They need to do more damage and quickly.

So far they had kept the Golem spinning, but soon it would hit one of them and only Roxhard had enough Protection to take a blow from the heavy stone creature. Hall could strike from a distance, using *Leap* to get out of the way if needed, but the women could not get in close to the Golem, and the class spells they had would not do enough damage.

Pike swooped down from the ceiling, flying fast at the Golem. The walking stone ignored the dragonhawk, thinking it a nuisance and nothing more. Opening his beak, Pike let out a loud screech followed by a crack as lightning shot out. The blue-colored bolt sparked and jumped in the air as it slammed into the shoulder of the Golem. More pieces flew off as cracks appeared in the Golem's rocky flesh. Another strike from Pike and a large chunk slid off, falling to the floor and shattering into pieces. An arm reached up for Pike, but the agile dragonhawk was already back up near the ceiling waiting for his Energy to recharge for another lightning attack.

The Golem pivoted between Sabine and Hall, closer to the Skirmisher, but drawn back to the Witch with each *Shadow*

Bolt. Hall heard running feet, boots slamming against metal, and saw Roxhard back in the fight.

Running, but not using *Battle Rush*, the Dwarf swung his axe at the back of the Golem's legs. He used the flat of the blade like a hammer. The weapon connected with all of Roxhard's considerable strength, larger chips flying out. Roxhard ran past, pulling up just beyond and turning to face the creature.

The Golem's health bar was a little more than half gone, most of the damage from Leigh's lucky cudgel strike.

"We're not equipped for this fight," Sabine called out, switching to her wand as her Energy was too low for another *Shadow Bolt.*

Smaller, less powerful, blasts of energy flew from the wand like missiles. Each struck the Golem, exploding in a flash and leaving a small drift of smoke.

Hall knew she was right as he stabbed out with the spear, narrowly avoided the Golem's answering swing.

"Just keep hammering at it," Hall shouted as Pike soared down.

The dragonhawk scored another lightning breath attack, more cracks forming along the Golem's shoulder. Roxhard darted in, slamming the flat side of his axe against the Golem's exposed back. The blow pushed the Golem forward a bit before it settled back solidly on its feet and turned to the Dwarf.

They needed bashing weapons, something none of them had or were trained on. Hammers, maces, weapons with heavy and flat ends. Swords and axes, with the sharpened edges, were not the right weapon for this monster. But that was all they had.

Hall shifted his feet, trying to set them around the shards of stone that now littered the floor. Evidence that they were damaging the black stone creature, but also a negative. The loose stone slid underfoot, the bigger pieces making them off balance.

Behind the Golem, he saw Leigh getting up. She had numerous small cuts along her arms and a giant bruise on her upper right arm. That arm hung limp by her side. She was unable to lift it, but she clutched her epic weapon in her left hand, stalking toward the Golem.

"Stop," Hall shouted at her.

She did, looking at him confused. She knew her cudgel was the only weapon that was truly harming the Golem.

Using *Leap*, Hall jumped over the Golem. With *Leaping Stab*, he scored a glancing attack, doing little damage. He landed behind the Golem, in front of Leigh.

"One more hit from it and you're done," Hall said quickly, looking over his shoulder at the Golem.

Roxhard was keeping it busy, keeping its attention. And paying the price as he barely blocked a swinging fist with his axe. The Dwarf buckled under the strength of the Golem's fist, somehow remaining standing.

"I know," Leigh said, looking past him at the wound she had made. "But this is the only thing that seems to harm it."

"Yes," Hall told her, reaching out and gently taking the cudgel from her. "But you're our healer. We can't afford to have you go down."

Leigh wanted to protest, started to but stopped. She knew that Hall was right. Didn't mean she had to like it, but he was right. She knew it was a tactical decision. He wasn't trying to protect her but was trying to protect the group. If they survived, they would have wounds that only she could treat.

And during the battle, her best course of action was to heal them as needed so they could keep fighting and defeat the Golem.

Hall let his spear drop to the ground, the wooden shaft and

tip landing with a thud. He held the cudgel in his right hand, examining it quickly.

IRONWOOD SHILLELAGH
OF THUNDER
DMG: 4d6 +2
Strength: +1
Durability: 19/20
Weight: 3 lbs.

On a successful hit has a 25% chance of casting Thunderclap. Effect of dealing additional +10 physical damage and stunning opponent for 15 seconds.

It appeared that the Golem was immune to stuns. Which made sense. It was an automaton, not thinking, programmed for one task. There was no mind in which to stun.

The *Thunderclap* special attack only processed twenty-five percent of the time. That didn't mean that one out of every four attacks would activate the *Thunderclap*. It meant that each attack had a twenty-five percent chance of activating.

Hall needed it to activate on his first swing.

He stepped up toward the creature, hating that the cudgel gave him a much shorter reach than the spear. He had to get that much closer to the creature and within reach of those arms. Now he understood what it was like to be a tank, having to melee the mobs and not have freedom of movement.

Roxhard saw Hall trying to stealthily approach the Golem. He doubled his attacks, slamming the axe against any part of the Golem he could. Cracks formed, small chips fell, but the Golem did not stop.

The steady stream of missiles from Sabine's wand stopped, drained of energy for now. She started moving to the side, waiting for the wand to recharge, while getting a clearer shot at the Golem where Hall would not be in the way.

Pulling his arm back, cudgel extended, Hall waited until the Golem's back was fully exposed. He swung, the cudgel slamming into the Golem's back. Cracks formed at the impact but nothing else. No *Thunderclap*. Hall cursed and dove down to the side into a roll, the Golem's arm swinging where his head had been, glad for his class' *Evade* ability.

He heard the sound of Sabine's missiles over his head, the small lights slamming into the Golem, followed by another *Shadow Bolt*. The Golem turned to her and Roxhard struck, his axe blade taking chips out of the Golem's stone hide as well as the axe head itself.

Pike swooped down once more, lightning crackling from the dragonhawk's beak. It struck the Golem, a line cutting across its chest. Large arms tried to hit the fast-moving bird, but Pike avoided them and managed to get another attack in before flying back out of range. The lightning strikes had done some damage.

Hall drew one of the throwing knives from his bracer. The knives themselves would do no damage to the stone hide but they also did lightning damage and Pike had proven that would hurt the Golem, more than anything else they were throwing at it. The knives wouldn't do much, but at this point, every little bit helped.

He threw the first one, the small weapon slamming into the stone Golem's cracked shoulder. A small chip fell off as the knife exploded in a bright spark. The second one was launched twenty seconds later, aimed for and striking the Golem's exposed inner stone where Leigh's cudgel strike had shattered a large hole. The knife stuck in a crack, sparking and sending lines of lightning across the opening.

Striding forward, Hall waited for a chance to get in close and strike. He shifted position, out of the range of Sabine's attacks and not getting in Roxhard's way. He saw Leigh was moving to be almost directly opposite Sabine, her staff in hand and ready to assist in any way she could. Her only offensive spell, *Splinter Storm*, would be wasted on the Golem.

The opening came and Hall attacked with Leigh's cudgel. He slammed the knotted wood end against one of the cracks across the Golem's stone exterior. Stone chips flew off, one cutting a thin line across his cheek. The crack widened, smaller ones splintering off from the point of impact. Still no *Thunderclap*.

Hall cursed, pulling his arm back for another strike when the Golem reacted quicker than before. It spun around, catching Hall off guard, a stone arm slamming into the Skirmisher. He fell down hard, barely able to roll out of the way of a smashing foot. The metal ground shook with the impact. Hall kept rolling, each time he landing on the shoulder the Golem had struck he gasped in pain.

A notification flashed across his vision.

-20 Health

-8 Vitality

The Golem's blow had hurt. His leather armor had done nothing to protect against the bludgeoning damage. His shoulder felt numb, lifting his arm was painful. Half his Health gone in one blow.

But how had the creature moved so fast? Hall stepped further back, watching the Golem. It was moving quicker. Its attack speed and reaction time increased as it was losing health.

The fight got a lot more dangerous now.

Hall pushed himself up, grunting as pain shot through his arm and shoulder. He tried to lift the cudgel, and managed it but through a haze of pain. His arm was stiff, getting tighter.

He made a couple of practice swings as the others kept the Golem spinning between them, with Pike adding another lightning attack. The cudgel swings were slow, lacking in power, but it would have to do.

He felt a rush of air as a furry form barreled past.

———

"Angus," Leigh yelled out as the cow charged the Golem.

Tired of standing in the background, Angus felt he had to do something. Hall winced as the animal; over a couple hundred pounds of bulk, muscle, and momentum; slammed into the Golem. There was a loud crack, more stone chunks falling, but Angus stopped hard. He didn't bounce away, just fell to the ground unmoving. The Golem rocked back, forced to take a step to the side, but showed little reaction.

"Get him out of there," Hall yelled to Roxhard.

The Dwarf was the only one strong enough to pull the weight of the unresponsive cow.

Which meant that Hall had to distract the Golem.

He charged in at the Golem, swinging the cudgel. The weapon slammed into the rock hide, stone chips falling, cracks lengthening, but still no *Thunderclap*. He rolled underneath the swinging arm, anticipating the Golem's attack and knowing the creature's increased speed. Hall was thankful for his higher Agility and the *Evade* Ability. He glanced over and saw Roxhard struggling to pull Angus away from the Golem.

As he stood up, avoiding the backswing of the Golem's arm, he saw an unexpected opening and took it. The throwing knife was still lodged in a crack, still sparking lightning somehow as the knife had not struck fully it had not discharged. He slammed the cudgel against the end of the knife. A weak swing, it still forced the knife deeper into the crack as well as striking the rock.

The explosion threw Hall back. He slammed hard against the metal ground. His head cracked against the hard floor, whipping his neck. He blinked away the bright flashes.

Thunderclap had finally activated, and with the extra lightning damage from the throwing knife, it had combined into a larger effect. Somehow. Hall didn't spend long thinking about it, pushing himself up and staring at the Golem.

It had stopped attacking. Everyone had stopped, watching. Stone struck metal floor, small pieces and large. The Golem stood still, one arm outstretched, the other hanging useless by its side and barely held on to the body. A body that was mostly shattered.

The gash that Leigh had made was now doubled, most of the Golem's chest gone, the shoulder a thin strip of stone. The waist was missing, somehow the leg still connected.

It started to move, more pieces still falling, somehow lifting the leg. The Golem was slower because of the immense damage but still faster than it had originally been. One step, two steps. It was fixated on Roxhard and Angus, the two barely out of its way.

The Golem's health was much lower. The way it was barely held together, one good charge would probably end it. But the two capable of that charge, Roxhard and Angus, were in no position to do it. Sabine sent another *Shadow Bolt*, taking some damage from the Golem but not enough. Leigh ran toward Angus and Roxhard, ready to heal.

Hall was too far to run in before the Golem would get to Roxhard and the cow. He looked at the cudgel in his hand. The ability was called *Leaping Stab,* not Leaping Bash, but it was worth a try. At the least, it would distract the Golem for a couple of precious seconds.

Activating *Leap*, he adjusted the arc to bring him just over the Golem. Arm back, he swung the cudgel at the stone head. Wood connected with stone, a solid hit, the impact jarring and altering Hall's jump. He wavered in the air, wobbling, his arm numb and tingling. The impact activated *Thunderclap*, the explosion pushing Hall higher and further out.

He slammed, back first, into the metal shelves, stopping his flight and falling to the ground. Landing hard, the cudgel fell from his now numb fingers. He gasped, trying to catch his breath, every part of his body hurting. Hall forced himself to look at the Golem.

Pieces of stone fell, a dust cloud forming as more and more hit the metal ground. The body was much the same, the shoulders all gone and no head existing. It did not move, a shuddering wracking the body as it started to shake itself apart. The Golem collapsed into a pile of black stones.

SLAIN: *Elite Dark Stone Golem*
+60 Experience
+50 Elite Bonus

Skill Gain!
Polearms Rank 2 +.2
Light Armor Rank 2 +.1

"Damn," Roxhard said, sitting down and breathing heavy, as the dust cloud settled to the ground.

CHAPTER FIVE

HALL MANAGED TO SIT UP, HIS WHOLE BODY ACHING. HIS shoulder was still numb, his arm too sore to lift. His back felt bruised, maybe another rib broken, from slamming into the thick shelving and falling to the ground. A knee was difficult to bend, each movement sending pain through his leg.

Sabine rushed to his side, helping him stand up. He took pressure off the hurt knee, trying not to put too much weight on her. Together they made their way over to the others.

A light blue glow was surrounding Angus, the cow starting to stir as the healing magic of Leigh's *Nature's Touch* coursed through his body. He gave a soft lowing sound, feet twitching. Pike perched next to the cow, watching intently. The dragonhawk gave a small squawk as Angus mooed.

"How is he?" Hall asked as Sabine helped him to sit down next to Roxhard.

"He'll live," Leigh said, relief in her voice. "He's a tough little guy." She looked up at Hall, noticing the small cuts and bruising on his face, how he held his chest and side, the one arm useless. Her eyes widened in shock and guilt. "Oh Hall, I'm low on Energy. I'm sorry. I should have saved some."

He held up a hand, stopping her, and forced a smile.

"I'm fine, he looked worse than I feel," he said, thinking he had cracked a joke but not sure it had translated well.

Leigh smiled, a little grateful.

"I can take an Energy potion," she offered.

Hall shook his head. He was in pain but he could wait for her Energy to regain. It would only be a couple minutes, and they had so few potions. No need to waste it. All his injuries were from impact, no slashing, so he couldn't even use bandages and raise his Triage skill. He sighed as he stretched out his leg, trying to loosen the knee. Raising that skill had cost money, and he hadn't even gotten to use it yet.

"Did it really get faster as it got damaged?" Roxhard asked, moving his shoulders to work the muscles. His own Health was down but he could wait until Hall was taken care of.

"Yes," Sabine said. "It had high Protection and Resistances as well."

"Guess we know what this place was used for," Hall said, wincing as he tried to lift an arm to indicate the large room around them.

Leigh was at his side, laying her hands on his shoulder. Warm to the touch, he felt the magic flowing from her and into his body, her hands glowing a soft blue color, spreading up her arms along her tattoos. Some of the pain went away, tired and sore muscles relaxing, ribs starting to mend. He felt the cut on his cheek start to close up.

Leigh casts Nature's Touch
+15 Health
+5 Vitality

He noticed that he regained some of his Vitality from the magic. Like the points lost from restless sleep, he'd only regain the last few points after his body got real rest.

"I'll do more after I get my Energy back fully but that should help," Leigh said.

"This is good," he said and forced himself to stand up.

He walked a couple steps, limping as the knee was still not cooperating fully. His shoulder felt bruised, but he could move the arm. While his entire body was still in pain, at least he could think and move somewhat.

Walking over to the pile of stone, he shifted some of the smaller and loose ones on top with his foot. He saw a faint glow coming from within the pile.

"What's that?" he asked, kneeling down and shifting rocks.

Roxhard and Sabine, now both seeing the glow, knelt on either side of him. Together they moved larger pieces of the broken Golem out of the way. Buried near the middle of the pile, giving off a strong blue glow, was a large gem about the size of a closed fist. Hall could not describe the shade of the glow. It was like the sky but brighter but not quite that color. The glow seemed to come from within the gem and diffused by the crystal. It was multifaceted, each face the same size and an even number of them. Oval in shape, it was a style and color none of them had seen before. There was something artificial about it, Hall realized as Sabine picked it up. It was carved. There was no natural way it could ever form.

You have found: Golem's Heart

"What do we do with it?" Sabine asked, turning the still-glowing object around in her hand, examining all the sides.

"Any gathering skill gains?" Hall asked.

Sabine shook her head. Nothing.

No one had an idea what the *Golem's Hearts* purpose was so Sabine tucked the gem inside her pouch, the glow disappearing.

Hall stood up, with effort, and looked around the room.

From what he could see, none of their weapons or equipment that had been dropped in the fight were buried under the stone. He could see his spear against the tables and Leigh's cudgel at the edge of a globe of light near the wall.

He was glad. They could not afford to lose equipment. Only a couple days out from Skara Brae, they still had a long way to go before getting to Silver Peak Keep. There was no telling what they would face along the way. But he knew there would be no more side trips to satisfy curiosity.

This one had proven to be enough and they had nothing to show for it.

He started to move to where the cudgel lay when he noticed the sliding door along the back wall was still open. It had never closed when the Golem came out and while it was pitch black inside, the room had to be big enough to hold the thing. Maybe there was something else worth investigating? He turned and headed for the back wall.

Pausing at the threshold, he examined the door and the sliding mechanism. The craftsmanship was exceptional, the track and the rollers moving with barely a sound. The door panel looked heavy, but it was held in place with no warping or uneven pressure against the tracks. There was no handle on either side of the panel, nothing that he could see that would open or close the door. The best engineers and smiths in the realms, Hall didn't think even the Dwarves were capable of what he was looking at.

Looking inside the room; letting his racial *Limited Night Vision* adjust to the shadows; he saw a space that was twice that needed to house the Golem. There were marks on the ground that indicated where the Golem had sat for a long time, dent-like impressions in the stone flooring where the weight of the Golem had pressed down. Shelves lined the three walls made of the same metal as the walls. Long, flat pieces of thick metal plates laying on brackets.

Most of the shelves were empty, but there was a small chest sitting on the middle one against the back wall.

Maybe this won't be a waste, after all, Hall thought as he stepped lightly into the room. He hesitated before placing his weight on the floor, leery of traps.

The floor didn't drop out from beneath him, nothing shot out from the walls, no spikes or spears rose from the floor, and he didn't hear the grinding that was a sign of the ceiling descending. It appeared to be trap-free.

Taking another step, he heard a familiar clicking from up near the high ceiling. Glancing up, he saw a small spark that ignited into a brighter light, revealing a large globe suspended from above. This one light lit up the room, showing a ten-foot by ten-foot space. He could see the metal shelves clearly, the dents from the Golem and the one chest across the room.

Stretching his arms, loosening them up, he walked fully into the room. He paused, waiting, expecting something to happen. Nothing did. Looking over his shoulder, he saw Sabine waiting outside, watching. He shrugged and walked the rest of the way to the chest.

About a foot long, a foot deep, and about six inches high. Made of wood, the chest was banded in bronze. It was unlocked.

Taking a deep breath, Hall quickly lifted the lid. He had to hold it up, the next shelf too close to push the chest's lid back. The insides were lined with velvet, a deep purple. Stitched into the velvet along the upper lid was the same symbol from the center of the rune circle. The symbol of Bastian the Sage. Inside the low chest, stacked end to end, filling up the space, were assorted coins. Mostly silver but also a handful of gold.

Not a fortune but a decent amount.

Hall picked up the chest and forced it into his inventory pouch. The chest seemed to shrink and stretch as it was pulled into the leather pouch. He pulled open his inventory menu, seeing that the coins did not automatically add to the total he already had. Something about the chest prevented them from stacking with the others. Closing the menu, he left the room.

"What was in the chest?" Sabine asked.

"1,000 silver and 100 gold," Hall answered.

"Not bad," she replied. "Between that and the experience, it makes the beating we took from the Golem almost worth it."

Hall nodded, feeling pain throughout his body. Almost worth it was right.

Something about it all bothered him. The Golem was some kind of guardian, but to protect only the chest? That seemed like overkill. There must have once been more here. It took a lot of material and magic to make a Golem. The materials alone would be worth a small fortune, much more than what was in the chest, so maybe it had been left behind after the workshop had been emptied.

But then why leave the one chest and the guardian if everything else was removed?

He was missing something; he was sure of it. But what?

"Guys," Roxhard shouted excitedly from across the room. "Check this out."

Standing below one of the globes along the wall, he was staring up between it and the wall, pointing. The globe was made of thick crystal, polished and sanded until it was clear and smooth. Perfectly round, the light from within shone out in all directions. Hall realized the bronze used everywhere served as a reflector, directing more light back into the room. Attached to the back of the globe, holding it to the wall, was a bronze tube. A plate was bolted to the globe, curved to match the surface, and another bolted to the wall. Looking into the globe, Hall could see that the tube was hollow and a much smaller one made of some flexible material was fed into the globe through a hole. The flexible tube ran down to the bottom and was pulled up and into the base of a pedestal that was held up in the middle of the globe by four crystal rods affixed to the sides of the globe. On the pedestal was another crystal, this one a cloudy white color and shaped like the end of a torch.

"What is in that tube?" Roxhard asked.

"Has to be some kind of oil or gas," Hall answered. "Something in there must have lit a spark when we activated the lights."

"I've never seen anything like this in the realms," Sabine said over his shoulder.

Hall looked over toward Leigh, who had been examining one of the tables, running her fingers over the runes. She shook her head. It was new to her as well.

It was interesting. The whole room was. But there were more pressing matters.

"Did anyone check to see if the door unlocked?" he asked, stepping away from the light.

No one answered.

With a sigh, Hall headed for the long hallway.

———

The door had slid open, presumably when the Golem was destroyed.

They walked out and stopped where the rough stone tunnel curved. Hall could see sunlight just ahead. He looked back at the open door, lights still on in the Golem's room.

"Should we close it?" Roxhard asked.

As if in response, the large door started moving on its own. It slid forward on the track in the ground. They watched, awed, as the two doors slammed shut. The light from beyond was cut off, the doors once again smooth.

"Wow," Roxhard said.

"Let's go," Hall said and headed for the light outside.

CHAPTER SIX

"I was always partial to Paradise Gangstas," Roxhard said with a sigh.

The four sat around the fire, Hall poking a branch into the ashes to stir them up. The moon was high in the sky, the stars out and bright. The islands above positioned so they did not block out the light from the moon. Hall did not like those nights, when the moon was behind the higher islands and the world was as dark as a cave.

"That's a stupid name," Sabine remarked.

She was laying down on her bedroll, blanket around her, using her pack as a pillow. She poked at the pack, trying to make it more comfortable without much success.

"My brother came up with it," Roxhard muttered.

Hall shot Sabine a scowl, the Witch not seeing it in the dark.

"It was a fine name back then," Hall said.

It wasn't, but he didn't want to say it. He knew how Roxhard thought of the brother that he would most likely never see again. Older by a couple of years, the fourteen-year-old Roxhard loved and idolized his brother. From the few conversations they had about Roxhard's family, Hall didn't think the brother felt the same way. It seemed the older brother had been a bully and mean, resentful of the tag-along younger brother. But Roxhard would never see it that way.

Especially not now.

"What was yours?" the Dwarf asked Hall.

"Dragon Riders," he answered. "And no, that's not going to be it either."

Roxhard laughed, Sabine grunted.

Hall watched the smoke drift up from the fire. He had it banked, keeping the smoke low, but still, a tendril curled up into the night sky. Camped at the edge of the mountains, the land sloping down around them, protected from the wind by a screen of boulders, he had a good view out over the rocky highlands. The land rose and fell, rugged and beautiful.

Angus mooed in his sleep, causing Leigh to shift. She was sleeping in her customary position, using the cow as a pillow. Pike slept on top of Angus, shifting slightly. The cow's lowing rolled across the foothills.

"What about..." Roxhard started but shook his head. "Naw, never mind."

"We don't need a name," Sabine said, not for the first time.

Roxhard ignored her.

When Hall had first awoken, reloaded into the game because of the Glitch, supposedly two years after the event had happened, the Guild names had been visible. He didn't know when they had faded away. It could have been almost immediately. He had stopped paying attention that first day.

Hall agreed with Sabine. He didn't see a need for a Guild name. The new game system didn't have a Guild tab, so the name would just be a name. There would be no special significance. In the old game system, the Guild was a way to communicate and organize. A loose, or sometimes tight, group of people all playing together. Friends and acquaintances. It allowed for long-distance communication.

Leigh had mentioned something about being able to form Factions, which were similar to Guilds but more like the old-style Factions. It was something to look into for the future. He didn't see a need for all that, not now. The new game system felt more real and seemed to be taking out mechanics that had broken the game's immersion while adding features that made it more immersive. Like hunger.

Reaching into his pouch, Hall pulled out a piece of jerky. He pulled up the inventory menu, a quick look at the remaining stock of the supplies they were carrying. They were in decent shape for now but would need to start conserving.

It had been over a week on the road from Auld and not a chance to resupply in Hall's new village of Skara Brae. The ruins had offered nothing. There had been a couple animals they had managed to find and skin and enough meat to eat, but that was it. They just had what they had bought in Auld before they left.

Hunger and thirst were now a concern. Something that had never existed in the game before the Glitch. He had thought they had planned well enough when leaving Auld, packing enough, but it didn't appear as if they had.

Silver Peak Keep was still a good distance away, Hall knew, wondering if there was anything in between.

Mentally opening the Interface, Hall brought up his map of Edin.

It was weird, he thought as he zoomed into the south-western section where they were, what the developers chose to keep and what they got rid of. He could physically take his map out but was still able to mentally access it.

Most of the island of Edin was blank, not yet uncovered or

explored. He could see the route they had taken from Auld, the port city they had taken an airship to after leaving Land's End Port on the island of Cumberland, to Skara Brae and the Grove as well as the route along the mountains they were on now. That was it. He had experimented with the map, trying to discover how it uncovered areas. It appeared that his eyes controlled the extent of the visible map.

Which made sense. If he couldn't see it, why would it be revealed?

But he had his memory. Which regretfully wasn't a huge help. Before the Glitch, the weird effect that had trapped him and the others in the game of Sky Realms Online, he had explored every inch of the realm of Edin. There had not been many villages. None that he could think of between Skara Brae and Silver Peak Keep, the town in the southwestern corner of the island.

Skara Brae hadn't even existed before.

There could be other ruins, villages, or almost anything now. They had found a new village and a new cave. Even the village Leigh said she was from, Cliff Fields, was new. There could be more of everything that was new.

He was starting to realize he had to forget most of what he knew of the game, what he had learned from years spent playing the original game. This was a new world.

Snores drifted across the night, coming from Roxhard who had fallen asleep. Sabine grunted and rolled over. Hall poked at the fire, spreading the ashes, before throwing another large branch on. Wood was scarce in the rugged foothills, they had lucked out and found enough for the night. The previous one that hadn't been so lucky, and it had been a cold night.

He leaned back, still studying the translucent map.

Maybe he was approaching the problem wrong, he thought. Both Land's Edge Port and Auld had been greatly expanded from what they had been. A city of only a couple dozen structures was now hundreds of buildings and people. Could that apply to other places in the game as well?

Hall zoomed out on the map, getting a wider look at the southwestern area of Edin. He tried to remember all the quests that were available in the zone. A very large zone, there had been numerous quest hubs. Besides the cities of Auld and Silver Peak Keep, there had been smaller ones scattered around.

One in particular.

Not just a quest hub, but a place with its own reputation and rewards. The gear found there had quickly been outpaced by other quest rewards in the northern areas of Edin, but that would not be why they would be going there. Not this time.

But where was it? he thought, trying to remember the old map.

To the southeast, where the foothills gave way to the moors, there was a forest, Fallen Green. The road from Auld to Silver Peak Keep ran along the southern edge of the woods, between it and the island's edge. Somewhere in that forest was a village. A Firbolg village.

———

"You sure about this?" Sabine asked as they finished up a cold breakfast, after Hall had told them his thoughts about where they should go next.

Hall shrugged.

"It's not that far out of the way," he replied. "We can resupply, heal up fully, and maybe even get some experience."

Sabine looked across the highlands to the southeast. Hall assumed she was trying to remember her own time in Edin and in the Firbolg village. Would it be worth the extra couple days side trip?

"We're not in a hurry," Hall added.

Which was true. He was eager to get back to his village, Skara Brae, and start rebuilding it. He still had no idea how he would manage it, but every day the pull grew. Leigh would also be in a hurry to return as well. As the new Custodian of the Grove, she would be eager to start cleansing it.

Or would she?

Hall knew she had been reluctant to accept her duties as a Druid but just as quickly as he had accepted lordship of Skara Brae, almost too eagerly for both of them, she had accepted being the new Custodian. Had she done it out of guilt or truly because it was something she wanted? The only way to find out was to go back. But like before, when she was tasked to discover what had happened to the Grove, she had been hesitant and in no hurry to do so. Would it still be that way?

She had demonstrated new abilities in Greenheight Vale, staring to cleanse that forest. How eager was she to learn those new abilities and put them to use?

"What do you know of the village?" Sabine asked Leigh.

"Of this village?" Leigh replied. "Nothing. There was a Firbolg village near my home of Cliff's Field. A peaceful folk, the villagers traded with them regularly."

Sabine turned back to the southeast. She got a vacant, faraway stare, and Hall knew she was opening up one of her menus. Most likely the map. Her eyes refocused, and she shrugged.

"Why not," she replied. "Besides, they're going to be your neighbors. Might as well meet them," she said to Hall as she walked past to gather her gear.

That was something he had not thought about. Hall remembered there were many menus he had seen on the village's Interface, most of which he had not reviewed yet. There had been an *Allies* and a *Trade Partners*. What would happen if he forged an alliance with the Firbolgs? The

Valedale Gnomes were listed as *Allies*. What was the difference between Allies and Trade Partners?

Only one way to find out.

He looked over his shoulder where Pike was sitting on Angus. The cow was laying down near the smoldering remains of the fire, mooing quietly to himself. Content. The dragonhawk was curled up on top of the cow, eyes closed.

Staring at Pike, Hall called out through the mental link they shared. Eyes opening instantly, Pike stood up and spread his wings. He squawked, causing Angus to wake up. The cow groaned and shook as Pike's claws dug in for purchase.

Flapping his wings, the dragonhawk lifted into the air. He landed on one of the boulders they had used as a windbreak. With another cry, Pike pushed himself into the air. Wings spread wide, flapping, the dragonhawk soared high into the sky.

The others all watched Pike as he flew higher and higher, powerful wings spread to catch the wind, holding him aloft as he circled. A tiny dot in the sky, they watched it disappear as the dragonhawk flew to the southeast.

Hall sat down, looking in the same direction, eyes focused on nothing, activating *Shared Vision*.

In his mind, he saw the highlands spread out before him. So much land, so much detail. Pike was high enough to see for miles in all directions, eyes sharp enough to pick out many details. The hills rose and fell, small streams flowing between them. Rocky outcroppings, small forests, the hills mostly covered in smaller boulders. A small mouse that Hall had to force Pike to ignore.

Pike flew further out. Good-sized ponds could be seen in the valleys between hills, one on a flat top that was at least a half-mile long. The dragonhawk lifted higher, losing details but seeing more. And there, on the edge was a line of darker green against the lighter green and grays of the highlands.

Circling where he was, Pike's view changed. Through the dragonhawk's eyes, Hall could see the edge of the forest and then to the mountains. He couldn't see the particular rock formation they were at, not from this distance, but he saw enough to get a general idea of what direction to head.

Hall had to fight to stop from getting dizzy. Somehow the circling and changing views didn't bother Pike, but it was bothering him. He closed his eyes, canceling the connection between the dragonhawk and himself. Opening his eyes, he saw the highlands spread out before him but lacking the amazing detail of Pike's vision. He had a momentary sense of loss.

Hall stood up, shaking his head, clearing it.

Looking up in the sky, he saw a dark speck miles out as Pike flew back.

"Pike saw the forest," Hall said to the others. "About two days that way. Maybe three," he added, pointing toward the speck that was the dragonhawk.

Walking back into the camp, Hall started pulling his gear together. Roxhard took up the last stick and spread out the ashes from the fire. He stepped into the small circle of rocks they had made, stomping on the last ember that was glowing red. Sabine and Leigh were already standing further down the hill, waiting.

Most of his gear went into the pouch on his belt, the rest into the traveler's pack he was carrying. Adjusting the straps so his cloak was not held down tightly, Hall grabbed his spear from where it had been laying against a rock. He could see rips and tears in his armor, both his chest and gloves. The leather on his legs was worn, stitching coming loose. Pulling his short sword out of the sheath, he saw nicks and scratches that a whetstone would not remove. Weapons and armor needed repairs.

Would the Firbolgs have a smithy capable of repairing both?

He didn't think there had been a smith in the original village. The only NPCs that could be interacted with had been the ones associated with the quests and a general goods dealer. He hoped there was a smith now.

CHAPTER SEVEN

It took them two and a half days to reach the edge of the forest. They had managed to avoid any random encounters, finding herbs and animals for food and skins. Turned out that along with Hall, who was not sure he was going to keep the Skill, both Leigh and Sabine had the Herbology Skill. They took turns claiming the various plants they found, each getting a couple skill gains.

Because of the hills and valleys, the going had been slow. Up a hill, down into a valley and back up again. The landscape was rugged, not easy hiking. They were tired, hungry as rations needed to be conserved, and starting to get on each other's nerves. Each carried wounds that magical healing could not deal with. Healing spells were great for closing wounds, stopping bleeding, and getting a body well enough to fight again. But it did nothing for the after-effects. Tight muscles, sore joints. Lingering aches and pains.

The hill sloped down to the forest, an uneven line of tall trees. Thick trunks, low branches, the forest was old growth. The edge ran for miles in both directions. The maps showed it to be deeper than it was long, possibly three or four days to go from one end to the other.

Hall tried to remember where the Firbolg village was. Almost dead center, he thought, getting some disagreement from Sabine. Roxhard, like usual, didn't protest or have anything to add. The Witch thought the village was more to the east, closer to the Auld side of the forest. Leigh stood back, scratching Angus behind an ear, waiting for someone to make a decision.

"Whatever," Sabine said finally, motioning for Hall to lead the way.

He bit back a response. It wasn't worth it.

They walked into the forest, the sun darkening as it fought to penetrate the thick canopy above. There was some space between the trees, but not much. It would have been impossible to ride a mount through this forest, which Hall remembered doing in the pre-Glitch version. Low bushes covered the ground around the base of some trees, enough space to walk through. Exposed roots stretched out across the forest floor.

The sound of birds rang through the branches, leaves shaking as small animals ran from branch to branch. Hall was glad to hear some noise, some animal activity. The wide-open and hilly highlands had been empty with barely any sound. He had forgotten how active a forest could be. Oaks, maples, pines, and birches dominated, other species scattered.

Hall led the way, Pike on his shoulder, Roxhard in the rear. He tried to stay focused on watching the forest but his thoughts kept drifting to the past. Called the Fallen Green Forest, there had been about a dozen quests. Most had come from the Firbolg village of Green Ember. The peaceful Firbolg were having troubles with their neighbors, a tribe of Badgin. An old truce had been broken by the bloodthirsty Badgin. The Players had progressed through the quest chains, raising in reputation which could be used to gain new recipes and items from the Firbolg.

Then there had been the Demons.

When he had first suggested coming to the forest, he had forgotten the Demons.

Hall pushed the thoughts away, concentrating on where they were. Using the old game as a guide could be dangerous, as they were learning. This forest alone was five or six times the size it had been in-game. A Player on a mount could have ridden from one end to the other in half an hour. Now it would take them days of walking to get through and the trees would prevent riding.

They had spent the first night in a small clearing beneath a fallen tree. The second night was in a small and unoccupied cave. A small fire, smoke curling up into the air, gave them warmth as the light and heat reflected off the stone behind them. Hall woke up, ready to take the last watch, just as he had every night.

It was something he had started doing back on Cumberland without really discussing it with the others. He always took the last watch, wanting to be the first up and preparing for the day ahead. Just another thing that pointed to him being the leader of the group.

His realizing it was happening had been slow, but the process had not. It had just happened naturally. He had somehow become the leader of the group. It was not something he had tried for. Truth be told, he hadn't wanted it to happen. But it had. Dyson, the merchant they had befriended, had said it was obvious. Hall hadn't seen it then. To an extent, he still didn't.

He found himself the leader of the party and the Lord of a small town. He had been happy to find that one of the governing options for Skara Brae had been one where he could be hands-off. Leading a party in combat, that he knew how to do even if it was reluctantly. Leading an entire village, that he had no experience with.

But the village was something he wanted to do. It felt right. He would start the rebuilding process, help it to become a real home, and then let others take care of it. He knew himself though. There was no way he would fully stop being involved.

He just had to hope that he didn't mess it up too badly.

With a sigh, Hall pushed himself up. He left his bedroll laid out, taking the blanket and cloak with him. His javelin harness was laying on the ground, and he left it there, taking the spear and belting on his short sword. The fire had gone down, the last few hours of the night cold. Just outside the cave, sitting cross-legged on the ground, was Leigh. Walking around the others carefully, quietly, Hall made his way out of the cave.

Laying the blanket on the ground, he sat down, pulling his cloak tighter around him. He laid the spear down alongside, in easy reach, adjusting the sword in its scabbard. He felt the joints in his legs protest.

"Evening," he whispered to Leigh.

She turned and smiled. The light from the moon seemed to catch her in that moment, and Hall was captivated by her beauty. He realized that every day, he was finding her more and more attractive. Not just her physical beauty but everything about her.

"Sleep well?" she asked, breaking into his thoughts.

"Not really," he admitted. "Got a couple hours but wasn't the most comfortable."

She chuckled quietly.

Hall had the urge to offer her his blanket. She was dressed in a leather skirt, the sides exposed and held together with lacing. Her top left her arms and waist exposed, showing the light blue tattoos that curled up her arms. Curly and wild red hair with two braids hanging over her shoulders, blue eyes, and pierced ears. No gloves, but leather bracers, and calf-high boots. Next to her on the ground was her epic quality magical cudgel, found in a treasure chest on Cumberland, and her gnarled staff.

As a Druid, he wondered if she had some means of dealing with the cold. She must, he had never heard her mention feeling it. It didn't appear she felt the night's chill now.

"How do you do it?" she asked after a minute or so of silence.

He looked at her, wondering what she meant.

"Waking up," she clarified. "Everyone else, me included, needs to be woken up for our watch. But you just seem to know when it's time."

Hall shrugged, wondering if she could see the movement. It wasn't something he had given thought to or realized he did. When it was his turn for watch, he just got up and took it. Taking the morning watch, the last watch, was a conscious decision. But waking up in time?

Back in real life, when he had been working a nine-to-five job, the same thing had happened. His alarm had been set for a certain time, and without fail, he would wake up a couple minutes before the alarm went off. Even on weekends and vacations. He still got up at the same time, just was able to fall back to sleep.

"Don't know how," he finally said. "You can go to bed, get a couple more hours sleep."

"In a minute," she replied.

Angus mooed loudly behind them, and they both turned. The cow was shaking a bit in his sleep, legs kicking. Some kind of dream. The others did not waken. Hall and Leigh had been speaking in whispers, not wanting to disturb the rest of the group, but if they hadn't woken over Angus' mooing, they weren't going to.

Leigh chuckled.

"The shaggy guy makes a great pillow," she said, a smile

and laugh in her voice. "But not when he has dreams. I've been kicked a couple of times."

"You said he was in a herd near your home in Cliff Fields," Hall prompted.

"Yeah," Leigh said, still looking back at the small cow. "Our farm was next to it, the herds fence the boundary with our corn crop. When helping my da in the fields, I'd see the cows in their pastures. They'd come to the fence and I'd pat them, sometimes crawling through onto their side. Large, but they're generally gentle. So one day, probably three years back, one of the cows was pregnant and giving birth. Premature."

She leaned back, looking up at the stars barely visible through the thick canopy of trees, lost in the memory. Hall could tell that Leigh did miss her home. He remembered why she had left, not exactly by choice.

"The calf was small, a real runt," Leigh continued. "They didn't think he'd survive but he did." She again glanced back at Angus, the cow's feet still kicking in the midst of the dream. "I had seen the birth happening, ran through the fence, and helped the little calf."

Leigh paused, tilting her head as she looked at Angus.

"I wonder if that was when my nature magic first manifested," she said absently.

Hall had never been a big fan of playing a casting class. He enjoyed having them as part of the party and the utility and range they brought. But he had always been drawn to the melee classes. Leigh's comment about her magical power manifesting was interesting. Players never had to worry about that, as they started out already with magical abilities. NPCs never had either. But it would make sense that such a moment happened. He was just surprised that the developers had bothered coding such a moment in for the NPCs. Just another example that it seemed there was more to Leigh than most NPCs.

"It became my responsibility to help feed him, bring him back to full health," she continued. "He never did gain the size he was supposed to. I think he'll always be on the smaller side. When I left, I felt horrible about having to leave him behind. The farmer had promised me that he'd look after Angus, but I knew it was a lie."

She fell silent, looking down at the ground. Hall figured she was right. No way would the farmer have kept Angus around. As the runt, Angus was useless to the farmer and just took up space.

"The first night out of Cliff Fields, the old Druid and I were awoken by a strange noise," Leigh said looking up and turning to face Hall. She was smiling at the memory. "Narya, the Druid, had a giant cat for a Companion. It wasn't growling, just looking into the trees around us, not bothering to even get up. That's when Angus walked out of the trees and rushed right over to me."

Hall smiled, glancing back at the sleeping cow. Angus' legs were no longer moving, the dream passed and the cow restful once more. He saw that Pike had moved off the cow's back, settling down on Hall's empty bedroll.

"Somehow he broke out of the pasture," Leigh continued. "I was surprised to see him. There was no way he should have known where I was or that I had even left. Narya said that it meant he was to become my Companion."

They had been speaking in whispers, Hall certain their voices were not carrying out into the woods. The fire, small though it was, should have been enough to keep predators at bay. Which was why he was surprised to hear a noise in the shadows of the trees.

A branch breaking, or being stepped on. Just a small snap, but he had heard it. Hall held up his hand, silencing Leigh, and slowly stood up. He reached down to grab his spear, Leigh shifted to grab her staff, when the voice spoke out of the dark.

"Do not," it said.

Deep, strong. Where Dwarf voices were also deep and strong, theirs was the strength of the stone, the deepness of the mines. This voice had the strength of the trees and the deepness of the woods. Hall knew it belonged to a Firbolg.

He watched as eight of them stepped out of the trees. How they had moved so silently, he did not know. Firbolgs were seven to eight feet tall, broad and heavily muscled. They resembled humans, just larger. It was too dark to make out details, but Hall saw each wearing a mix of bark and leather armor. A couple carried shields and hammers, others bows. The leader, the one that had spoken, stepped forward a couple paces. He bore a large warhammer, the head carved from wood, and a shield four feet high and two wide. The shield was held out to the side, in his left hand, the head of the hammer was pointed at Hall.

"Who are you and why are you in our lands?" the Firbolg demanded.

———

The Firbolg had spoken loudly, intentionally. He had wanted to wake the others.

Behind him, Hall could hear Roxhard and Sabine waking quickly, hands most likely going for weapons or starting to cast before stopping and realizing they were surrounded and outnumbered. They would see eight large Firbolgs, all armed, with Hall and Leigh at the front of the cave. Neither going for their weapons. They would relax, wait for Hall to make the first move.

At least that is what Hall hoped was happening behind him. He didn't dare look back, locking eyes with the Firbolg leader.

He cursed himself for again thinking of this as just like the old game.

When he had first come to the Firbolgs village, it was simply just riding in and finding the quest giver. He had been given a quest in Auld about the village and its troubles. There had never been roaming patrols. Now he had no such quest, no real reason to be in the forest, and to the patrol, they were trespassing. He didn't think saying 'we want to earn some reputation and do some quests' would work.

Firbolgs were generally peaceful. Allies of the Druids, they worked to protect their forest homes. When provoked, they were quick to anger and would unleash their great strength on anyone or anything that threatened their homes. Strong and tough, Firbolgs were fearsome warriors. The argument over which was a better Warden, Dwarf or Firbolg, always seemed to creep up in the forums for the game.

But they were never openly hostile to strangers that were caught in the forests, not until those strangers did something wrong.

Hall and party had done nothing. They should have been ignored until they were closer to the village. Had he been wrong in his estimate of its location? Was it closer than he had thought? Seeing the Firbolgs here and now caught him by surprise. He had not expected to see any of them this soon into the forest and not in the night.

"We are from Skara Brae," Hall said finally, not sure where the inspiration came from. "A village to the northwest in the mountains. We came to speak to your elders and meet our closest neighbors and perhaps set up formal trade relations."

He felt the surprised eyes of his companions on him. He wanted to look back and shrug but kept his gaze focused on the lead Firbolg. The leader had stepped closer, and by the small light from the fire, Hall could make out some details. He still couldn't tell skin color, as all Firbolgs tended to have brown or tan skin that was really a light fur covering over their entire body. The leader wore no helm, his hair thick and long, falling past his shoulders. He had deep eyes, a golden color, with a wide and flat nose. His ears were slightly pointed, the tips barely poking through his hair. His gaze was angry. Hall thought the Firbolg looked young, maybe around the same age as he was.

"I have never heard of this village," the leader growled.

Hall shrugged. Now that he had set them on this course, he felt some confidence. It was a good direction, he realized. Almost perfect. Being Lord Hall, ruler of a town, could open a lot of doors that being Hall the Skirmisher could not.

"We're new," Hall said lamely, his confidence in the plan weakening a little.

The Firbolg looked past Hall, studying the others. His eyes widened seeing Pike and Angus, the cow now standing with Pike back on the cow's shoulders. Hall was looking back, seeing that Roxhard and Sabine were standing near their bedrolls and weapons, neither grabbing for anything but each ready.

"You are a Druid of the Grove," the Firbolg said to Leigh.

"Custodian of the Grove near Skara Brae," Leigh replied.

The Firbolg looked closer at Leigh.

"The only Branch of the World Tree near is—" He stopped and glanced at Hall.

Growling, the leader jumped back and lifted his warhammer. The others around him all tensed, readying their weapons. Hall held out his hands, hoping the others took the signal to relax. He knew if they reached for their weapons, they would not survive.

He mentally pulled the Firbolg leader's status bar.

Skill Gain!
Identify Rank 1 +.2

Jackoby of the Brownpaw
Firbolg Warden

His *Identify* skill was too low to get any real information but at least he had a name and class. That was something to start with. He wanted to get more information on the other Firbolgs but Jackoby had to be his focus for now. It was also odd that the Firbolg had been given a name. Other times when he had used the skill, there had been no name. He quickly looked at one of the other Firbolgs to compare.

Skill Gain!
Identify Rank One +.1

Brownpaw Hunter

Interesting, Hall thought wondering what the difference between the two Firbolgs was.

"The only Branch near is corrupted," Jackoby spat on the ground, cursing. "It is to the northwest where you say your village is."

Hall was glad that this Jackoby was giving them time to explain. He now understood why they were alert and ready to fight.

"It was corrupted," Leigh said calmly. "But no longer."

"Explain yourself," Jackoby commanded.

"We killed the former Custodian," Hall said.

They really hadn't. Vertoyi had beaten them, could have killed them all. The corrupted Druid had been blinded by his power, apparently making a deal with Demons to gain that power. He could not see the damage he had caused to the Grove, not until Leigh made him see it. Vertoyi had chosen to die, to start the healing process in the Grove.

What Hall said wasn't really a lie. They had been the ones

that caused Vertoyi to see how far he had fallen. They had been the ones to push him toward taking his own life.

Jackoby lowered his wooden hammer but did not fully relax. Behind him, the other Firbolgs still held their weapons at the ready.

"There were ruins at the Grove," one of the other Firbolg said.

With another growl and a quick glance back, Jackoby silenced that one. Turning back to face Hall, Jackoby studied him for a long time.

"He is right," the Firbolg leader said finally. "There was a village there, but it was in ruins. You have claimed it as yours." A statement, not a question.

"I have," Hall replied.

Taking a couple steps back, never turning, Jackoby kept his warhammer pointed at Hall.

"The elders must learn of this," he said, stopping beneath the trees, a shadowed form. "Do not leave this spot until we return. Moving deeper into the forest will be considered an aggressive act and will be treated as such." His voice faded as he disappeared into the trees.

One by one the others followed until each was gone and only silence remained. Hall still couldn't believe how silent they had been. He waited a couple of minutes before letting himself somewhat relax. Hall knew there were Firbolgs in the trees watching, probably more than just the eight that had shown themselves, possibly just waiting for the party to do something stupid.

"What now?" Sabine asked.

"We wait," Hall answered.

CHAPTER EIGHT

They did not wait for long.

It was midafternoon when the Firbolgs returned.

The morning and early afternoon had been tense. Without being able to leave the cave, they mostly sat around. Waiting. Which would have been boring but they were on edge, fully expecting a cloud of arrows to come flying out of the woods at any moment. Each of them kept glancing into the depths of the trees, looking for the Firbolgs they knew were watching. Hall had walked to the edge of the clearing, taking a couple of steps into the trees. Nothing had happened, but he could feel eyes on him.

With nothing to do, having forced free time, they took the opportunity to examine their Character Sheets and study their Skills. Hall felt like an idiot, that he hadn't taken the time to do so before, but things had been hectic and nonstop since day one of his new life in Sky Realms Online. It was not something that could happen while traveling, and they had found themselves with precious little downtime. After walking so many miles a day, when they finally camped and settled down, they were too exhausted. When not traveling, it was time to sleep.

He had given the Skills a quick review, noticing the addition of the Activity and Environment skill groups, but this was the first time he was able to really look into them. Mentally pulling up his Character Sheet, he opened the Skills tab. Divided into Combat, Magic, Environment, Activity, and Professions; there were a lot of choices to make. The problem was that he did not know the maximum number of skill points available. There was a complete lack of help menus now. Mentally clicking on a skill would give a description, but that was it. No hard numbers about what the skill would do to things like Attack Power, Attack Speed, and the other Statistics.

Glancing at Leigh, the only one that did not have the faraway look that meant someone was accessing the Character Sheet, he realized that she already knew everything about the Skills. He didn't need access to a Wiki page; he had access to someone that had been essentially born into this world. Leigh knowing about levels and classes most likely meant she knew about Skills as well.

"Dumb question," he said, catching her attention. It was weird looking at her through the translucent Character Sheet hovering in the air before him. "But what is the maximum number of Skill points?"

Leigh gave him that look she gave him a lot. The one that said it was a strange question, and he was a strange person. So far, she still trusted him and wanted to spend time with him, but he was afraid that at some point he'd push her away with the questions that were obvious to her. The ones that showed he knew nothing about the world he lived in. He hoped it never came to that.

"Dumb but not that dumb," she answered. "Scholars have been debating for ages why there's no total given anywhere, but it was discovered through trial and error. Combat or Magic depends on your Class, and there's a 200 point maximum."

Hall saw that Roxhard and Sabine were paying attention.

"I don't need to explain the difference between Combat and Magic, do I?" Leigh said with a laugh.

Roxhard laughed with her, Hall smiled, and Sabine scowled.

"Activity and Environment are 150 points in each," Leigh continued. "With Professions being 150 but..."

"We know the Profession restrictions," Sabine interrupted.

Leigh shrugged, not bothered by the Witch's irritated tone.

"If there's only 150 points in Professions, that means there's 50 points maximum per skill," Hall said, doing the math quickly.

Professions were divided into Gathering and Crafting. A character, or person Hall thought now, could only have a maximum of two in either Gathering or Crafting.

"Right," Leigh said. "Five ranks in each skill."

They fell silent as each again returned to their individual Character Sheets. Hall had his Combat skills already. *Light Armor, Polearms, Small Blades,* and *Thrown.* He could have substituted *Small Blades* for something else, but he wanted to have some close-quarter combat capabilities and a fall back if a spear was broken. As a Skirmisher, he did not have access to any Magic skills. Already in Activity he had *Triage* which he knew he'd keep along with *Identify* which would come in useful someday, just not right now at lower levels. Environment was *Tracking, Camouflage, Stealth,* and *Survival.* He would have to drop something or not raise two to their maximums. Or drop those completely to pick up something else. *Negotiation* would probably be a good Skill to have especially in forming alliances and trade for Skara Brae. For Professions, he had his two Gathering, *Herbology* and *Skinning,* and his Crafting with *Cartography.* He did think about taking up another Crafting Skill, to supplement his income. But which? Leatherworking? Blacksmithing? Would that be a waste since eventually, hopefully, they would have skilled and dedicated crafters in the village? He filed the thought away to the back of his mind. It was something to figure out once the village had started growing and he saw where he might need to fill in gaps.

Looking at his Character Sheet, Hall realized he had an unassigned Stat point, gotten when he had leveled to four. He wanted to put it into Strength, Agility, or Wellness but decided on Charisma. Considering what he hoped to accomplish in the Firbolg village, he would probably need all the Charisma he could get.

For now, Hall was satisfied with where he was heading. Along with the Class Abilities he would gain as he leveled, the additional Skill Abilities he would gain at higher ranks would help his arsenal of offensive capabilities.

He spent some time looking through the available skills, ones he knew he wouldn't be raising. Some were things he thought only NPCs would use. Skills like *Farming* and *Dancing*. He was about to ask the others what they had chosen when the Firbolgs arrived.

Jackoby came out of the trees, as silent as before. The trees were empty and then they weren't, Jackoby and four others just appearing as if out of nowhere. He did not look happy. His shield was slung over his shoulder, Hall taking that as a good sign.

In the daylight, Hall got a good look at the Firbolg. Tall, he seemed to tower over even the others. At least seven and a half feet tall, as wide in body as Roxhard. Jackoby had light brown fur-like skin with thick tufts at his shoulders. His hair was thick and long, hanging down well past his neck. Eyes that were still golden stared at Hall, not with anger but annoyance. There were darker patches of fur around the eyes, extending up his temples. Stripes of the darker fur ran up his bare arms. He wore a light leather chest piece but with thin plates of a dark wood stitched into the hide. The wood plates bent with the Firbolgs movements, thin enough to stretch and move, but they still looked strong enough to deflect a blow from a weapon. Leather covered his wrists and his feet.

The head of his warhammer was easily eight inches long and six high. Circular, it resembled a tree trunk cut into a smaller piece. Which it most likely was, Hall realized. Strange symbols were carved into its smooth surface.

Like during the night, Jackoby pointed at Hall using the warhammer.

"Come with us," Jackoby growled. "Now."

Hall and the others stood up, grabbing their weapons and packs. They had already cleared up the camp, stowing their gear, anticipating having to move quickly to either follow the Firbolgs or fight and possibly run away.

Jackoby took the lead, followed by Hall and the others. Two Firbolgs took the rear behind Roxhard. The other two disappeared into the forest, one to a side.

"The bird does not fly or it will be shot down," Jackoby warned, looking over his shoulder.

Hall nodded. He had thought about sending Pike into the air for an overhead view, allowing Hall to map their movements easier. But not now.

The Firbolg set a quick pace, forcing them to hustle to keep up. They were moving too fast for Hall to keep track of where they were heading, unable to pull up the map and pay attention to where they were walking. The Firbolg was taking a very winding route. Between the speed and the route, none of them could say exactly where they were going or where they had been.

Hall knew that was Jackoby's goal.

———

They walked for hours.

The sun was barely visible through the thick canopy of

trees, but Hall was able to see it at times. He knew they had started out heading south and then had turned to the east before heading south again. At one point, he could have sworn by the sun's position that they had swung back north.

Jackoby never looked back. He kept the same steady pace, up hills and across brooks. The Firbolg assumed the group was following. If they weren't, he did not care. It was obvious that Jackoby wanted nothing to do with them.

Hall had a quick thought that the Firbolg might have been leading them somewhere only to kill them but that would have been a waste. They were easy enough targets back in the cave. No, Hall knew Jackoby was leading them to the Firbolg's village. Just the long route.

They didn't speak during the trek. There was no time, as they had to concentrate on walking. The terrain was rough, no trail. They pushed through the bushes, over fallen trees and brooks. They walked along the edge of a long ridge that extended for miles in both directions, the floor far below at the bottom of a steep grass and rock covered slope. A river flowed along the bottom of the ridge, the forest divided. The view from the top of the ridge was spectacular, the land lower and flatter from the bottom of the ridge all the way to the island's edge. They could see more islands floating in the distance, the edge of Edin miles away and the thin line of the Auld to Silver Peak Keep road. A sea of green treetops spread out below, the forest far larger than Hall had remembered or assumed it to be.

The forest was beautiful, the parts they saw of it.

Tall trees, the trunks getting thicker and the branches higher the deeper they walked into the depths of the Fallen Green Forest. Old growth that had not been disturbed, allowed to spread and reach for the sky. Grass-covered hills, with flat boulder-covered tops. Valleys and dells, streams running along the bottoms. They passed by two decent sized ponds, watching the surfaces ripple as something passed beneath.

Eventually, they arrived at the outskirts of the village.

———

The first sign was the disappearance of the animal noises. The woods had been alive with the sounds. Squirrels running through the trees, rustling the branches. Birds chirping and flying, their wings beating as they soared through the sky. Pike squawked in frustration, wanting to fly off and hunt or soar over the woods, but Hall kept him grounded. He felt the talons as Pike squeezed his shoulder, the dragonhawk watching a chipmunk dart up a tree.

Now, there was no noise, and Hall knew they were close.

Ahead, two Firbolgs stepped out from behind large maple trees. Each wore the strange leather and wood armor over their chests, lower legs, and arms, and each wore a helm carved to resemble antlers. The guards carried a shield and warhammer. They nodded as Jackoby walked by, giving hard glares to Hall and the others.

Hall studied them, pulling their basic information, remembering to do so. It was hard, he realized. Seeing the status of a target, friendly or not, had come naturally before. Now, he was forgetting how some older, common game mechanics translated into this new life. Looking at someone to get information about them was not something he would have done in the real world. It was part of no longer thinking of Sky Realms as a game.

Skill Gain!

Identify Rank 1 +.2

Brownpaw Border Guardian

Brownpaw Border Guardian

Just past the guards, a trail cut into the forest. On either side of the trail stood two tall totem poles. Eight feet tall, two feet in diameter, carved from a shining and dark wood. Hall realized it was ironwood. Which was odd as he didn't remember any growing in this forest. Ironwood was a high-level, harvestable material used by crafters, the same material as his new spear. The totems were richly detailed, every line tight, without any wear showing. Each totem showed a large bear standing on its hind legs, growling head staring into the woods. Perched on top of each bear was an eagle with wings spread.

The totems were beautiful, shining in the sun. The level of detail was amazing, each feather intricately carved, the fur of the bear's hackles standing up. The carvings were polished, the darkness of the wood having variations. Hall was impressed by the workmanship.

They stood six feet or so apart, the trail just wide enough for two Firbolgs to walk side by side. The floor of the trail had been worked smooth, roots and stumps removed from the path, the ground hard-packed, branches along the sides pruned.

Jackoby did not wait for them to examine the totems. If anything, the Firbolg Warden increased his pace. Hall and the others had to rush to keep up, the Firbolgs behind them prodding them on. He saw that the two Firbolg Hunters that had been flanking them were now in the rear with the others. The trail curved to the south, and they continued for another hour.

More totems lined the path, stone walls in other spots. They passed what looked to be fields with no buildings visible, just wide-open lands for farming. Some Firbolgs could be seen working in the fields. Large beasts that looked like moose, called Alcest, were hitched to wagons or plows. They had shaggy hair around their forelocks, thick hooves, standing as tall as a Firbolg's shoulder. Wide and strong looking animals, they had large heads with tusks that grew out from the underside of their heads. Wide antlers with many points grew from the forehead. Shaggy coats in whites and browns, with a few black.

Herds of wild Alcest roamed the highlands to the north, and Hall had been unlucky enough to fight some. The animals were strong and fast, using the tusks and antlers in combat as well as kicking out. They looked like moose but had many traits of horses, which is why they served as the mounts for the large Firbolgs.

The fields gave way to forest again, thick and old. Ahead, through the trees, Hall could see the canopy thinning. A clearing just ahead. The trail opened onto the ridge, showing the view of the forest below. They followed the path as it turned, paralleling the ridge, a wooden fence along the cliff-side. Trees on the other side and an almost sheer drop on the other with the railing alternating with a low hedge. The land started to slope down.

Hall knew they were approaching the Firbolg village of Green Ember. He recognized the path as it was similar to the one leading to the village in the game. Ahead, the trail would curve away from the ridge, which in the game wasn't as high, and open into a large clearing with a dozen homes. Firbolg homes were large but simple. Built of logs with low-pitched roofs. Green Ember homes had all faced a central square. He was expecting something different. All the cities were different. Larger, more full of life.

He discovered that even expecting Green Ember to be different, he was still very wrong.

The forest ended, the path continuing down a gentle slope with Green Ember spread out before them. Terraces, eight levels, were cut into the side of the hill sloping down to the forest below at the bottom of the ridge. The path widened, becoming a road that met with others leading to the top terrace, other roads visible far below that led away from the lowest terrace. The road switchbacked as it continued down terrace to terrace and ending at the lowest, a long line cutting across the hill.

Buildings, homes, and shops were built along the terraces. Some were two stories, the upper story having an entrance on the higher terrace, others a single story with flat roofs that became gardens or areas of grass. Wooden staircases ran alongside those. Between some of the homes were steep ramps or sets of stairs going from terrace to terrace. Parts of the homes could be seen extending into the hillside, putting them under the roads above. The exposed parts were made from logs with thick glass-filled windows. Each story was taller than any Human dwelling.

The central terrace widened out, a large statue in the middle with benches arrayed around it. Firbolgs, men and women, could be seen wandering the streets, moving from home to home. Trees and planters were spaced along the street, provided color and shade. A small pond, the water crystal clear, was below the steep cliff a short distance from the village proper, homes along the shores.

Hall counted at least a hundred buildings, with more scattered around the lower forest floor so far below. Green Ember was much larger than he had ever imagined it would be. And peaceful, full of light. The original village had been surrounded by trees, the canopy thick and blocking most of the sun. This village, town really, was open. The ridge was exposed, open to the land around.

"Wow," Roxhard said, voicing what Hall was thinking.

"Come," Jackoby growled, impatient, from further down the path.

The Firbolg had kept walking while they had stopped in

amazement. Hall nudged Roxhard, and they started walking again, the Dwarf's eyes wandering the village.

They followed the path to where it became the road, continuing past the first row of buildings. Each log that made up the buildings seemed to be at least a foot in diameter, carefully smoothed to remove all bark, polished and sanded. They fit tightly together, the top ones just below the flat roofs, were longer, sticking out a foot or two past the walls. The ends of each of those were carved. Bears, eagles, great cats, and even otters.

The level of detail was amazing, Hall thought as he looked up at one as they passed. He noticed images carved into the logs over the doors. Pictures of animals, runes, and other symbols.

Jackoby turned down a set of stairs, leading them to the next terrace. Stone, made from the granite of the ridge, the stairs were set for Firbolg size. The rise of the steps just a little off for Hall, even more for the shorter Roxhard, who had a hard time walking down them. Turning to the right, Jackoby led them to another set of stairs between two houses.

Down they went, zigzagging their way down the terraces to the central one. They passed by one shop, the front open to the street, and Hall didn't notice Sabine stopping until she called his name. Walking back to join her, he looked into the shop.

A lone Firbolg woman, her tan fur showing streaks of gray that marked her age, was standing in front of three young Firbolgs. Two boys and a girl, no older than sixteen if that. The elderly woman had a hand raised, fingers outstretched, and was tracing them across the surface of a stone tablet she held. Where the fingers passed, a line of green followed. It glowed, softly, the line solid as if painted onto the stone. She finished and held the tablet for the Firbolg children to see. Green lines crossed over others, a square forming around a circle.

Pulling her fingers into a fist, she snapped the first two, and the green light flared and disappeared but a faint outline was etched into the stone. Setting the tablet down, she stepped back, motioning the children to do the same. Once they were clear, she barked a single word and the lines drawn onto the tablet flared once again and a shaft of green flames shot out from the glowing carved lines. A small column, only two feet high or so. It died out a couple seconds later. The woman smiled and asked the younger Firbolgs a question in their language.

"What was that?" Sabine asked, staring at where the green lines had been floating.

The older Firbolg woman noticed them looking. She studied Sabine for a moment before turning and motioning at the younger Firbolgs to bring their attention back to her. They had all turned when Sabine had spoken, watching the newcomers with fascination.

Hall wondered if they had ever seen Humans or Dwarves before.

"Move," one of the Firbolg behind them said, stepping forward and motioning with his hammer.

Jackoby had paused at the top of another set of stairs. He scowled at them. Sabine started walking, but her head turned back to look at the building and the older Firbolg inside.

The Firbolg leader led them to the large square in the center of the terrace. The statue was made of ironwood polished to a dark sheen. A bear, sitting on its haunches. Easily fifteen feet tall, the statue dominated the square, wooden benches set in rows facing it.

Turning, Jackoby led them to a building that faced the square. The largest in town. Three stories, a balcony off the top, with a steep, sloping roof. A log formed a ridge beam that ran past the walls a couple of feet, the end carved into a roaring bear. Each of the corners under the roof held similar totem heads. All bears, different poses.

Standing outside the large building, to the right of the doors, was a Settlement Stone. Like the one that stood in Hall's village of Skara Brae, this stone was four to five feet tall. A light gray obelisk, square that tapered to the top. Nine inches wide at the base, six wide at the top where the four sides came together into a point. Runes were carved across its surface as it sat on a wider pedestal a couple inches off the ground.

The stone granted many powers to the ruler, or rulers, of a village. All functions of the village were accessed and somewhat controlled from the stone. Hall had just barely touched the surface of what the stone's menus showed.

Open double doors, nine feet tall, led inside. Jackoby motioned for them to follow as he entered the building. The first floor was wide open, two stories tall, a set of stairs along the right-hand sidewall. Four great pillars stood in the corners of the room, more totems than structural, running from floor to ceiling. Animal heads were carved into them, rows of carved symbols between the heads.

A firepit was in the middle of the space, sunk down, the wooden floor leading up to it and stopping a foot or so shy. Logs were stacked in the pit, none lit. Tapestries hung on the walls, finely made but lacking in colors. Grays, browns, and blacks, nothing bright. They depicted Firbolg in battle, Firbolg farming. Armed Firbolg lined the walls, ten to each side and four near the doors. Hall could hear noises coming from the room above, most likely more guards.

Hall thought they were all there because of the party. He had wondered why they had been allowed to enter with their weapons. Now he knew. They were badly outnumbered. He wondered if it was a test of some kind. Give them their weapons and see if they could be pushed to attack.

At the far end was a single chair on a raised stage. Sitting in the chair was the oldest Firbolg that Hall had ever seen. She was stooped, hunched over, a thick wooden and gnarled staff held in hand. Her fur had gone to all gray, and she wore a simple green robe. Darker gray stripes lined the exposed fur of her arms, bands around her eyes that turned and ran down her neck. Her eyes were bright still, showing interest as Jackoby led them forward. Next to her was a Firbolg male, similar coloring to Jackoby, but taller. This one had dark stripes along his cheeks.

"Come closer," the elderly Firbolg, the village leader, said. Her voice was strong. "What have you brought to us, my son?"

Hall glanced at Jackoby in surprise. The Firbolg was the son of the village leader?

Her gaze fell on Hall. He felt her sizing him up, studying him.

"You are Hall, the new Lord of Skara Brae?" she asked and didn't bother waiting for a response.

He wondered how she knew his name. There had been no introductions exchanged. Back in Grayhold on the first day when Guard Captain Henry had known his name, Hall thought it part of the game's coding. NPCs had always automatically known Players' names. It had ruined the immersion but had saved time. Is that what happened with a high enough *Identify* skill? Everyone could just *Identify* the person and find out the name. Hall now realized that was how Henry had known his name.

The elderly Firbolg's gaze fell upon Leigh.

"Leigh, is it not? You are the new Custodian?"

Leigh nodded, shrinking under the gaze, but then she stood straight, finding her confidence, matching the elderly Firbolgs stare.

"I am."

"How did such as you—" the male Firbolg standing next to the elder started to ask and paused, his voice a growl. He made

Jackoby seem friendly. He shook his head and barked a laugh. "There is no way you defeated the Custodian. None of you are above Level Four."

Hall looked at the Leigh, Sabine, and Roxhard; they all looked to him, waiting to follow his lead. He sighed. Thoughts of lying passed through his mind, quickly. That was not a good way to start off an alliance and that was what he was there for.

"We got lucky," he said. "Vertoyi, the corrupted Custodian, would have killed us but she," he pointed at Leigh, "showed him the corruption he had caused. In the end, he took his own life to end that corruption."

He had never looked to see what level Vertoyi was. Twelve at least. Higher than they had thought the Druid would have been. By taking his own life, Hall and the others had missed out on a good amount of experience.

But they also had not died. It was a tradeoff Hall was fine with.

The Firbolg warrior laughed, mocking, but the elder smiled.

Skill Gain!
Identify, Rank 1 +.4

Yarbole of the Brownpaw
Level 15 Clan Chieftain

Baskily of the Brownpaw

He was surprised that he got a level reveal on the elderly Firbolg but not the other. He looked at Yarbole and saw her smiling. Had she allowed her Level to be viewed?

Hall didn't know exactly what a *Clan Chieftain* was exactly. The NPC class, what its role was at least, that was obvious. But what were the Class Abilities and what were Yarbole's skills?

The elderly Firbolg was one of the highest Levels they had encountered yet. He thought about what Leigh had said. Higher Levels were rare. Most people living in the realms, the NPCs, were Level Four to Six with some rare going higher and almost legendary figures making it to Level Twenty. It was almost unheard of for a person to get to Level Twenty-Five.

Adventuring was the best way to gain experience, and there were few people that took up that path. Too dangerous. Most people took the safer road, gaining experience through their class quests and other minor occurrences. Which was why they were so low.

Baskily, the younger Firbolg that stood on the platform, was going to be trouble, Hall knew. He seemed older than Jackoby and not just in Level. Hall hoped it didn't mean Baskily was going to be the future Brownpaw chieftain. Or elder. Or whatever the clan of Firbolgs called their leader.

She hadn't said much, but Hall just felt like Yarbole would be the easier one to deal with. There was a grandmotherly aura to her.

"It does not matter how Vertoyi died," Hall started, wanting to get on some solid footing, thinking that he would invest in the *Negotiate* skill. "It only matters that he is dead. Leigh is the new Custodian, and she will cleanse the corruption."

Baskily started to say something, but Yarbole held up her hand. The other quieted instantly.

"The Grove is far from here," she said in her cracking voice. "But all things are connected to the Branches of the World Tree, even the forest we call home." She motioned with her staff, making a circular motion. "We felt the corruption of the Grove, saw its effects. It is good that the corruption will end," she finished and gave a respectful nod to Leigh, who returned it. Angus mooed, and the old Firbolg chuckled.

Hall started to speak, but she held up a hand.

"My son..." She made a motion toward Jackoby who had moved off to the side. The Firbolg glared at Hall and the others. "He tells me that you wish to discuss trade relations with the Brownpaw."

Here we go, Hall thought.

"I do," Hall said to her. "But my first goal was to meet our new neighbors."

"You have met us," Baskily growled. "Now you may leave."

The elderly chief of the Brownpaw laughed and shook her head. She reached out her free hand and laid it on Baskily's arm.

"Calm yourself, my son," she said, gently scolding him.

If anything, his glare intensified.

"Your village is in ruins, is it not," Yarbole stated.

Hall nodded.

"For now," he said, trying to sound confident as a leader of a thriving community would. He felt out of his depth, unsure what to say. Finding someone else to serve as Skara Brae's ambassador, its spokesperson, moved to the top of his long list.

"A trade agreement between peoples is based on each having equal standing," Yarbole said. There was no arrogance in her voice. She spoke like a teacher. "Or when unequal, one side has something of value that other wants. What do you have to offer us?"

Hall thought about, trying to come up with different plans. There had to be something that he could offer Yarbole. He wasn't sure he really needed a trade agreement, or alliance, with the Firbolgs, but he was sure they didn't need one with him. There was nothing Skara Brae had to offer and might never have anything of value.

Finally, he just shook his head.

"Nothing," he admitted in defeat. "We have nothing that would benefit the Brownpaw."

Baskily barked a laugh. Jackoby looked angry, upset that his time had been wasted.

Yarbole looked thoughtfully at Hall, studying him. Her fingers tapped on the wooden armrests of her chair, a pattern of some kind.

"If you have nothing to offer the Brownpaw," she said finally. "Then there can be no trade agreement."

CHAPTER NINE

HALL SIGHED. IT WAS THE ANSWER THAT HE HAD EXPECTED, BUT it was still hard to hear. He felt defeated, like he had failed. He hoped that Yarbole would at least let them spend the night, get some rest and restock before they left.

"But," Yarbole said, drawing everyone's attention. "There is much that we can do for friends of the Brownpaw."

Baskily looked to his mother in surprise, shocked. He was about to say something, but she held up her hand, sharply cutting him off. Yarbole lowered her hand and looked at Leigh. Her gaze was sharp, measuring.

"As I said, the Grove is connected to our lands. Before the corruption, the Brownpaw were allies and friends of the Custodians. We can be so again," Yarbole told Leigh. The elder's gaze was not unfriendly, but there was no warmth in it either. A warning, Hall took it. Yarbole telling Leigh that the Firbolg would do her part and Leigh would need to do hers.

"I would like that," Leigh replied and nodded her head.

Yarbole's gaze softened, and she looked at Hall.

"It would be years before your village could offer anything to the Brownpaw," she said, not unkindly, just stating facts.

"There could never be a trade agreement between us, but we can be allies and friends."

"I would like that," Hall said.

Yarbole nodded.

"But friendship is not freely given," she said, raising a finger and pointing it at Hall. "Trust and friendship must be earned."

Now, Hall felt he was in familiar territory. Sky Realms Online had a robust reputation system, even before the Glitch, and it seemed to have gotten bigger post-Glitch. Earning reputation, which led to friendship, with different factions was a staple of MMOs.

"What can we do to show the Brownpaw our friendship?" he asked, choosing his words carefully.

"To earn the trust of the Brownpaw, you must shed blood for the Brownpaw," Baskily said in response. His tone was still angry but now resigned. His mother, his chieftain, had chosen a path, and he had to follow it.

Hall knew what was coming. A quest. He remembered the original game and the series of quests involving the Badgin that were creeping in on Brownpaw territory. The first quest had been to thin their numbers, then find out why they were encroaching on Brownpaw territory and finally defeat the Badgin chief. Three or four parts in total. With some repeatable aspects to raise reputation with the Brownpaw.

Yarbole was offering a quest. Just not the one he thought.

"Our resources are stretched thin," Baskily admitted. "The Badgin are creeping around the edges of our territory in the west, Trow to the north. We do not have the warriors to send east."

"What is to the east?" Hall asked, recovering from his surprise.

In a way, he had been looking forward to fighting the Badgin. The ferocious little humanoid beasts had been some of the most entertaining fights he had. The quests had been basic, but the fights had made up for it. He had hoped for something more familiar from the original game, but again, Sky Realms Online post-Glitch had surprised him.

Baskily shook his head, some fear creeping into his eyes. Yarbole put her wrinkled hand on his arm, but it was Jackoby that spoke. A dark growl.

"Undead."

————

"What?" Hall exclaimed.

Undead in Fallen Green? There had never been Undead on Edin before. They were rare on all the islands. There were few practitioners of the dark magic needed to raise the dead. Necromancy was a Skill that could be learned by Witches, a magic to supplement their Class Abilities. Very few Players had chosen it as the Skill Abilities weren't that useful. NPCs had it, but by the Lore, they were shunned by most civilizations and were hunted down. Most Undead were weak, Zombies and Skeletons that could be easily taken out. Their main threat was in numbers. But there were higher level Undead, vampires and revenants, which posed more of a challenge.

"It started two weeks ago," Baskily started. "They appeared as if out of nowhere. Dozens of Skeletons. We dispatched them easily enough but then more appeared."

"And kept appearing," Jackoby muttered.

"We sent warriors out to find where the monsters were coming from, but none returned," Baskily told them.

Hall studied Yarbole. She appeared sad, guilty that her people had died.

"So instead of sending more of your people, you're going to send us?" Sabine asked, an edge to her voice. "Nice way to make friends."

Baskily let out a low growl, taking a step forward, angry with fists clenched. Sabine stared at him defiantly, hands ready to raise and start spell casting. Yarbole glared at Sabine sharply but put a restraining hand on Baskily. The Firbolg did not take another step but did not back down.

"Yes," Yarbole answered. "There is more, but as you say, we are sending you. As my son said, to become friends of the Brownpaw, you must shed blood for the Brownpaw as we will for you."

"When?" Sabine muttered, but quieter than before, looking away from Yarbole's unwavering stare.

"As the Spirits will it," Yarbole replied, turning away from the Witch. "You came to us, asking for the friendship of the Brownpaw. This is how you earn it."

You have come seeking the friendship of the Brownpaw. Yarbole, Clan Chieftain of the Brownpaw, requests that you discover the cause of the Undead plaguing her lands. Do this and the Brownpaw will be in your debt and will provide aid and support to your fledgling village.

Journey to where the Undead are and seek clues to what is raising them.

THE ROAMING DEAD I
Slay 0/12 Undead
Find a Clue to the Cause of Undead Uprising 0/1
Reward: +500 Brownpaw Firbolg Reputation
+50 Experience

ACCEPT QUEST?

Hall glanced at the others. Leigh and Roxhard nodded, agreeing to go with his decision. Sabine just shrugged. He accepted the quest and looked at Yarbole.

"We need rest and healing," Hall told her. He glanced behind him, out the doors of the building and the setting sun. "It is getting late. May we stay here tonight and set out in the morning?"

"Of course," Yarbole replied. "Jackoby will show you to rooms and where to find food."

The Firbolg did not look happy at being told to escort the party.

"Thank you," Hall said, turning to leave but stopped and looked back at Yarbole. "I know it may be too much to ask, but my companions recently leveled and could use training."

A brief scowl crossed Yarbole's face before the serene smile and calm returned. It seemed she was starting to get annoyed. She nodded, accepting his request.

"My son will show you where the Warden and Druid can receive training," Yarbole said and glanced at Sabine. "I am sorry but we do not have any Witches in Green Ember."

She did not appear sorry.

Sabine nodded. She looked down at the floor, shuffling a foot. It was obvious that Sabine wanted to say something, or ask for something, but was afraid to.

"Speak, child," Yarbole said gently.

"As we were escorted through the village," Sabine started, looking up at Yarbole and choosing her words carefully. "We saw a Firbolg using a strange kind of magic."

Yarbole looked confused for a second but then understood.

"Ah, you saw Tyrenda," the Clan Chief said with a nod and smile. "She is a Shaman with the Rune Magic skill."

It was Sabine's turn to look confused.

"What is the Rune Magic Skill?" she asked hesitantly. Sabine wanted to know more, that was obvious, but was realizing her snarky attitude earlier might cost her that knowledge.

"Tyrenda can explain it better," Yarbole replied. "Why

don't you go and ask her? She may even teach you how to perform Rune Magic."

Sabine's eyes lit up. She had not expected that.

"Thank you," she said and gave a slight bow.

Yarbole nodded, raising her wrist and giving a slight flick. A clear signal that it was time for them to leave.

CHAPTER TEN

THE MORNING DAWNED BRIGHT AND CLEAR, NOT A CLOUD IN the sky.

Hall walked out of the one-room building the four of them, plus Pike and Angus, had shared for the night. Some kind of bunkhouse. There had been eight beds set up along the walls, a long table with benches in the middle. It had been empty, on the lowest terrace of Green Ember, one level up from the lower forest floor.

His Vitality had been fully recharged. The first time in a long time.

Success!
You have gotten a Full Night's Rest.
Your Vitality is fully restored.

Jackoby had led them there, showing them the location, before bringing them around to meet the trainers. They had left Roxhard with a group of Wardens. Leigh had wandered off by herself, with Angus, to where the Druids Grove had been pointed out.

Druids could be confusing, Hall had thought. All places of Druid activity were called Groves but all did not contain a Branch of the World Tree. To an outsider like Hall, a Grove was a Grove, but Leigh had assured him there were differences that only a Druid would recognize.

Sabine had left to return to the upper terrace and the Rune Magic user.

That had left Hall alone. Jackoby had left as soon as the two had returned to the small bunkhouse. While not outright hostile, like his older brother Baskily was, Jackoby was not friendly either. It was obvious he saw them as a nuisance, wasting his and the tribe's valuable time. Food was brought to him. No meat. Bread, vegetables, fruit, and cheese. Pitchers of water were provided. Not what Hall had been hoping for, but he wasn't going to complain.

Leigh was the first one back. She was smiling, scratching behind Angus' ear.

"All set?" he asked.

"Yeah. I learned *Gust of Wind* and *Earth Shield*," she said proudly. "I also got some training in the Plant Magic skill."

Hall nodded. Both the Abilities and the Skill would come in handy. Unlike the Melee classes, which had Combat Skills available to all, the Magic classes had specializations that augmented their spells. For Druids, it was Beast, Plant, or Spirit. That Leigh had chosen Plant Magic meant she was setting herself up for more powerful defensive abilities.

Spying the food, she practically ran to the long table in the middle of the room.

"I'm starving," she said and took a seat.

Hall chuckled and remained at the door.

Roxhard was the next to return. He moved slowly, stretching out his arms which showed them to be stiff and sore, his face a giant bruise. Leigh gasped when she saw him, momentarily forgetting about the food and rushing to the

Dwarf's side. She lay her hands on either side of his face, her tattoos glowing light blue as healing energy flowed into Roxhard.

"Thanks," he said, his cheeks red from Leigh's closeness and touch.

"Did you learn your next Ability?" Hall asked, trying to get Roxhard's attention.

The Dwarf was focused on Leigh, staring at her with a dumb expression. His eyes snapped into focus, and he glanced at Hall.

"Huh? Oh, yeah, I did," Roxhard said, smiling as Leigh stepped back. He moved his arms, no longer feeling the stiffness. "*War Cry* and *Combat Tactics*."

It was at least an hour after the sun had set fully before Sabine returned. The Witch had a contented smile on her face until she caught sight of Leigh. The other three were at the table, the plates with Sabine's share of the food pushed aside. They had been playing a card game with a deck that Roxhard had found on one of the bunks. A game called Steps. They had looked up when Sabine had entered.

"Why didn't you tell us about the other Magic Skills," she said, a tone of accusation in her voice. She sat down on the bench, pulling at the food, her hunger overriding her annoyance.

"What do you mean?" Leigh replied, genuinely confused. "I thought you knew."

"Other Magic Skills," Hall asked.

"Rune, Light, and Arcane," Sabine answered as she ate. "It appears that Magic classes can learn these new types as part of their two hundred points in Magic Skills."

"Sorry," Leigh said. "I really did think you would know about them."

Sabine started to reply, but Hall cut her off, not wanting an argument to start.

"Did you learn Rune Magic?" he asked.

The Witch shook her head.

"I learned Arcane instead."

"What's the difference?" Roxhard asked, throwing a card down and giving a triumphant look to Hall, who just rolled his eyes. Leigh chuckled.

"Rune magic is about creating timed effects. You mark something and activate it later. Kind of like the runes on magical weapons. Arcane is about the manipulation of energy. It will give me some more defensive and offensive capabilities."

They had all gone to bed soon after, falling into a deep sleep. Hall had thought about setting watches but decided not to. Like in the cave, the Firbolgs had plenty of opportunity to harm them and did not. And why would they kill them? Weren't they going to risk themselves for the Brownpaw in the morning?

Which bothered Hall as he stood in the doorway looking out onto the morning. Firbolgs moved about the buildings below them, some heading to the pond and early morning fishing. The body of water had looked small from atop the ridge, but it was bigger than Hall had first thought.

He didn't know why the quest was bothering him. The basics of it were nothing new, the storyline was fairly standard for RPG games. The people are being threatened, seek out the threat and stop it. The same type as the first quest out of Grayhold post-Glitch.

It was the nonchalant way the Firbolgs had admitted to using Hall and his friends so no Firbolg would be risked. *Used* was a good word. Before he felt like he was doing a service. This felt different.

Sighing, he knew it didn't matter. They were still going to seek out the source of the Undead. They were adventurers; this is what they did. And the Firbolgs had provided training, he had to admit. It was all part of the plan that was half-formed.

If he wanted to make Skara Brae into something, anything really, he needed friends and allies.

He needed the Firbolgs.

Three of the Brownpaw walked toward him. Jackoby was in the middle, large warhammer and shield in hand.

Skill Gain!
Identify Rank 1 +.2

Brownpaw Hunter
Brownpaw Hunter

Hall thought he recognized the two Hunters from the first walk to the village yesterday, but he wasn't sure. He had not gotten a good enough look. Wearing leather armor with the bark plates, they each carried a longbow and quiver, the bows almost twice as big as anything a Human or Elf would use. Longswords were belted at their waists.

Glancing back into the building, Hall saw that the others were done with packing up their gear. He turned back to Jackoby.

"We're ready to go," he said.

"Good," Jackoby answered gruffly. "Follow us."

———

They walked for almost an hour following a wide path along the shore of the pond, Firbolgs out in the water fishing from large canoes. The path wove around trees, passing between trunks as they encroached close to the water's edge. Near the far end of the pond, the path turned southeast into the woods.

Small totems, standing about four feet high, lined the path at set intervals. Bears with the mouths open with stone plates set in. Pausing at one, Hall saw the remains of wax on the plate. Others had candle stubs. The path itself was smooth, no plants or roots along the surface, hard-packed, well maintained. The branches along either side were cut back, pruned, not allowed to extend out over the path. Thick canopy above blocked out most of the sun, dark shadows everywhere.

The three Firbolgs walked slowly, not pushing. They were nervous. The further away from the pond, the more nervous they got. Hall wasn't sure why. The woods seemed peaceful enough, the totems indicating the path was frequently traveled.

Another half an hour later he found out why.

They heard the noise, an odd shuffling as if leaves and sticks were being pushed forward. Branches snapped, followed by a low moaning sound. The three Firbolgs stopped, moving off to the side. Hall stepped forward, glancing at Jackoby before turning to where the sound was coming from. Jackoby motioned Hall forward.

"Look," he said in a whisper, or what was meant to be a whisper for the deep-throated Firbolg.

With a quick glance back at the others, Hall stepped off the path. He moved quietly, each step careful.

Skill Gain!

Stealth Rank One +.1

The noise grew louder as Hall walked through the woods. He saw a shadowed form about ten feet away, its gait awkward and shambling. It continued, ignoring him, ignoring everything and just moving through the woods with no purpose that he could see. It thumped into a tree with a squelching sound, shifted a bit and kept walking.

Hall paralleled it for a bit, waiting for a break where he could see it clearer. When he got a good look at it, he wished he hadn't.

It stood about seven-feet tall, or would have if it wasn't

sagging forward. The thing walked as if its spine and muscles could not fully support the upper body weight. Taller, thicker, and wider than Hall, the creature was a Firbolg. Or it used to be. Rotting flesh fell from the body, exposing muscles and bones. Clothes were falling off, what remained of them. Patches of fur and scraggly hair, eyes that stared out at nothing showing no life.

A Zombie. A Firbolg Zombie.

That explained part of the Brownpaw clan's reluctance to take on the threat of the Undead. It was their ancestors, their loved ones, that were being reanimated.

Skill Gain!
Identify Rank One +.1

Rotting Brownpaw Warrior

The wind changed direction, and Hall got the scent of the creature. The smell assaulted him, foul and rank. He fought back the gag that threatened to erupt. He had never smelt anything so horrible. It made his eyes water.

Rotting Stench
The smell attacks your senses and clouds your mind, distracting you.

Your Attack Power is decreased by 2.

Your Attack Speed is increased by 1 second.

Your Protection is lowered by 2.

There was no timer associated with the debuff, which told Hall it was a constant effect. The negative effects might even increase the closer he got to the Zombie. Would it stack with more Zombies around? That would be bad if the Protection debuff stacked. Protection was the stat that reflected how well a blow from an enemy was avoided or how much damage was mitigated. It was a reflection of Agility, actual armor worn, and other factors. One of those was the ability to avoid the blow completely. The *Rotting Stench* debuff lowered the Protection stat by making it harder to focus and avoid attacks.

Zombies were not a tough foe when faced one-on-one. They did not use tactics; they just attacked. Magically strong, a hit from one could do some damage, and they sometimes hit with a Rotting Touch attack that added a little Poison Damage, but they were slow and easy to put down. A Zombie's true threat was in numbers. A pack of mindless Zombies could overwhelm almost anyone.

Because there was no controlling a Zombie, they were rarely raised.

Hall listened for more. They would not be quiet; it was impossible for a Zombie to not make noise. Hearing nothing, he crept forward, coming up behind the creature. He moved carefully, not making a sound. Somehow a Zombie's senses were heightened. The slightest sound would alert it, and the creature would have its target, not stopping until the target, or it, was dead.

Skill Gain!
Stealth Rank One +.1

Holding his spear, he jabbed it forward. The ironwood tip punctured the Zombie's chest, slamming out the front in an explosion of gore. The Zombie stopped moving, not even looking at the long shaft of wood sticking out of it. The creature tried to turn but could not as the spear impaling it kept it facing forward.

It was strong, constant movement as it tried to turn to get

at Hall. He had to keep rotating, holding the spear shaft between arm and body. If the Zombie had tried to step forward, it could have pulled itself off the spear, but it was too dumb. It just wanted to get at Hall.

Holding the shaft tight, keeping the Zombie away from him, Hall pulled out his short sword. Raising the sword, getting it ready, he pulled the Zombie toward him. When it was close enough, he swung the sword.

The Rotting Brownpaw Warrior's head landed on the ground with a wet thud. The body sagged, and Hall let it fall to the ground, pulling his spear out of it. He shook the tip, pieces of Zombie flying off. Hall grimaced at the disgusting mess left along the smooth wood spear.

SLAIN: *Rotting Brownpaw Warrior*
+25 Experience

Skill Gain!
Polearms Rank Two +.1

THE ROAMING DEAD I
Slay 1/12 Undead
Find a Clue to the Cause of Undead Uprising 0/1

He studied the rotting body, trying to see if there was anything useful to gather. Not seeing anything, and not wanting to sift through the rot, he headed back to the others. Once he got about twenty feet from the body, the *Rotting Stench* debuff disappeared, and his stats returned to normal.

Crazy distance, Hall thought, wondering if more than one Zombie would increase the range. Could wind direction factor in as well? Would it make sense to attack from downwind?

He stepped out onto the path behind the others, all of them turning swiftly.

"Well?" Sabine asked.

"We saw the quest notification," Leigh added.

They weren't in a party yet the quest was shared? Hall found that interesting. They had tried to party up at various points from when Hall had met Roxhard outside Grayhold, but it had never worked. It seemed that was because it was unnecessary.

"Zombie Firbolg," Hall said, looking at Jackoby.

The large Warden seemed to deflate, his normally angry eyes turning sad.

"Yes," Jackoby said. "Whatever is doing this has been using our own dead."

Hall knew he should have assumed that would be the case. What else would a Necromancer use? The only dead around would be Firbolgs. Suddenly, he knew where Jackoby was taking them and it worried him.

"We're going to the Fallen Green, aren't we?"

Jackoby nodded.

CHAPTER ELEVEN

HALL LOOKED OUT ACROSS THE CLEARING AT WHAT GAVE THE forest its name.

The Fallen Green was an immense tree laying on its side. Twenty feet in diameter, one hundred feet long. Just the trunk with knots where the branches had been removed long ago. By who, no one knew. Just like how no one knew why a hundred-foot tree had fallen in the first place. The stump was off to the side, itself twenty feet above the ground with a smooth top. Jagged edges had been removed from the stump but not the end of the great tree. The tree had fallen, not been cut.

It lay in a large clearing, something preventing other trees from growing. Only grass covered the clearing, tall and waving in the breeze. Some flowers scattered here or there but mostly on top of the mounds. The entire clearing was covered in burial mounds, still more on the other side of the tree.

Burial mounds that were open, dirt piled on the side as something had dug its way out.

Zombies and Skeletons roamed the clearing, the Zombies wandering aimlessly, the Skeletons with some purpose. Hall counted about two dozen. Luckily there were more Zombies than Skeletons.

Where the Zombies were mindless, just walking slabs of meat, the Skeletons were not. In Undeath, the walking pile of magically strong and connected bones possessed almost all the skills and training they had in life. That made Skeletons very dangerous and unpredictable since it was hard to tell what they had been when alive. They carried an assortment of weapons, rusting and rotted, or nothing at all. Warhammers and a couple swords, some shields, and a scythe.

Skill Gain!
Identify Rank One +.5

Brownpaw Bone Warrior
Brownpaw Bone Hunter
Brownpaw Bone Blacksmith
Brownpaw Bone Leatherworker
Brownpaw Bone Border Guard

Hall picked Skeletons at random, using the *Identify* skill. Only some of them had fighting Classes. Which would make it easier. It seemed the Necromancer had not been picky when raising the bodies. Which, with Undead, it didn't matter. Zombies and Skeletons, it was the numbers that mattered.

He had never understood how Skeletons retained the skills from life. The mind was gone, any soul gone. It was just a pile of animated bones. In one of the forums, someone had tried to explain it as a type of muscle memory but had been trolled fairly quickly. Skeletons were bones, not muscle. Hall had given up trying to figure it out. Skeletons were animated by magic, that was why they worked. Logic had nothing to do with it.

Really, the only important thing was how to destroy them. Which was pretty simple, just hit them until they broke.

"How do you want to play this, boss?" Roxhard asked in a whisper.

They were hidden at the edge of the clearing, behind bushes and trees, slightly higher than the clearing, giving them a good view. Hall peered up into the sky where Pike circled. Closing his eyes and then opening, he looked down upon Fallen Green. The tree nearly divided the clearing in half, the tip at one edge and the stump at the other. Zombies and Skeletons roamed on both sides of the immense tree. There was nothing else, just the mass of Undead.

He closed his eyes again, dismissing the *Shared Vision*. Looking around at the others, they all watched him, waiting for his command. He silently cursed, hating that he had somehow become the leader.

"Will you three fight with us?" Hall asked, staring straight at Jackoby. The look told the Firbolg what Hall expected the answer to be.

"Yes," Jackoby said a little reluctantly.

Hall couldn't blame him, not really. The Undead were his ancestors and his people. Hall wondered what he would do when faced with the possibility of fighting his zombified grandfather.

"It's just a body," Leigh said, picking up on Hall's concern.

Jackoby nodded. Hall could tell the Warden understood but it still didn't change the facts.

Hall watched the movements of the Undead. It was hard to plan as there was no pattern, and with the way the creatures reacted, they would be hard to pick off one by one without getting swarmed by the others. He wished one of them was a Shaman. *A good Fireball or Chain Lightning spell would be great*, he thought, remembering the lightning spell that Vertoyi, the corrupted Custodian, had used on them.

"What we need is a place that will limit the number of

them we will face at once," Hall said, eyes darting around the clearing, looking for anything.

He remembered what Fallen Green had been before. The burial mounds had been there, the great tree itself, but no Undead. Just Badgin grave robbers. The land was the same, just more of it, as he tried to picture it in his mind. The tree, stump, mounds, grass. There had to be something they could use to funnel and control the Undead's movements. Hall looked to Jackoby. This was his home; he should have some idea.

The large Firbolg shrugged.

"It is all open land," he replied.

Hall cursed. So much for that idea.

"What about the stump?" Roxhard asked, pointing toward what was essentially a large hill made of wood. "That's a ramp around it right?"

"Yes, it is," Hall said, cursing his own stupidity.

Twenty feet high, twenty in diameter, the top of the stump had been smoothed by the Firbolgs for their ceremonial use. A thin ramp had been carved into the side of the stump, spiraling to the top. It was perfect.

———

They crept carefully along the edge of the woods, eyes watching the clearing and the Undead for signs of movement. Spread out, keeping space between them, they all worked to keep the noise down.

Hall could hear the clack of bones as the Skeletons moved, each motion a popping of the magically held joints. The Zombies just uttered their low moans, feet shuffling across the ground.

The one drawback in the plan was that using the stump would open them up to all the Undead on both sides of the

Fallen Green. It was high enough that none of the Undead could climb up the steep sides, and the ramp was thin enough that only a couple of the Undead would be able to go up at a time. Control of the numbers but it still would be a lot of them.

It took a fair bit of time to move across the wide clearing at their pace. Stepping carefully, quietly and watching where they were going as well as the Undead in the clearing. Hall stopped about thirty feet away from the bottom of the ramp, a direct line with no burial mounds between. There were a few Undead, Zombies, shambling about.

He motioned to Roxhard, pointing to one of the Zombies. The Dwarf nodded.

"On my signal," he told the others, not bothering to look back at them, concentrating on the movements of the Zombies. "Run for the ramp."

"What is the signal?" Jackoby asked.

The Firbolg seemed annoyed. Had been since Hall had come up with the plan. The top of the stump was where the Brownpaw performed many ceremonies. It was kind of sacrilege to fight from there, but Hall wasn't caring. Yarbole hadn't specified how they were to accomplish their task, so Hall would use what was available.

"This," Hall said and activated *Leap*.

He arced out over the clearing, a good ten feet or so high. The Zombies, three of them, looked up as he soared overhead. He stabbed down, and the ironwood tip of his spear sliced right into the rotting meat head of a Zombie. Hall didn't even need to pull the spear out, his own momentum and the rot did it. The Zombie fell backward, arms and legs kicking uselessly.

Hall landed and pivoted, thrusting out with the spear and catching another Zombie in the side as it tried to get at him. Standing up, he twisted with the spear, pulling the trapped Zombie, moving it away from the group's path. He saw the third Zombie go down hard, the barreling form of Roxhard slamming into it. Guts, muscle, and bone flew everywhere as the Dwarf's momentum blew the Zombie apart.

The others raced by, heading for the ramp. The three Firbolgs stopped, watching the Skeletons and Zombies start to react to the noise.

"Go," Hall yelled.

They started moving again. Hall watched as Pike swooped down from above, diving for the first Zombie Hall had skewered. The dragonhawk hovered in the air, screeching and released a jagged bolt of blue lightning. The strike slammed into the Zombie's chest, gore exploding outward. Pike flew off and the Zombie stopped moving.

Slain: *Rotting Brownpaw Farmer*
+10 Experience

Skill Gain!
Polearms Rank Two +.1

THE ROAMING DEAD I
Slay 3/12 Undead
Find a Clue to the Cause of Undead Uprising 0/1

Rotting Stench
The smell attacks your senses and clouds your mind, distracting you.

Your Attack Power is decreased by 2.

Your Attack Speed is increased by 1 second.

Your Protection is lowered by 2.

Hall stumbled as the Zombies' *Rotting Stench* attacked his

senses. His back was to the clearing, facing the forest, and he could hear the sounds of the Undead approaching. Some would be chasing the others, but most would be coming to attack him. He cursed as the impaled Zombie tripped and fell, almost pulling the spear from Hall's hands. Holding it tight, the Zombie just slipped off the weapon. He glanced at Roxhard, seeing the Dwarf was following the others, the Zombie he had knocked over unmoving. That was the extra kill he had received counting for the quest. Roxhard had killed one and they shared it.

He turned and watched the line of Undead slowly marching toward him. Pike flew down, blasting a Skeleton in the face with a lightning bolt. The creature tried to bat at Pike, but the quick and agile dragonhawk soared out of reach. Hall reached for his javelin, meaning to impale the creature that Pike had attacked but realized the weapon would no longer return to him. He didn't want to lose the weapon, not yet.

Instead, he pulled one of the throwing knives from his bracer. Taking aim, he launched the magical weapon. It slammed into the Skeleton's chest bones. A normal knife would have ricocheted off, doing minimal damage, but this one exploded on impact. Sparks erupted, spreading all over the Skeleton's chest. It hesitated before starting to walk again, smoke drifting up from the charred bones.

The rest of the Undead kept marching, ignoring the one that was smoking.

A quick glance to the ramp showed the others were already at the top, Jackoby and Roxhard midway down and attacking the few Undead that were following up the ramp. It was then that Hall saw the flaw in his plan.

And it was a big one.

The Undead did not care that the path up the stump was only wide enough for two to stand side by side. They just kept going, the ones behind pushing the ones ahead. There were not many at the moment, but Hall could see more and more of the Undead in the clearing heading for all the noise. It was only those on the far edges that did not react. The mass of Undead would just keep pushing up the ramp and his companions would have no choice but to keep retreating.

Hall cursed his stupidity. Once on top of the stump, they would have nowhere to go.

From the top of the stump, he saw the two Brownpaw Hunters firing arrow after arrow into the Undead, not the ones on the ramp but the ones still advancing. Which was smart. Each arrow found its mark in a Zombie's head, instantly stopping the creature. Another smart move. The arrows would have been wasted on the Skeletons. Hall was glad that Jackoby had brought experienced fighters with him.

Sabine and Leigh were casting spell after spell down at the Undead. The Witch alternated between *Hexbolts* at the Undead on the ramp and *Shadowbolts* at the others. Leigh was using her *Gust of Wind* to push the Undead into others, causing them to attack each other. *Splinter Storms* launched into Zombies in the clearing.

THE ROAMING DEAD I

Slay 4/12 Undead

Find a Clue to the Cause of Undead Uprising 0/1

Roxhard's axe lifted from a Zombie's head, the Dwarf pushing the creature into the ones behind it, causing confusion and giving himself a quick breather.

Hall estimated the distance from where he stood, pushing back a Zombie with his spear, to the top of the stump. It would be close, but he could make it with *Leap*. Crouching, about to activate the ability, he paused, seeing something glinting in the sun at the base of the large tree. It wasn't the shine of metal. Possibly a jewel of some kind.

He was going to ignore it. The spot was clear of Undead. For now. But it would make it harder for him to get back to the top of the stump. Not worth it until he remembered the quest. They had to find a clue to the cause of the uprising. He had played Sky Realms Online, and other games like Dragon Scrolls and Elder Age, long enough to know that an object that was purposefully drawing the Player's attention was usually special in some way.

Whatever it was, it practically had an arrow above it in bright lights saying 'vitally important'.

Worth the risk, Hall thought and activated *Leap*.

He soared over the heads of the Undead, not bothering to attack. Landing in a crouch, Hall sprinted the last couple of feet toward the Fallen Green. There were no Undead, but he could hear the sound of some of them turning and starting to shamble his way.

The trunk of the Fallen Green was a light brown and rough, the thick bark cracked. In a normal-sized tree, the ridges of bark and crevices between were small, not even wide enough for a finger. But the Fallen Green was not normal-sized. The crevices in the bark were easily wide enough for a finger to grip. The tree had fallen with such force that it had pushed into the ground, burying part of the curve under feet of dirt. The curve of the trunk was visible, moss and plants growing over the surface.

Where the curve hit the grass, there was a small object resting on the ground. The glint he had seen. It was green and about the size of a softball. Perfectly round, a bright spot of light seemed to glow from within. He reached down and picked it up.

Success!
You have found Eye of Death's Gaze.

THE ROAMING DEAD I
Slay 6/12 Undead
Find a Clue to the Cause of Undead Uprising 1/1

Hall had no idea what the object was, but it had satisfied the Quest conditions. They would have to figure out what the object did after dealing with the Undead. He saw that the others had killed more Undead, but he had not received any experience. Basically, it was what he had thought. There was shared experience if two or more dealt some amount of damage to the same target, but there was no shared experience across Quests.

Something else caught his eye. Just to the side of the object, he found a footprint. Human-sized, booted. Another one just beyond. They led down the side of the trunk, heading for the stump.

Skill Gain!
Tracking Rank One +.1

Hall was tempted to follow the trail, but the Undead were too close now. Glancing around, dropping the *Eye of Death's Gaze* into his pouch, he saw the creatures converging from three sides. He was going to find himself trapped and over-whelmed. Where he stood, at the slight depression in the grade, he couldn't see beyond the Undead to see if there was a safe space to land after using *Leap*. It wouldn't do him any good to jump out of one group of overwhelming Undead to land in another.

But he did have one direction which he knew was clear.

Activating *Leap*, Hall jumped straight up.

He adjusted his angle slightly, arcing over the wide trunk of the tree. He landed near the edge where it curved, almost slipping and falling but adjusting his balance. Carefully, he walked to the middle of the tree, Pike swooping by and squawking.

"Yeah, not that graceful," Hall said in reply.

Walking quickly but carefully, he made his way to the back of the tree, where the trunk was ripped and torn from falling. He could hear the moans of the Zombies and the clacking of the Skeletons fading. The creatures could not figure out where he had gone and were not following.

He stopped at the end, looking down at the stump a good thirty feet away. Long strips of bark and broken lengths of wood shot off from the end, none of them looking like they'd take his weight. Roxhard and Jackoby were midway down the ramp, holding back the pressing herd of Undead. Sabine and Leigh had spread out, one on either side of the Firbolg Hunters. The ranged attacks were doing damage, keeping wandering Undead at bay, but were not thinning the numbers greatly.

THE ROAMING DEAD I
Slay 9/12 Undead
Find a Clue to the Cause of Undead Uprising 1/1

Judging the distance, Hall thought he could make it with *Leap* but the difference in elevation between the top of the trunk and the stump would mean he'd land with some added force. It would hurt.

Stepping back ten feet or so, Hall set his feet. Taking a deep breath, he sprinted toward the end of the trunk, activating *Leap* at the edge. He soared over the air, arcing up. He saw Undead all around the stump, heard Pike flying above him. There was a good view from the apex of his arc, looking out over the forest. He thought he saw an odd structure further away, surrounded by trees, before he started falling downward. The air rushed, the wooden top of the trunk coming closer. He could see the hundreds of rings set into the stump, the wood worn smooth after countless years of feet and work. It was coming up fast.

Hall braced himself, landing hard. He felt the impact through his body, grunting in pain, as he tucked into a roll, dropping his spear on the stump. He stopped near the far edge facing the forest beyond. Somehow, he had managed to not snap the javelin in his roll.

DAMAGE!
HARD IMPACT!
Health 40/46
Vitality 18/20

Standing up, a little shakily, Hall looked down the edge of the stump. There was no ramp on this side, but he did see some vines and branches. The forest was not that far away, a twenty-to-thirty-foot sprint. It gave him an idea.

Hall grabbed his spear and headed to the opposite end and the others.

"How's it going?" he asked Sabine, the closest.

He pulled a throwing knife from his bracer and let it fly. Sparks erupted from the head of a Skeleton that Roxhard was facing off with, cracks forming in the bone.

"There is a lot of them," the Witch answered, firing bolts of energy from her wand.

The weapons were unique to Witches, granting them the ability to attack offensively when their Energy was depleted. There was a skill associated with the magical weapons, allowing the Witch to do more damage as the skill was raised. Wands were not unlimited, having to recharge themselves, but doing so fairly quickly. They did not deal a lot of damage, but every little bit counted.

"Only need three more," Hall answered, taking his second throwing knife and launching it at the Zombie facing Jackoby.

He struck the creature in the shoulder, bright sparks erupting on impact. The Zombie staggered and Jackoby managed to get in a good swing of the warhammer. The creature's head exploded, the body slumping to the side and being pushed off by the next Undead in line. Hall didn't receive any experience, which told him the damage had not been enough to grant him a shared kill.

The Firbolg looked at him, giving a brief nod in acknowledgment of the assist before giving the Skeleton now in front of him the full attention of his warhammer.

You have earned +50 Alliance points with Jackoby, Warden of the Brownpaw.

You are now "KNOWN" by Jackoby. The Warden acknowledges your assistance in the fight. He is less hostile toward you.

Hall dismissed the prompt. Up until that point, he hadn't thought Jackoby as anything special as far as NPCs were concerned, but there seemed to be more to the Firbolg.

"I found the clue we were looking for," Hall told Sabine. "Now we just need to get time to examine it."

"Easier said than done," she replied, slipping her wand back through her belt. She raised her hands and staff, gesturing as she cast a *Shadowbolt*. "There are a lot of these things."

"I've got an idea about that," he said.

She glanced at him, expecting more, but Hall just smiled and moved over to Leigh.

"How is Angus at climbing?"

CHAPTER TWELVE

"Switch," Hall yelled, having to speak up over the sound of the Undead herd.

The creatures had pushed Jackoby and Roxhard further up the ramp. The Dwarf swung his axe, slicing into a Zombie. He pulled the weapon out, gore following, and kicked the Zombie back into the ones behind.

QUEST COMPLETE!
You have defeated enough Undead to satisfy the Brownpaws. You have discovered a clue as to the cause of the uprising.

THE ROAMING DEAD I
Reward: +500 Brownpaw Firbolg Reputation
+50 Experience

You have become KNOWN to the Brownpaw Firbolg of Fallen Green. They are thankful for your assistance in dealing with the Undead.

Hall expected to see another quest prompt appear. Roxhard's last kill had completed the first step in a chain; there should have been a second quest. *Maybe something else triggers it*, Hall thought and tapped Jackoby on the shoulder.

He gasped as the *Rotting Stench* debuff activated. The smell from so many Zombies was almost overpowering.

The Firbolg whipped around quickly, warhammer raised, face angry, before realizing it was Hall. Jackoby turned back toward the herd in front of him.

"Switch," Hall repeated, and almost reluctantly, the large Firbolg did.

Hall used his spear to reach around the Warden, stabbing into the first Zombie and pushing it backward. The creature lost its footing, falling into the ones behind it.

"We're getting off of here," Hall told the Firbolg, who looked confused.

"They'll tell you how," he shouted and motioned to the top.

Still confused, Jackoby ran the small distance remaining to the top of the stump. Hall noticed lots of small cuts and scrapes across the furred arms.

"When I tell you to run, do it," Hall told Roxhard.

The Dwarf just nodded.

He also had lots of small wounds across his arms. Hall noticed each swing of the heavy axe was slower, not as strong. A screech told them that Pike was making an attack run. The dragonhawk swooped down, and instead of focusing on one target, he let out his lightning breath and shot it across multiple Undead.

That's new, Hall thought, watching as the lightning arced from Zombie to Skeleton to Zombie, each taking small amounts of damage.

Hall kicked out, sending a Zombie stumbling backward, and giving him time to swing his spear over his shoulder, sliding it into the harness he wore. The weapon was great for keeping enemies at a distance, but it was a hindrance in this situation. He drew his short sword and sliced through the neck of the Zombie that had lurched forward.

The creature's head nearly fell off, the thing moaning as the momentum of the swing sent it tumbling down the side of the stump. Its head slammed into a rock at the bottom, bursting into a pile of muscle and gore.

SLAIN: *Rotting Brownpaw Farmer*
+10 Experience

Skill Gain!
Small Blades Rank Two +.1

"Cut the legs," he shouted. "Block the ramp."

Hall adjusted his swing, aiming for the Skeleton that had appeared in front of him, replacing the Zombie. He struck the creature's knees with the flat of his blade. It did a little damage, making the Skeleton wobble. He slammed the sword into the knee again, ducking beneath the grabbing arms, hitting it with the edge. A tendon or something was sliced, somehow breaking the magical bond, and the Skeleton fell to the side. It landed in a heap of bones at his feet, arms still reaching for his ankles.

He stepped back, avoiding the arms, and smiled. It had worked. Somewhat.

Beside him, Roxhard had better luck. The single-bladed weapon, even when the flat of the head was used, had enough strength behind it that it turned a Zombie's knees to pulp. The creature fell to the wooden ground of the ramp with a disgusting squelching sound. The next Zombie in line tried to walk forward but got caught in the pile of bones and muscle that was the first Zombie. It stumbled forward, catching the swing of Roxhard's axe. The head went flying through the air, the body falling into a slump, blocking that part of the ramp.

"Run up to the top, follow the others," Hall told the Dwarf.

"But—" Roxhard started to say.

"GO!" Hall ordered.

He shifted into the middle of the ramp, short sword swinging in a wide arc to keep the Undead back. He heard, not seeing, Roxhard run to the top. He thought he could make out the heavy steps of the Dwarf across the surface of the stump. Hall waited, counting down the seconds, needing to give Roxhard enough time.

The Undead pushed him back, a step at a time. They pushed through the makeshift barrier of bodies, ignoring it by sheer mass. Hall's short sword didn't have the reach to really damage the mass of Undead, but it did help keep them back.

Hoping he had given Roxhard enough time, Hall activated *Leap* and jumped up. He landed on the flat top of the stump, pivoting quickly. He could hear the herd of Undead moving up, slowly, their moans and clacking of bones coming closer. Running across the flat surface of the stump, he got to the other side and looked down.

He watched Roxhard land on the ground, jumping down the last few feet. The others were in a long line stretching to the treeline, Leigh and Sabine already under the cover of the canopy. There were no Undead on this side, the noise of their fight had drawn all the creatures to the ramp. They were working to keep quiet, but it wouldn't last. Already the first Zombie was stepping onto the flat top.

Sheathing his sword and swinging his leg over the side, Hall grabbed one of the vines. He watched a second Zombie and a Skeleton step onto the stump and let himself down. He slid down the vine, using the rough bark for footholds. Quickly, he climbed down the side of the stump and landed on the grass.

"Go," he said to Roxhard, and the two took off running toward the treeline.

He didn't look back as he heard the sound of thuds, splats,

and breaking bones of the Undead following him off the stump and smashing into the ground.

———

The small group gathered beneath the trees, all looking back to the clearing and the Undead.

"Why..." Jackoby started to say, his voice angry.

Hall slashed his hand through the air, stopping the Firbolg. Shaking his head, Hall motioned toward the forest. The others picked up on the idea, even Jackoby, and they all moved quickly and quietly deeper into the forest. Hall pushed to the front, hoping he had the direction right.

He led them a couple hundred feet into the thick woods, finally thinking it was safe enough and far enough away to stop and talk.

"Why did we run?" Jackoby asked angrily, pushing his way through the others to confront Hall. "Your plan failed," the Firbolg spat, standing close to Hall and looking down. Hall stared back, looking up but not giving an inch. "We need to find out what is raising the Undead."

Hall looked up at the Firbolg, fighting the urge to punch out. He hated people invading his personal space and especially hated when others used their size to try and intimidate. He kept the stare locked for almost a minute before responding.

"And we will."

"How?" Jackoby growled. "We ran. The Undead are back there. We have no clue."

Hall wanted to laugh but knew it would only anger the Firbolg more. He had forgotten that Jackoby did not have access to the Quest text. He did not know a clue had been found.

"We have this," Hall said and pulled the small stone out of his pouch.

He held the *Eye of Death's Gaze* in his palm, pushing his hand out so Jackoby had no choice but to take a couple steps back.

"What is that?" Jackoby asked, almost shying away from the object.

"No clue," Hall replied with a shrug. "But it's called an *Eye of Death's Gaze*. I don't know about you, but that just screams Necromancer to me."

Jackoby calmed but did not offer an apology.

"I also saw a line of tracks leading away from Fallen Green," Hall added, putting the *Eye* back in his pouch. "Leading the same way we're going, coincidently."

The Firbolg studied Hall, eyes curious. Finally, Jackoby nodded. Hall was satisfied with that small gesture. Respect, apology, and thanks all in one.

"There was a structure of some kind this direction as well," Hall said, pulling out the physical manifestation of his map

The parchment was rolled tight, brown paper with ends cracked and curling. The words and images were faded but still legible. Lots of notes covered the map, more than Hall had realized he had added. His *Cartography* skill allowed him to make notes on his map, but he did not remember adding this many. Had the skill made notes based on his thoughts?

Jackoby studied the map and looked at Hall again, a new respect in his eyes.

"You are a Cartographer?" Jackoby asked, a little bit of that respect in his voice.

"I guess so," Hall replied and pointed at the map. It showed the clearing around Fallen Green in detail, the scale adjusted so the clearing was large and the focus. "I saw it while falling onto the stump," Hall started. "So, the scale might be off but I think it was about here," he finished and pointed to a spot about a mile or so from where they now stood.

Skill Gain!
Cartography Rank One +.1

Jackoby studied the map for a time, eyes roaming from where Hall pointed to the clearing and to the village of Green Ember.

"There is an old tower in that general area," Jackoby finally said, standing up and looking in the direction they had been going. "It has been unused for almost a century. Forgotten by many."

"Whose was it?" Sabine asked, suspicion in her voice.

Hall wished they had known about the tower earlier. They could have avoided the entire fight with the Undead. All RPGs had one thing in common. A lone and empty tower in the middle of the woods, or anywhere, was always anything but empty.

"An old Elf Shaman," Jackoby answered and glanced at one of the Hunters.

"Yorsif," the Hunter supplied.

"That is where we must go," Jackoby said, his voice strong and brooking no argument.

Jackoby of the Brownpaw wants your assistance in investigating the Tower of Yorsif the Shaman to see how it is connected to the Undead Uprising plaguing the Brownpaw Firbolg.

THE ROAMING DEAD II
Investigate the Tower of Yorsif the Shaman 0/1
Reward: +200 Brownpaw Firbolg Reputation
+50 Experience

Accept Quest?

Hall looked in the same direction. He was estimating how long it would take to get to the tower, comparing it to the amount of day they had left. It was barely noon. They could push on and get close to the tower. He wanted more distance between them and the Undead. He was about to tell the group to get moving when an unpleasant thought entered his mind.

"Did this Shaman die in his tower?" Hall asked.

Jackoby shrugged before the impact of what Hall asked hit him. Sabine groaned and cursed.

"I do not know," Jackoby answered.

Great, Hall thought. *We might have a Lich to deal with.*

CHAPTER THIRTEEN

HALL HAD GUESSED THE DIRECTION ACCURATELY. IT TOOK about an hour of walking through thick forest growth before they came upon the tower, looking like what Hall had quickly glimpsed as he jumped from the Fallen Green to the stump.

Three stories tall, it barely reached above the tallest trees, which helped shield it from view. Made of a light gray stone, large blocks fit carefully together. Square with crenellations along the parapet. The walls were straight, about thirty feet long, with small windows set into the stone. Each of the windows was boarded up with shutters that hung rotting from hinges.

Vines grew up the face of the tower, thick, the cleared space in front overgrown. The trees had been cut back a good fifty feet around the tower, isolating it in the middle of the clearing.

It looked like no one had been there for decades, but Hall could see broken grasses, pushed asides branches, that indicated someone had passed recently.

That and the two giant Undead creatures standing guard outside.

Skill Gain!

Identify Rank One +.2

Shambling Rotten Oak Craobh (Blue)
Shambling Rotten Birch Craobh (Blue)

Hall had never encountered Undead Craobh before. Living trees, they moved and talked, protectors of the forest. The Undead Craobh were pitted and cracked, the bark falling in many places. Worms and other insects crawled across their surfaces. Long limbs ending in clawed fingers, thick legs, barely any face just the markings of eyes in the bark, long branches extending above that would have been covered in leaves but were now bare. One was gray and thicker around while the other was thin, having white bark with black stripes.

The Oak Craobh was at least fifteen feet tall, the Birch only ten feet.

And they were now showing Difficulty, something that *Identify* had not done before. Quickly checking his Character Sheet, Hall saw that he was now at 5.1 points for *Identify*. Difficulty must have been triggered by reaching 5 points in the Skill. Each name was in Blue. If he remembered how it had worked before correctly, Blue enemies were only one or two Levels above his.

"I didn't think there were any Craobh in Fallen Green," Hall said quietly as they all huddled in the treeline. He glanced at Jackoby.

"There aren't," the Firbolg Warden replied just as confused as to why the living trees were here and why they were now Undead. "Not usually," he added after some thought.

"Oh?" Hall prompted.

"Once a year, some make a pilgrimage from the forests to the north down here to see Fallen Green," Jackoby said. "But that had been months ago."

Hall just shook his head. It really didn't matter why. What mattered was that the Craobh were now here and in their way. He studied the tower, sending the Firbolg hunters around to the back and one side, Leigh taking the other, to watch the windows for any sign of movement. It was midafternoon, the sun starting its descent. He didn't like the idea of having to camp in the forest with the Undead roaming around. If they didn't assault the tower soon, they would have to return to the Firbolg village and try again.

He was tempted to do that anyway; return to Green Ember and come back in the morning with more Firbolg warriors. The scream from the rear of the tower changed those plans. One of the Firbolg hunters. The two Craobh turned, alerted by the sound.

They would never get a better chance.

"Roxhard, the Birch," Hall ordered. "Jackoby, the Oak."

The Firbolg Warden glared at him, trying to decide if he should listen or run to the rear to see to his clanmate. In the end, he turned away from Hall and activated his *Battle Rush*.

Hall watched as both Wardens sped off toward their targets. They were blurs, feet pounding hard on the ground. They pushed through the grass, the wind from their passage blowing across the clearing. Jackoby outpaced Roxhard, his strides longer.

The Firbolg slammed into the heavier Oak Craobh. Bark exploded on the impact, the inside of the creature beneath the rotting bark was soft. Pulp covered Jackoby as his warhammer slammed into the living tree's stump thick legs. It groaned, almost falling forward.

Roxhard hit his with more force. The Birch Craobh cracked, two of its long branch fingers snapping off. The creature howled. Arrows shot out from the trees, striking the Craobh. Hall smiled, glad to see the other Firbolg Hunter had decided to help Roxhard.

"Pick a target," he told Sabine as he ran out of the treeline.

He didn't look to see what she chose to do, just kept running. He angled toward the Oak Craobh that was trying to turn around to get at Jackoby. The Warden kept moving, keeping the creature's back in front of him.

Activating *Leap* when he was close enough, Hall jumped into the air. He stabbed down at the Craobh, high enough to avoid the branches so his attack did minimal damage. Every little bit helped, and it was not his intent to battle that Craobh.

He landed just beyond it, legs bent to absorb the impact. He resisted the urge to use his Attack of Opportunity on the Craobh, instead pushing forward. Dashing around the corner of the tower, he stopped and cursed.

Just as he feared.

The Firbolg Hunter lay with his back against a tree, smoke rising from his leather and bark armor. He was weaponless, in obvious pain as he glared across the open space. Smoke rose from the ground around him, the tree behind scorched and blackened. Near the tower's wall was a tall figure. Judging by the slimness of the Skeleton and the overall height, it had once been an Elf, now just a Skeleton in rotting robes. The skull was bare, exposed, the hand and finger bones sticking out of the robe's hem, moving in complicated gestures. The empty eye sockets glowed with a sickly green light.

Above the animated Skeleton was a balcony coming off the stone tower. Open doors led inside to where the Lich must have come from before spying the Firbolg Hunter.

Leigh stood off to the side of the Hunter, staff extended and splinters spraying out toward the Skeleton. Angus was next to her, the cow mooing angrily.

Skill Gain!
Identify Rank One +.1

Yorsif the Undying Lich (Orange)

A Lich. An Undead magic user. The fire damage meant it had been a Shaman. And it answered Hall's question to Jackoby. The Shaman that built the tower had died there.

The splinters from Leigh's staff flew straight and true, speeding to their target. The Lich raised a hand, moving it from left to right and a gust of wind blew across the clearing. The splinters were caught in the gust, all of them blown harmlessly aside. The glowing eyes turned to the Druid.

Hall *Leapt*. He arced over the Lich, spear stabbing down. The Ironwood tip slammed into the Lich's shoulder, knocking the thing off balance and disrupting its casting. Hall landed and pivoted, jabbing out with the spear. He caught the Lich in the chest, slicing through the rotting robe and pushing the Lich back.

He pulled its Status Bar, seeing only about one-eighth of its life gone.

"The Firbolg," Hall shouted to Leigh as he jabbed at the Lich again.

The Lich would be a tough opponent, Hall knew. Having the Firbolg Hunter up and helping in the fight was needed especially with the group split up among three tough enemies.

The glowing green eyes of the Undead Shaman stared at him with hatred, the creature not uttering a sound. It staggered back with each jab of the ironwood spear. Small bits of health dropping. Hall knew he had to keep it from being able to cast a spell.

The Lich staggered as Angus slammed into the back of the creature. It fell forward, Hall stepping out of the way, falling to the ground. Hall stabbed out with his spear, scoring repeated hits as Angus stomped down hard on the Lich's bony legs. The cracks were audible, as were the moans of the creature.

Moaning loudly, the Lich jerked his hand and Hall felt the

rush of wind blast through the trees. It hit him with force, lifting him up and throwing him ten feet through the air. He landed hard, rolling to a stop, barely holding onto his spear. His Heath Bar flashed red, a bit of Health disappearing. Angus mooing was loud, ending in a pained cry, as the small and shaggy cow was slammed into the side of the tower.

Hall pushed himself up, using his spear. The impact had hurt, the ground hard and unyielding. Grass brushed against his face as he stood up to see the Lich staring at him with the glowing green eyes. Hall could almost feel the hate in that gaze. The bony fingers moved in intricate motions that should not have been possible.

Light flared as the fingers carved through the air and a line of fire shot out.

Diving to the side, Hall felt the heat of the blast. It scorched the earth, burning away the grass, leaving a black smudge of ash. In one smooth motion, Hall stood up, pulling the javelin from the harness across his back and let it fly. The weapon soared through the air, slamming into the Lich's chest where it stuck, caught between bones. More health dropped from the Lich's bar, but it still had plenty left.

Moaning in a way that sounded like a growl, the Lich slashed a hand through the air sharply, the other weaving another pattern. Hall braced himself, ready to move one way or the other, or stand still and try not to be blown away. Yorsif the Lich had so far shown itself as having a fire spell and a wind spell. Hall couldn't remember enough about the Shaman class to know at what Level those spells were granted, and there was no way to know what Rank they were.

A bright ball of light shot out, not in a straight line but staggering as Hall moved. The ball seemed to follow him as he dove to the right. It slammed into his chest, his cry of shock loud. Pain spread throughout his body, spasms of strange energy. It didn't feel like electricity but it behaved somewhat the same. A chill filled his bones, cramping his muscles. At the same time, he felt a jolt of adrenaline. His body wanted to move, but the chill would not let him.

What the hell, he thought, having never felt the effect before.

He had been hit with all the different kinds of magic during the years he played Sky Realms Online. The game system had dampened the pain so it was barely even noticeable, but it had translated the effects so the Player felt them. A fire spell caused a slight burning sensation, cold would make the Player shiver.

What he had just felt was new.

After training, Sabine had mentioned three new types of magic, one of them being Arcane. Had he just felt his first Arcane spell?

It had taken a decent amount of his Health away.

Another gust of near hurricane-force winds blew through the area, slamming Angus against the stone wall of the tower when the cow had charged in at the Lich. Angus hit hard and did not move this time.

Moving quickly, the Lich cast another glowing ball of light. It streaked toward Hall, who knew he could not avoid it. He braced himself for the pain.

The earth rumbled at his feet, a wall of dirt and roots shooting up in front of him. The ball of light slammed into the earthen wall, sparks erupting and streaking across the surface. The wall shook hard, the section where the ball hit pushed out, pieces of dirt falling back to the ground.

He looked over at Leigh, standing up above the wounded Firbolg who was struggling to stand. She nodded and turned to face the Lich, casting a *Splinter Storm*. The shards of wood shot out from her staff, slamming into Yorsif. Hall stood up and used *Leap*. He jumped over the earthen wall, over the Lich, stabbing down with his spear.

The Lich had raised its ratty and threadbare robe, catching

many of the splinters. Some got through but not enough to do real damage. But Yorsif was not ready to defend against Hall's *Leaping Stab* or his attack of opportunity when he landed.

Both blows landed solid hits, chunks of the Lich's Health disappearing.

Yorsif tried to turn, to face Hall and start casting, but could not as grass and roots crawled up its bony legs. It struggled to lift its legs, an angry moan as bony claw-like fingers reached down to pull at the grass and roots. The javelin still sticking out of its body hindered its movements, preventing it from pulling up all the grass.

Wishing he had a Bashing weapon, Hall jabbed his spear at the Lich's neck bone. The ironwood tip, hard as steel, grazed the bone, taking chips off. Hall cursed. He had hoped to take a good chunk off, weaken the bone. Instead, he just made the Lich angry.

It turned quickly, unnaturally fast, bony arm outstretched. It grabbed the spear and pulled, yanking Hall forward. The Lich was strong, Hall now off balance. He dug his feet into the ground and let the spear go. With no resistance now, Yorsif lurched back. An arrow slammed against the Lich's skull, scratching the bone as it skidded off to the side.

The Firbolg Hunter was back in the fight.

Hall drew his short sword as the Lich's attention turned to the Hunter. Flames shot out, two streaks heading for Leigh and the Firbolg. Both moved aside, the fires hitting the trees, scorching bark and burning away leaves. Luckily, the magical fire did not set the wood ablaze. Hall swung out with the flat of his blade, connecting with the Lich's shoulder, pushing the creature back.

EXCEPTIONAL SHORT SWORD
OF FIGHTING
Damage 2d4 (+3)

Agility: +2
Strength: +1
Durability 15/20
Weight: 5 lbs.

A quick glance at the weapons stats showed that striking the magically hardened bones had knocked a point of durability off the sword. Hall cursed. The sword was a good weapon. Rare level, the stats showed Blue. It would be a while before he found something better. He couldn't afford to keep smacking at the Lich with it.

He needed his spear back. The Lich had tossed it aside, standing between Hall and his main weapon. No space to get around between it and the tower, and going in front would be to invite an attack. A screech from above told him that Pike was circling, waiting for a chance to attack.

Perfect, Hall thought and mentally gave the dragonhawk instructions.

The Lich turned back toward him and he jabbed out with the sword, the Lich moving aside to avoid the blow. Hall swung the sword to the side, the Lich again moving. Deliberately keeping the attacks slow, the Lich could easily avoid them.

A screech filled the air, the sound of something diving from above. The Lich looked up and caught a blue-white lightning bolt in the face. Pike's attack sent exploding sparks everywhere, lines of lighting across the creature's skull. The brightness flared and disappeared.

The green eyes still stared out from the skull's eye sockets, strong as ever, but the bleached white of the skull itself was blackened with small cracks across the surface. Hall wished they had lightning attacks, either Leigh high enough in Level or their own Shaman. The damage that Pike's small breath attack had done was more than anything the others had managed.

With another screech, Pike came in for a second attack. The Lich moved its hands quickly and Hall felt the force of the wind gust against his back. It struck Pike, the dragonhawk unable to withstand the wind's pressure and was blown off course. Flipping end over end, Pike was pushed into the trees. Hall watched as leaves exploded out as the dragonhawk was thrown through the branches, the sound of limbs cracking and breaking.

He mentally reached out to Pike. The dragonhawk was hurt, battered, but alive.

Thankful, the attacks had done what Hall needed, as he dove to the ground and rolled past the Lich. He sprang up, reaching out and grabbing his spear. Leigh launched a *Splinter Storm* just as he rolled past, all of the wooden shards striking the Lich. Its Health bar was down just below half now.

Hall could hear the sound of fighting from the sides as the others dealt with the Shambling Craobhs. He had hoped those fights would have ended quicker and they could have attacked the Lich with more numbers.

Sky Realms Online had always had a friendly fire component, where ranged and magical attackers had to be aware of their allies or else catch the allies in the crossfire as all fought against the same target. In old MMORPGs, it hadn't mattered. Allies had been safe from friendly fire, and everyone could attack at the same time. Sky Realms had changed that, added a sense of realism to how things were targeted.

Hall was preventing Leigh from launching more *Splinter Storm* attacks or the Hunter from firing more arrows. He could easily be caught in those attacks.

More melee would have been good. Someone to attack from the Lich's blind side where the flanking bonuses would apply.

No way of knowing if that help would arrive.

Hall knew they had to end this fight and quickly. The

longer it took to take out the Lich or the Craobhs, the more time it would give the Necromancer time to get involved. He wondered why the Necromancer hadn't made an appearance yet. There was no way the loud fights were being missed. Was the caster even in the tower?

Spear in hand, Hall jabbed out, catching the Lich in the shoulder and pushing it back. The roots holding it in place were gone, shrinking back into the earth from where they had come. Yorsif stumbled back and Hall jabbed out again, pushing the Lich further away. An arrow struck the creature's shoulder, catching in the folds of the robe.

The constant moaning got louder. Hall could start to feel the sound, not just hear it.

The tip of his spear sent more bone shards flying off the creature, ripping the robe even more. He pulled it back quickly out of reach, before the Lich, which was surprisingly fast, could grab it. More movements of the bony fingers and another blast of flame shot out. Hall moved aside, feeling the heat waves. Rolling on the ground, he pushed up with his spear, catching the Lich under the jaw. The head snapped back, a cracking sound, and a good amount of Health disappeared from its bar.

Another *Splinter Storm* attack took more Health away. The Hunter got lucky and an arrow lodged into the joint between spine and skull. The Lich's head tilted at an awkward angle. The fingers moved and flames shot out toward Hall who jumped out of the way, the blast catching his leg.

He felt immense pain, his leathers protecting his flesh from burning, but the heat was intense. His Health dropped some more as he rolled in the grass to put out the flames. Pushing himself out of the way, he sprung up and leveled his spear.

The Lich ignored him, turning to face Leigh and the Firbolg. Still moaning, louder with an edge, the Lich waved its arms and two of the globes of strange energy shot out. One struck the Firbolg, pushing the Hunter backward against a tree. His body spasmed and he dropped to the ground. Leigh was struck, her body lurched, made rigid, and she screamed in pain. The Druid fell to the ground, her body shaking as she tried to get up.

Hall pulled her Health bar, seeing that it had dropped by half. More shocking was that the Arcane globes had taken three-quarters of her Energy as well.

The green eyes seemed to shine with satisfaction as the Lich turned back to Hall. They dared him to attack.

He did.

Hall took a couple steps, leading with the spear. The Lich grabbed it with both hands, the skull splitting into a bony grin, stopping Hall in his tracks. He pushed, trying to slide the Lich backward, but the Undead creature was the stronger. It held its ground. Hall struggled, trying to jam his spear into the chest of the Lich. The tip wavered, unmoving.

He let the weapon go, jumping back as the Lich was again unbalanced. Pulling a throwing knife from his bracer, he launched it at the Lich. The small weapon caught the creature in the shoulder, sending up bolts of lightning across the bones. The light flared down, showing scorch marks along the shoulder and small cracks.

Drawing his sword, he used *Leap* and jumped into the air. Without a spear, he couldn't attack mid-*Leap*, so he adjusted his jump to land right behind the Lich. With his back to the Lich, he spun around, putting all the power of the momentum into the swing.

The sword slammed into the Lich's shoulder, knocking the creature to the side. Bone chips flew from the impact, the arm hanging limp as the connections were severed. Yorsif's Health dropped to below a quarter left.

Staggering back, the Lich's green eyes dimmed, but the hatred, somehow visible, only deepened. The moaning increased, louder, the strange edge stronger. Hall could feel it, and now it echoed through his mind, digging into the corners. Pain grew from within, his head pounding. It felt like his brain was being crushed. Spasms of pain wracked his body, dropping him to the ground. He dropped his sword, clutching at his head.

Undying Moan

The constant moaning of the Lich starts to enter your mind as the creature's health drops. The sound fills your mind, the only thing you can concentrate on, causing intense pain. Health drops by -2 every 3 seconds for duration. Energy drops by -2 every 3 seconds for duration. Vitality drops by -4. Moan lasts until the Lich is dead.

Hall crawled back, feeling blood leaking from his nose and ears. The pain was intense. He could barely see, everything a blur, but he knew the shape in front of him was the Lich. It was coming for him, reaching down. He rolled to the side on instinct and kept rolling. He stopped, staggering as he tried to stand. Reaching down, he felt something in the grass.

His spear.

Grabbing it, in desperation, he activated *Leap*. Hall arced over the Lich, instinctively stabbing down. He overbalanced, the moaning in his mind breaking his concentration. The arc fell short, closer to the Lich then intended. His aim was off but he was so close it didn't matter.

The ironwood spear point hit the Lich in the already cracked skull. It exploded in a ball of dark green energy. The shockwave pushed Hall up, and he fell back to the ground hard, rolling to a stop and unable to get up, his body battered.

Yorsif's headless body stood still, the moaning stopped. Green smoke drifted from the neck where the skull had been. Then, it just collapsed, falling to the ground in a heap.

> **SLAIN:** *Undying Lich*
> *+30 Experience*
>
> **Skill Gain!**
> *Polearms Rank Two +.2*
> *Small Blades Rank Two +.1*
> *Light Armor Rank Two +.1*
> *Thrown Rank Two +.1*

Hall lay on the ground, breathing heavy. He could think again, the pain in his head stopped. He thought he had bruised his ribs, didn't think anything was broken, but he had no desire to move. He just wanted to lay there and sleep.

But knew he couldn't.

He could hear the sounds of fighting coming from the sides of the tower.

CHAPTER FOURTEEN

HALL TRIED TO STAND, PAIN LANCING THROUGH HIS BODY AS HE sat up. He leaned back down. A glance at his Health showed it below a quarter. The fight had been close. Reaching out with his mind, he found Pike, the dragonhawk sitting in a tree and nursing his own wounds. From where he lay, Hall looked across the clearing. He could see the pile of bones that had been the Lich. Angus was pushing himself up, the cow standing shakily. At the treeline, the Firbolg Hunter still lay against the tree where he had fallen. Leigh was running to him.

Hall smiled as she crouched down at his side, laying her hands across his body. They glowed a light blue, and he felt the warmth of the healing energy flowing through his battered body. His Health bar started to go up.

"Thanks," he said, at last able to sit up.

Leigh nodded. She looked exhausted. Her Health was stabilized but her Energy was low. Multiple healing spells were draining her physically and mentally. She left his side and went to Angus, the cow mooing softly.

Using his spear to help him stand, Hall looked from one side of the tower to the other. Sounds of battle came from each. To his left was where Roxhard had gone, with a Firbolg Hunter, against the Birch Craobh. On the right was Jackoby and Sabine, facing off against the Oak Craobh. Battered, his Vitality down, Hall tried to figure out which side to aid first.

Health 37/46

Energy 50/67

Vitality 12/20

"How is he?" Hall asked, motioning toward the Hunter against the trees, realizing he didn't even know the Firbolg's name.

"Resting," Leigh replied. "He was close to death."

Nodding, Hall turned to the left. He wanted to say that the choice was practical. It was only Roxhard and the Hunter while the other side had Sabine, a Witch, and her debuffs that would greatly aid Jackoby. He wanted to say it, but he knew it was because the left was Roxhard. Hall felt protective of the Dwarf, a fourteen-year-old kid trapped in that body. It wasn't the protectiveness of a big brother, not yet, but it was getting there.

Sprinting to that side, he saw the large Birch Craobh swinging a long arm ending in sharp branch-like fingers. Strips of white and black bark were peeling away, sap running down its side, the wood beneath rotten. The creature moved slowly, shambling. Large chunks of the Craobh were missing, arrows sticking out of the bark in almost a dozen places.

The Firbolg Hunter stayed in the back behind the Dwarf, lowering his bow. No more arrows were fired, the quiver empty, but the Firbolg could not find a spot for a melee attack. The Craobh was too big, taking up the entire space between tower wall and forest. Roxhard was swinging his axe wildly, in close to the Craobh so the Undead walking tree could not use its long arms. Pieces of wood went flying with each blow.

Roxhard was slowly but steadily whittling away at the Craobh's Health.

Hall activated *Leap*. The tall tree was too high to jump over, especially as tired as he was, but he had planned on that. He didn't activate *Leaping Stab*, instead landing on the shoulders of the Craobh. Grabbing onto a branch with his free hand, he stabbed into the Craobh's head with his spear, sending shards of wood flying. He angled the weapon, aiming for what the Undead creature used for eyes. Instead of moaning like the Lich had, the Craobh made no sound beyond the creaking and cracking of the wooden joints.

He felt the spear tip strike something other than softwood. It penetrated deep into the Craobh, Hall feeling thick sap splash out against his gloves and bare arm. The Undead tree's arms lifted into the air, trying to reach for Hall on its shoulders. The angle was wrong; it couldn't grab him.

Roxhard shifted his attack and started chopping at just one leg of the creature. Large pieces flew with each swing of the axe, the perfect weapon for fighting a walking tree. The Craobh stumbled, overbalanced, and started to fall forward. Using *Leap*, Hall jumped off its shoulder, activating *Leaping Stab* for a quick jab that didn't do much damage. He landed in the tall grass, skidding a short distance.

The ground shuddered as the walking tree crashed. Hall heard the snap of branches, the cracking of the trunk. Looking over his shoulder, he saw Roxhard and the Hunter jumping onto the creatures back and starting to hack away at it.

Satisfied they had it under control, Hall ran around the front of the tower just in time to see the Oak Craobh fall to the ground. The earth shuddered at the impact, Hall glancing at the tower to make sure it was steady after the quakes caused by the two falling Craobh.

Sabine stood at the treeline, firing bursts of small blue-white energy daggers from her outstretched hand. Each one slammed into the head of the fallen Craobh. Hall now recognized the tell-tale sign of Arcane magic. Jackoby climbed onto the Undead tree's back and started bashing away at it with his warhammer. No pieces of wood flew off. Instead, the bark cracked and snapped under the impact of the hammer, the wood beneath being smashed to a pulp.

Hall came to a stop in the middle, between Sabine and the Craobh's head. He stayed out of her line of fire, seeing the small daggers of energy fly past. Behind the Craobh, where its legs kicked as it tried to right itself, stood Angus. The small cow had rammed into the back of the Craobh, knocking it down, and now the cow was thrashing his horned head back and forth across the Craobh's back, taking small pieces of wood off with each horn thrust.

SLAIN: Shambling Rotten Birch Craobh (Blue)
+10 Experience

Skill Gain!
Polearms Rank Two +.1

Using his spear to hold himself up, Hall took a couple deep breaths. He was tired, his body battered. Jackoby walked across the back of the barely moving Oak Craobh. The large Firbolg stood over the creature's head, a foot on each shoulder, his warhammer held in two hands. He raised the hammer and brought it down, the Craobh's head bursting apart on impact.

The Firbolg jumped off the Craobh.

"Where were you?" he grunted, seeing Hall.

"Killing a Lich," Hall replied with a shrug.

"Where is Herkilo?" he asked, eyes widening with worry.

So that's the Hunter's name, Hall thought as he pointed behind Jackoby.

The Firbolg Warden turned around rapidly, watching as

the Hunter walked slowly toward them. Leigh was at his side, almost protectively. Jackoby turned back to Hall, nodded, and moved to the other side as Roxhard and the last Hunter were coming to the front.

Hall glanced up to the treetops as Pike soared into the clearing. The dragonhawk slowly circled the tower, before gliding down and landing on Hall's shoulder. He winced as the weight of the dragonhawk settled on a sore spot.

"Is everyone good?" he asked.

They all nodded. Roxhard and Jackoby both stretched sore muscles that were tightening. The two Wardens eyed each other, sizing each other. Hall rolled his eyes, wondering if that was going to become a problem but then not caring. They wouldn't have Jackoby with them for long. Leigh smiled wearily, laying her hands on Roxhard to heal his wounds.

"I'll heal you when my Energy raises again," she said to Jackoby.

The Firbolg Warden nodded before he started talking quietly to Herkilo in their language. The Hunter nodded, gesturing to Leigh and Hall as he talked.

"Here," Leigh said to Hall, holding out her hand.

In her hand was a ring, a thin band of silver with writing along the edge.

"Found it on the Lich," she said.

Hall studied the band, trying to see what stats it had but couldn't get anything from it. They would need to get a high enough level Witch to cast *Scry* on it. A level six spell, it would be a while before Sabine could cast it.

"Keep it or give to Sabine," Hall said. "Probably geared for a magic Class."

Leigh looked at the small silver ring, moving it around in her hand, before finally giving it to Sabine.

The Witch looked shocked but nodded her thanks.

"What about the Necromancer?" Roxhard asked, looking at the tower.

"I don't think he's home," Hall replied. "It's not like we were quiet. He'd be out here by now."

"Or he's just waiting for us inside," Jackoby said.

"Possibly," Hall agreed. "But now would have been a good time to attack while we were all low on Health and waiting for healing."

The Firbolg Warden grunted.

"Either way, we're going inside," Hall said and lifted his spear, starting to walk toward the tower.

———

He paused at the large double doors. Solid wood, banded in iron, they were Firbolg-sized in height and width. There were no markings, no detailing on the doors or the stone around them. The whole tower was plain, unadorned. He leaned closer, examining the door, the wood, and the stone, looking for obvious signs of traps or wardings.

"Either of you have Detect Traps?" he asked, looking back at the Firbolg Hunters.

They both shook their heads.

Of course they don't, Hall thought as he stepped back and raised his spear, butt end pointing at the door.

Motioning the others back, he tapped on both door panels with the spear. He started at the bottom, then moved to the top and the middle before tapping all along the edge. Nothing happened. He didn't hear a click or see the heavy doors move. The tapping had been light. He hoped it didn't echo inside the tower, but there was no help for it. He wasn't going to be stupid enough to just pull open the doors without checking first.

Two large iron rings were mounted to the door, and Hall reached out for one, motioning Jackoby to take the other. The

Firbolg was reluctant but finally stepped forward and grabbed it. Looking at each other, Hall nodded, and both pulled.

The doors slid open reluctantly, Hall straining but Jackoby opening his with ease. There was no explosion, no loud noise, no gas. Hall breathed a sigh of relief that the doors were untrapped. He was doing that far too often, risking traps. They needed to find someone with Trap-related skills soon.

They looked past the open doors and into the dark tower. Only enough space to walk through, the doors did not let much of the fading sunlight in. They could see a large hall, a set of stairs in the middle leading to a landing with what looked to be more stairs up to the second floor. It appeared that the balcony Hall had seen on the back side of the tower came off the landing. Two doors were on either side of the central stair. There were no pictures, no decorations, just bare stone walls. No furniture.

Hall didn't know how long the tower had been vacant but there were always remnants of occupation. Broken and cobweb-covered furniture, fading tapestries, mildewed paintings. But here, there was nothing. It was silent inside the tower. The sunlight caught particles of dust floating in the air.

Slowly, they filed in, leaving Angus outside to act as a guard, the Firbolg Hunters with their bows ready to draw. They fanned out, putting space between them as they walked across the stone tiled floor.

"How many rooms?" Hall asked in a whisper. Something about the place made him want to speak quietly. He wasn't worried about sneaking up on anyone, that time had long passed, but the nature of the seemingly empty tower pushed at him and made him whisper.

"I do not know," Jackoby said, his tone of voice almost offended that such a question would be asked. "I have never been here. No Brownpaw has."

"Isn't that convenient," Sabine muttered.

"Watch the doors," he told the Hunters before starting up the stairs.

He saw them glance at Jackoby, who nodded.

Pausing, Hall sent a mental command to Pike. The drag- onhawk released his grip on Hall's leather-clad shoulder, spreading his wings and lifting into the air. They all watched as Pike flapped his wings, flying in a circle before heading over the stairs, turning at the landing and flying up the next set of stairs to the second floor.

Closing his eyes, through Pike's vision Hall could see the stairs and the dark hallway they led to above. They entered the second floor on the end, the corridor running along the front of the tower with windows looking out into the forest, rooms off the other side of the corridor. In the middle of the floor, between the rooms, another set of stairs led to the third floor. Flying quietly, barely flapping his wings, Pike flew down the set of stairs leading down to the landing on the other side of the tower. He settled on the stone railing.

With his eyes now open, Hall led the way to the top of the landing. He thought about splitting up, sending Jackoby and possibly Sabine up the other side, but decided not to. In MMORPGs, there had never been a reason to split the party. The mechanics just didn't work that way. And in the old pen and paper RPGs he had played, splitting the party was a sure way to get the Dungeon Master to kill the party.

He picked the stairs to his right as that was the set Pike had flown up. It seemed as good a place to start as any. Moving slowly, they started up to the second floor.

———

The upper floors were empty. A few rooms, with no furnishings or decorations, just cobwebs and dust. No animal bones. Noth- ing. The layout of the rooms and tower size prevented any secret compartments to exist, and none of them could sense or find anything magically hidden.

Which is why Hall now found himself standing in front of the entrance doors. He faced the two doors that led underneath the landing, coin in hand. He had decided the door on the left was going to be heads. No reason other than it was the one on the left.

The gold coin was from Essec. It had the tower of Spirehold on one side and the standard of Essec on the other. Each kingdom and race had their own style of coins. Different sizes, shapes, and weights but long ago it had been decided that the value of each was going to be the same. A gold coin from Essec was worth the same as one from the Highborn Confederacy. This made trading easier and a person could end up with a variety for different coins when making deals.

"Call it," Hall said as he flipped the coin into the air.

Leigh and Jackoby looked at him in confusion. Roxhard glanced at Sabine and made a "all yours" motion to her.

"Tails," she replied, watching the flight of the coin.

It landed on the ground, flat and shaking. It settled and Hall reached down, picking it up and showing it to the others before placing back in his pouch.

"Tails it is," he said and pointed at the door to the right of the stairs.

He walked over to the door as the Firbolg Hunter, the one that wasn't Herkilo, stepped to the side. The Hunter moved away, clear of the door and any potential explosion.

"What's your name?" Hall asked.

The Hunter looked surprised to be asked, glancing at Jackoby before looking back at Hall.

"Tertion," he answered.

Hall nodded and grabbed the door handle, Pike flying off his shoulder to wait on the stair railing.

Standing on the hinge side, Hall pulled it open, using the wood of the door as protection.

Nothing happened and he peeked around the door, looking at a landing and a set of stairs that headed down, coming off the landing to the left. He stepped around the door and onto the landing. Letting his eyes adjust, he could see the steps descending and turning into the tower. The walls were smooth stone, the stairs stone. His *Limited Night Vision*, a Racial Ability for being a Half-Elf, showed nothing out of the ordinary.

But he did hear noises coming from below. A person, male from the sound, talking to himself.

Hall almost laughed but managed to keep it in.

That was why the Necromancer hadn't heard them. Whoever it was had been beneath and surrounded by tons of stone. No sound would have penetrated.

They still had the element of surprise.

Slowly, one step at a time, he started down.

CHAPTER FIFTEEN

THE STAIRS WERE NARROW, A CHILL COMING UP FROM BELOW.
Hall could feel it through the exposed parts of his armor,
almost cold enough to make his breath fog. The voice got
louder as he descended. Stopping at the turn, he waited.

Behind him was Roxhard, followed by Sabine and Leigh.
Jackoby took up the rear, leaving the other two Firbolgs up top.
Hall wasn't happy with the Firbolg in the rear. This was their
land they were fighting to protect it, but Hall knew that he and
the others were expendable for this quest. He wasn't sure if
earning the favor of the Firbolgs would be worth this effort. At
least in the short term, it wouldn't be. Long term, there was no
way to tell.

It was too late to second guess now. They were in too deep,
literally.

Peeking around the corner, Hall saw another fifteen or so
stone steps with a light at the bottom. It appeared to be a large
room, the voice coming from deeper. Not close to the stairs.

"I am tired," it said. Or at least that was what Hall thought
it said.

Definitely male. The voice was speaking Traders, the

central language of Hankarth, but Hall could not place the accent. It sounded like it was moving away from the stairs.

Hugging the wall, Hall took the last couple steps down, pausing before he entered the room.

Square, larger than the tower above, the room was stone, lit by blazing torches set in braziers placed evenly spaced on the walls. Floor, walls, and low ceiling all unmarked and the same stone blocks. There was only one opening on the far side, an arch that led into shadows. There were no furnishings or decorations save a bedroll and a couple blankets in the middle of the room. There was a pile of wood to the side, the remains of a fire near the bedrolls. A couple travel packs were stacked in a pile next to the bedding.

Someone was living down in the tower's cellar.

And not living well.

Hall could feel the cold and damp, leaching through the stones from the ground. No sun, no ventilation. The air was stale to breathe. Why would anyone choose to be down in the cellar when there was an entire tower?

He got his answer a couple seconds later as a shadow stepped out of the opening at the far end of the room. The shadow became a person as it stepped into the light from the torches. Tall and thin, almost gaunt, dressed in flowing black robes. The figure carried a thick wooden staff topped in what looked to be the skull of a wolf with red jewels in the eye sockets. Pale skin, long blond hair hanging haggard. Sharply pointed ears poked out of the thin hair.

An Elf. One of the Highborn.

Of the two Elven races on Hankarth, the Highborn were the most populous but also the most segregated. They considered themselves the most civilized race on the fractured islands, and in many ways, they were. They were also arrogant. Highborn kept to their lands, for the most part, the island of Arundel and their controlled territories. It was rare to see any in the other realms that were not merchants. They thought themselves superior to all the other races but especially their cousins, the Wood Elves.

Where the Highborn lived in cities of breathtaking beauty, tall and thin spires with elegant carvings, the Wood Elves lived in the wilds of the world. Their homes were in the trees, along the plains. They were as wild as the lands they called home. And all Players were Wood Elves, including Half-Elves like Hall. The Highborn had never been a playable race.

This Highborn was young. Hall didn't know why he thought it; he just knew it was true. It might have been the way the Elf carried himself, the way he talked to himself. The voice sounded young, not haughty like the older Highborn. The race was tall and thin, but this one was more so. He looked like he had not eaten a good meal in days. He looked tired, run down. The black robe was dirty and the closer to the middle of the room the Elf walked, Hall could see that it was ripped and torn.

Everything about the Highborn looked haggard, not at all what Hall was used to seeing from members of the race.

"I found it," he said as if talking to someone, but Hall could see nothing. "I am sorry it took so long. Please do not be angry."

The voice sounded tired, worn out. Pitiful. Not like a threat.

Hall felt sorry for the Elf.

He glanced back at the others, motioning for them to wait. Taking a deep breath, he stepped out into the room.

"Why are you down here?" he asked, as calm and gentle as he could.

The Highborn's head shot up, surprised and afraid when he caught sight of Hall. He raised the staff and pointed it toward the Skirmisher. Leaning his spear against the wall, Hall held up his hands, keeping them away from the sword belted at his waist. The ceiling was too low for him to *Leap*, but he knew he could still *Evade* most attacks while the others entered the room to confront the Elf. Looking at the Highborn, Hall figured that Roxhard and Jackoby could defeat the Elf with just their *Battle Rush* abilities.

Skill Gain!
Identify Rank One +.1

Highborn Witch (White)

"Stay back," the Elf said. "Don't make me hurt you."

Hall had to fight the urge to attack the Elf. That was what normally was required. It was obvious this Elf had something to do with the Undead plaguing the Firbolg and the quest requirements usually dictated killing the NPC. *There had to be more here*, Hall thought, as the current quest condition had not been met. It was a reason to not attack, but Hall knew he also didn't attack because he felt bad for the Elf.

"I'm not going to hurt you," Hall said, silently adding 'not yet anyway'.

"Who are you? How did you get down here? Where is Yorsif?"

Hall could see the staff quivering, shaking as the Highborn held it. The Elf looked terrified.

"Dead," Hall answered, taking a chance.

The Lich had been higher Level than Hall, but not that much. Not the most powerful Lich, it still was strong and would have been hard for this Highborn to control. The Undead could only be controlled by someone strong of will and this Highborn was not that.

When Hall said the Lich was dead the Highborn seemed to brighten a bit, back straighter, the tip of the staff lowering.

"Really?" he asked and Hall knew for certain the Highborn

would have been considered a teenager by that race. His experience with Roxhard, a youth trapped in an adult body, had taught him to recognize the aspects and mannerisms of youth.

"Yes."

The Highborn looked over his shoulder at the dark opening. Hall looked past, trying to see if there was something there but all he saw were dark shadows.

"The Craobh?"

"Dead," Hall answered. "Why are you down here?" he asked again.

"How did you kill them? Just you?" the Elf asked.

"No," Hall replied. "I have friends."

He gestured to the stairs and motioned the group to come out. He hoped they would do so with weapons sheathed. Each of them moved out slowly, spreading out and keeping space between them. Jackoby was the last out. He had his hammer still in the harness across his back, but his shield was held protectively in front of him.

Upon seeing them, the Elf Witch's eyes widened in fear. They darted from one to the other, staff moving with the eyes. He took a step back.

"Why are you sending Undead to attack us?" Jackoby asked, his deep voice soft.

The Firbolg Warden was hesitant, confused. This Highborn was not what he had been expecting.

"What?" the Highborn asked, shocked. The staff lowered, the jeweled wolf's eyes pointing at the ground. "I did not... I do not know..." He was at a loss for words.

"The Undead, Skeletons and Zombies, have been attacking my home," Jackoby said. "Our honored ancestors have been pulled from their graves at Fallen Green and wander the forest, finding their way to our homes and our fields."

"But I did not," the Elf started to say but stopped, head

tilting, eyes clearing in thought. "Fallen Green? Is that the clearing with all the mounds and the huge tree?"

The Elf hung his head, almost crying. His shoulders sagged, the staff drooping.

"Oh no, no, no," he said, shaking his head. "I did not mean...It was not my fault...He made me..."

"Who? Yorsif?" Leigh asked, her voice soft and soothing.

The Highborn nodded, up and down, crazy and chaotic.

"Yes," the Elf said. "He needed them. The necrotic energy." Looking up at them, moving from one to the other, the Elf's eyes showed desperation. He needed them to understand. "And me. He needed me for the summoning."

It was confusing trying to follow the Highborn. The Elf spoke quickly, the thoughts scattered, but Hall had clearly heard the last word. He didn't like the sound of it. Nothing made sense. The Elf had raised the dead, had to have raised Yorsif the Lich. Was that the summoning? It still didn't explain why the Highborn was in the cellar.

"What summoning?" Hall asked, afraid to hear the answer.

"I am sorry," the Elf said, sagging, the staff dropping to the ground. "Please forgive me." He was openly crying now, great sobs.

Hall glanced at the others, worried now. He grabbed his spear from where it lay against the wall, Jackoby and Roxhard drawing their weapons. Leigh and Sabine moved back, the others stepping in front of them.

The Highborn dropped to the ground, sitting on his knees, arms wrapped tightly around himself. He sagged, moving back and forth as he cried. Hall's eyes were drawn toward the dark opening. They waited, tense, feeling like something was coming. He felt it, a presence, powerful.

Waves of energy seemed to flow out of the opening. Almost physical as they brushed against Hall. He shivered, involuntarily, not from cold but fear. Nervously, he gripped his spear, seeing the others all reacting the same.

Touch of the Grave
You feel cold, a chill as if someone walked across your grave. Fear grips your heart, making you want to run.
Attack Speed +2 seconds.
Attack Power -2.
Wellness -2.

Hall looked at the debuff and cursed as his Health dropped. *What the hell*, he thought as his body shivered again. He forced himself to look at the opening as his mind tried to make him cower away.

There was no sound, but Hall saw something large and heavy step out of the shadowed opening. It was tall and broad, wearing leather and bark armor. A Firbolg, covered in black and gray fur and markings. In one hand, it carried a large warhammer, and in the other, a large shield. Both were made of wood. The weapon and armor should have been rotten, molded from the moisture and dampness of the cellar, but they were not because the creature was not real. Not solid. Hall could see the walls beyond through the Firbolg. Blurry and indistinct, tinged by the light blue color the ghostly creature glowed.

Skill Gain!
Identify Rank One +.2

Elite Firbolg Warden Revenant (Purple)

Hall cursed again, hearing the others do the same.

A Revenant. One of the strongest Undead. And this one was **Elite**.

CHAPTER SIXTEEN

THE CREATURE ADVANCED INTO THE ROOM. ITS EYES, SMALL sparks of green in black pits, the only thing that looked solid on it, moved from one to the other. It was measuring, judging.

"Spread out," Hall ordered. He thought about telling them all to run, but it was too late. The Revenant knew them, saw them. There was no escaping. That was what made the ghostly creatures so dangerous. They would not stop until the target was dead, or they were destroyed. And doing that was not easy.

Revenants were one of the strongest of the various types of Undead. The spirits brought back more than just the physical body. Angry spirits. Vengeful spirits. Magically given powers greater than they had in life.

The creature stopped at the side of the Highborn, ignoring the broken Elf. It opened its mouth and a sound came forth, a moan that reverberated against the walls, bouncing back and forth in the enclosed space. Hall felt it through his bones, every nerve, feeling as if a great weight was settling on his soul.

Elite Firbolg Warden Revenant attacks with Wail of the Soulless.

-5 Health

-5 Energy

You resist stunning effect of Wail of the Soulless

Closing its mouth, the red eyes glinting evilly, the Revenant stalked toward them.

Hall glanced at the others. Leigh and Sabine clutched their heads, the pain from the wail stunning them. Roxhard shook his head, fighting the effects as Jackoby roared and charged.

The large Firbolg ran across the space, too close for *Battle Rush*, but he used his *War Cry* ability. The shout seemed to shake the foundations of the room, mortar dust falling to the floor. The Revenant staggered back as the shout slammed into it. Pulling the creature's Health bar, Hall saw a small fraction disappear. There was a lot left. The Purple coloring of the Revenant's name told Hall it was considered a Boss-level monster.

Jackoby swung his warhammer. It slammed into the Revenant's shield, the sound of wood on wood, the ghostly shield as solid as a real one. Pushing out with his foot, kicking the Revenant, Jackoby growled in pain. Cold seemed to creep up his leg, and he had to stagger away from the Undead. The Firbolg Warden limped, and Hall saw frost on his lower leg.

The Revenant swung its warhammer, Jackoby catching it on his shield. There was a bright flash of blue, Jackoby pushed down under the blow. He stepped back, frost spreading across his wooden shield.

Hall circled to the side, watching the Revenant and the Highborn. The Elf was on the ground, crying, sagging, not looking at anything, but Hall didn't trust that to last. As far as he was concerned, they were facing two enemies. But he didn't want to draw the Highborn into the fight, content to let the Elf cry. But he would keep an eye on the black-robed Elf.

He sent a mental call out to Pike as he pulled a throwing knife from his bracer. Taking aim, he let it fly across the room. The small blade struck the ghostly blue of the Revenant, sparks erupting on impact. More of the creature's Health dropped, another fraction. Pulling the javelin from the harness, he let the weapon fly, The Revenant ignored him, concentrating on Jackoby in front of him. The flying spear struck the creature in the shoulder, passing through the body to slam against the stone on the other side. There was a cracking sound as the weapon snapped in half on impact.

Another small fraction had disappeared from the Revenant's Health bar.

He threw his second knife, following it with a charge at the Revenant.

The knife struck, sparks erupting, as Hall jabbed out with his spear into the Revenants back. The tip seemed to pass through the blue glowing bark and leather armor. Hall could see it within the Revenant.

BONUS DAMAGE!
Flanking Attack +7

Hall was thankful for Sky Realms Online's flanking mechanics. The bonus damage was a nice addition to his normal damage. Any attacks from behind or the sides were able to ignore most Armor Protection values, as well as any Agility Protection bonuses. The idea was that those were the unprotected sides, with no way to use a weapon or shield for defense or to evade the attack.

The Revenant turned, red eyes fixed on Hall. It lashed out with its right arm, but Hall managed to step back, avoiding the attack. He felt the cold that fell off the creature in waves. He shivered and jabbed out with the spear, scoring another hit.

He stepped back quickly as the Revenant stumbled

forward. Roxhard was behind it, swinging with his two-handed axe. The blade passed through the creature pulling a trail of glowing, fog-like material with it. Jackoby was on the other side, swinging with his hammer, the Revenant catching the weapon on its shield.

A bolt of purple lightning slammed into the Revenant's shoulder, lines of energy spreading across its body. The creature moved, the bolts flaring. It seemed to shake, fighting against the constricting bolts. But it still swung its warhammer, not as fast or strong but still plenty powerful. The weapon slammed into Roxhard's shoulder, sending the stout Dwarf flying. Blue lights exploded on contact, lines of frost spreading across his shoulder. He cried out, slamming into the floor. Leigh rushed to his side, her tattoos glowing light blue as soon as she laid her hands on Roxhard's shoulder.

Sabine cast a *Shadowbolt*, the line of black slamming into the Revenant. She moved her hands in a complicated gesture, and a light blue-white energy dagger shot out, the *Arcane Missile* striking the Revenant. She fired another one, and another, as rapidly as the cooldown would let her.

Hall shifted to the side, giving her a wider target to hit. The game had flanking damage to aid the attackers, but it also had a friendly fire mechanic. Sabine could just as easily hit Hall or Jackoby instead of the Revenant. That was the problem with fighting one foe, trying to allow everyone to attack. It had been one of the aspects of the game that Hall had liked the most. It made for challenging Raids as the Players had to coordinate the timing of their attacks. He had played older MMORPGs where forty people could be attacking the same single target. A large mass, just hacking away with spells and ranged attacks ignoring the friendlies.

The Revenant raised its warhammer, the red eyes flaring, as flames spread out across the weapon. The fires crackled, flickering shades of blue. The eyes seemed a little dimmer, not as bright as before, as if it was taking the energy from within.

Which it was, Hall realized. He remembered what the Highborn had said. Something about raising the Skeletons and Zombies because he needed the necrotic energy. The Revenant was running on borrowed energy, not its own.

That fact did Hall no good as he jumped back, avoiding a wide swing of the warhammer.

Another *Shadowbolt* struck the creature, its eyes turning and locking on Sabine. She took an involuntary step back. She tried to cast another spell, her fingers fumbling as they shook with fear.

The Revenant pointed the end of the warhammer at her, the fires gathering at the tip and shooting out at the Witch. Gripped by the magical fear, she couldn't move out of the way, the icy blast striking her in the stomach. She doubled over in pain, lines of white frost where the blast had hit, her skin turning a shade of blue.

Roxhard stepped in front of her, axe raised, as Leigh crouched next to the Witch.

Pike swooped in, flying low, at head height. The dragonhawk flew straight at the Revenant, beak opening and shooting out a bolt of lightning. The blast hit the Revenant in the chest, sparks spreading across the body. More Health dropped, but they had still barely made a dent.

Jackoby and Roxhard stood apart, facing the Revenant, making it turn from one to the other. It seemed to be able to with ease, blocking Roxhard's attacks with its shield, parrying Jackoby's with its own warhammer. None of the three were able to score direct hits, but the cold damage from the flames around the warhammer was eating away at both Wardens' Health.

Hall threw another throwing knife, the blades magically

reappearing in his bracer. Pike scored another lightning attack, more damage taken from the Revenant. It pointed the warhammer at the swooping dragonhawk, another blast of icy fire which Pike avoided. The fight rotated, forcing Hall to step to the Revenants side as the Highborn was in the way. The Elf didn't move, didn't even notice the battle raging behind him. The cold aura of the Revenant didn't seem to affect the Highborn.

Even with using his spear, not having to get in close, Hall could still feel that intense cold. It sapped his Health, very little at a time but still eating away at it.

They were chipping away at the Revenant and could eventually possibly destroy the creature, but they couldn't afford to make a mistake. Numbers were on their side, and they had to keep up the pace to stop the creature from counterattacking.

Opening its mouth again, the Revenant let out a wail. Both Roxhard and Jackoby fell backward, crying out in pain. So close to the creature, they couldn't resist the full impact of the Wail. Hall felt it, felt the pain clutching at him, trying to stop him from moving, from thinking. He fought through the pain and stabbed out with the spear. The tip passed right through the Revenant, bursting out the other side with a spray of ghostly material.

Turning quickly, the Revenant forced the spear from Hall's hand. The shaft stuck out of the creature, the end of the wood slamming against the head of the Highborn. The young Elf grunted and fell to the ground, unmoving. Hall stepped back as the Revenant turned to face him, tip of his own spear pointing his way.

It took a step toward him, stopping as a swarm of splinters passed through its body. The shards hit the stone wall, falling to the ground. The Revenant turned and saw Leigh, her staff pointed at it. Sabine was standing next to the Druid, her own staff raised. A purple bolt shot out, striking the Revenant and sending purple tendrils of energy across its body. The new *Hexbolt* replacing the old that had run out.

Roxhard was up, axe swinging, passing through the Revenant. Hall drew his short sword, stepping up and attacking from the side. He had to step in close, feeling more of the cold from the creature. It seeped into his bones, sapping his strength. He scored a solid hit but couldn't step back in time. The Revenant hit him in the shoulder, knocking him to the ground. His shoulder felt numb at the impact, lines of frost crawling down his arm.

Pike dove back in, a lightning blast pushing the Revenant back. A hit from Roxhard to its shoulder turned it toward the Dwarf. The next swing was caught on the shield, and Roxhard couldn't avoid the warhammer that slammed into his chest. The Dwarf fell to the ground, forcing himself to roll out of the way.

He was replaced by an enraged Jackoby. The Firbolg caught the Revenant's hammer on his shield, pushing it out of the way, and slammed his own hammer into the creature's chest. The face of the hammer passed through the creature, pushing aside the ghostly material which flowed back in and around the hammer.

Seeming to grin, the Revenant grabbed Jackoby's hammer with its shield hand. Holding the Firbolg in place by the hammer, it twisted its body and stabbed the tip of Hall's spear into Jackoby's side. The Firbolg grunted, feeling the ironwood tip of the spear slice into his stomach. Red blood started to flow, dripping onto the ground.

Hall stood up, grabbing the end of the spear with one hand and pulled. He yanked it out of the Revenant, dropping the weapon on the ground. Jackoby staggered back, shield hand clutching his side. The Firbolg glared at the Revenant.

Roxhard rushed in, striking at the Revenant and got the shield to the face. The Dwarf fell to the ground. A shaft of black streaked at the Undead creature, who caught it on the shield. The bolt splashed against the glowing blue shield. Stepping forward, the Revenant kicked out at Roxhard, catching the Dwarf in the head. It turned and pointed the flaming hammer at the two casters. Streaks of blue flame shot out, Leigh catching one in the shoulder and being thrown backward. Sabine moved but got caught in the leg, blue flames and frost covering the lower part of her leg.

Swooping in, Pike got hit by the shield; the Revenant was ready for the dragonhawk. Pike fell to the floor, rolling to a stop, staggering to stand.

The Revenant took a step toward Jackoby, who still clutched his side, holding his hammer weakly. The Firbolg growled, eyes filled with hate and defiance. Jackoby was moving along the wall, turning the Revenant away from the women and the downed Roxhard, exposing the creatures back to them. He didn't move fast enough to avoid another blast of fiery frost. Grunting in pain, he staggered to the ground, brown fur tinged in white frost.

Another step, raising the warhammer, the Revenant prepared to strike Jackoby. The Firbolg was unable to defend, staring at his death coming.

The hammer descended and struck Hall as he dove in front of the Firbolg. He collapsed to the ground, clutching at his side where the ghostly hammer had struck. Frost covered his leather armor and his exposed arm.

Hall's spear stuck out of the Revenant's face, the tip piercing the skull. Somehow while being hit by the hammer, Hall had managed to strike the Revenant. The creature staggered back, shield arm reaching for the wooden shaft. Roxhard swung his axe at the thing's legs, coming from the side. The axe sliced through both legs. He stopped the movement of the axe, and swung back in the other direction, again through both legs.

Sabine's *Shadowbolt* struck the Revenant in the back, splashing against the glowing translucent body, black spreading from the bolt. Standing up, Jackoby stood protectively over Hall, reaching for the wooden handle of the spear.

He pulled it out and immediately jammed it back into the Revenant's face. The creature tried to open its mouth and moan but the spear cut through, somehow blocking the sound. Again, Jackoby removed the weapon, and again, he stabbed the Revenant with it. Roxhard kept hacking at it, the Revenant unable to mount an offensive attack. It couldn't even defend itself.

Pushing himself along the ground, clutching his side, Hall tried to get out of the way. He thought his ribs were cracked, probably broken. Breathing was hard, each breath painful. His body felt cold, spreading from where the hammer had hit him. He hadn't thought about what he was doing, he had just seen Jackoby about to die and acted. Hands grabbed at him, pulling as he crawled. He looked up and saw Leigh. She was watching the fight as she pulled.

A safe distance away, Hall felt her hands on his side, saw them glowing and felt the warmth of her healing magic spread through his body, driving the cold away. He felt the pain in his side lessen, no longer as painful to breathe. It still hurt, but he could breathe, and that was what mattered.

Leigh helped him to stand. He leaned against the wall watching Jackoby and Roxhard attack relentlessly. Sabine shot *Shadowbolt* after *Arcane Missile* after *Shadowbolt* after *Missile*, an unrelenting barrage. Hall looked at the Revenant's Health. It was barely past half. All the damage they had done and the Revenant was not in danger yet. They couldn't keep this up.

Already the creature had landed a couple of strong blows to them. The chances of that continuing would only increase.

Jackoby, still in immense pain, slipped and almost stumbled. The Firbolg dropped Hall's spear and managed to get his shield up in time to block the Revenant's weak attack. He pawed around at the ground until he found his warhammer.

There had to be a way to end the creature. They couldn't just hope to keep chipping away at it.

The Highborn was still unconscious, somehow managing to avoid being trampled. He would be no help. Hall drew his sword, pushing off from the wall. Leigh started to protest but stopped, knowing it would be useless. He took a couple steps, each one hurting. The healing had helped, but his body still hurt. Watching the combatants, he waited for his chance for an opening.

He thought about all the ramblings that the Highborn had said. The Elf had talked about necrotic energy, gathering enough. The Zombies and Skeletons had been raised to provide energy to eventually summon or raise the Revenant? How had that worked? How had the energy gotten to this place?

Taking a step closer to the Revenant, he thought of something he had forgotten about. It was what had first led them to the tower. Reaching into his pouch he brought out the *Eye of Death's Gaze*. The small orb glowed, pulsing. Holding it out, he saw the Revenant turn his way. It started to take a step, but attacks from Roxhard and Jackoby stopped it.

Hall looked down at the orb and back at the Revenant. He examined the orb closer. Perfectly round, perfectly smooth, glowing with a green inner light. The pulsing was new. It had not been doing that when Hall had first found it.

The sound of someone grunting drew his attention. He thought Jackoby had been hit again, the Firbolg already weakened, but it was Roxhard. The Revenant had backhanded the

Dwarf, hitting him full-on with the shield. Skidding across the floor, Roxhard pushed himself up, frost covering the side of his face where the shield had hit. The deep-set eye was black, puffing up.

Leigh ran to Roxhard's side. She wanted, needed, to get to Jackoby, but the Firbolg was too close to the Revenant and would not back away. Her hands touched Roxhard, face and chest, glowing and spreading the healing warmth.

Smiling, Roxhard stalked back to the Revenant, but Hall got in his way, taking the position he had been.

Holding the orb in one hand, attacking with his short sword, Hall tried to get the Revenant's attention away from the Firbolg. Stronger, a heavier weapon, Jackoby was doing more damage. He needed the Firbolg free.

"Behind," he yelled at Roxhard, motioning with the hand holding the orb.

The movement caught the Revenant's attention, the eyes fixed on the orb. The green glowing eyes. Hall lifted his hand, the orb moving up, and the Revenant's eyes followed. It ignored the Dwarf that moved behind it, only turning away from the orb when Jackoby's hammer slammed into its side. Hall struck out, cursing the Firbolg for distracting it. His sword stabbed into the Revenant's head, tip poking out the other side.

It didn't seem to care.

He could feel the cold from the creature, so close he was almost touching it.

Roxhard attacked from the side, axe slicing through the Revenant. Jackoby's hammer slammed into its shoulder, forcing Hall to step back.

"Stop attacking," Hall shouted at the Firbolg.

Jackoby gave him an odd look but didn't stop.

"Dammit," Hall cursed. "I need you to smash this," he yelled, thrusting the *Eye of Death's Gaze* at Jackoby.

Again, the Firbolg Warden gave Hall an odd look but then

saw how the Revenant's attention was drawn to the glowing orb. Quickly, Jackoby grabbed the orb, stepping back out of reach as the Revenant made a grab for it. Hall intercepted the creature's hammer strike, barely catching it on his sword. He grunted in pain, the impact felt through his bones and especially his cracked ribs.

Jackoby moved to a corner of the room, away from everyone else. The Revenant tried to follow, but Hall and Roxhard got in the way. That was what told the Firbolg the small orb was important. It was the only thing the Revenant paid attention to.

He placed it on the ground, taking a step back and aiming his hammer. He sneered at the Revenant and brought the hammer down with all his strength. It slammed into the orb.

There was a cracking sound, small and quiet but somehow audible to all. No great explosion or light or force. Just the cracking. Jackoby lifted the hammer to see shards of glass, dust and green smoke swirling away.

The Revenant stopped. The green glowing eyes flickered. Then the body started to flicker. It disappeared, came back, disappeared and came back even more translucent than before. The eyes still glowed, but not as bright, a dull green. Checking its Health, Hall saw that most of it had disappeared, dropped. Just a thin bit of red showed.

Reaching down he grabbed his spear in his left hand. He jabbed with the spear, sliced with the sword. Roxhard swung the axe, sideways, up and down. More bolts of magic came from Sabine. Jackoby wanted back into the fight, but Leigh stopped him, finally able to heal the Firbolg.

The attacks continued, the Revenant unable to do anything. It stood there, trying to mount a counterattack, to do anything, but failed. Bit by bit, the Health dropped, quicker than before.

Until there was none left.

Roxhard's axe sliced through the Revenant's chest, not just passing through. It left a large gash in the translucent body, the wispy substance no longer flowing back into place. The Revenant stumbled, shaking, looking duller and duller. Sheathing his sword, Hall grabbed his spear with both hands. He lined it up and stabbed it forward. Through the Revenant's head.

It flickered, appearing solid and then disappeared.

SLAIN: *Elite Firbolg Warden Revenant*
+100 Experience

Skill Gain!
Light Armor Rank Two +.1
Polearms Rank Two +.2
Small Blades Rank Two +.2
Thrown Rank Two +.1

QUEST COMPLETE!
You have investigated the Tower of Yorsif the Shaman and found him returned as a Lich along with a summoned Revenant and a Highborn Elf Necromancer that has been living in the tower's cellar.

THE ROAMING DEAD II
Investigate the Tower of Yorsif the Shaman 1/1
Reward: +200 Brownpaw Firbolg Reputation
+50 Experience

You have defeated Yorsif the Lich and the Firbolg Revenant but are no closer to discovering why the Undead are plaguing the Brownpaw Firbolg.

THE ROAMING DEAD III

Discover why the Undead have risen 0/1
Reward: +50 Brownpaw Firbolg Reputation
+25 Experience

ACCEPT QUEST?

Hall sighed. It appeared they were not done yet.

CHAPTER SEVENTEEN

"WHY DID YOU DO THAT?" JACKOBY ROARED, STANDING IN front of Hall, looking down at him.

Hall clutched at his side, still feeling the pain of the broken ribs even though Leigh had cast *Nature's Touch* on him again. They were all still sore and in pain from the fight with the Revenant. Even the Highborn Elf, who was still out cold.

"Do what?" Hall asked. He wanted to push past the Firbolg and prod the Elf awake. He had questions, but Jackoby was much bigger. It would probably be easier to push through a wall.

"Save me," Jackoby growled.

Hall looked at him confused, wondering what that meant. He hadn't thought about it, he had just reacted. Jackoby, while not a friend or even someone he liked, was part of Hall's party. That meant if he was in danger, Hall would work to save him. The way Jackoby was acting, it was like Hall had committed a grave offense.

"You're welcome," Hall muttered and stepped around the fuming Firbolg.

Jackoby turned but didn't follow. Hall could feel the eyes

boring into him. He had thought to get a Reputation increase for saving the Firbolg, but this was not close to anything he had imagined. Anger? That made no sense.

Setting his spear against the wall, Hall grabbed one of the torches and walked through the dark opening. The light didn't show much, but he could make out that the room was smaller than the other chamber, maybe half its size. It was empty except for a raised dais in the middle, two steps up. Hall walked closer, mounting the steps, more light coming into the room as Sabine walked in with another torch.

On the platform was a stone coffin, the heavy lid in two pieces on the ground where it had been pushed. There was no detail to the coffin. Looking inside, Hall was not surprised that it was empty, most likely where the Lich had been resting. Behind the coffin was a stone statue. A Firbolg wearing bark and leather armor, carrying a warhammer and shield. An exact match for the Revenant.

Hall stepped closer to the statue, noticing an odd deformation on the stone chest. Pulling the torch in, he saw there was a space, a half globe taken out of the statue. Softball size. Just the right size of the *Eye of Death's Gaze* to sit. As he pulled back, he noticed that the warhammer and shield were reflecting the torchlight, the glare catching on the metal banding.

The weapon and shield were not stone.

Handing the torch to Sabine, Hall pulled the warhammer out of the statue's grip. It rested snugly in the carved stone hand, but it slid out. He was able to pull the shield off the statue's arm. Using *Identify*, he saw both items were blue.

Skill Gain!
Identify Rank One +.2

TORKLIR'S SHIELD
Protection +2
Health +5
Earth Resistance +15%
Durability 20/20
Weight 8 lbs.

On a successful Block has a 25% chance of reflecting damage back on attacker.Attacker receives damage equal to one-half of what would have been a successful attack.

TORKLIR'S HAMMER
Strength +2
Health +2
Durability 20/20
Weight 8 lbs.

On successful attack has a 25% chance of Stunning target for 10 seconds.

The Revenant had a name.

The statue was carved so it appeared to be standing protectively over the stone coffin. There was a story here, Hall knew, and maybe the Highborn Elf knew it.

Together, Hall and Sabine gave the room a good searching. There was nothing else of value, no loot, just the shield and hammer. Bare stone walls, unmarked coffin.

"I miss the days when everything dropped loot," Sabine muttered.

They walked back out into the main room, replacing the torches. The Highborn was still out but someone had moved him so he was sitting up and not lying down anymore. Jackoby was standing over him.

"Here," Hall said, handing the shield and hammer to the Firbolg.

He looked at Hall in confusion.

"None of the rest of us can use them," Hall replied. "Seems a waste to leave them down here."

"Thank you," Jackoby said slowly, looking at the items. His eyes widened as he Identified them, seeing their stats and bonuses. Again, he looked at Hall in confusion, unsure.

"That was the only loot," Sabine said, a little annoyance in her voice. "If you don't take them, we'll just sell them."

Still slightly shocked, Jackoby opened his pouch and placed his original hammer into it. Hall watched as the strange distortion happened when the large hammer sank into the much smaller pouch. The shield followed, an even bigger distortion. A waviness to the air, the wooden object twisting and turning in on itself until it was small enough to slide into the pouch.

Jackoby took the shield first. Like his old, it was made of wood and banded in metal. Somehow the wood had survived being down in the damp cellar for years. A diamond shape, a band of iron ran along the edge, two thin straps across the single plank of a cherry colored wood. There was no symbol or insignia inscribed on the surface. It was plain, looking nothing special.

The hammer was different.

Jackoby adjusted the straps on the shield, testing the fit before taking the hammer in hand. The same length as his old, the head was thinner and the shaft was wrapped in leather. Instead of barrel-shaped, the head was squat, a flattened triangle atop the head. Made of a dark gray wood, there were some etchings along the surface of the weapon.

Stepping back from the others, he gave the hammer a couple practice swings. He nodded, happy with the weight and swing.

"Thank you," he said again.

You have earned +200 Alliance points with Jackoby, Warden of the Brownpaw. Confused by your gift of the hammer and shield, Jackoby is unsure how to feel. He is still distrustful of outsiders but is starting to shift his thinking.

Hall nodded, glad the gifts had helped his reputation with Jackoby. Every little bit helped. He didn't need the Warden to be his friend, but an ally in the Brownpaw would only help Yarbole decide to the alliance with Skara Brae.

"Can we wake him?" Hall asked, pointing to the unconscious Highborn.

Leigh crouched down in front of the Elf, laying her hands on either side of his head. The tattoos on her arms glowed and the light transferred to the Elf. His eyes shot open. They were unfocused at first but widened in fear as he realized where he was and who was staring down at him. He tried to push himself away from them, scrambling in fear, hands digging at the stone.

"Calm down," Hall said, he tried to keep menace from his voice but failed. "If we had wanted you dead, you wouldn't have woken up."

The Highborn slowly nodded, calming down a little. There was still fear in his eyes, but he wasn't trying to back away.

"Who are you and why did you raise the dead?" Jackoby asked, growling.

Hall rolled his eyes. Not the way he would have handed it, but a direct approach with questioning would probably be quickest.

"Quinthetal," the Elf stammered, eyeing Jackoby nervously. "I didn't want to," he said, pleading, turning to Hall.

"Didn't want to what?"

"Raise the dead," Quinthetal replied. His eyes were still terrified, but he was calming down enough to talk. "My great-grandfather. He made me."

"Who made you?" Hall asked but thought he knew.

"Yorsif," the Elf answered.

Hall had been right and was reevaluating the age of the Elf. Quinthetal was young. Very young. Which, for an Elf, could mean he was fifty years old.

"The Lich," Sabine asked.

Quinthetal nodded, eyes darting around as if looking for the Lich to just appear. He seemed more terrified of that thought than he did of Hall and the others.

"How could a Lich make you do anything," Sabine stated more than asked. There was skepticism in her voice.

Quinthetal started to speak, but Hall held up a hand.

"From the beginning," he said.

Nodding, the Elf started to speak.

"I live in Ersofir," he said. "That's..."

"On the edge of Northern Edin, the Highborn Confederacy port," Hall broke in, motioning with his hand for Quinthetal to speed up and stick to the relevant stuff.

"My great-grandfather, Yorsif, had been driven out by our people. He had been practicing necromancy. My grandfather had been young and even though it was years ago, our family still suffered from the dishonor," Quinthetal started slowly, his voice growing in confidence as he spoke. There was bitterness, hidden anger. "Even as I grew up, I had to learn to live with it. We could never forget even though no one heard from Yorsif again once he was banished. One day, a couple weeks ago, I was going through some old chests and found a couple of his old journals. Or what I thought was journals." He hung his head, shaking it sadly. "I wish I had never found those. I read some passages and quickly hid them again once I knew what they were."

"Why didn't you destroy them?" Leigh asked. She still crouched down next to the Elf. There was pity in her eyes, compassion.

"I don't know," Quinthetal replied sadly. "I thought about it, but something made me just hide them. The voice wasn't talking to me yet but maybe it."

"Voice?" Roxhard interrupted. "What voice?"

"That night, I started hearing it," the Elf said. "At first in my dreams, but then when I was awake. It wanted me to read more from the book and so I did. It was the only way to make the voice stop." He paused and looked from one to the other, pleading for understanding. The only ones that showed it were Leigh and Roxhard.

"I read more and then more. Each night I would read more pages, and each night the voice would get stronger and more compelling. Eventually, I left home in the middle of the night and came here."

Hall knew what came next, and he was starting to feel sorry for the Elf.

"You were able to raise Yorsif, and the Lich forced you to use the Eye of Death's Gaze to gather the energy needed to raise the Revenant? That was why you started raising the dead in the Firbolg's graveyard?"

Quinthetal nodded, looking almost relieved to have the story out.

QUEST COMPLETE!
From Quinthetal, you have learned why the Undead have risen from the Firbolg graveyard at Fallen Green. With the Eye of Death's Gaze, Yorsif the Lich and the Revenant destroyed there should be no more dead to harass the Brownpaw.

THE ROAMING DEAD III
Discover why the Undead have risen 1/1
Reward: +50 Brownpaw Firbolg Reputation
+25 Experience

Silence fell, the Elf exhausted. The rest of them were relieved. With the prompts, it meant that the quest chain was over and they could return to the Green Ember.

"What do we do with him?" Roxhard asked, pointing to Quinthetal.

PART TWO
THE GUILD

CHAPTER EIGHTEEN

THEY BROUGHT THE ELF WITH THEM. HIS FINAL FATE, ALL HAD decided with some coaxing for the more reluctant Leigh and Roxhard, should be in the hands of the Brownpaw. It was their people that his actions had endangered. While not entirely his fault, the Firbolg had still been in danger from the Undead.

It was late and so they decided to spend the night in Yorsif's tower. It was warm and out of the elements but the stone floors were not comfortable. They stayed in the main hall, still setting watches throughout the night and keeping Quinthetal tied up. The Elf didn't complain, probably just happy to still be alive.

Jackoby was silent for most of the trip, occasionally giving Hall a strange look. He would study the shield and warhammer, the only loot from the Tower, study Hall and stare unseeing into the forest. The Firbolg Warden seemed to be struggling with something.

The sun was bright as they walked back to Green Ember. It was a short hike. They made good time and by late afternoon were in front of Yarbole. Baskily was in the same spot next to her. The old Firbolg was smiling. He was not.

"Were you successful?" she asked, looking questioningly at Quinthetal.

The Elf's head was downcast. He walked slow and dejected. No one replied, Jackoby still lost in his own thoughts, so after a second or two, Hall stepped forward and answered.

"We were," he said and explained about Quinthetal and Yorsif.

As he spoke, he saw Baskily getting angrier by the word. Hall knew what that one would do to Quinthetal. It was none of his business, but he found himself hoping the Elf would live, get a second chance.

Once Hall was done, Baskily took a step forward. Yarbole laid a hand on his arm, stopping him. She studied the Elf, thoughtful.

"Do you still hear this voice?" she asked.

It took Quinthetal a bit to realize she was addressing him. He looked up, sad.

"No," he replied. Tears started running down his face. "I'm sorry. I'm so sorry."

The Elf collapsed to the ground on his knees.

Baskily looked angry, not caring, but Yarbole looked at Quinthetal with pity. She motioned to two of the guards stationed along the hall's side. They approached and each grabbed one of Quinthetal's arms, lifting the Elf up. He didn't protest, didn't help them either, just hung as dead weight. Crying the whole time. They carried him out the door and disappeared.

"What is going to happen to him?" Hall asked, watching them go and turning back to Yarbole.

"You almost died fighting the things he summoned," Yarbole replied. "And yet you feel pity for him?"

Hall shrugged.

"Not pity," he replied. "He did cause all this, did almost kill us. He does deserve some punishment but..." he paused, trailing off. Turning to look out the entrance where Quinthetal disappeared, he sighed. "I guess I do feel some pity. He's just a kid."

"It is hard to feel compassion for our enemy," Yarbole said, leaning forward. She rested her hands on a thick wooden cane, the rough wood carved in many symbols. "But sometimes it is the right thing to do."

Hall nodded. He glanced at Baskily, who had settled back behind his mother again. The larger Firbolg didn't look happy, or friendly, but he wasn't staring back with hate. That was an improvement.

"You have shed blood for us," Yarbole said after letting the silence linger, studying Hall the whole time. "You did it knowing that there might not be a reward for you. And still you did it anyway."

She leaned back, fingers tapping on the cane. Yarbole smiled.

"I think the Brownpaw can be friends with the people of Skara Brae," she said and then chuckled. "The few of them there are."

You have earned +250 Faction Reputation points with the Brownpaw of Fallen Green. You are now KNOWN and TRUSTED. Yarbole, Clan Chieftain of the Brownpaw, has decided that the Brownpaw can be allies with your village of Skara Brae. The relationship is one-sided for now.

"Thank you," Hall replied with a deep nod. On his shoulder, Pike gave a quiet squawk.

"Formal trade agreements will come when you have something to trade," Yarbole said, not unkindly, just stating fact. "But the Brownpaw will always be your allies."

"Unless you cause us not to be," Baskily said, an edge to his voice.

Hall wondered if his first alliance would last once that one took over the clan. Thoughts for the future, he opened his Settlement Interface.

Skara Brae Town Stats:
Lord: Hall
Status: Ruins
Morale: N/A

Government: N/A
Appointed Officials: N/A

Population: 4
Production: N/A

Faction: None
Allies:Gnomes of Valedale
Brownpaw of Fallen Green
Trade Partners: N/A
Enemies: N/A

"You all look weary," Yarbole said, glancing at her other son, Jackoby, who was still deep in thought. "Please, rest. We will talk more in the morning."

Hall smiled, fighting back a yawn, not realizing how tired he was.

———

The next morning, afternoon really, they all gathered at the lowest level of Green Ember, alongside a road that led deep into the forest in a southwesterly direction. It was a heavily traveled path, two Firbolgs wide, the edges cleared of branches. Jackoby stood on one side of Yarbole, still lost in thought as he had been all night. Baskily was on the other, not friendly but not angry. Leaning on a cane, Yarbole was smiling.

"This path will take you to the Silver Peak Road and The Season's Goose," Baskily said, pointing down the path. "A roadside Inn and Trader's Post that we deal with. From there it is a week's walk to Silver Peak Keep."

Hall pulled up his map, changing the scale and paging it around to show all of the Fallen Green forest and the road to the south. He was surprised to see so much revealed, wondering if because Baskily had described it, the map had filled in. Using the measuring scale he had devised, he shifted it to make the distance from where they stood to the edge of the forest about two days.

Skill Gain!

Cartography Rank Two +.1

Dismissing the map, he nodded his thanks to Baskily and turned to Yarbole.

"Thank you," Hall said with a bow.

"I have a feeling the relationship between Green Ember and Skara Brae will not be one-sided for long," Yarbole said with a chuckle. Reaching out, she took Hall's hand in both of hers, patting it. He could feel the light fur covering her hands as well as the many wrinkles.

With a screech, Pike lifted off Hall's shoulders and into the sky where he circled before flying away, heading southwest. All the eyes, except Jackoby's, followed the dragonhawk's flight.

"I was honored to fight alongside you," Hall said a little formally to the Firbolg Warden.

He didn't know if honored was the right word, but it seemed to fit. Facing Jackoby, he held his hand out, waiting for a warrior's clasp.

The Firbolg stared at the hand. The tension grew,

becoming awkward. Hall was a little embarrassed, holding his arm out.

"Right," Hall said and withdrew the arm.

The others were further back, waiting, and Hall turned to join them when Jackoby stepped forward. He raised his head, looking at Hall with an intense glare before turning back to his mother.

"The Half-Elf saved my life," he started, his large hand grasping the warhammer he held tighter. It was obvious to all that this was hard for Jackoby. The Firbolg looked to the skies, sighed, and continued. "I owe him a life debt."

Baskily reacted quickly, stepping forward to stand in front of his brother. Hall could see the similarity between the two. He had no idea what Jackoby meant by life debt. He had saved the Firbolgs life, but they were in a group on a quest together. That was just what was done. He didn't expect payment of some kind.

"Brother," Baskily said, almost angry. "You cannot."

"I can and I must," Jackoby replied.

"Mother," Baskily said, stepping away. "Talk some sense into him."

Hall looked back at the others. They all shrugged, not sure what was going on.

He was tempted to just start walking but something held him back.

Yarbole walked up to Jackoby, looking up at him. He smiled down at his mother, staring into her eyes, and just nodded. Since the return from the Tower, Jackoby had appeared lost. Now he looked focused, sure of his direction. His mother reached up, tenderly running a hand down his cheek, smiling. She stepped back and turned to Hall, her smile gone and a serious look on her face.

"Take care of my son," she said.

Hall started to have an idea what Jackoby meant by life debt. He turned to the Firbolg and held up his hands.

"That's not necessary," he said. "There's no need for..."

"You saved my life," Jackoby said, locking eyes with Hall, who could see the uncertainty and nervousness hiding behind the strong gaze. Hall's protest died away. "I will see that debt repaid."

You have received:

Life Debt of the Brownpaw

For saving his life, Jackoby of the Brownpaw has pledged his life to yours. He will fight
alongside you until he feels that his debt to you has ended.

Hall nodded.

CHAPTER NINETEEN

THE SEASON'S GOOSE WAS A LARGE BUILDING, BUILT OF LOGS
with a shingled roof. Two stories, windows in the gable ends
indicating a third story under the sloped roof. Old, the building
didn't look worn but had the look of a place that had been
there for a while and was comfortable. Next to it were two
smaller buildings, a barn and what had to be the Trader's Post
that Baskily had mentioned.

There was no need to visit the trader. None of them had
any loot to sell, and each had barely any gold so there would be
no purchasing, and the Brownpaw had given them plenty of
travel rations and other supplies.

Now that Hall thought about it, he had been surprised by
how much Yarbole had given them. Jackoby had none of his
own, apparently not fully committed to coming with them until
the last minute, but it seemed Yarbole had known what was in
her son's heart. She had sent along enough for him as well.

When they had started the walk, tension had been thick in
the air. Jackoby, as sure about his choice as he was, did not
appear happy to be there with them. The others weren't sure
what to make of the whole situation. Neither did Hall.

"Just don't jump in front of arrows for me, okay?" Hall said with a chuckle, trying to be funny. But he was somewhat serious. He didn't need the Firbolg purposefully getting in the way in hopes of eliminating the debt.

Jackoby just grunted and picked up his pace, taking the lead.

Hall shrugged and the walk continued.

He had noticed that his Alliance standing with Jackoby had not changed. Which was a surprise. He had thought that the Life Debt would have raised the standing instantly. It had not. Jackoby still barely tolerated him.

Which was not ideal in a traveling companion.

It didn't improve over the day, night alongside the path and the rest of the next day before they got to the Inn.

They walked into the nearly empty Inn, Angus curling up outside with Pike settling on his back. A large open room, two fireplaces on the ends, and a long bar across the back wall. Pictures hung between the windows, a large double-headed axe behind the bar. The barkeep was an older man, Gael, with gray hair and beard. He was polishing a glass, chatting with two men at the bar. They looked like farmers fresh from the fields.

Hall figured there had to be a couple small villages, or farms, around, and it was still somewhat early. The farming dinner crowd would still be an hour out.

A single waitress, dressed in a simple wool dress and shirt, moved about the large room filled with many different sized tables. Broom in hand, she was cleaning up, flashing them a large smile when they walked in. She stopped cleaning and hustled through the door in the back of the room, behind the bar, to tell the cook that dinner guests were starting to arrive.

"Take a seat," the barkeep said. "Not that many empty spots, I'm afraid," he said with a chuckle.

Leigh laughed, which meant Roxhard laughed. Hall just

smiled. Sabine scowled and Jackoby said nothing, waiting until the others had taken their seats. The Firbolg stood, looking toward the bar before grunting and sitting down. Hall wondered if Jackoby had thought about sitting away from them. Hall just shook his head. Two days into this Life Debt, and he was already annoyed.

"What can I get you?" the waitress asked. "Cook just put some venison over the fire."

"Sounds good," Hall said. "Also need two rooms."

She looked at the group, eyebrow lifted in amusement. A Half-Elf, two female Gael, a Dwarf, and a Firbolg. The waitress was trying to figure out the sleeping arrangements.

"Three and two," Hall supplied.

Nodding, the waitress took their drink orders and headed over to the bar. Hall glanced at Leigh quickly, before shifting his gaze, wondering if there would come a time he would share a bed with her. There was mutual attraction, but there hadn't been a time to act on it.

No one talked, enjoying the silence and rest, until the waitress came back with their drinks. Four ales and a wine. Hall put down a couple of silver coins that quickly disappeared into the waitress's hand.

They all took long pulls of their drinks. Except for Jackoby. The Firbolg stared angrily at his mug, pushing it away.

"Something wrong?" Hall asked.

"I will pay for my own food and drink," he replied.

Hall sighed. *Best get this over with*, he thought, leaning forward and pushing the mug closer to the Firbolg.

"I get it," he said, waiting to continue until Jackoby was looking at him. "You're not here by choice, not really. If I could just say something and end this Life Debt I would, but I've played enough..." he paused. He was about to say 'games'. He had played enough games. It had been a long time since he thought of this life as a game. "Look, I get how these things work. I can't just make it go away. And as that's the case, we are stuck with each other. So let's make the best of it."

Jackoby nodded. A sullen nod, but a nod. He didn't reach for his mug.

"As for that," Hall continued and pointed at the mug. "You're part of the group, and as such, you share in the profits. And expenses." He smiled. "You'll get your turn to pay soon enough."

He leaned back and waited, watching. Jackoby grunted and picked up the mug, taking a long pull. Hall raised his own mug in salute to Jackoby and took a drink.

You have earned +100 Alliance points with Jackoby, Warden of the Brownpaw. Jackoby appreciates your gesture and it has softened his ire at being there.

"That reminds me," Roxhard said. "We still need a name for our Guild."

Sabine audibly groaned.

———

The next morning, they set out early. Hall had thought about trying to see if there was a merchant caravan leaving for Silver Peak Keep. Hire on as guards and ride in wagons for the week's journey. But he decided not to wait. Any caravan would catch up to their walking pace anyway.

Before they left, he opened his map and marked the Season's Goose location on the map, seeing where their path through the Fallen Green Forest from Green Ember had been traced.

Skill Gain!

Cartography Rank Two +.1

The road was wide, enough for two wagons to pass side by side. Well-traveled, it was decently maintained. Relatively smooth, hard-packed dirt with few ruts and holes. It wouldn't last. The further from the Inn in either direction, the road would worsen. Trees lined the north edge, grass spreading out to the south, a long slope that led toward the jagged edge of Edin a couple miles away. A dark line in the distance, blue sky and clouds beyond with dark specks that were the other islands.

Unlike Cumberland, which had the shadow of Edin floating above it, there were no islands close enough to cast their shade over Edin. There were a few higher, like Arundel where the Highborn Confederacy had their capital, but that was further south and away enough that the sun never cast its shadow over Edin.

The trees provided some shade, making the morning nice and pleasant.

He set a leisurely pace. They were in no hurry. Fully rested, stocked up on supplies to get them to Silver Peak Keep, the walk would give Hall plenty of time to organize his thoughts and plans. He still wasn't sure why he had felt the need to ally with the Brownpaw. The Firbolgs were not that close, a week of traveling through hostile country. Even if he built up Skara Brae, what could the Firbolgs offer?

Yarbole had to know this. But she still had done it.

Long-term thinking on her part? A generation down the road? Actual creation of a road between the two villages?

He was glad he had made allies of the Firbolg, just not sure why yet.

The shopping list for Silver Peak Keep was long. Materials were a big item but so were people. They needed craftspeople to work in the village, to at least work to fix it up. Farmers, carpenters, blacksmiths.

Even if they made it just a home for the four, now five, of them, it would end up costing a lot of gold to keep heading back to Silver Peak Keep or Green Ember for supplies. They could spend most of their time doing that instead of adventuring.

That had been his first thought, making it a place to rest between adventures, but the more he thought of it, the more that idea just didn't work.

To make anything of Skara Brae, they needed people to live there.

But how to get those people there?

"Silver Skarans?" Roxhard asked, his deep voice breaking the silence.

They had all been lost in their thoughts, Pike scouting overhead, as the miles trudged by. Roxhard speaking up startled them.

"No," Hall replied.

"Yeah, not really that good," the Dwarf said and fell silent, eyes looking away at the edge of the island.

Jackoby stared at Roxhard strangely. The Dwarf didn't act how a Dwarf of his age should act. Mannerisms, speech patterns. None of it was what a hundred years, or more, old Dwarf would say or do. Hall wondered when to let Jackoby in on the secret. Not that it was really a secret but how to explain it? They hadn't needed to with Leigh. She just accepted Roxhard how he was.

"Look," Roxhard exclaimed, drawing their attention.

He was pointing, iron-mailed hand outstretched, at something in the sky, a couple hundred feet above the island, over the nothing below, just off the edge of Edin. It was moving, a black object against the blue sky, heading in their direction. It never came close, staying just off the island, but they could see some details, the shape coming into focus. A long body, angled at the front and flat at the back, two larger objects at the high point in the back, vertical facing large squares. The shape of an airship.

That's what we need, Hall thought, watching the ship as it sailed through the air. An airship. A quicker way to get from Skara Brae to Silver Peak Keep and anywhere else. But how to get one? It was a dream, he knew, never going to happen.

He watched the ship drifting through the sky until it was out of sight.

Turning his attention back to the road, they continued walking, having days of travel ahead.

————

They could see the walls of Silver Peak Keep first. The land rose higher, the road switchbacking up the slope to a large and flat plateau on the edge of Edin. Stone walls, twenty feet high, ran along the edge, made of gray blocks in uniform sizes. Small figures, guards, could be seen patrolling the top of the walls. Towers were spaced at intervals, two larger ones framing the wooden gate. To the north of the city was where the Thunder Growl Mountains started, the infamous Silver Peak itself the first. Its top was lost in the clouds, the sides of the bald face of rock immediately below them shining almost silver in the sun, giving the mountain its name. South was the plateau and open plains below which continued to the east where they had come from, the forest stopping a day or so back.

Because of the angle of the land ahead, all they could see was the walls of the city getting larger the closer they got. Dark shadows on top of the landscape at the horizon from miles away, looming larger and larger as the miles disappeared until from a mile out all they could see was the sloping grass-covered hill and the walls above. It was as if the world ended at those walls.

The closer they got, they could see the shine of the walls, made from the same stone as the mountain, containing flecks of whatever material it was that gave the mountain its name. Small points of silver along its entire length.

Hall had never been a big fan of Silver Peak Keep. An ugly city, the plateau in the original game had been so much smaller, but the wall had still loomed ahead as they approached. Consisting of only a couple dozen stone and wood homes, it had been a major quest hub. He had spent a lot of time there while leveling in this realm.

The city, because of its construction, had never seemed to fit in with the rest of the Realm. Hall was curious what changes this new version of the game, this new version of his life, would have for Silver Peak Keep.

Pike soared down out of the sky and settled on Hall's shoulder as they started up the long slope of the plateau. They could see a line of wagons ahead of them, stopped at the gate, as city guards looked them over. Silver Peak Keep had two gates. There was the aptly named East Gate that led to the Silver Peak Road and Auld at the other end. The other was on the southern side of the city and led to the farmlands as well as Peakdock.

There was no harbor for airships in Silver Peak Keep itself. The edge of Edin at the city was too jagged, the land sloping up and dropping down sharply. There was nowhere to construct a safe harbor on the height of the plateau, so the docks had been built a short distance away down on the plains. In the original Sky Realms Online, there had been a quest chain that led to a complex under Peakdock, the home of a thieves' guild. The catacombs had been considered one of the Raid Dungeons, where a party was needed to complete the dungeon.

Slender towers of a whiter stone could be seen where the stone perimeter wall and the mountain met the Keep itself.

The Keep was lost from view as they got to the top of the slope, to a strip of flat land between the top of the slope and the wall. The wagons had moved on, the guards impatiently staring at the group and waiting for them to approach.

Skill Gain!
Identify Rank One +.1

Silver Peak Watchman (Orange)

Hall assumed the guards were around Level 12, like those in Grayhold had been. Possibly lower. There wasn't much that threatened the people of Silver Peak Keep. The Trow, Caobold in the mountains, Centaurs and Boarin in the plains. But none of those usually came close to the Keep. The farmlands got threatened more but still not much opportunity for the Peak Guards to Level. If they were appearing Orange in comparison to Hall's own Level Four, then they couldn't be more than Level Nine.

Besides the quest in Auld that led the Players to Silver Peak Keep, the first quest had come from a Guard at the gate. Hall studied the two on either side of the wooden doors that swung out. Each wore a chain shirt, leather pants and helms, carrying swords and shields. The symbol of the city, a silver tower in front of a mountain, was painted on the metal shields and stitched into silver and blue tabards they wore over the chain-mail shirts. Neither of them appeared special, neither was named. There was nothing to indicate either was a quest giver.

Neither of them said a word or even looked at Hall and the others as they walked into the city. Hall was disappointed. He had been looking forward to getting some quests while in the city. Being only Level Four, he felt odd. In the past, being on Edin, he would have been at least around Level Twenty.

They walked through the thick stone gates and into the city. It wasn't as noisy as Land's Edge Port had been. The two- and three-story stone houses blocked most of the city sounds. It was noisier than the plains had been, but nothing that was overwhelming.

Most buildings had a first floor made of small gray stone blocks, small glass windows with wooden shutters and wooden doors. The second, and sometimes third stories, were made of wooden planks placed vertically. Roofs were steeply sloped with wooden shingles. The homes of those with gold had two stories of stone. The really wealthy had all three stories made of the gray stone.

Already, Hall could see the city was vastly different. Besides being larger, which he was coming to expect as the new normal, Silver Peak Keep was not as structured as he had remembered. Before, the dozen or so homes had been laid out in a grid pattern. Straight streets and alleys between, all leading out of the round open gathering spot in front of the Keep. There was none of that in evidence. The street they were on ran straight for a couple of blocks before turning ninety degrees to the right. There didn't appear to be a reason for it. The road just turned.

They could see the Keep, a large square building, solid walls on three sides as it was built against the mountain a little higher up the slope from the city proper. Two towers at the corners of the wall, with a larger central tower coming out of the center with a connecting bridge leading into the mountain.

It dominated all the views, looming over the city. Glimpses were caught between buildings as they walked, the central tower always visible just over the roofs.

Pulling up his map, he was disappointed to see that most of the city was grayed out, just the portion they had already walked appearing, and that was only a block or two away from their path, the areas of the city that were visible to the eye.

Skill Gain!

Cartography Rank Two +.1

He tried to remember where the Trainers had been but was drawing a blank. There were Inns and stables around the edge of the Town Square, which was really a circle, facing the Keep. One Inn at least, that was what the original game had. He assumed, like Land's Edge Port, there would be more now.

They found the first one as the street turned again and emptied into the Town Square. A small fountain occupied the center of the Square. A stone Roc with its wings spread, water shooting out of its mouth and into the basin around it. The water made a pleasant splashing sound as it hit. A road with stone pavers led up the slope to the gate into the Keep. Guards were posted at the closed Keep doors, another set at the bottom of the stone ramp.

The Peak's Shadow Inn had all three stories made of stone. An ugly building, stone walls with no decorations, like every other in the City, the door was open and inviting. They entered and saw a nearly empty common room. It was midafternoon, not yet time for the Inns and taverns to start serving food.

"What can I do for you?" the innkeeper asked from behind the bar, polishing a mug as was the habit of all bartenders.

"Rooms," Hall replied. "Two and for an extended stay."

"How extended?"

Hall shrugged. "Not sure. Couple days, at least."

The bartender tilted his head to the side, staring at nothing as he thought, still polishing the mug.

"One gold a night," he finally said.

Hall stared at him, shocked. That was expensive. It was just past the line and into rip-off territory. He sighed. They had money, but not that kind. And what they had would be needed for supplies, training, and provisions for Skara Brae.

The innkeeper must have read that in Hall's face.

"The Inns down in Peakdock are cheaper," he said, not unkindly. "But you get what you pay for."

Hall nodded and headed out of the Inn.

CHAPTER TWENTY

PEAKDOCK WAS SPRAWLING. LOTS OF WOODEN, SOME STONE, one-story buildings with a few that were two. No three stories. It was almost a mile south of Silver Peak Keep, down the slope and following the wide road that led to the farmlands. Five docks jutted out past the edge of Edin, warehouses and other support buildings facing them, the other structures haphazardly built behind. It had the look of a city that had just grown organically, starting out as the few buildings by the dock and the rest built as needed. No rhyme or reason.

The original Peakdock had been a half dozen small wooden structures and two docks. This version of the city might have started out like that, but it was so much more now. A true city. Hall thought there had to be close to a hundred buildings, if not more.

There was a lot of activity on the docks. Airships coming and going, the cranes never stopped unloading. Wagons brought goods to and from Silver Peak Keep, a long train of them slowly moving up and down the hill.

They stood at the south gate, looking down the slope at Peakdock. Smoke rose from the many chimneys, casting a pall over the small city. It looked dirty, rough, not exactly welcoming.

Sabine looked over her shoulder and into the city, her blonde hair longer now. They all had longer hair, Roxhard and Hall's beards unkempt and in need of a trim. Hall hadn't really noticed that hair was growing, it never had before. Hunger, sleep, hair growing, and other body functions. Things they never had to worry about before.

Could they catch a cold now?

"Are we sure we really want to try those Inns?" Sabine asked, looking back at Peakdock. "I doubt they'll have baths," she moaned.

"Too expensive," Hall replied. "We're not rolling in gold."

"Which is odd," she muttered as they started walking down the sloped road. "We should have more by now. Should be higher Level as well."

Hall nodded. She was right. Leveling had been much faster pre-Glitch, the weird event that seemed to have stranded a bunch of Players in the game. Making gold hadn't been that much faster, but he remembered having more than the handful he had now at Level Four. There had been more quests as well. More random quests.

They kept to the edge of the road, mostly in the grass alongside, to avoid the wagons and horses. Dust was kicked up by the passage of so many wheels, causing Angus to sneeze a couple of times and Pike to decide flying was better.

It took almost an hour to hit the outskirts of Peakdock, and the city looked worse close up. The many buildings were not hovels, but they were not that good either. Rough planks, a few glass windows, and low sloped roofs. Some with shingles but many thatched. There were many personal gardens, small fenced-in areas next to or behind the homes. Some were back to back, others looked shared between the homes.

People could be seen moving about what could be called

streets but were really just random lanes between the front of the homes. They wore wool clothing, rough spun and worn, with many patches. Everyone looked happy enough, and Hall figured that they had to make enough to live comfortably. Obviously not that comfortably, but well enough.

A hardy folk. The kind that he would need as villagers in Skara Brae.

He asked for directions from one of the women tending her small garden and got rough directions to the two Inns in Peak-dock. Both were near the docks, as he had assumed, and while the directions were hard to decipher with the haphazard warren of streets, they managed to find The Listing Deck easy enough.

Two stories, the wood aged gray. The building appeared to be well maintained, and they could hear some noise and music coming from within. It was past dinner time and the tavern would be filled with sailors and workers even though the docks were still operating and would do so until completely dark.

Roxhard volunteered to stay outside with Pike and Angus while they tried to rent rooms. There didn't appear to be a stable attached, but there would be one nearby. The Dwarf sat down on the steps and looked out across the docks. His mood had soured the further from Green Ember they had gotten, and Hall wasn't sure what was wrong. Even Leigh couldn't break him from the dour mood.

In the morning, Hall figured he'd pull Roxhard aside and try to find out what was bothering him. It was getting late and they needed rest.

The inside of the Inn was pretty much like all the others. A long bar across the back wall with doors leading to the kitchen, a stair along a sidewall, hearth on the other with a stage next to it. On the stage sat a Skald playing a lute and singing. The crowd filled the common area, tables everywhere. Two barmaids went from table to table, taking orders and dropping off mugs and food. The music wasn't that good, but it was better than just the normal sounds of a tavern.

Hall led them toward an empty table in the far corner, furthest from the stage and the barmaids. Jackoby scowled, eyes staring at everything and everyone. He was not impressed it seemed. Hall wondered if the Firbolg had ever been in a tavern like this. Possibly not. Most likely he had only ever been in The Season's Goose on the Silver Peak Road. And that Inn was a far cry from The Listing Deck.

Raising his hand, Hall tried to catch the attention of one of the barmaids as they sat down. She nodded and gave him a wave, indicating she'd be over as soon as she could. Settling in the chair, Hall looked the room over. He was looking for other Players, as he had every time they went anywhere. He had even looked to see if there had been some in Green Ember. It was hard to tell a Player from an NPC and getting harder every day that passed. The lines that separated the two were blurring.

At least for him. For Sabine, it seemed the lines were still thick. Her mood had also gotten worse as they traveled. Hall thought it was because the trip to Green Ember, which hadn't even gotten them any loot, had been a waste in her mind. In a way, it was. In the short term, anyway. But he was thinking long-term now.

Sabine had never been the nicest or most enjoyable traveling companion, but since Green Ember, she had gotten worse. Hall wondered how long she would stick around as he worked to rebuild Skara Brae. She was jealous he had gotten the village and not her. Had her worsening mood started then? Weeks back.

He pushed those thoughts away. If she stayed or went, that would be her choice. Not much he could do about it.

His eyes still roamed the room, studying everyone. He stopped on a woman sitting alone at the bar. Not quite sure why she had grabbed his attention out of the entire crowd.

Almost a foot shorter than him with Gael features but dark skin. Her long hair was done up in thin and tight dreadlocks. A pretty face, dark eyes. No visible tattooing. She wore a reddish colored leather kilt that left her upper legs bare, a pair of calf-high, dark-colored boots. Leather armor covered her body, with small pauldrons over the shoulders, her dark arms bare except for a pair of bracers. Straps crossed the armor, a pouch on a belt at her side. She wore two thin-bladed swords.

A Duelist.

And Hall was pretty sure the woman was a Player.

She must have sensed him looking at her because she turned away from the bar. Her eyes studied him and rose in surprise, a bright smile across her face. The woman was excited, grabbing her mug and pushing her way quickly through the crowd. Patrons shot her angry glares as she crossed the room. She ignored them.

"Wow," she said, voice filled with excitement. "Are you real?"

The woman was full of energy. She seemed to be around Hall's age, maybe a couple years younger.

Skill Gain!
Identify Rank One +.1

Hall was surprised there was no other information revealed. In a way, it confirmed she was a Player as the NPCs gave basic information.

"If you mean, are we Players?" Hall asked with a glance at Jackoby and Leigh. "Some of us are."

The woman's eyes darted around the table, resting longer on Sabine and quickly passing by Leigh and Jackoby. *Is she using the Identify skill?* Hall wondered. Was she realizing the same thing he had?

"May I?" she asked, indicating the other chair at their

table. Hall nodded and the woman sat down, leaning forward. "To be honest, I had given up hope about seeing some other Players. It had been so long."

She talked fast, the words jumbled together. Pausing, she took a drink from her mug.

"I'm Caryn," she said, placing the mug back on the table.

"Hall," he replied.

The others gave their names, Leigh as friendly as usual and Sabine and Jackoby fighting over who could be the surliest.

"I'm sorry," Caryn said. "I'm not normally this..." she paused, searching for the right word.

"Hyper," Sabine supplied.

Caryn smiled sheepishly, nodding.

"All this is new to me. I'd only been playing for a couple hours before that weird lag thing happened."

She would have kept talking, but Hall held up his hand, stopping her. He looked to Sabine, who was as surprised as he was.

"Wait, hold on," he said. "You had just started playing Sky Realms Online when the Glitch happened?"

Caryn nodded.

"Three hours to be exact. I was wandering around outside Grayhold on my third or fourth quest when I got that lag spike and the follow-up message. My girlfriend had been playing for a while and finally convinced me to give it a try."

Her eyes clouded over with sadness, and Hall didn't ask any follow-up questions about the girlfriend. She was obviously not there now, probably hadn't been one of the few that had been uploaded into the game.

"The Glitch, huh? Is that what it's called?" she asked, focusing back on the present. "I haven't seen any Players since then, weeks ago now. Any NPCs that I've talked to give me a blank look, ignoring it." She looked at Jackoby and Leigh, motioning with her finger. The two NPCs were staring off into space, which Hall had noticed Leigh did when talk of the pre-Glitch days came up. "Just got that email from Electronic Storm explaining what happened."

It was interesting that she hadn't run into any other Players but if she hadn't gone back to Grayhold, she would have been ahead of the Players like Hall, Roxhard and Sabine that got trapped within the game. As the days went by, as evidenced by her being on Edin, Caryn had just kept ahead of them as they spread out into the world.

"You've been alone ever since?" Sabine asked.

Hall knew Sabine would sympathize with Caryn. The Witch had yet to reveal what happened, but she had dropped enough hints that her experience right after Hall had first met her in Grayhold to when they encountered each other at River's Side had not been enjoyable. She had met up with some bad Players. Hall knew no more, but he had guesses as to what happened.

It had not been that long post-Glitch before Hall and Sabine ran into each other again. He couldn't imagine what it would have been like to be totally alone for as long as Caryn seemed to have been.

"Not really alone," Caryn said and leaned in closer. "I ran into an NPC and started a quest chain that led me here. Been kind of working with him since."

"Working with?" Hall asked.

There was a naivete and innocence about Caryn, and Hall wondered how old she had been in real life. Was she like Roxhard? A teenager trapped in an adult body? He didn't think it was that extreme. He thought her not that much younger than his own age and was probably right. She was a just new gamer enjoying the experience.

"Ran into him just outside Grayhold," she explained and glanced around the Inn to make sure no one was in earshot, lowering her voice. Hall found the behavior odd. "Had a quest that I accepted and part of it was following him to that city at the end of the road out of Grayhold."

"Land's Edge Port," Roxhard supplied and Caryn nodded.

"That's the one. Followed him there, did a couple jobs, and he brought me here," she finished, waving her arms to indicate Peakdock.

"What kind of jobs?" Sabine asked suspiciously.

Caryn smiled but looked embarrassed, eyes darting around the inn again.

"You know..."

"What did you steal?" Hall asked, lowering his voice.

He glanced at Leigh and Roxhard, both looking shocked.

"Some gold, a couple potions," Caryn said with a shrug. "Got a lot of skill levels," she said beaming, excited. "It was thrilling. Very exciting."

"And dangerous," Leigh added with mild reproach.

"I suppose," Caryn said and Hall knew she left out the "but it's just a game" part of her thought.

Hall thought about the other Player they had met back when first landed on Edin. Davit or something, his name had been. A Bodin Duelist. Besides Davit and now Caryn, they had not met any other Players themselves, not since Sabine joined them in River's Side. He found it odd that there weren't that many of them running around. In the original game, anywhere you went you came across another Player. Now there were barely any.

Caryn was far different from Davit but similar in a way. He had been a relatively new Player and had embraced the role of a killer. NPCs were just playthings for him. Were they that way for Caryn? But instead of killing them, she stole from them.

The door to the Inn opened and a tall man stepped through. Black hair, nut-brown skin with angular features. He stood a couple inches over six feet and was all wiry muscles. He moved with an easy grace, eyes darting around the room taking it all in. He wore dark breeches and a tight tunic, two swords on his waist. The dual swords would indicate a Duelist, but as an NPC the man could be some other Class. Hall, judging by his skin and features, thought the man to be Arashi, from the higher islands.

His eyes focused on Hall and his group but still looked around the room. Nothing seemed to escape his review. But he did it in such a way that it didn't appear he was examining everything. If Hall hadn't been looking right at the man, he wouldn't have known. Moving away from the door, he headed toward them.

"I think that's your friend," Hall said to Caryn.

She leaned back, looking over her shoulder. She jumped up, waving her hand so her small form could be seen over the heads of the crowd. Hall saw the man's easy gaze turn hard, quickly disappearing. He did not approve of Caryn's reaction.

He stopped a short distance away, behind Caryn, making her turn around in her seat. His eyes roamed the table, stopping on Sabine for a while, and he smiled as she glowered at him. His eyebrows rose at the sight of Jackoby. He finished his review of them by stopping on Hall. There was a challenge in that stare, Hall knew, along with appraising.

"Who are your new friends, Caryn?" he asked. His accent was Arashi, his voice smooth as silk.

CHAPTER TWENTY-ONE

STILL SMILING CARYN INTRODUCED THEM ALL TO THE newcomer. His gaze never left Hall's. Caryn didn't seem to notice.

"And you are," Hall prompted when it became obvious the man was not going to supply his own name.

"Oh, I'm sorry," Caryn said instead of the man. "This is Berim, the friend I told you about."

Berim's face again showed the quick flash of anger and disapproval before the easy smile was back. He bowed his head slightly.

"A pleasure."

Skill Gain!
Identify Rank One +.1

Berim (Orange)

Hall wasn't surprised he didn't learn more. No class like he had gotten when first *Identified* Jackoby. He wondered how many levels higher this Berim was. Orange meant he was at least three levels higher, but Hall thought it might be more.

Berim leaned down, eyes finally leaving Hall, coming in close to Caryn. The eyes moved around the table as he spoke. He wasn't quiet even though it appeared he wanted to speak to Caryn alone. Hall wondered why.

"We need to leave," he said to her. "We cannot be late."

"Oh right," she said and stood up. "It was nice meeting you all," she said, waving at the group. "Are you going to be in town long? Maybe we can get together again?" There was an almost pleading note to her voice at the last question.

"A couple days," Roxhard replied and it was Hall's turn to disapprove, but his face didn't show it.

There was something about Berim he didn't like. The man was obviously a thief, which was reason enough not to like him, but there was more. Hall just wasn't sure what that was.

Together, Caryn and Berim left the Inn. Hall didn't think it would be the last time he saw them.

———

"You need them where?" the carpenter asked.

It was the next morning and Hall stood in the carpenter's shop within the walls of Silver Peak Keep. Just barely within the walls, it covered a large amount of ground. The store faced the street, a large workshop and supply yard behind with eight-foot-high fencing around. The fencing wasn't a true barrier from determined thieves, but no true thief would ever think to rob a carpenter.

The carpenter stood behind the counter, the shelves and floor in the shop lined with all manner of wooden items. Tables, chairs, spoons, bowls, toys, bookcases. Hall had examined some when he and Leigh, with Jackoby waiting impatiently outside, had entered and found the quality to be excellent. The reception they had gotten wasn't as good.

The carpenter, a man that introduced himself as Herbert, had listened to Hall talk and explain what he wanted and then had almost laughed. Herbert had held it in, though.

"Breakridge," Hall explained again. "Where the Thunder Growl and Frost Tips meet."

"That's what?" Herbert asked, looking up at the ceiling and doing some calculations in his head. "Two weeks or more up rough country?"

"A week," Hall replied. "Give or take a day."

He needed building supplies and someone with the knowledge to use them properly. His village, Skara Brae, needed to be rebuilt. For that, they needed the supplies and the experienced carpenter. Hall had hoped to hire one and buy the other in Silver Peak Keep. It didn't look like that was going to happen.

Herbert shook his head. The carpenter looked sorry.

"And how would we be getting the materials there?" he asked, not unkindly. "No road means no wagons."

Hall nodded. He understood and was angry with himself. In some games he had played, there had been building mechanics. When the quests or events had started, the tradesmen and materials would just show up and the construction would start. He had never had to worry about actually getting the materials to the site. Ever since the Glitch, he had accepted that the game was his new reality and had accepted the changes in the mechanics to make the immersion more real, the game more lifelike. And it had been. He had been treating it like it was his life, which it was. But in this instance, he had hoped the mechanics would be more game-like. There were some instances where game overruled real, but this did not look to be one of them.

"I'm sorry, lad," the carpenter replied.

"Thank you," Hall said and turned to leave.

He was a couple steps toward the door, Herbert heading the other way, when he noticed Leigh was not alongside. She was facing the door, had taken a couple steps, and stopped. The Druid looked deep in thought.

"Leigh?" Hall asked.

She turned back to face the counter.

"Master Herbert," she called and the carpenter stopped, looking at her. "What about hiring only a carpenter? Someone with the knowledge and experience to rebuild the village?"

Herbert walked back to them, Hall also returning to the counter. *Why didn't I think of that?* he thought, liking Leigh's idea, doubly glad she had come along. He was happy that she had chosen to spend the day with him. Nowhere else to go, nothing else to do, she had said but Hall had seen her smile at the idea of spending the day with him. Her idea was good; he had gotten hung up on the idea of the carpenter and the materials. But there was a forest and possibly a mine nearby. The materials could be made with some work.

The carpenter was still shaking his head but not as sad as before. Hall could tell he was thinking about the idea, pushing some thoughts around.

"You have a way to make the materials?" he asked. "Boards, nails?"

Leigh nodded and Hall didn't contradict. They didn't have the means now but could get it. Eventually. Someday. But no need to advertise that for now.

"That's a bit different," Herbert said, tapping his fingers on the counter. "I wouldn't do it myself. Couldn't pick up the family for something so risky." He stopped tapping his fingers and looked at Hall, his face serious and warning. "That's the biggest problem, lad. The risk. Not just from the wild animals, monsters and such, but from what could be a years' long project and little to no pay. This person would basically become a citizen of this village of yours."

"With the chance to be the village carpenter," Hall said. "The only carpenter," he added.

Herbert nodded.

"Yeah, the only carpenter in a village that could either grow or never be more than ruins," the carpenter replied.

It was Hall's turn to nod, an acknowledgment of the true risk.

Herbert was silent for a while, stepping back and leaning against the wall. Hall waited patiently. He liked the way this was feeling, like it was meant to happen.

"I do know a fellow," Herbert said finally. "Good carpenter." He paused and sighed. "Or he used to be."

"Used to be?" Hall asked.

Herbert motioned them to come closer to the counter, and he leaned in close.

"Duncant is his name. A Bodin. Good fellow. Did excellent work but ran afoul of some trouble and can no longer work in the city."

"What kind of trouble?" Leigh asked.

"You'll need to ask him yourself," Herbert replied. "I'll just say that he can't work in Silver Peak Keep or Peakdock again. He might just be looking for a new place to call home."

He finished speaking and leaned back. Hall thought about it. He would need to learn what exactly had caused this Duncant to lose his ability to work in the city. But he just might be what Hall needed.

"Where can we find him?"

"He does odd jobs for the farms around the city," Herbert answered, stepping back from the counter and back to the door that led to the yard outside. "Rents a room down in Peakdock, near the market."

"Thank you," Leigh said and waved as she and Hall turned to leave.

They walked out of the shop, the door closing behind them. Hall squinted at the bright noonday sun, not realizing how dark the interior of the shop had been. He saw a large bird circling high above, glad to see that Pike had not gone far. Angus was sitting on the ground with Jackoby leaning against the wall next to him.

The Firbolg grunted and pushed off the wall, lifting his warhammer. He didn't bother saying anything to either Hall or Leigh, just waited. Hall sighed. He had hoped that the relationship with Jackoby would have gotten better by now, but it had not. Since entering the city, Jackoby had gotten noticeably colder.

"Back to Peakdock to find this Duncant?" Leigh asked.

Hall nodded.

───────

It took some asking around but they finally found Duncant.

The maybe-carpenter sat alone in a tavern, one of many ringing the docks. This one was called The Sailor's Wind and was decent as far as dockside taverns went. Which meant it wasn't absolutely disgusting and rundown but it was close. A two-story building, with rooms to rent on the upper, the lower was a large and open room. The long bar ran down one side, the doors directly across. Stairs to the upper floor were on one side. Tables filled the rest of the space. Mismatched, some obviously on different sized legs. Stains covered the floor, light barely coming in through dingy windows. Tired looking barmaids, older women, walked the room dealing with the few customers at this hour.

Duncant was the lone person sitting at the bar counter. He

was the only Bodin in the room, so it had to be him. Using the Identify skill confirmed it.

Skill Gain!
Identify Rank One +.1

Duncant, unGuilded carpenter

Hunched over the counter, sitting on an upside-down pail on the bar stool. It allowed him to be at just the right height for the counter. A near-empty mug and a plate cleared of food sat in front of him. The Bodin stared down at it, looking sad and lonely.

Hall hesitated near the door, watching the small man. He glanced at Leigh, who shrugged.

Together they made their way through the maze of tables, stepping over some strange stains on the floor. Ale or blood or something else.

He took the seat next to the Bodin, the smaller man glancing up briefly before staring back down at his plate. Lank blond hair hung long, greasy looking. Dark bags under dull blue eyes. His fair skin, tanned from being outside, had a weathered and beaten look. As did the entire Bodin. His clothes were patched but with new holes.

Duncant looked to his left at all the empty seats, stealing another quick glance at Hall. He returned his look to the plate, one hand wrapped around the pewter mug.

"Are you Duncant? The carpenter?" Hall asked. Even though he knew, he felt it polite to ask.

The Bodin looked up sharply, a little scared and angry. He studied Hall, looking the Half-Elf up and down, then leaned forward to take a look at Leigh who sat next to Hall.

"You're not one of Hucard's boys," Duncant said, some of the fear leaving his eyes. "Who are you?"

"Master Herbert told us to seek you out," Hall said in reply. "We're looking for a carpenter."

Duncant started to say something but stopped, his eyes brightening for a second, before he hung his head and barked a bitter laugh. It was an odd sound coming from a Bodin's light voice.

"Herbert has you wasting your time."

"So, you're not the carpenter?" Hall asked, hoping to hit the man in his pride. "Herbert said Duncant the carpenter was good, and we have need of a good carpenter."

Now Duncant did look up. He looked intrigued.

"He's right about that part at least," Duncant said. "I am a good carpenter."

Hall studied the Bodin. There was some pride there. He wasn't sure why the carpenter was no longer working. It most likely had something to do with this Hucard he had mentioned. A debt collector of some kind? That would explain why Herbert thought Duncant would be eager to relocate. As would the unGuilded part. He had the carpenter's attention now; it was time to bait the hook.

"The job is a long one," Hall began, watching Duncant's reactions. "We're looking to rebuild a village. It's been in ruins for years and needs a lot of work. About twenty buildings for now but with more needed."

"There are no villages near here that need that kind of rebuild," Duncant said, now very much intrigued. The carpenter was nibbling at the bait.

"It's not near here," Hall supplied.

Duncant sat up straighter, eyes brighter. He was taking the bait.

"Not in Silver Peak Keep or one of the surrounding villages?" Duncant asked, his voice hopeful.

Hall shook his head.

"It's a week or so travel to the north in the mountains,"

Hall told the Bodin. "There really isn't any pay to begin," Hall said, deciding it was best to be honest. Duncant seemed to deflate a little, some of the sadness creeping back in. "But you would be in charge of rebuilding the entire village. Room and board taken care of."

Duncant was caught between the sadness he had when they had arrived and excitement at the opportunity. Hall watched, letting the Bodin come to his own decision.

It didn't take long.

"The whole village?" Duncant asked.

Hall smiled and nodded.

They spent a solid half hour talking over details with Duncant. Hall described the village, its current condition and what he thought the first steps should be. Duncant made a couple comments, adjusted some plans and made suggestions of his own.

Hall was feeling good about the addition of the Bodin to the village.

Arrangements were made for Duncant, and his tools, to join them on the return trip to Skara Brae. The Bodin didn't seem fazed by the idea of a week or more journey through the wilds. He seemed eager to get out of Silver Peak Keep and get to work. He didn't drop any hints about why he wasn't able to work in the city, and after talking to the Bodin, Hall didn't care.

Whatever the reasons, it just meant he could check one to-do item off his long list.

He and Leigh, with Jackoby trailing behind, left The Sailor's Wind and headed back to their Inn. It was almost noon. Duncant had asked if they would join him for a meal at The Sailor's Wind, which would have been paid for by Hall of course, but Hall had declined. Hall would not trust any food coming out of a place like that. Instead, they had said their goodbyes and made their way to The Listing Deck.

Where they ran into Roxhard.

The Dwarf was sitting on the steps outside, eyes roaming the people walking around the docks, which were busy. Airships were docking and leaving, large wooden cranes lifting crates of goods out of the ship's holds. Others lowering crates of goods into empty holds. Sailors wandered around, porters and teamsters with wagons. It was organized chaos. For all the randomness the wagons portrayed as they were pulled around the dock by teams of horses, none got in the way of the others.

When Roxhard saw them, he jumped up and ran the last couple feet between them. He looked anxious and agitated.

"We have a problem," he told them.

Hall sighed. So much for a drama-free time in Silver Peak Keep.

"What happened?" Leigh asked.

"It's Sabine," Roxhard answered. "She's been arrested."

CHAPTER TWENTY-TWO

Since they were in Peakdock, they headed toward the Constable's office there.

It was at the edge of the dock city, alongside the road that led to the plateau and Silver Peak Keep. Hall had remembered passing it when they had come to Peakdock, but he had not paid much attention at the time.

He did now.

It was a large two-story building. The entire bottom floor was made of a dark stone, tightly fit together. A heavy oak door, banded in iron, was the only opening on that level. The upper story was wood, with a flat roof. Guards could be seen on watch in the corners. He was about to open the door when Leigh spotted a set of stairs to the side.

They walked up the stairs, Angus staying below and Pike circling ahead. The guards craned their heads and watched the dragonhawk flying.

At the top of the stairs was a single door, wooden like the walls. Turning the handle, Hall walked inside. Most of the space was a single large room. Two doors in the far wall led to what was most likely private offices. There were a couple of small desks in the open space, shelving along the wall with hooks beneath. It was a kind of mustering room for the guards. Along one wall was a staircase that led down.

The room wasn't empty.

A lone guard sat at one of the small desks. Hall tried to see beyond into the offices but couldn't from his angle at the entrance. The guard looked up. He was dressed in leathers with a tabard bearing the mark of Silver Peak Keep. Next to him, on top of the desk, was a metal helm.

Skill Gain!

Identify Rank One +.1

Sergeant Brient of the PeakGuard (Orange)

Hall noticed that Brient did not seem surprised to see them. Light brown hair, brown eyes, rugged-looking face with a nose that looked as if it had been broken and not set properly. He had a scar down his right cheek. Burly looking, he fit the image of what Hall would think a veteran guardsman should.

"I take it you're the friends of the Witch," he said, more statement than question.

Hall exchanged quick glances with the others as they spread out inside the room. The four of them, all in their armor and carrying weapons, looked imposing, but Brient didn't seem to care.

"You match the descriptions," he continued, eyes taking in each of them, measuring them, finally stopping on Hall. "Took you a while to get here."

"What?" Hall managed to say. He was confused. Brient, somehow, had expected them. Sabine must have given descriptions.

But from what Roxhard had said, it had been pure luck that he had seen it happen. The Dwarf was returning to the inn, a couple buildings away, when Sabine had been escorted out by six Silver Peak Guards. One of them was a Witch and was casting *Silence* on Sabine so she couldn't cast her own spells. A couple of the Guardsmen looked shaky, as if they were fighting off the after-effects of a *Hexbolt*. He had thought about trying to rescue her but was outnumbered and it was Guardsmen, the law in the city. Instead, he had waited for Hall and the others, feeling guilty the whole time. Hall agreed with what Roxhard had done.

They had immediately headed to the Constable's Office. But if Roxhard had not been lucky enough to arrive at that moment, none of them would have known she was arrested and it would have been hours, or the next day, before they came here.

So how had Brient been expecting them this soon?

"Why did you arrest Sabine?" Hall asked.

"Get you lot here," Brient replied, and it was not the reply that Hall had expected. Hall started to say something, but Brient held up a leather-gloved hand to stop him. "She was the last to see a merchant alive. A man named Gregorn, an apothecary, was found dead minutes after she left the shop. Evidence of magic being used. People outside his shop gave her description, and I knew her to be part of that adventuring company had come in earlier. Asked her nicely to come in for questioning. She didn't want to." Brient stopped and shrugged, as if it was just another day.

"How'd you know she was with us?" Hall asked.

"Peakdock isn't all that big," the Sergeant replied with another shrug. "One road in and out if want to go to the Keep." He motioned behind him with his hand, the city at his back. "There's a reason why we built the Constables right on that road."

"Sabine wouldn't have killed the merchant," Leigh said and Hall hoped she was right.

He didn't think the Witch would have either, but he really didn't know her that well, even after all the weeks they had been traveling together. Sabine wasn't the nicest person he had ever met and didn't seem to have the same respect for NPCs that he and Roxhard had. Could he see her getting angry and killing an NPC? Yes. Did he think she would have? No.

"I know," Brient said and smirked.

Hall's next question was forgotten by Brient's remark. None of this was making sense.

"Hold on," Hall said. "Let's start over."

"No," Brient replied. "Let's not." He stood up, standing a couple inches taller than Hall. Walking around from the desk to stand in front, Brient continued talking. "I have need of your services and having your Witch tied to the scene of a crime was a lucky break and good way to get you here."

Hall took a breath, keeping his anger down. Brient seemed to be smiling, knowing he had somewhat of the upper hand and was able to keep Hall and the others on uneven footing.

"You arrested her to get us to work for you?" Leigh asked, shocked.

Again, Brient just shrugged.

"Pretty much."

"Why the hell—" Hall started to say but forced himself to calm down. "Why not just ask?" Hall said through gritted teeth.

"Couldn't," Brient said. It was his turn to sigh and he leaned against his desk. "Look, I wish it didn't have to be this way but it is. I can't publicly hire you to do anything. Politics and all that. Can't have the Guard looking weak but that's where we are. Weak. Can't do anything."

Hall studied Brient. The man wasn't apologetic in any way but he did appear to be genuine.

"What is going on?" Hall asked.

"A guild war," Brient said. "Between two thieves' guilds. One of them, the new one edging in on the old guild's turf, I suspect has some deep ties to the Guard and the leadership up in the Keep."

Which explained why Brient had said the Guard was weak, Hall realized. The leadership would prevent him and the other Guard from doing what they needed to do in favor of allowing this new guild to gain ground. Like in real life, in-game criminal organizations fostered ties with law enforcement. Hall had no desire to get into the middle of a turf war, but it seemed he wasn't being given a choice. Not if he wanted to free Sabine.

"Why us?" Hall asked.

"Lots of people saw you talking with Berim and one of his guildmates yesterday," Brient explained. "That connects you with the guild." He held up his hand as they started to protest. "Doesn't matter if it's true or not. Appearances and all that."

"Which is Berim's?" Hall asked after taking another deep breath to calm down.

"The old," Brient replied. "I've had quite a few run-ins with him through the years. They call themselves the Dooor Knockers." He chuckled. "Yeah, not the most fear-inspiring name, but they know their business. The newcomers call themselves Silver Blades."

"You are paid by the Door Knockers," Jackoby said, his voice full of contempt. It was the first time in a long time that the Firbolg had spoken, and Hall was surprised to hear him now.

Brient pushed himself up from the desk and glared at the taller Firbolg. There wasn't an inch of backing down in the guardsman's stare. He was angry. He stared daggers and Hall was afraid a fight was going to break out. Brient clenched his fists, the leather creaking. He took a couple deep breaths and somewhat relaxed. The reaction convinced Hall the Sergeant wasn't on the take. It was too quick, too angry to be faked.

"The Knockers aren't good," he said, not bothering to defend himself. "But they're not as bad as the Blades have been in a short amount of time. With the Knockers, we all knew where we stood and they knew what lines not to cross."

"Like the murder of an apothecary," Hall said and Brient nodded.

"This war isn't good for the people of the Dock or the Keep," Brient said. "I just want them kept safe. By any means."

Hall was starting to understand Brient better. Here was a man that was hamstrung by the people in charge. A man that just wanted to do his job. Hall could understand that frustration. But was there really anything he could do about it? Anything he should do about it?

"I'm going to release your Witch," Brient said. "No matter what you decide. She was just a means of getting you here to talk. One that neither Guild, or my superiors, could question."

Brient looked hopeful as he stared at them, waiting for a reaction. Roxhard glanced up at Hall, who didn't appear as if he was going to respond. Jackoby just glared at the guardsman. Leigh was thoughtful. After a minute of awkward silence, Brient sighed.

"Okay," he said. "I get it. How about some incentive?"

He moved back around his desk, sitting down and pulling open a drawer, taking a stack of papers out. He set the parchments down on the desk and started thumbing through them.

"I did some digging into you," he said. "It seems you have a village further up the mountain range." It wasn't said as a question. "And are looking for people to help rebuild. The problem is getting people and materials up there from here. No roads, dangerous lands. Duncant is a good choice by the way," Brient said and looked up with a wink. He tilted his head in thought. "Helping me with my problem might actually help him with his," he said with a shrug.

Hall was surprised how well informed the Sergeant was. They hadn't been in the city for long and the conversation with Duncant had happened before coming to the Constables. Brient must have had them watched. Hall was angry at himself for not spotting the tail.

Brient pulled out a piece of paper from the stack, holding it up triumphantly.

"This should work," he said and stood up again. "So, if you help me out with the Guild war problem, I'll help you out with your problem."

"Which is?" Hall asked, knowing what was coming. He knew this was all leading to a quest, and Brient was holding the reward.

"No Guilded craftsmen would run the risk of the trip to your village," Brient replied. "Too long away from the city and they'd lose their Guild status if they weren't here to produce the Guild's share of their goods. So, this piece of paper here," he waved the parchment in his hand, "will give them an exemption for the length of your job."

Hall sighed. And there it was. The reward.

"You still need to figure out a way to get them there safely of course," Brient added.

Sergeant Brient of the Silver Peak Guards wants your help in dealing with the impending Guild war between two rival thieves' Guilds, the Door Knockers and the Silver Blades. Even though his methods of enlistment were not honorable, his goal is. The Guild war will bring strife and danger to the streets of Silver Peak Keep and Peakdock, harming innocents.

RIVALS IN THE DARK

Prevent the Guild war 0/1

> *Reward: +100 PeakGuard Reputation*
> *+500 Alliance Reputation with Sergeant*
> *Brient*
> *+50 Experience*
> *Crafting Guild Exemption Writ*

ACCEPT QUEST?

Grumbling, Hall accepted the quest. He looked to the others, who all nodded that they received it as well. He hoped that also applied to Sabine, who was still locked up downstairs. Or Hall thought she was down there. Brient hadn't said and they hadn't seen or heard her.

Brient smiled, taking the writ and placing it on top of the stack which he quickly returned to the desk drawer.

"Good, good," he said. His smile was large. "I do apologize about how I got you here," he added.

None of them responded.

"Where do we start?" Hall asked.

"The Door Knockers usually stayed away from the higher end shops in the Nobles Square," Brient said. "Part of the arrangement," he added with a grimace. Hall had thought the Sergeant to be okay with the agreement between the Guild and the city, but apparently, he wasn't. "The Silver Blades have been starting in that territory, where the Knockers weren't. This, of course, is making the Knockers angry. Understandably. They view it as a violation of the agreement. Which it is." Brient shrugged. A 'what are you going to do' gesture, which was different from his other shrugs. The man could communicate books with just his shrugs.

Hall just shook his head. It was complicated, and he really didn't need to know the particulars. He just wanted to know where to find the Silver Blades so he could get this quest over with. That Writ from Brient would help a lot with the rebuilding of Skara Brae.

"The Blades have their enforcers out hitting those shops, which is angering the nobles and the merchants. They had protection from the Knockers and none from the Blades. At least, not yet. I figure that's the end goal of whoever is in charge of the Blades. Anyway, the Blades have their enforcers out in the Square. I'd start there."

Sergeant Brient has tasked you with stopping the upcoming Guild war by eliminating the
newcomer Silver Blades Guild. He has given you a probable location for a Silver Blades
operation. He suggests you start your hunt there.

THE NEW BLOOD I
Disrupt a Silver Blades Operation 0/1
Question a Silver Blades Guildmember 0/1
Rewards: +50 Door Knocker Reputation
+50 PeakGuards Reputation
+50 Alliance
Reputation with Sergeant Brient
+50 Experience

ACCEPT QUEST?

Accepting the quest, Hall pointed at the stairs. Brient got the message. With a nod, he got up and walked down the stairs. Hall glanced at the desk, remembering which drawer Brient had put the Writ. He was tempted to move to the desk and grab it but knew that would lead to more trouble for Sabine.

They could hear the sound of a metal door creaking open

from below, Brient's muffled voice, and then Sabine's angry reply. And did she sound angry.

Her beautiful face was a mask of barely contained rage as she walked up the stairs. She ignored Brient, pushing through the others as she marched toward the door.

"Let's go," she muttered.

Hall gave Brient a last look as they left. The Sergeant just shrugged.

CHAPTER TWENTY-THREE

Hall closed his map, the translucent image disappearing from his vision.

Before him were two- and three-story homes and shops. The lower floors were made of small stones or red bricks, the upper stories in wood with shingled roofs. It was evident in the craftsmanship that this section of Silver Peak Keep was where the richer citizens lived. The more well-to-do merchants, that dealt in higher dollar items, alongside the minor nobility.

Originally a fortress city, Silver Peak Keep didn't have true nobility like other cities. It was governed by a Chancellor, who used the title of General, as a call back to the old days when it was a General that led the city. This General was supported by a three-member council, made up of rich merchants, that were each responsible for running a different aspect of the city. From there, it was the few nobles the Keep did have that formed the ruling class. These nobles were second and third sons, cousins and uncles, of the greater noble houses that lived in Auld and other Edin cities further to the north.

As such Silver Peak Keep had no true noble's quarter but a small section of the city in the western shadow of the Keep and the mountain had become what was referred to as Noble's Square. A large fountain was in the actual square itself, the prized and expensive real estate fronting the open space. The streets were paved in cobblestones, the lamps lit by gas.

There was a visible change in the city as one went from the wider area to the Noble's Square. The homes became nicer, the streets paved in better material, everything cleaner and brighter.

And cheerier, Hall thought as they walked through the side streets, avoiding the main thoroughfares of the Square. There was a saying back in the real world that money couldn't buy happiness. But there, as well as Hankarth, Hall saw evidence that it certainly helped. In Peakdock, there was an air of futility. The denizens barely made enough to survive but, in the Square, the opposite was true. Every person here made more than enough to survive and had much more beyond.

That was evidenced in the shops. None of the clothes was utilitarian. Here, it was all fashion over function. Decorative over useful.

Sabine had barely spoken since being released. Hall could tell that, besides angry, she was embarrassed. They were stuck in a quest chain now because she had let herself get captured. Leigh had said that it could have happened to any of them. Which was true, and Sabine knew it, but she didn't like that it came from Leigh. Sabine didn't have a high opinion of the NPCs, and Hall wondered how this incident would affect that.

The streets of Nobles Square were noticeably less crowded. Mostly well-dressed women with servants following, some with armed bodyguards. Most likely more for show but with the threat of the Silver Blades, that probably wasn't true anymore. The breaking of the agreement had to have the rich nervous. It could mean kidnappings would soon begin.

In part because of the wariness and worry, along with how they were armed and dirty in comparison, Hall and the others received a lot of lingering looks. Disapproving looks as well. They avoided the main streets for that reason.

Brient had given them a general description of what the Blades might look like. It wasn't much to go on but it was all they had. The Sergeant wasn't sure of their route either. He didn't know where in the Square they were operating, just that they were.

Hall wasn't sure where to go or what to do. Any other game, there would have been markers on his map indicating where the band they wanted would be found. Here, there was nothing. They could spend hours, even days, wandering the streets of Nobles Square and not find anything.

Brient had been explicit in his instructions. They were not to be noticed and any fights were to be out of the public eye. Restrictive but it made sense. He had explained that they were on their own; he could not protect them if they got arrested by the guard and Brient fully expected the guard in the Square to be on the Blades' payroll. And the longer they wandered aimlessly, the more likely it was the guard would take notice of them.

They walked for a couple hours, moving from street to street and finding nothing. Sabine grew angrier by the minute, and the rest grew more annoyed and frustrated. Including Hall.

"Enough of this," he finally said. "This is ridiculous."

"It is," Sabine added. "We should just ignore that damn guard and leave. This isn't our concern."

Hall ignored her, not in the mood. In a way, she was right. But he wanted that Writ. And it had been a while since they had last been in combat. He was kind of missing it. Combat, and quests, had been more frequent in the previous version of the game. He didn't know why they were so infrequent now, but he was used to fighting almost constantly. He wanted a fight.

He thought about their situation. They couldn't just wander the streets. It was boring and would accomplish nothing. There had to be a better way and he thought he knew what it was.

"Come on," he said, turning and heading in a direction that would take him out of Nobles Square.

Sabine smiled. "About time we abandoned this quest."

"We're not," Hall said and got a scowl from Sabine. "We're just taking a different angle."

"Brient said we had to start here," Roxhard said, confused.

Hall nodded. In the previous game, the quests were fairly linear. Go to a location and do a thing, then go to the next location. There hadn't been much free choice, but Hall didn't think that was still the case.

"Yes, but the quest doesn't specify where we have to disrupt an operation," Hall pointed out.

"What are you thinking?" Leigh asked.

"If we can't find a Silver Blade, then we find a Door Knocker."

———

They found Caryn in the same spot. Almost the same chair at the bar in The Sailor's Wind. She was waiting for food, a mug of ale in front of her. When she caught sight of them, she smiled and practically ran over to them.

"Hey," she said with enthusiasm, and Hall realized she was one of those few people that were always bubbly and happy. The kind of people that usually annoyed him. "How are you doing? Sorry about yesterday and leaving so abruptly but duty called."

"That's why we're here," Hall said.

Caryn's smile faltered a bit, and Hall knew she realized exactly why they were there to see her.

"Which part?" she asked, the smile back. It was obvious the Duelist was stalling. "Abruptly leaving?"

Hall just stared at her.

Caryn sighed.

"Fine," she said and motioned them to a table at the side.

It was past noon, past lunchtime, and the tavern was pretty much empty. There were a few customers, mostly dock workers and teamsters, waiting for their next assignment or the next arriving airship. None of them seemed interested in the conversation. Hall wondered if any of them were working for the Door Knockers or even the Silver Blades.

He hated that the map wasn't showing who was good, for now, and who was potentially aggressive. There was no way, beyond observation, to know the allegiance of the tavern patrons.

"What do you know about the Guild war?" Hall asked as they all sat down.

He had kept his voice low, but she still looked around anxiously, eyes darting around the nearly empty tavern. She leaned in closer.

"How do you know about that?" she asked.

Hall waved away the question, just stared.

"Look, I had no idea what was happening when Berim recruited me outside Grayhold. At that point, I had gotten the email about the Glitch and tried to log off but couldn't. I was close to panic when I encountered him," she explained. "I was new to these kinds of games. Like I said, my girlfriend got me to play. She was always the gamer. So, when I met Berim and got a quest, I followed him. I didn't know what else to do."

She looked from one to the other. Hall wasn't sure if she was looking for sympathy or understanding.

"I did a couple jobs here and there along the way. Got lots of Skill Gains, a couple of Levels. Things looked good. I could forget that I was trapped here. But what I hadn't realized was that I was getting in deeper with Berim."

She paused as a barmaid came by, carrying her food and new drink. Caryn smiled in thanks as it was set down. The barmaid looked at the others. They all shook their heads no. Annoyed, the barmaid stalked off.

Caryn took a drink from the mug, staring at the food, pushing it around with a fork.

"I guess I did," she admitted, still not looking up. "But did it matter? I hadn't seen any other Players; as far as I knew there were no others. What else was I supposed to do?"

Hall nodded. He understood. Roxhard, Sabine, and himself had all ported into Grayhold by use of their old Town Stones. He had assumed it was that way for all the Players now trapped in the game. But there had to be some playing through the Glitch and never ported. But the more he thought about it, the more it didn't make sense. The message from Electronic Storm said it had been two years since the Glitch, and they were reactivated. Wouldn't Caryn have been reinserted as well?

A question for another time. They were here for a purpose.

"The Guild war," he prompted.

She glanced up at him and sighed.

"We landed in Auld and hitched a ride on a caravan here. Turns out the caravan was owned by the Door Knockers. I was inducted into the Guild as a recruit and settled into my life."

Hall thought about the timeline. If she and Berim had come straight to Silver Peak Keep, they would have gotten here about the same time as Hall and the others had found the treasure in the mountains in northern Cumberland. And that had been weeks ago, a month or more.

"Soon after the Silver Blades started moving in on Knocker territory," she continued. "It's been pretty quiet, both sides keeping it that way for now. But how did you know about it?" she asked again. "Why are you getting involved?"

"Not by choice," Sabine muttered.

Caryn looked at her strangely, turning back to Hall.

"We've basically been hired by the PeakGuards to stop the Guild war," Hall explained. He had thought about not telling her, making something up, but why bother? It wouldn't hurt for anyone to know. Might help them in the long run if they could work with the Door Knockers.

Work with a thief's Guild? Why not?

"Why you?" she asked.

"We're not connected to the politics of Silver Peak Keep," Hall explained. "And we're expendable."

"Why not just leave?"

"Can't burn bridges in the city," Hall replied and explained about Skara Brae and how Silver Peak Keep was the nearest city and would be the place they would need to trade with.

"Makes sense," Caryn said. She leaned back, watching each of them before sighing. "Okay, come with me."

———

They followed her through the warren of streets that created the maze of Peakdock. Some were wide enough for a wagon, most would be classified as alleys in the city up on the plateau. They had to walk single file through those. Angus trotted along between Hall and Leigh, near the front of the line. Pike was flying just above the rooftops, able to see between the homes and watch for ambushes.

Hall didn't trust Caryn. Not yet. He knew she was taking the long way, a winding route that would lead them lost and unable to find their way back again. A sound safety precaution. Hall didn't fault her for that.

He wondered how loyal to the Door Knockers she was. From the way she acted, what she said, he didn't think she was invested in the Guild. They had helped her and it seemed that Caryn was working with them out of a sense of debt.

But even if she wasn't fully a member, Hall knew she would most likely side with the thieves if it came down to it. Not that he thought it would. He wanted the Door Knockers as allies, not enemies.

He was going to make plenty of those over time that could threaten Skara Brae. Starting with the Silver Blades.

Caryn stopped at the back door to an unassuming home. Two stories, all wood including the shingles. The upper floor hung out over the alley a foot or two, and Hall had to step back and really crane his head up to try to look in the second-floor windows. He saw nothing, but he could feel the itch at the back of his head that meant he was being watched.

She tapped a pattern on the door. A series of loud and soft knocks, quick taps and long pauses. It was random, designed to be hard to remember on a single listen. Hall didn't even bother trying. Finishing the coded knock, Caryn stepped back and waited. She appeared a little nervous, not looking back.

Anxious, she had pushed them quickly through the maze of buildings and streets, wanting to arrive at the destination before she could change her mind. She glanced back at them often, smiling nervously. It didn't do anything to set Hall at ease.

Now she didn't even look at them, just stared at the door.

The minute stretched to two, then three. Caryn reached for the door as if to knock again and stopped, hand dropping to her side. She waited, impatient, nervous. Hall looked back at the others, giving a slight nod. No weapons were drawn, but some hands hovered closer to hilts and handles, and others moved to the sides to be freer to move in the motions of spell casting.

They waited like coiled springs, ready to move.

Finally, the door opened and a figure stepped out of the

shadowed interior. He was short, an inch or two shorter than Caryn, and wide. Taking up the whole doorway, he looked strong. Thick arms, broad shoulders. Bald with a black tattoo swirling around his right eye and along his skull, he stared at them without a bit of friendliness. He wore leather pants, bracers, and a sleeveless leather tunic. More tattoos swirled up and down his muscled arms. Two maces were hanging from his belt, one head smooth and the other covered in knobs.

The perfect doorman.

"Who are they?" he asked looking past Caryn.

Skill gain!
Identify Rank One +.1

Ulysses (Blue)

"Friends," she replied. "We need to see Berim. They want to help with our problem."

"We dun't have a problem," the man, Ulysses, said and spit on the ground.

He studied Hall and the others, Caryn sheepishly stepping aside. The doorman's eyes roamed over all of them, appraising them as he would an animal at market. The eyes widened a bit when they settled on Jackoby, showed surprise at the sight of Angus, but otherwise showed no concern or curiosity at the mixed group.

"Ain't a damned tavern," he told Caryn, eyes never leaving the group, hands crossed over his chest, but Hall knew Ulysses could grab the maces quickly if he wanted to. "Turn around and take 'em back where ya found 'em."

"But—" Caryn started to say but Hall stopped her.

He wanted to take a step forward, move around Caryn to better see the doorman but he knew that wouldn't go over well.

Try as hard as he could, he couldn't see the archers he knew had to be in windows around them.

"We are here to help with the other Guild," Hall said, choosing his words carefully, hoping that showing discretion would help.

"Ha," Ulysses barked. "The Witch was recently a guest of the PeakGuard," he said and pointed at Sabine. "Ya lot were last seen goin' inta the Constable's Office. So, what kind of deal did you strike with ol' Constable Morjack? Huh?"

Hall glanced at the others, surprised. The Door Knockers were incredibly well informed, seemingly having eyes everywhere. Or was it just one place? Hall had a suspicion he knew who had told the Door Knockers and decided to play that hunch.

"Since you know all that," he began and did take a step to the side to be clear of Caryn and in line with Ulysses. He felt the others tense as he did so. No one made a move to attack and Ulysses did not react, which told Hall all he needed to know. "I wonder what else Sergeant Brient told you."

Ulysses' features did not change as he stared at Hall. Then he laughed, big and loud.

"I like you," he said to Hall, still laughing. "Got some big ones, ya do."

The laughter stopped and a hard glare came to Ulysses' eyes, his face set in stone. It was a look that told Hall to not mess with the man, to do what he said.

"We've ben expecting ya," Ulysses said and Hall couldn't tell if it was a good thing or not.

CHAPTER TWENTY-FOUR

THE INSIDE OF THE BUILDING WAS NOT WHAT HALL HAD expected. The house had been small, the walls only thirty feet long. The inside was dark, lit by candles placed at odd intervals around the open space. Just a single room, no walls, the windows all boarded up. There was another door directly across that exited out onto one of the wider streets.

Hall could see four men in the room, spaced out between the candles, drawn weapons reflecting the weak, flickering flames. There was a mix of swords and daggers. All of them dressed in dark clothing.

Skill Gain!
Identify Rank One +.2

Door Knocker Enforcer (White)
Door Knocker Enforcer (White)
Door Knocker Enforcer (White)
Door Knocker Captain (Blue)

He thought they could handle the group, including Ulysses,

but it would be a tough fight. Caryn would tip the odds in favor of the Door Knockers. In the confined space of the building, as open as it was, the impact of Angus would be minimal and Pike had been told to wait outside. The dragonhawk had protested but settled to wait on a neighboring roof. So many combatants in the space would also limit Hall's abilities as well as the two-handed attacks of Roxhard. Casting would be difficult without taking out friendly targets.

All this passed quickly through Hall's mind in a matter of seconds as he looked around the dark space. Featureless, at least what was revealed by the weak light. There didn't appear to be any chairs or tables. Not even a staircase to the upper story.

Where were they to go? he wondered.

In answer, Ulysses walked to the middle of the room. He looked back at Hall and scowled, clearly unhappy. Leaning down, still looking at Hall, his thick knuckles rapped on the floor in another coded knocking pattern. This one different from the entrance door.

He waited a couple seconds, knocked again, and then stepped back.

Hall heard a light thud, and then a crack of light appeared in the floor. A rectangle shape, the crack grew thicker as a panel was lifted up. Four planks held together from the bottom with brackets for handles. Two pairs of hands pushed the panel up, and two of the men along the wall rushed forward to grab it.

A stair down was revealed. Well lit, bright, and welcoming.

"Come on," Ulysses said as he walked down the stairs.

Hall followed, pausing at the top.

The stairs ran straight, made of stone with stone sides. Square blocks fitted tight together made up the walls, the stairwell barely wide enough for Ulysses to walk down. It was going to be a tight fit for Jackoby and Roxhard.

Hall glanced at Angus.

"He going to be okay?" he asked Leigh.

"Should be," she replied, unsure.

Nodding, Hall started down. There was nothing they could do. Either Angus would make it down the stairs or he wouldn't. The only other option would be to leave the cow at the top of the stairs, and no one wanted that. Everything seemed okay with the Door Knockers. For now. And they did seem to be invited. But accidents could happen.

Angus came with them.

They moved down the straight run of stairs, walls to either side. It emptied out into another large room, this one made of stone. Walls, floor, and ceiling were all stone blocks. Light came from torches set in brackets along the wall. Fifteen feet or so to a side. Empty, with only one opening directly across.

Ulysses waiting in the middle of the room until the last of the group was down, waiting as they spread out into the space.

"I would ask ya ta leave yer weapons here but doubt that would be happening so why bother," he said with a shrug and a smirk.

Hall didn't even bother replying.

Ulysses laughed and started walking toward the other opening, an arch set into the wall. The tunnel beyond was lit, torches spaced evenly, and Hall could see that it ran for a good hundred feet or so. The ceiling was arched, the walls and floor smooth, but unlike the previous room, only part of the walls and floor were stone blocks. The rest was finished off dirt and soil. Not rough, but smoothed and worked. Tightly packed. Some roots were visible, snaking across the ground. But nothing that was a tripping hazard.

They followed Ulysses, single file and spaced apart, down the tunnel. The Door Knocker didn't show any concern or worry, which made Hall start to worry. It was all too casual. Even if they had been expected, he would have thought there would be guards stationed along the route. He was sure there was some kind of hidden security but thought some would be obvious and visible. A show of force. But there was nothing.

The Guild was too calm.

Hall stepped out of the tunnel, not that far behind Ulysses and Caryn, and into another room. A round one this time, with multiple tunnels branching off. And another empty room. Ulysses stopped in the middle and turned, looking at them. Caryn didn't move away from the group, which helped Hall's nervousness. If she had moved, he would have expected an attack. Instead, he expected to be kept waiting for a long time.

He was wrong.

The sound of footsteps, boots against the stone floor, came from one of the side tunnels. It echoed through the round space, the sound carrying. Hall turned and watched Berim step out of the tunnel and walk over to stand next to Ulysses. The dark-skinned man looked them over, studying them as he had the Inn the previous day.

"Why did you bring them here?" he asked, looking at Caryn, ignoring the others. His tone held reproach and disappointment.

"You already know," Hall answered, wanting to have some control over the conversation and encounter. "How long has Sergeant Brient been in your pocket?"

Berim was silent for a minute. If he was annoyed at Hall for interrupting, the man didn't show it.

"He's not," Berim finally answered. "At least, not usually. Brient is probably the most honorable and honest man in the PeakGuard."

"Then why does he want us to help you?" Leigh asked.

"You have a village, do you not?" he said to Hall, not directly answering Leigh or waiting for an answer of his own. "One thing you will learn, maybe the most important thing, is that a good leader knows that compromises need to be made sometimes. In the case of the good Sergeant, he knows that a guild war is very bad for the city, and that out of the two guilds, the Door Knockers are good for the city."

"How can any thief be good for the city?" Roxhard asked.

Berim looked at the Dwarf and shrugged.

"You must be young," he said. "Every city of any size will have crime. There will always be crime. Which would be better? Disorganized anarchy, where any two-bit cutthroat feels like they can steal anything from anyone? Or organized with rules that need to be obeyed? Organized where some things are not allowed?"

Hall nodded. He understood what Berim meant even if Roxhard didn't. The world, any world, was not black or white. There were shades of gray, and sometimes it was better to work with the enemy you knew than the one you didn't.

"Brient's hands are tied," Hall said. "He knows the stability in the underworld that the Knockers bring but he can't openly aid the Guild."

Berim nodded.

"Hold on," Caryn said, stepping in front of Hall and taking a step toward Berim. "If you knew they were going to help you, why the hard time about bringing them here?" The Duelist was angry.

"Appearance," Hall answered, eyes never leaving Berim. Caryn looked back at him. "The Knockers can't appear as if they need outside help to deal with the Blades. That would make them look weak and make others start to question their power."

"Just so," Berim said and looked to Caryn. His eyes flashed anger. "It was also not your place to bring them here," he said and waved his hands to indicate the room they were in. "You forced our hand by doing so publicly."

Caryn chewed on her bottom lip, nervous and a little ashamed. Hall felt sorry for her. She was working in a world she knew nothing about, not really, and one where she didn't seem to belong. He wondered what her overall experience and life had been like before Sky Realms Online. She had been playing only for a couple hours, but outside the game? What had she been doing? This encounter, the situation the Knockers found themselves in, was not unique or even new.

"I assume you're going to point us at the Silver Blades and then disappear," Hall said, diverting Berim's attention away from Caryn. The young woman had been shrinking under the man's unrelenting glare.

"Something like that," Berim answered. He glanced at Ulysses and nodded.

The wider and shorter man stepped forward and pointed to one of the side tunnels.

"This way," he said and started walking, not looking back, expecting them to follow.

Hall started to but stopped with one last glance at Berim. The thief watched him, face impassive. Turning away, Hall started down the tunnel.

"You go with them," he heard Berim say and knew the thief was taking to Caryn.

———

The tunnel Ulysses led them down started wide and got progressively shorter and thinner as they walked. The stone of the walls, ceiling, and floor became older and cruder. Eventually, the stone floor disappeared, becoming hard-packed dirt with puddles of water. Before long they were walking in water an inch or so deep. Their boots splashed as they walked, more water dripping from the ceiling above. Moss appeared on the now damp and slick walls.

Jackoby had to crouch in spots, muttering angrily to himself. Only Ulysses and Roxhard did not feel affected by the shrinking tunnel. There were still torches mounted to the wall, but further apart and some not lit. Hall's *Limited Night Vision* was next to useless. There was too much light for his vision to fully switch.

They walked for what felt like an hour, through twisting and turning tunnels. At one point, Hall was sure they crossed back along their path but said nothing. Ulysses finally stopped at a four-way intersection, the flowing water deeper in the middle. Next to the short man was a metal ladder running up the wall, the top lost in the shadows.

"Up ya go," the man said and pointed.

"What about Angus?" Leigh asked, the cow moving in close to her. His four paws were wet and muddy, drops hanging from the shaggy fur under his belly.

"Figure it out," Ulysses replied.

"What's up there?" Hall asked, reaching into his pouch and pulling out some rope.

He was glad he had thought to bring the rope. It was normally in his travel backpack, which was in his room at the Inn, but he had switched out some items that morning. He walked over to Angus, the Highland cow, studying him. When he started to tie the rope around the cow's chest, the animal stepped back and mooed loudly. Ulysses laughed as Leigh held Angus steady so Hall could tie the rope securely.

"Empty warehouse," Ulysses answered and stepped away from the ladder. "Should be empty."

Hall didn't like the way he said the word *should*. Keeping up appearances was one thing, but the Door Knockers could be doing a better job of helping, Hall thought as he grabbed ahold of the ladder. Climbing up with his spear and javelin in the harness would be difficult, which is why he wanted to go first.

He got to the top of the tunnel with the ladder continuing through a small shaft. Pausing, Hall glanced down at the group, measuring the size of Angus. The cow would fit. He thought about telling Ulysses to lead them back to the surface another way but knew it would be useless. Lifting his leg, he put it on the next rung and continued. The shaft grew dark, no light coming from below and just a thin line above.

The line of light grew brighter, thicker, and Hall knew he was at the top. He reached up, thankful his harness didn't keep his weapons that high above his head. Gloved fingers hit wood, and he could feel the different planks. Pushing lightly, the trap-door lifted. He wasn't worried about traps. The Door Knockers would have disabled any already.

Through the separation between door and floor, Hall could not see much. He heard no noise, nothing to indicate someone had seen the trapdoor lifting. No blades stabbed through the space, no foot slammed down on the door.

Someone could be waiting for Hall to fully show himself, but it was a risk he would have to take.

Pushing the trapdoor open more, Hall stepped out of the shaft and into the warehouse.

It was empty, just like Ulysses had said. A wide-open space, wooden columns equally spaced the length and width of the room. Large, but not such that the ends were lost in shadows. He could see the far walls easy enough. Vertically laid wood planks with studs behind, running from column to column that held up a pitched roof above. One story tall, no windows and just a set of double doors on the far end. There were no crates, no barrels, nothing to show that it had ever been in use. A layer of dust coated the floor, enough that footprints would have stood out. There were none.

Stepping away from the trapdoor, Hall spun slowly. He took it all in, all of the nothing. Mentally reaching out to Pike, he could feel the dragonhawk. Pike lifted off from the roof he had been waiting on, woken up by Hall's connection. The bird flew south and slightly west. Hall linked his vision with Pike's, seeing what the bird saw, trying to get an idea of where in Peakdock they were.

From what he could see, they were near the docks on the western edge. A couple streets back from the open area of the docks, close enough for quick wagon travel but far enough away to avoid the commotion and activity of the docks. And avoid watchful and curious eyes.

Breaking the connection, Hall moved back to the trap door. Jackoby was stepping onto the floor, coiled rope in his hand. Hall looked down and saw Leigh looking nervously up. He smiled, trying to reassure her.

Stepping back, Leigh nudged Angus so the cow was standing alongside the ladder. The rope crisscrossed his body, looping under him at his front and back.

"Ready?" Hall asked with a glance to Jackoby.

The Firbolg grunted and handed the end of the rope to Hall. They set themselves in a line before the trap door and started to pull. Hand over hand, the two pulled the rope out of the shaft. They could hear aggravated mooing, and small cries of pain as the cow bumped into the walls and ladder. Hall grimaced, not liking that he was hurting Angus but not seeing another choice. There was no way that Ulysses would lead them back through the tunnels, and they'd be lost without the Door Knocker.

Finally, Hall could see the cow's horns poking through the opening. He ran forward, grabbing the small cow around his head and neck, pulling to get the front hooves on the floor. Angus scrambled once his hooves touched wood, almost knocking Hall down. He may have been small, but Angus was still heavy and strong. With some more effort, the cow was finally in the building.

Jackoby sat down, breathing heavy. Angus walked over and nudged him, Jackoby grunting but reaching up and patting the cow behind his ear. Hall walked over, reached down to pet

Angus and jumped back as a horn poked at him. Jackoby laughed and Angus gave an annoyed moo.

Hall shook his head, stretching out his arms that were sore after lifting the cow.

One by one the others all came out of the shaft, except Ulysses. The small man poked his body out enough to grab the trap door.

"Not coming with us?" Hall asked. He has assumed the thief wasn't but had hoped for a surprise."

"Yer on ya own now," Ulysses said with a dark chuckle. "Good luck."

The Door Knocker went down the shaft, pulling the door closed behind him. Hall could hear what sounded like a locking bolt sliding into place.

"Not going back that way," he said with a shrug. "Let's get this over with."

CHAPTER TWENTY-FIVE

Hall opened the single door slowly and carefully, afraid it would make a noise and alert whoever was outside. He knew there would be someone out there. Berim would not have sent them to an empty building, and Hall doubted the Door Knocker would have sent them to an easy target either.

Whatever was out there was going to be tough. Berim was using them, sending them at a target he wanted removed. The thief could have easily sent them to the target that Brient had directed them toward, a much safer target, but instead had sent them here.

He either wanted the Silver Blade operation removed or wanted something they had. If Ulysses had stayed, Hall knew it would be something the Blades had. Instead, without a Door Knocker present, Berim just wanted the operation removed. Hall didn't think Caryn counted as a Door Knocker, not anymore at least. Her days in the guild were numbered.

With the door open a couple inches, Hall couldn't see much. The angle was bad, the slit revealing wooden walls across a dirt street. No movement, no shadows indicating anyone standing outside. Just wall.

Opening his mind to Pike, Hall had the dragonhawk circle the street. It was dangerous to use Pike. Any Silver Blade watchers would be suspicious of a dragonhawk circling, but it was the only way to get any idea what they were going to face. All he could see was a door almost directly across from theirs. It was a two-story building with a shallow-pitched, wooden-shingled roof and windows on the second story. Pike's sharp eyes couldn't see any movement in the windows but did pick up two men lying flat on roofs to the left and right of the target. One of them was looking up at Pike.

Hall quickly ordered Pike to fly away and broke the connection. Pulling the door closed, he motioned the others further away. He quickly explained the layout and where the two men were.

"Could they be Door Knockers?" Caryn asked without any real conviction.

"Ulysses would have told us if they were," Hall said, not adding that if they were Door Knockers, they were just there to watch, not aid. "No, they have to be Silver Blade watchers."

"What do we do?" Leigh asked.

"Nothing," Sabine muttered. They all looked at her. "This isn't our fight."

Hall knew she was still bitter about being arrested and used as bait, but she did have a point. It was a short-term concern though. Long term, they needed to be able to operate in Silver Peak Keep and that would not happen if they angered the PeakGuard or the Door Knockers.

"Like it or not," he said to the group, focusing on Sabine and to an extent Jackoby. "This is our fight."

"Fine," Sabine said, obviously still not happy. "Since we're going to do this, how are we going to do it?"

Hall looked back at the door, picturing the other in his mind. It had swung the same way if he remembered right, swinging in. He smiled.

―――――

Leigh pulled the door open fully and quickly. With a loud moo, Angus charged out. The cow ran straight for the opposite door, full speed and head lowered. They could hear the surprised shouts from the rooftops above, the two watchers following the speeding cow's progress. They didn't notice Hall and Sabine step out of the door and into the street.

Hall took the left, Sabine the right. He didn't bother with trying to *Identify* the Silver Blade. There was no time. He saw the flash of purple as Sabine cast a *Hexbolt* at the watcher above. Activating *Leap*, Hall jumped into the air, angling toward the roof of the next building over. As he did, he summoned Pike, hearing the screech of the dragonhawk far out over the plains around the city.

Landing on the roof next to the surprised Silver Blade, Hall managed to keep his balance. He had pulled his spear out mid-flight and now jabbed straight out with it. The Blade had to roll to the side to avoid the spear, which is what Hall wanted. It bought him time to set his feet solidly on the wooden shingles. He rotated his body and stabbed out with the spear again, driving the Blade further back.

"Who the hells are you?" the Blade cried out, rolling to avoid another spear thrust and getting to his feet in a smooth motion.

From the street below, Hall could hear the others racing across the open street. Leigh and Caryn would be following behind Jackoby and Roxhard, using the two Wardens as shields. They didn't know what to expect inside the building, so the Wardens would crowd the doorway and get an idea of the opposition. Leigh was there to provide healing as needed.

If there was too much, they were all to immediately retreat and run deeper into the warren of streets. Hall would follow when he could, either into the building or in retreat.

For now, he was occupied.

He thrust the spear forward, the Blade knocking it aside with his now drawn short sword. The weapon wasn't fancy, a blade in decent shape and an unadorned hilt. Hall could tell the Silver Blade knew how to use it. Both held their ground, watching the other and waiting. The roof pitch was shallow but there was enough of it to make the footing uneven and treacherous. The shingles were rough, providing a good grip, but a misplaced foot would spell doom.

Skill Gain!
Identify Rank One +.1

Silver Blade Cutthroat (White)

The thief was equal level to Hall, maybe even one below. Tall and lanky, blond hair and pale skin, dressed all in black with a lowered hood and half-mask. The only visible weapon was the short sword, but Hall assumed there were more. At least a throwing knife or two, a dagger in a hidden sheath.

He jabbed with the spear, keeping the Cutthroat moving and off-balance. He couldn't hear much from the street. It sounded like the group had entered the building. Fighting the urge to look over his shoulder to check on Sabine and her opponent, he took a step forward toward his.

The Cutthroat changed the angle of his blade, bringing the edge down to slice at Hall's spear. Quickly pulling it back, Hall rotated it around his body, grabbing the blunt end with his other hand. He knew the ironwood could probably take the slice of the blade, turning it, but didn't want to take the risk. Holding the spear by the blunt end, he completed the rotation and swung it at the Cutthroat. The weapon was at its maximum length and slammed into the side of the Silver Blade.

A blunt force hit, the shaft of the spear caught the Cutthroat in the side. The man grunted and staggered back, closer to the edge. He had the presence of mind, and the speed, to try and grab the spear's shaft but Hall had halted the swing and was bringing it back. Once again, he rotated the weapon around his body and held it with the sharp end pointing at the thief.

Quickly stabbing out, he caught the Cutthroat in the shoulder. Black cloth ripped, exposing pale shoulder and a bloody wound. Stumbling back, the Cutthroat barely kept his balance and Hall caught him with the spear again. This time, the weapon opened a large gash along the thief's side. Crying out in pain, the Cutthroat took two more steps back, the edge of the roof closer. He looked over his shoulder, fearful, and turned back to Hall.

With a cry, the Cutthroat charged, taking a slicing blow from the spear but ignored it. Hall waited and stepped to the side, further up the roof, barely avoiding the charge. He swung out with his hand and caught the Cutthroat in the back of the head. The man fell forward, stumbling, and lost his balance completely. Too far forward, he leaned over the edge and kept going.

There was a loud crash, followed by a cracking sound.

SLAIN: *Silver Blade Cutthroat*
+25 Experience

Skill Gain!
Polearms Rank Two +.1
Light Armor Rank Two +.1

Hall knew the thief was dead, but he still stepped to the edge and looked down. The body lay against the wall of the next building, head against the ground and bent unnaturally to the side, legs up against the wall, broken crates underneath.

He looked across the rooftops toward the other guard, watching as the man spasmed with bolts of purple energy around him. Sabine cast a *Shadowbolt*, catching the man in the chest, which caused him to fall forward. The thief stumbled but somehow managed to keep his balance. He overcompensated and ended up falling backward, landing hard on the roof and out of view from Sabine.

Reaching for his javelin, Hall felt a familiar presence streaking his way. He glanced over his shoulder, seeing the dark orange and green form of Pike coming closer. The dragonhawk's wings, over three feet in length, flapped quickly. Pike screeched and Hall sent a thought to the dragonhawk, lowering his hand.

On the other roof, the Silver Blade was pushing himself up, keeping well back from the edge and the angrily muttering Sabine. With his back turned, he didn't see Pike until it was too late. Hearing the wings flapping in the air, the thief turned and caught the raking talons of Pike across his shoulder. He screamed in pain as the dragonhawk circled and let out a screech. A bolt of lightning shot out, catching the thief in the head. Smoke rose up and the smell of burnt flesh drifted across on the wind as the body fell to the ground.

SLAIN: *Silver Blade Cutthroat*
+10 experience

Activating *Leap*, Hall jumped down to the street two stories below. Sabine turned to face him, still angry. Hall motioned toward the open door and the Witch followed, fuming. He told Pike to keep circling and to let him know if anyone approached the building.

The first floor was a wide-open space. Thick columns held

up the roof in the front half of the space and an upper story in the back half. Unlike the building they had started in, this one was not empty. Large and small crates filled the space, some organized into neat rows and stacked on top of each other, while others were laid randomly in no particular order. Sacks of different sizes were set on top of crates, on the floor, and piled on top of others. Then there were the bodies.

Three of them. Dressed like the ones that had been on the roofs.

All were clustered near the door. Two of them had no weapons drawn, the other had a sword lying just beyond his reach. They had been caught by surprise, unprepared for the violent assault.

An assault that had stalled.

Roxhard and Leigh, with Angus, were behind crates to the right. Jackoby and Caryn were crouched behind some on the left. None of them looked too badly hurt. But none were capable of moving.

The upper story in the back half of the building was lined with doors, offices of some kind, with a walkway and railing in front. Standing at the railing were two Archers and what looked like a Witch and a Shaman. The Archers were firing arrows at the crates as fast as they could draw them, the Witch and Shaman waiting for their chance, arms raised and ready to cast spells.

They caught sight of Hall and Sabine just as Hall saw them.

"Cover," he yelled, waiting a second to make sure Sabine had heard.

She dove to the side, landing hard and crawling quickly to crouch behind a small crate. Hall went to dive just as he saw a shaft of dark energy streaking his way. He landed on the hard ground, the shaft slamming into his side. It had barely caught him, but that was enough.

He felt pain spread throughout his body. An icy pain, body stiffening. Grunting, biting back a yell, he pulled himself behind a large crate. The pain still racked his body. Glancing at his Health, he saw it had gone down by a quarter. He cursed. The stinging icy feel faded, but he still hurt.

Now he knew what their enemies felt when Sabine struck with a *Shadowbolt*.

An arrow clattered against the wooden crate, the shaft snapping.

He cursed at himself. They should never have just rushed the building. He should never have let the Door Knockers push them into this.

They were pinned down. There was no way to distract all four Silver Blades. He could try and charge, having Jackoby and Roxhard follow, but they didn't need all four of the ranged attackers to deal with that. One, maybe two, would be waiting for when Sabine and Leigh tried their ranged spells. Rushing just one would be death for that one. The same thing would happen, two of the ranged would concentrate on the attacker, while the other two kept the rest pinned down.

And the Silver Blades just had to wait. Reinforcements or the PeakGuard would be drawn by the noises.

"Are there more?" Hall shouted, hopefully just loud enough to be heard by his friends and not the Silver Blades.

"Not that we know of, but I think one got out," Leigh answered.

Which meant reinforcements would definitely be coming. And there could be an unknown number waiting in the offices.

Hall grumbled. He had been thinking in game terms again. A suicide run was the first step in doing any raid dungeons. Without knowing what was ahead, and knowing the Player would just respawn, there was no reason to not just rush in and get an idea of what they faced. They would get killed, respawn, and then be able to plan.

Without consciously doing it, Hall knew he had followed that same strategy.

And it could cost them.

Angry at himself, Hall tried to come up with some plan. Any plan.

Could they retreat without getting hit? That could be their best option. Run away. Try a different angle to get at the Silver Blades.

He glanced at the open door, sunlight streaming in. The dirt street outside was empty, nobody walking and no wagons. But he caught a glimpse of a shadow, small and moving. It disappeared and then came back. As if something was circling above.

Pike.

Hall got an idea.

"Get ready," Hall yelled out, again hoping he was only heard by his friends and not the Silver Blades.

But if they did hear him, it could only help. There was no way they could anticipate what was coming.

"For what?" Jackoby growled.

Hall didn't answer. He just shifted position so he could get up and run quickly.

———

The screech was loud.

All heads turned toward the open door, watching as a blurry green something darted into the building. It flew straight and fast for the second story at the far end. The Archers tried to track the blur but could not, so startled were they. The casters lost their concentration, spell casting disrupted. Summoned energy harmlessly disappeared, back to where it was pulled from.

As Pike sailed over his head, Hall got up and started

running. He kept low, heading for the far wall and the set of stairs that led to the second level. He could feel the looks of the others, confused at first but then realized what was happening. They were slower to get up, but they did and started following Hall.

He could hear Sabine and Leigh behind him, voices raised in casting.

The dragonhawk streaked for the catwalk and pulled up in front of the casters. All four Silver Blades looked at the bird in surprise and then fear as the sharp beak opened and a jagged bolt of lightning shot out. The blue streak slammed into the Shaman. The man fell back against the wall, sagging to the ground, smoke rising from the wound on his chest.

Pike gave one more screech and let himself drop close to the ground before pumping his powerful wings and flying off to the side, out of the way.

Jagged streaks of purple energy replaced the dragonhawk. Each struck one of the Silver Blades, even the fallen. Bolts of energy spread out from where the streaks impacted, causing the Blades to spasm in pain. A swarm of flying splinters followed, striking the wooden railing, the office walls beyond and the three Silver Blades still standing. Each yelled in pain as dozens of small splinters cut into them.

Hall smiled as he activated *Leap*. The ceiling was high enough and he arced up and across the distance. He felt himself leave the ground, powerful legs pushing up, air rushing past. The far wall and the catwalk rose, coming closer. He could see the surprised eyes of the Silver Blades watching him coming closer to them. In a matter of seconds, he landed on the walk next to the Witch. Using his *Attack of Opportunity*, Hall struck out with his spear and caught the Witch in the chest. The ironwood tip plunged in deep, the Witch falling to the side. Hall pulled out the spear and slammed the butt end into the Archer's side. The Blade stumbled back, tried to move and spasmed as the *Hexbolt* activated.

Rotating the spear, he stabbed down at the fallen Shaman. The Blade moved, dodging out of the way. Hall cursed, knowing his surprise attack was done. He now had to prepare to defend himself and he was outnumbered.

The Witch was slower to recover, clutching at his side, blood leaking between clenched fingers. He stared at Hall with hate. Dressed all in black, with blond hair and blue eyes. Hall turned and jabbed out with the spear, pushing the Archer back and preventing the man from counterattacking. Smiling, the expression, confusing the Archer, Hall turned away to face the Witch.

Pike screeched and let out another bolt of lightning. The Archer was flown forward, slamming into the wall, dropping his bow, as the bolt slammed into his back. Smoke rose from the wound, the Archer trying to push himself up. The dragonhawk continued his flight, talons raking across the upraised arm of the Shaman.

Across the struggling Witch, the other Archer raised his bow. Hall stopped, ready to *Leap* away but knowing he wouldn't get away before the arrow hit him. There was no way to evade it. The string pulled back tight, the Archer taking a deep breath before releasing.

The thick black line slammed into the Silver Blade Archer, pushing him to the side. He grunted in pain, side coming numb, the bow lowering, the arrow dropping to the ground. The Archer turned, tried to step away from the railing and out of Sabine's view, but he stopped and stiffened as he saw the heavy hammerhead swinging his way.

Jackoby was on the walk, leading with his hammer. The weapon slammed into the Archer's chest, the impact pushing the Blade into the railing. Wood cracked, splintered, and the Silver Blade fell to the ground.

The wooden walk shook as the large Firbolg angrily swung the hammer at the Witch who had managed to stand, hand still gripping his side. The Blade stepped back, avoiding it but hit the weakened rail. He stumbled and Hall caught him with a spear thrust into the unwounded side. The Witch stepped to the side, foot past where the railing ended and hanging over nothing. He stumbled, prodded by another thrust from Hall, and the Witch followed the Archer down to the ground.

Glancing down, Hall saw Roxhard finishing off the two Blades. Turning around, leaving the Shaman to Jackoby, Hall jabbed at with the spear at the last Archer. The man cried out in pain as the tip sliced cleanly and easily through his black clothing. He fell back, landing on the ground, and Hall stepped up. A final stab finished the Archer off.

Raising the spear for an attack, Hall turned and relaxed. Jackoby stepped back from the Shaman. The Silver Blade was unmoving.

Notifications flashed across Hall's vision.

SLAIN: Silver Blade Archer

+15 experience

SLAIN: Silver Blade Witch

+15 experience

Skill Gain!
Polearms Rank Two +.2

Hall stepped back against the wall, away from the broken railing. He leaned against it, breathing heavy. His eyes looked at all the openings, waiting for something or someone to step through. No one came.

Stepping to the railing, he looked down. Roxhard stood over the two black-clad forms of the Silver Blades. Leigh and

Sabine were looking toward the entrance. Caryn was examining some crates off to the side.

"Did we keep one alive?" Hall asked.

"This one," Roxhard said and pointed at the Archer.

"Barely," Sabine muttered. "Leigh had to heal him to keep him from dying. He still might. His chest is crushed." She glanced up at Jackoby with annoyance.

Hall looked at the large Firbolg, who just shrugged.

He glanced at the notifications again, seeing nothing for the related quest. Muttering a curse, he motioned to Jackoby, pointing at the doors. The Firbolg didn't move even though Hall knew Jackoby knew what Hall wanted.

With another curse, he walked to the furthest door to start his search.

CHAPTER TWENTY-SIX

Cautiously, Hall opened the door.

Oak, solid, iron hinges. Nothing special and a quick search had shown no runes or traps that he could see. Still, he used his spear to push it open. Behind him, Jackoby stood with weapon ready. The Firbolg was there to honor the debt he owed Hall, not to do anything else. Nothing happened as the door opened into a dark room so Hall stepped inside.

His *Limited Night Vision*, a racial ability granted by his being a Half-Elf, showed an empty space. Not large, ten-foot by ten-foot. An office of some kind.

Leaving the door open, he stepped to the next one and repeated the opening by spear. No traps and another empty room. The third was the same. And the fourth.

All the rooms on the second story were empty. No furniture, no shelves, no windows. A thick layer of dust had covered the floor of each, showing the rooms had been unused for a long time.

Hall sighed. He had hoped to find something in one of the rooms. What, he wasn't sure; just something that would satisfy the quest requirements and bring them to the next step.

He returned to the first room, the furthest down the walk. There had to be something he missed. Stepping back inside, he started tapping the walls and the floor with the spear, listening for hollow spaces. He examined the ceiling, looking for anything different. A hidden trap door or loose board. Jackoby just stood in the doorway, watching.

"You could help," Hall said.

Jackoby grunted and didn't move.

Hall continued his search. He moved on to the second, searching the same way. Tapping with the spear, pushing against the ceiling. Still finding nothing.

"Look out!"

Jackoby turned and started running down the walk, the Firbolgs heavy footsteps slamming against the wood. Hall ran to the railing and looked down.

He saw Roxhard charging across the warehouse using his *Battle Rush* ability. The Dwarf was a blur of pumping legs as he ran toward the entrance. Just inside the door, pushing through the opening, were two large humanoids dressed in leathers and carrying large swords. Each was the size of a Firbolg, but they were something else. Pale green skin was visible around the pieces of leather armor, metal plates on the shins and chest, scales were visible over their arms that extended across their chests. Each carried a curved sword and small shield. Slanted yellow eyes and sharply pointed ears were on large heads, bony ridges down their noses. One had black hair cut to leave a strip down the middle of his head that hung down his back where it was braided. The other was bald, a long beard hanging loose over its chest. They separated as they entered the building, four Humans with swords and daggers behind them.

Hobs.

How had the Silver Blades managed to recruit Hobs? Hall thought as Roxhard slammed into the first one. The creature took a step back but didn't fall or get stunned. Roxhard seemed to bounce off the Hob, falling down on his backside. He managed to jump up and catch the Hob's sword on his two-handed axe.

The Hob's health had barely gone down.

Skill Gain!

Identify Rank One +.2

Silver Blade Hob Enforcer (Blue)
Silver Blade Hob Enforcer (Blue)

Hobs were not native to Edin. They lived on other islands further to the east. Tribal creatures that lived in a militaristic culture, they sometimes hired on as mercenaries. They fought with each other as much as they did others. The Highborn were their enemies, the two sharing some of the same islands. Vicious, brutal, and cunning.

The second Hob stepped aside as Leigh's *Splinter Storm* shot out. The attack missed the Hob but landed squarely on one of the Humans behind. It didn't evade the *Hexbolt* from Sabine, which caught both of the Hobs. They spasmed as streaks of purple energy cascaded around their bodies, but they fought through the pain, grinning.

Caught by Leigh's spell, the Human fell to the ground, crying out in pain. The Hobs and the other Humans ignored him. Roxhard exchanged blows with the Hob he faced, the second advancing on Sabine and Leigh.

Caryn stepped in its path, both her swords ready. The Hob swung with its longer sword and Caryn darted out of the way. She turned in a circle, attacking with one sword that the Hob caught on its shield, but she continued her pivot crouching down low and her second sword scored a hit on the Hob's chest below the raised shield.

Duelists were dancers in combat. They turned, jumped, ducked, twisted, and moved out of the way of attacks always somehow able to make one of their own with a weapon as they evaded. Watching a Duelist fight was like watching poetry in motion. They were a blur of feints and strikes, their speed meant to distract the target from where the real attack was coming from.

And Caryn was good. Hall could see that from where he stood on the railing.

Pike sat on the railing next to him, waiting for a command. Jackoby was running across the warehouse to intercept one of the Humans that had moved past the fighting pair of Hobs. Everyone was too close for Leigh and Sabine to use spells. Not yet, not the way they were moving. Each waited their chance. Angus stood in front of them, a heavy barrier.

Hall could see more Silver Blades just outside the entrance, at least four, waiting to come in. Including another Hob.

The reinforcements had arrived and he doubted they'd be getting any from the Door Knockers. Three Hobs and seven Human Blades. Hall just hoped none were casters.

He watched as the Blade that Leigh had hit with her spell was starting to get up. He pointed and mentally gave Pike a command. The dragonhawk lifted off the railing, flapping his wings and dove straight for the wounded Human. Screeching, Pike let out a bolt of lightning that slammed into the Human. The man fell to the ground, leather armor smoking, as Pike circled around.

Jackoby's hammer slammed into one of the other Humans, who had been distracted by Pike. The man staggered back, his arm breaking with a loud crack. The Blade screamed in pain but managed to duck another attack by Jackoby.

Skill Gain!
Identify Rank One +.4

Silver Blade Cutthroat (White)
Silver Blade Cutthroat (White)
Silver Blade Cutthroat (Blue)
Silver Blade Cutthroat (White)
Silver Blade Cutthroat (Blue)
Silver Blade Cutthroat (Blue)
Silver Blade Hob Enforcer (Blue)

Hall breathed a sigh of relief. None that he could see were casters. But that didn't mean there weren't any waiting outside, just out of view. There was only one way to find out.

Using *Leap*, keeping his arc low and long, he jumped off the railing and soared across the warehouse. He landed next to the Hob that Roxhard was fighting and jabbed out with his spear. The Hob managed to turn out of the way, just catching a slicing blow across its chest. Another quick jab, which missed the evading Hob, and Hall was past and charging at one of the other Cutthroats.

He sidestepped an attack by the Cutthroat and slammed the side of his spear shaft into the man's side. The Blade grunted as Hall dropped the spear and pulled out his short sword. There wasn't enough room to use the spear effectively. The Cutthroat got an attack in that Hall caught on his bracer. He could feel pain shooting through his arm. The sword's edge did no damage but the force and the impact still hurt as a glance in the corner of his vision showed his Health bar drop. He hadn't recovered fully from the first fight. Grunting, biting back the pain, Hall twisted his body and slashed out with the sword. He cut the Cutthroat across his chest, the blade slicing cleanly through the black clothes the Blade wore.

Hall could feel resistance as the blade cut into the body of the Cutthroat. The Blade cried out in pain, body jerking backward and away from Hall's sword. Reaching up, Hall caught the loose black fabric, twisting his sword so it was point out, and pulled the Blade into the sword. The man cried louder, the sound ending, blood dripping from his mouth. Hall pushed the Blade down and pulled out his sword.

He sliced it through the air and caught the descending blade of another Cutthroat.

Metal clanged on metal, the weapons screeching as they slid along their lengths. Hall pushed, trying to drive the Cutthroat back. He glanced behind him, seeing the three Hobs occupied. Roxhard, Caryn, and now Jackoby were holding their own against the bigger opponents but had been maneuvered so they blocked any attacks from Sabine and Leigh. The Cutthroats were all inside, spreading out, a couple moving to flank the three fighting the Hobs. One was moving to Halls unprotected side while the others waited to see where they would be needed.

The sound of something heavy stomping on the floor of the warehouse filled the air, and Hall felt the wind as Angus charged past. The cow slammed into one of the waiting Humans. The Blade was sent flying, lifted off the ground, and slammed into the wall of the building. He struggled to get up, only to have the cow's horns slam into his stomach.

One of the flanking Blades screamed as a crack of lightning filled the space, the flash of light blinding. Pike screeched and soared higher into the rafters of the warehouse, looking for another opportunity to attack.

Hall kicked out, forcing the Blade back. He stabbed forward with his sword, making the other Blade take a step back. The man smiled, cocky, knowing Hall was outnumbered. Hall grimaced and jabbed again, the Blade casually batting the sword aside. Which was what Hall wanted. He let the sword go with his right hand and caught it in his left, the blade pointing down. He sliced up, catching the surprised Cutthroat with the tip.

Reaching behind him with his right arm, Hall pulled his

javelin out of the harness on his back. Since acquiring the magical throwing knives, he hadn't used the weapon much but still carried it. There were times when the javelin would be a better choice than the knives and this was one of those times.

Holding the weapon, he took aim. The Blade in front of him dove to the side, thinking the attack was meant for him. It wasn't.

Hall pulled back his arm and pushed it forward, letting the javelin fly. The weapon sailed through the air and caught one of the flanking Blades in the shoulder. It was a glancing blow, but it knocked the Cutthroat off balance.

He pivoted and swung his blade in an arch, missing both of the Cutthroats. The one to his right didn't miss him. Hall felt the pain as the man's weapon sliced a long gash down his arm. He bit back the scream, feeling his blood run down his arm and fall to the floor. His Health bar dropped, not a lot but enough. It was the Damage Over Time aspect of the attack that worried him.

GASH!

You have been wounded, the attack opening up a long gash in you.
The attack does 10 damage over 10 seconds.

A crackling bolt of purple energy slammed into the two Cutthroats facing him. Bolts erupted from the impact spots, streaking across their bodies. They tried to move but spasmed as the bolts caused intense pain through their limbs. Hall took advantage, changed his grip on his short sword and stabbed out with the blade. The first stab went through a Cutthroat's neck, the man's eyes widening in shock and pain. Hall sliced to the right, the sharp edge of his weapon sliding out of the Blade and through the air. It struck the other Cutthroat in the shoulder, slicing a deep gash.

Hall went to stab the man with his sword when the Blade

jerked. He was lifted up off the ground, crying out as he was caught on Angus' horns. The cow had gotten a little bigger and stronger. Grunting loudly, Angus shook his head rapidly. The Blade cried out and fell off the horns to the ground. Hall stabbed the Blade and the man's cries ended.

"Leveled, did you?" Hall asked Angus as he paused to catch his breath, trying to push back the pain of the wound on his arm. He could feel the Damage Over Time attack taking bits of his Health away every second.

Angus mooed and shook his head, drops of blood flying off the ends of his horns. His fur was matted with blood along the top and covering his hooves. The cow had stomped one of the Silver Blade Cutthroats to death but looked to have received wounds of his own.

Hall couldn't hear the sounds of fighting anymore, and he looked around. The three Hobs were dead. Jackoby stood over one, his eyes watching the two Cutthroats that had been trying to flank him. They stood about fifteen feet away, using some crates as cover. Roxhard's axe head dripped blood, more blood dripping from wounds along his arms. He held the weapon ready, watching the two Cutthroats to the left.

Caryn had stepped back, breathing heavy, standing in front of and between Sabine and Leigh, head moving from one group of enemies to the other. She held both blood-covered swords, ready to attack, but in a position to defend the casters.

Hall moved back and picked up his spear, holding it in his left and sword in his right. The shorter weapon was in his primary hand but he wanted the spear to use defensively. He looked from one group of Cutthroats to the other. Everyone, including the Silver Blades, waited.

Taking the time during this lull in combat, Hall glanced at the notifications he had received.

SLAIN: *Silver Blade Cutthroat*

+25 Experience
SLAIN: Silver Blade Cutthroat
+25 Experience
SLAIN: Silver Blade Cutthroat
+15 Experience

Skill Gain!
Polearms Rank Two +.1
Small Blades Rank Two +.2
Light Armor Rank Two +.2
Thrown Rank Two +.1

"You could surrender," Hall said to the four Silver Blades as he dismissed the notifications.

He didn't expect them to. It was a stalling tactic.

"This isn't your war," one of the Blades, female, said. One of the two to the right.

Hall turned to face the woman. Her voice had been sweet-sounding with a Gael accent, but the tone had been rough and harsh. She was not afraid, or at least it did not show in her voice. She sounded confident, like she was speaking from the position of strength.

"It wasn't," Hall admitted. "But it is now."

"Your funeral," the Blade said, again her tone matter of fact as if the outcome was inevitable. "The Cudgel does not like interlopers in his business."

Hall caught the name she used. The Cudgel. Presumably the leader of the Silver Blades. *An odd name for a group called the Silver Blades*, Hall thought.

You have learned the name of the one you think is the Silver Blade's leader. The Cudgel. Seek out more information on the mysterious man. Learn his or her identity and where to find them.

THE BLADE'S CUDGEL I

Learn the identity of The Cudgel 0/1
Learn the location of The Cudgel 0/1
Reward: +100 Door Knocker Reputation
+75 PeakGuard Experience
+50 Experience

ACCEPT QUEST?

Hall accepted the quest, glancing at the others to see if they had received it as well. Leigh nodded. He returned his attention to the talkative Blade. The second Blade had moved further behind her, a step at a time. He sent a command to Pike and the dragonhawk dove out of the rafters coming to a hovering stop behind the Blade that was trying to flee. He turned and saw Pike, stopping. The talkative Blade never turned. Hall shifted and looked to the left, seeing the other two had not moved.

He turned back to the talkative Blade and saw her glance to the side, looking behind Leigh and Sabine. His gaze moved sharply that way when Sabine cried out in pain.

An arrow was lodged in her shoulder, the tip sticking out with blood dripping down. She reached up, holding the injured arm. Behind her, where they had left him, was a Blade. He was standing, shakily, with bow in hand. He was reaching for another arrow. The wounded Blade.

Hall cursed. They had forgotten about him.

CHAPTER TWENTY-SEVEN

THE LULL CEASED.

Turning, the talkative Blade and the other ran to attack Pike. The dragonhawk was confused on which to attack and flew toward the closest. The man was prepared and got his dagger up, causing Pike to swerve out of the way.

Still shouting curses, Hall used *Leap* and sailed after the retreating Blades. They couldn't let them escape. He landed a couple steps behind the fleeing Blade and stabbed out with his spear.

One-handed, he couldn't get much strength behind the thrust, but it was added by his Class Ability's *Attack of Opportunity* as well as the undefended attack from behind. Gaining bonuses from both attacks, the thrust of the spear was enough to just catch the fleeing Cutthroat and pushed her forward, causing her to fall to the ground hard.

Hall dropped both his sword and spear, pulling a throwing knife from his bracer. Stopping, he threw the small blade and it spun through the air. It slammed into the shoulder of the Cutthroat, sparks of lightning erupting on impact. Bending down, Hall grabbed his spear on the move.

The female Cutthroat was trying to get up, and Hall stabbed down with the spear. He caught her in the side, and she fell back to the ground. He pulled out the spear and turned back to the other one. Pike had swooped down and attacked from behind.

Screeching, the dragonhawk let out a bolt of blue lightning. The blast struck the thief in the back, forcing him to the ground. Smoke rose from the wound as his body convulsed. Hall stepped forward and finished him off with the spear. He turned back to the female Cutthroat. She was on the ground, clutching at her bleeding side, not trying to get up.

SLAIN: *Silver Blade Cutthroat*
+25 Experience

Skill Gain!
Thrown Rank Two +.1

He turned around to see how the rest of the battle was going.

The Silver Blade Archer was down for the count most likely, as Jackoby had charged the already wounded man. The Firbolg stood over the body, hammer raised and ready to strike. The clash of metal on metal came from the other side of the building as Caryn and Roxhard were engaged with the last two Silver Blade Cutthroats.

Instead of trying to run, the two Blades had attacked them. *Which was odd*, Hall thought as he ran to assist them, commanding Pike to watch the wounded woman. Most thieves were cowards at heart and would abandon their Guildmates if it meant their survival, or even a chance of survival. Between the Hobs and these very loyal thieves, Hall was starting to think they had jumped in over their heads. This Cudgel didn't seem like a typical crime boss.

As he passed by, Hall glanced out the still open doors. There were no more Silver Blades, but the noises had started to attract attention from the citizens of Peakdock. Which wasn't good. Being identified by the people of the town was just as bad as letting one of the Blades escape. Eventually, the Cudgel would learn who they were.

He stopped and started to close the doors.

"Someone get the PeakGuard," a voice said from outside.

The doors slammed shut, and Hall looked for a plank to lay across them. He didn't think the PeakGuard would be quick to respond. They most likely knew the warehouse belonged to the Silver Blades and would assume it was a battle with the Door Knockers. But he was not going to take any chances.

They had to finish off the Blades and interrogate their prisoner. Somewhere else though. It was time to get away from the warehouse.

Hall leaned against the doors, taking a breath. He saw that the other two Cutthroats were down. Hopefully dead. He pushed off from the door, heading back to the female Blade. She was pushing herself across the floor, trying to get away. Pike was on the ground, watching her, squawking as she slowly made her way, a trail of blood behind her. She had gone maybe two or three feet when Hall stopped next to her.

"That looks like it hurts," he said.

She growled at him.

He stood up, looking back at the others who were looting the corpses.

"Anything?" he asked.

"Nothing major," Roxhard replied. "Some coins, that's about it."

Hall squatted back down.

"Do you have anything worthwhile?" he asked. "We have a healer," he added.

The woman paused, trying to take a deep breath. She

cursed, muttering as she grimaced in pain. More blood leaked out. Hall fought the urge to call Leigh over. They needed what this woman knew.

"We didn't make this our fight," he started. "We're forced into it, but we will see it through, and your side is on the wrong side as far as we're concerned. I really don't care which thieves Guild runs Silver Peak as long as neither goes crazy, which is what a Guild war will cause. Lots and lots of crazy. Lots of people dead for doing nothing because your boss, this Cudgel, doesn't like the Door Knockers." He paused and sighed. "Sounds pretty stupid really."

"What do you want?" she asked, forcing the words out.

"Information that will help end this war."

The woman relaxed or just gave up, Hall couldn't tell. He stood up and waved to Leigh. The Druid rushed over, took one look at the woman, and laid her hands on the Blade's shoulders. Leigh's tattoos started glowing blue, energy running down her arms and into the Blade. The Cutthroat did relax, breathing easier as the wounds closed up. Smartly, Leigh stopped the healing before too much was done. Just enough to make the woman comfortable, but not healed fully.

"The Silver Blades will win," the Cutthroat said and coughed. She spat a glob of blood onto the floor. Eyes fixed on it, she continued to talk. "The Cudgel will not give up. The time of the Door Knockers is over."

"Maybe," Hall said. "Remains to be seen. So, are you going to help us or not?"

The look the woman gave him was all the answer he needed.

———

They found the back door, the one the Blade's had been trying to get to, and left by it. Pike flew out and circled into the air, heading far out before coming back in to give Hall a view of the main doors. A small crowd had gathered, a dozen people or so, and he could see the sun reflecting off the armor of the PeakGuards that were taking their time getting there. Six of them.

Inside the warehouse, they'd find a lot of bodies and one woman tied up and gagged. It was a risk leaving her alive but Hall didn't think the Blades would try to rescue her. He had a feeling that the Hobs would be a distraction and might even push the PeakGuard to be more involved. Brient had mentioned nothing of them and having Hob mercenaries running loose in Silver Peak and Peakdock was not something the PeakGuard should stand for. They would have to do something.

Or so Hall thought and hoped.

But he wondered how far the corruption went. Brient blackmailed them into taking out the Silver Blades because the guards weren't and were essentially being told not to. That seemed to hint at a higher-up in the guards being aligned with the Blades.

None of it really mattered, he thought as they made their way through the alleys of Peakdock. They were still no further than they had been before the warehouse. They had some coins and some good experience but no leads.

"Where do we find Berim?" he asked Caryn sharply after he felt they were far enough away from the warehouse.

"We can head back to The Listing Deck and he'll find us," she replied.

"No," Hall said, an edge to his voice. "Where is he?"

Caryn didn't respond, hanging her head.

"In case you didn't notice, he just used us as fodder. Used you. Obviously didn't care if you lived or died as long as it thinned out the ranks of the Blades."

Hall tried to calm down. Like when he was letting the

female Blade suffer to get information, he thought he was being overly harsh on Caryn. He was just tired of being used and wanted to get ahead of everyone. Berim. Brient. The Cudgel. He had come to Silver Peak for training and supplies, a couple craftsmen to work on Skara Brae and maybe some citizens. He hadn't come to get involved in a Guild war. But here he was stuck in the middle of the war and neither side was going to make it easy on him.

He stared hard at Caryn. She kept her head lowered, feeling his gaze and finally sighed. She looked up at him, glancing at the others.

"You're right," she said. "I don't know why Berim sent us there. Maybe he did think you'd find what you needed to lead you to the Blades leadership. Or maybe he did just want you to thin out the numbers. Either way, he didn't care if we lived or died." She placed emphasis on the word 'we'.

"So, where is he?" Sabine asked.

———

Caryn led them through a maze of streets in a generally western direction. Not toward the docks like Hall had assumed, but more the outer edge of the city. The buildings were less congested the further away from the docks and the center they went. More space between them, wider streets. A better-looking neighborhood; at least for Peakdock, where better-looking was a relative term.

Hall couldn't see anyone, but he knew they were being watched. Had been since they had turned down this street. Homes lined both sides, wide paths between them. Two-story buildings, both made of wood, with wooden shingles. Solid oak doors and glass-filled windows on the first floor. Doors were all closed, most of the windows shuttered.

The sun was starting to set. Hall could see it through the

breaks in the buildings, just above the edge of Edin. He thought he had walked the whole of Peakdock in the last day or two.

He glanced at the buildings they passed, trying to see into the windows, between the buildings and the rooftops. Trying to find the people that were watching them. He sent his thoughts out to Pike, the dragonhawk circling above. Pike had a good view of the roofs, not seeing anyone hiding on them. That made Hall feel a little less paranoid.

The Duelist was leading them to the house at the end. Larger than the others with the second story overhanging the first a couple of feet. The roof was high, steep, with a railed walk on top. Widow's walks, Hall knew they were called. Or were on Earth, at least. Used for the sailor's wives to watch the ships coming into the harbor, waiting and hoping for their husbands to return. He had yet to see a building with one in Edin and tried to remember if he had seen any in other parts of the world. The house was far from the docks but the height would give it a decent view.

Caryn stopped at the unmarked door and raised her hand to knock. She hesitated and Hall reached past her to bang on the door. He stepped back and waited.

They heard footsteps behind the door, coming closer. The handle turned and the door opened. Ulysses stood there looking up at them.

"Took ya long enough," he said and stepped aside to let them in.

CHAPTER TWENTY-EIGHT

Ulysses led them up to the second floor.

The door opened into a large foyer, a hallway leading deeper into the house with a staircase to the side. Without another word, or even waiting for them, Ulysses started up the stairs.

Those opened into another hallway, and the short man led them to a door at the far end. Hall glanced around nervously, looking at the others. Roxhard and Leigh followed him. Caryn appeared nervous and afraid. Sabine was angry. Jackoby kept looking behind him, not anxious but not happy. Angus followed along behind the Firbolg, hooves clopping on the floorboards.

The door was open and Ulysses led them into a large office. Shelves lined the walls, filled with books of all kinds. Thin, thick, tall and short. Leather and metal spines. Some ornate, others plain. Other objects filled some shelves, between the books or entire shelves devoted to them. Knives on stands, gloves, globes, and things that Hall couldn't identify. On one wall hung a large painting, a couple of leather-backed chairs beneath it, a door to the side.

Vivid colors depicted an image of Silver Peak itself, the

mountain that gave the city its name. It glistened in the sun, shining like a beacon. An exaggeration as the real mountain was never that bright, but the artist had talent. A large window overlooked the backyard; Hall able to see the western plains and farmlands beyond Peakdock. A large desk, maple or some other similar wood, stood in front of the window, a high-backed chair behind it, and two similar chairs facing it. The desk was clear of everything. No quill pens, no ink jars, no books. Nothing.

But there was no dust. The room and desk got used. Hall stopped in front of it, a couple steps ahead of the others. Ulysses indicated he could take a chair and Hall ignored him. Glancing out the window, he saw the shadowed form of Pike circling through the air outside. That made him a little more comfortable.

He had again been knocked off balance. It seemed Berim was steps ahead of him. As was the Cudgel most likely. Hall was feeling out of his depth. He remembered a quest in the original game that was somewhat similar, but it had been pretty straight forward compared to what they were now caught up in.

Berim stood before the window, back to them. He pointed up at the dark speck that was Pike.

"Yours?" he asked as he turned around.

Hall ignored him.

The Arashi smiled and held out his hands, giving a brief nod.

"I take it that you're mad at me," he said.

Again, Hall ignored him. The others spread out through the room. Jackoby focused on the door behind them. Caryn stood in the middle, nervous, looking from one to the others as it was obvious they were preparing for a fight. Ulysses chuckled. The man appeared unarmed, so did Berim, but Hall did not expect them to be. They had weapons or easy access to them.

"I am in the same position as Sergeant Brient," Berim explained. "I cannot appear as weak to my people."

"Bull," Hall explained and Berim looked confused, not understanding the term, but Hall continued. Not caring. "You used us."

Berim nodded, understanding that.

"I did," he said with a shrug. "We had heard that the Cudgel had hired Hobs from Tarisk and needed to verify."

It was said matter-of-factly, as if Berim had ordered dinner.

"Without wasting any of your people," Hall said.

"Just so," Berim said with a nod. "My people are too valuable and you..." He paused and just shrugged again.

Hall kept his anger in check. Berim still wanted something from them, still needed them. Or else they wouldn't be in this room.

"What about me?" Caryn said, striding forward. As the Duelist moved, Ulysses did too and Hall rotated to block the small man.

Ulysses looked up at Hall with an angry look, the eyes telling Hall to move. Hall stared back, his eyes daring Ulysses to try. The small man glanced at Berim and backed down at a signal from the Arashi.

"You are not a Door Knocker," Berim replied, again in the flat tone. "Just an apprentice."

Caryn stood before the desk, hands hovering near her weapons. The small woman was angry. She stared at Berim. The man stared back.

"I could have been killed," she said, cutting each word short.

Berim nodded.

"Yes. And I would have missed you, but with this group..."

He waved his hand to indicate the others. "I did not see that happening."

Caryn seethed, the anger radiating off of her in waves. The room was silent, tense. Finally, Caryn backed down. She released the built-up tension in her body and stepped back. She stood between Leigh and Sabine, the Druid laying a comforting hand on the smaller woman's shoulder. Angus walked forward and butted Caryn's hand, the woman absently petting the cow.

Berim looked at her for a moment, his gaze softening before returning to look at Hall. The calm and emotionless facade came back, but Hall had seen the brief break.

"You don't have the strength do you," Hall said, things clicking into place.

The Guild leader, if Berim was truly that, did not have the people to go up against Hob mercenaries. That was why he needed Hall and the others.

Berim smiled, confirming Hall's guess. The thief said nothing, just the smile that quickly disappeared.

"I hate this city," Sabine muttered behind them.

"I recruited you for the same reason that Brient did," Berim said and Hall decided not to argue the point. They had come to Berim, he had not recruited them. "You are an unknown quantity to the Silver Blades. They know our strength but we do not know theirs. They know nothing about you."

The reasoning made sense to Hall, but he still did not like being used. By Berim and by Brient. He agreed with Sabine.

"The Blades spent months studying us," Ulysses said, speaking for the first time since greeting them at the door. The man did not seem bothered that a fight had almost broken out. "They learned everyt'ing bout us before they made ther move."

"Then why has it taken so long to destroy you?" Jackoby

said, his deep and rough voice drawing all attention. "If they have superior strength and know all your capabilities, they should have destroyed you instantly."

Berim nodded to acknowledge the point. He started to say something and stopped. He glanced at Ulysses and gave a small nod. Berim seemed to shrink, the confidence gone, and he looked tired.

"We don't know," he finally answered. "What you say is true. The Silver Blades could have wiped us out in a couple nights. A week at the most. But they haven't."

"The Cudgel seems intent on findin' somet'ing," Ulysses says.

"Something you have," Hall reasoned.

"No," Berim replied and Hall sensed the man was telling the truth. At this point, there was no need to lie or hide anything. "Not something we have but something they think we have."

The thief walked out from behind the desk, motioning Hall to follow him.

"Come with me," he said. "Ulysses will bring your friends downstairs where food is being prepared. We will join them there, but I need to show you something."

Hall started to follow but paused. He looked at the thief, Ulysses, and his friends. Sabine appeared even angrier, probably at being excluded. Caryn had calmed down, eyes not focused on anything and lost in thought. Jackoby studied Ulysses, deciding on his first target if needing to attack. Roxhard appeared as he always did, ready to follow Hall's lead. Leigh looked at him nervously, worried, but she smiled.

Berim waited at the thin door next to the painting.

Saying a quiet curse, Hall moved to the door and the thief.

———

The door opened into a thin hallway with a steep set of stairs. Hall had to duck to get by the low ceiling with his spear and javelin jutting out over his shoulder. Berim moved easily up the dark stairwell, Hall grumbling behind. They climbed a dozen steps or so when Berim stopped and pushed up with his arms.

Hall saw a thin crack of fading sunlight and then more as the trap door was pushed fully open. Berim walked out and Hall followed. They stood on the widow's walk, the city of Peakdock spread out around them.

"This isn't your house, is it?" Hall said.

Berim laughed.

"It actually is," he replied. "I own it. Under a different name of course."

Smoke rose from the chimneys of Peakdock. The docks were still busy, but the rest of the streets had thinned out as people headed home for their dinners. Pike squawked and landed near Hall, taloned feet grasping the thin railing that surrounded the flat walk. Berim paid no attention to the dragonhawk.

"This home used to belong to a former constable," Berim said as he looked out in the direction of the docks. "He would come up here every night to survey the docks. To survey his domain."

"And you do the same?" Hall asked. Instead of looking toward the dock, he turned to look out at the mountain. He felt safe enough up here. If Berim wanted him dead, up on the walk would be wasted effort. It would have been easier in the stairwell or below in the office. Or even in the street outside.

Silver Peak was immense, towering over the city and surrounding countryside. The strange rock of the mountain seemed to glow in the evening sun. Not hard to look at, but the mountain had a shine to it. It was breathtaking.

"I come up here to look at the mountain," Berim replied, coming to stand next to Hall. "No matter how powerful or strong I think I am, just looking at the mountain reminds me that I am not that powerful or strong. It keeps me humble."

Hall chuckled. Humble was not something he would ever think Berim could be.

"What are the Silver Blades looking for?" Hall prompted.

"To be honest, I'm not really sure," Berim admitted, not looking back at Hall. He kept his gaze focused on the mountain. "When they attack our safehouses, the Blades ransack them. They leave most of the gold and jewels, magic items, and so on."

"They're taking your territory so they don't need the spoils as they'll get it all going forward," Hall reasoned.

Berim shook his head.

"Only some of our territory," the thief said. "They are trying to eliminate us but only working in some of the territory. It's odd," he admitted. "I can't figure out why."

"Do you have any idea who the Cudgel is?" Hall asked.

He followed Berim's gaze toward the mountain. Silver Peak was spectacular. A unique sight. Lots of bright points of light surrounded by the gray of rock. Steep sides leading to a point high above, the tip breaking into the clouds. He could see shadows circling the peak, Shrikes in flight.

"No, but I suspect it's a merchant or a noble. I think it's someone that we," he paused and smiled, "wronged."

Hall just shook his head. This was getting him nowhere.

"What did you have to show me?"

At the base of the mountain, on the plateau, were the walls of Silver Peak Keep. The walk was not high enough to see over the walls, but Hall could see the small figures that were the guards on patrol. The road between Peakdock and the plateau was empty, all traffic ending with the oncoming evening.

"That," Berim said and pointed at a spot to the west of the road.

Hall saw farmland, fields bordered by stone walls and

wooden fence. Fields of food, not pastures for livestock. A small river flowed through the fields, passing by a mill building. There were other buildings in a cluster. A barn, a two-story home, the mill, a windmill in the fields and other smaller ones. A decent-sized forest was to the east of the river bordering the farmland. The water wheel turned as the force of the river pushed against it.

Leaning forward, Hall couldn't make anything out. He thought he saw the movement of people, but it was hard to tell in the fading light. He glanced up and spotted Pike. The dragonhawk flew down through Peakdock and out over the fields to the farm. Berim watched the bird go.

Hall focused and saw through Pike's eyes. The fields streaked by, the stalks of grain blowing in a breeze. Even though Pike was flying fast, everything was still detailed. Nothing was a blur. He flew over the buildings, and now Hall could see the people.

Some were dressed as he expected farmers to be. Wool pants and shirts. Leatherwork vests. Boots. They carried tools, moving from field to building, building to field, or building to building. Doing whatever their chores were. It was the ones just inside the doorways that had Hall's attention. Dressed in all black, weapons catching the setting sun.

Silver Blades.

Closing his eyes, he canceled the connection to Pike and looked at Berim.

"Every third night, a small boat comes down the river," the thief said. "The cargo changes. Sometimes it's people, sometimes it's crates of something. But there is always a boat."

Hall glanced at the sun and back to the farm.

"And tonight is the third night."

Berim smiled but Hall didn't catch it. He was studying the farm and the outbuildings, memorizing the layout and planning how to assault the place.

He stepped back from the railing and looked at Berim. The thief was all confidence and ego, sure he was pushing Hall where Berim wanted him to go.

"What does that," Hall began and gestured to the farm, "have to do with what the Silver Blades are looking for?"

Berim's ever-present smile faltered. Just for a second and he regained his composure.

"The farm?" Berim asked instead of answering, which told Hall the thief was trying to think of the best way to respond. It was clear that Berim did not want to answer, most likely because he did not know and did not want to show weakness, but he finally did. "Possibly nothing. Possibly everything."

Not an answer but Hall knew it was the best he would get.

For now.

He looked at the farm once more. Attacking the farm was again doing what Berim wanted, playing into the thief's plans. But it also would satisfy the requirements of the quest from Brient. It would give them the next step to complete the chain.

Which could even bring more information from Berim.

"After we take the farm," Hall began, turning once more to Berim and fixing the thief with an intent and serious look. "You will tell us everything you know."

Berim, still smiling, nodded.

Hall sighed. He sent Pike circling through the air, instructing the dragonhawk to make a couple of high passes over the farm. Ignoring the thief, Hall walked down the stairs to find the others.

———

They were in a long dining room, a space that ran the full length of the building. It was set in the rear, at the end of the corridor off the entrance. Large windows and glass doors opened onto a garden in the back. A tall wooden slat fence surrounding the well-maintained space.

Hall barely gave the garden a glance. He focused on the rest of the room. The table was long, seating for twelve, made of a dark wood. Thick and heavy-looking, lightly carved and adorned. Paintings and tapestries covered the walls, a single door in the corner to the kitchens, presumably.

Ulysses sat at the head of the table, leaning back in a chair, his leather booted feet on the table. The others were all clustered at the other end, plates of food in front of them. All looked up as Hall and Berim entered.

He quickly filled them in on the farm.

"Awfully convenient," Sabine said with a glare at Berim, who took a seat next to Caryn.

The Duelist gave the thief a dark glare, returning to her food and obviously ignoring him.

"Sends us after a warehouse full of his enemy, and once we eliminate that for him, he now has another target that just happens to fulfill one of the tasks Sergeant Brient gave us," Sabine added, angry.

Berim shrugged, pulling a plate over and piling it high with food. There were steaks of what Hall thought to be venison, ears of corn, potatoes, and cabbage. Mugs of ale and wine were in front of each, two in front of Ulysses. A tall and thin man, older with a balding head of gray hair, came out of the door to the kitchen. He had two more mugs in his hands.

The thief didn't reply to Sabine. He just grabbed a mug from the server and took a drink.

Hall sat down next to Leigh, taking a drink from the mug the older man set down.

"We head out in an hour," he said. He looked at Ulysses. "And you're coming with us."

The small man chuckled, thinking Hall was joking. Realizing Hall wasn't, Ulysses stopped laughing and leaned forward, feet slamming hard to the floor.

"Hells I'm not," he growled. "Ya on yer own."

"And five of your thugs," Hall continued, looking at Berim, ignoring Ulysses.

Sabine smiled. Roxhard kept eating, not sensing the tension in the room.

Berim lowered his mug, fingers tapping on the table. He glanced down its length at the fuming Ulysses and back to Hall. The thief didn't respond.

Smiling, Hall stood up.

"Okay," he said and motioned to the others. Leigh had to tap Roxhard to get the Dwarf to pay attention. "We're leaving."

"Enjoy ta farm," Ulysses said with a laugh.

"Leaving Silver Peak Keep," Hall added.

CHAPTER TWENTY-NINE

HALL CROUCHED AT THE RIVER'S EDGE, LOOKING DOWN AT THE water. It rushed past the rocks, white caps as it slammed against the stone. It looked cold. Clear and clean, but cold. At this point, a mile south of the mill's waterwheel, the river was only about twenty feet wide. Not that deep, but enough that a flat-bottomed boat could sail by. It thinned past the farm before it turned north, passing around the plateau, out into the plains and away from the city. Called the Silver Plains River, it ran into the plains for ten miles or so before turning back to the mountains and their heights, crossing the Silver Peak road as it came from Auld, disappearing across the plains.

He had remembered traveling across the bridge that spanned it only three miles or so north of where they currently were. He had seen the farm from the road as they had walked down the Silver Peak Road. Just a farm, that's all it had been then.

Now it was his target.

Pike had flown over the farm a couple of times and Hall had seen each one. The Silver Blades were staying undercover, a lot of activity centered near the larger barn which was closest to the river. A small dock lay alongside the banks, no boat currently tied up. A dozen workers moved about the fields and the grounds. There was no sign of a boat.

Not yet.

They were too far away to make out details, not even able to see the workers, but Hall was reluctant to head closer. Across the river on the east side, Ulysses and five Door Knockers were waiting for Hall's signal.

The small man had grumbled and growled the whole time after they had left Berim's house and gotten to the riverbank. But once there, he had settled down. A professional, Hall knew Ulysses would do his job. Which was a simple one. Distract the workers and as many Silver Blades as he could.

Hall and his friends had the more difficult task. Capture a Silver Blade as well as whatever cargo they were smuggling. Capture the cargo or destroy it. Berim was fine either way. The quest wasn't specific. It just said to disrupt a Silver Blades operation. Destroying the cargo would definitely do that.

Standing up, Hall waved his spear in the air. Across the river, he saw movement. The small form of Ulysses, agile and swift despite the man's stocky size, ran across the open fields. Five dark forms followed, dressed all in black. *Is all-black a thief's standard outfit?* Hall thought, hoping they would not get into the middle of the fight. There was no way they would be able to tell who was who in the chaos of combat.

Once Ulysses was far enough away, Hall started walking slowly forward. The others spread out behind him, a long line. Even Caryn, who had refused to go with Ulysses and the Door Knockers. She was pretty adamant about no longer associating with Berim and his Guild.

Even moving as slowly as they were, they covered the distance quickly. Hall had them stop a hundred yards away from the barn. They were crouched low, short plants of something Hall didn't recognize growing around them. It provided little in the way of physical cover but with night approaching it would work.

Skill Gain!
Camouflage Rank One +.1

Hall almost chuckled. He had forgotten he had the Skill. It was not high, not even a full point yet. But every little bit helped.

Farmers, or those that posed as farmers, walked out of the barn. Hall was starting to suspect it was for show. They didn't move like farmers but like soldiers.

Skill Gain!
Identify Rank One +.1
Durnpoole Farmhand (White)

The skill was no help except for the level. True farm-workers would be Level One or Two, most likely. They would show as gray to the skill. White would seem to indicate they were not simply farmers.

One of them, a man carrying a large scythe over his shoulder, stopped at the open doors to the barn. He began talking, facing away so Hall could not hear. It looked like he was conversing with someone inside. The farmer walked away and a black-clad figure stepped out. Pointing upriver, the farmer indicated something which Hall assumed meant the boat was coming. The black-clad figure said something else, returning to the barn.

Skill Gain!
Identify Rank One +.1
Silver Blade Cutthroat (White)

Hall shifted, getting more comfortable.

The sunset cast a reddish glow over the evening. Hall could see a spot of white coming down the river. A sail. One single mast. It was almost time.

Standing in a half-crouch, the others getting up as well, Hall started the slow crawl to the barn.

———

From high up where he circled, enjoying the last of the sun's rays against his wings, Pike saw it all. His sharp eyes picked up the riverboat, a flat-bottomed craft that was long and skinny with a single sail on a short mast, as it drifted down the river. A single man stood at the rail, hand on the tiller. Crates and boxes filled the open boat.

Pike didn't know what any of it was called. He just saw the objects and the Man he was bonded with, his rescuer, named them. The names were important to the Man. Pike did not care. All he wanted was to fly and hunt.

Two of the enemy, the ones that the Man wanted him to track, were on the wooden platform that stuck out in the river. These were dressed in wool clothing, carrying no weapons. The ones with the metal talons were in the buildings, waiting. Pike had spotted four of them in the largest building and three others in a smaller one. There were another dozen of the ones not in black. These were scattered around. Most were gathered at the edges of the fields, near the long strip of dirt the Man called a road.

The boat, as it had been named, bumped into the wooden platform. Ropes were tossed to the men waiting, who tied it off. The first of the men took a step onto the boat, and Pike screeched.

Just as he had been told by the Man.

Hall watched the sail getting closer. From his angle, he couldn't see the water, the boat, or the dock. Wooden steps led from the higher elevation of the farm to the lower river and dock. All he could see was the top of the sail. He knew two of the fake farmers had gone down.

He heard the screech of Pike circling high above.

The signal.

He stood up a little, staying low but enough to see the other side of the river.

Ulysses and the five Door Knockers stood up, crossbows in hand. They took aim and fired. The *thwacking* sound of the crossbows filled the silent night. As did the screams of the men on the dock. They echoed through the night.

And drew the black-clad Silver Blades out of the barn.

Hall was fifty feet away and stood up fully. He activated *Leap* and jumped into the air. His energy bar dropped as he landed, closer, and activated the ability again. He landed in the middle of the four black-clad Blades. The spear struck out, stabbing one in the back. Hall received the bonus from a rear flanking attack as well as a critical strike increase. The Blade jerked, falling to the ground.

Pulling the spear back, Hall swept it around his body. The three other Blades jumped back, drawing their weapons, as Hall used *Leap* again. He jumped back as more crossbow bolts flew across the river. Two of the Blades went down, leaving one alive.

The man looked from Hall to across the river, lost and confused. He couldn't figure out which way to run and which way the attack was coming from, so he just froze in place. He completely missed the streaking form of Pike. The dragonhawk came screeching out of the air, talons racking across the man's back. He screamed and pain. A small throwing knife slammed into his chest, lightning cracking at the impact. Staggering, the man fell to the ground.

SLAIN: *Silver Blade Cutthroat*

+25 Experience

SLAIN: *Silver Blade Cutthroat*

+25 Experience

Hall heard the sounds of others as they came running. Three more black-clad Blades coming out of the farmhouse, three fake farmers behind them. There were more shouts from the fields as the fake farmers reacted to the fighting. They hopped over stone walls, and Hall hoped the wooden fences that lined the fields would delay them. He glanced across the river to see the Door Knockers reloading their crossbows.

One of them fell, dropping his bow, as an arrow slammed into his shoulders. Surprised, Ulysses turned around to see a half dozen green-clad men come running out of the trees just beyond. One of them carried a bow, stopping to nock another arrow.

Skill Gain!

Identify Rank One +.1

Silver Blade Forester (White)

More noise drew Hall's attention back to the buildings as his friends ran forward to engage the enemy. Both Jackoby and Roxhard had activated their *Battle Rush* abilities. The two Wardens raced forward through the field and across the yard. Each slammed into a Silver Blade Cutthroat, the smaller and lighter men going flying. Hall focused on the new noises and saw more forms come running out of the barn.

Two Hobs.

Cursing, Hall activated *Leap* and landed between the two large Hobs.

He struck out with his spear, stabbing the right one in the side. The Hob staggered, pushed by the force of the thrust. Its leather armor and tough hide stopped most of the damage, but Hall saw the health bar drop a little.

Holding the spear, he slid it to the side, his left. The butt end slammed into the stomach of the second Hob that had just started to turn. It grunted and gave Hall time to step back out of their reach. He stabbed out with the spear, two thrusts, one to each Hob.

Caryn ran by him, a blade slicing out at one of the Hobs as she passed to intercept the fake farmers. She drew a thin line across the creature's side. It growled in pain and turned to attack her, but the quick Duelist was already past. It did leave his side exposed to Hall, and he received a spear stab in his shoulder. Hall's *Breakridge Ironwood Spear's* special ability activated, and he saw wood chips erupt from the tip of the spear, lodging in the Hob's shoulder.

Splinter!

Your attack causes a shard of wood to lodge in the enemy's wound, causing 3 damage every second for 15 seconds.

Hall saw an icon appear next to the Hob's Health bar. It was weird, he thought as he used the spear to deflect attacks from the other Hob. The creature's sword hit the wood, the Hob expecting to chop the spear in half, but the ironwood was as strong as steel. Hall was seeing more and more game elements appear in this new world, like he was adapting to it. The longer he was there, the more like the original game it appeared. There were still many things that were different, but the game elements seemed to come and go. At first, he had seen Guild names and such above the characters and NPCs, but those had faded, and he had to use the *Identify* skill. Now, icons were starting to appear and he could not remember seeing them before.

It was confusing, like the world itself wasn't sure where it was going.

He grunted, forcing himself back to the fight, as the Hob's curved sword slipped past his defenses and almost scored a hit. Hall twisted out of the way, taking a step back as the other Hob rejoined the fight.

Purple energy streaked past Hall, coming from both sides, and struck the two Hobs. Lightning crackled around their bodies as the *Hexbolt* took hold. They both tried to move, tried to attack, but the energy tightened and flared. The Hobs grunted in pain.

Hall took a step back and grabbed his spear with both hands. He aimed at the already wounded Hob and slammed the spear forward, right at the creature's unprotected neck. The sharp ironwood tip cut through the scaled hide. Greenish blood splashed out as the creature jerked and spasmed. Hall kicked out with his foot, pushing the dead Hob off the spear. Blood still dripping from the tip, he reversed his grip and stabbed out at the second Hob.

Still wrapped by the crackling purple energy, the Hob stepped back, stumbling but remaining upright. It growled at Hall and didn't see the *Splinter Storm* from Leigh. The shards of inch long wood sliced into the Hob. Most were deflected by the armor or the Hob's own scaly hide, but enough penetrated and got stuck. Drops of blood dripped down to the ground as the Hob staggered. It roared in pain, trying to move but unable because of the *Hexbolt*. It stared at Hall with hatred as a spear thrust took its life.

SLAIN: *Silver Blade Hob Enforcer*

+25 Experience

SLAIN: *Silver Blade Hob Enforcer*
+15 Experience

Skill Gain!
Polearms Rank Two +.2

Hall looked out across the battlefield, trying to decide where he needed to be.

Between the farmhouse and the barn, in the wide-open yard, Jackoby and Roxhard had finished off their first opponents and moved on to the next. Caryn was facing off against one of the fake farmers, while Leigh and Sabine shot out with spells when they could. Bodies lay across the ground. None of his people looked wounded. Angus kept a protective watch around Leigh and Sabine, the cow's eyes on the people rushing from the field.

They were getting closer, working their way through the fields, about a dozen of them. They were armed with scythes and shovels. Real farmers? It didn't matter. They were coming to attack and they'd be dealt with as if they were Silver Blades. Leigh and Sabine were already starting to fire spells off at them, Sabine mostly using her wand to conserve Energy. With a thought, Hall sent Pike to attack and harass the farmers.

He turned his attention to across the river. Ulysses and his Door Knockers were engaged with the Silver Blade Foresters. It was a pretty even fight, and Hall wondered if he should jump across the river to aid the Door Knockers. Ulysses killed the Blade he was fighting and double-teamed another. Hall stayed where he was. That fight would be over soon.

Stepping closer to Leigh and Sabine, Hall turned to face the farmers running in from the fields. There were a lot of them. Pike was dive-bombing them. The dragonhawk's talons ripped across the shoulders of one, his lightning breath attacking another. They stopped, swatting at him with their shovels, but Pike just flew out of range.

About to activate *Leap*, he stopped as he heard some new sound coming from the barn. He watched as a huge form rushed out of the building. It had to bend to step out of the wide and high door, stretching up to its full height.

It was about fifteen feet tall, dark skin the color of dirt, long and knotted green hair and beard, small dark eyes almost hidden by a thick forehead. Arms were as wide as both Hall's legs, as long as his body. Thick legs like tree trunks. It wore rough hides, pieces stitched together that covered its chest and legs only, and in its hand, it held a solid-looking club.

A forest giant.

CHAPTER THIRTY

WHERE DID THAT THING COME FROM? HALL THOUGHT AS HE cursed.

Skill Gain!
Identify Rank One +.1

Oak Crag Hold Giant (Purple)

All fighting stopped as the giant stepped into the yard. It roared, raising its arms up and smashing the club down into the ground. The earth shook with the impact, everyone in the yard knocked off balance. The Silver Blades took the chance and backed off, the few that were still alive. Jackoby and Roxhard turned to face the giant, spreading out and putting more space between them.

Hall looked from the giant to the farmers, along with the few Blades left.

They were badly outnumbered, and it would take time for the Door Knockers to cross the river. If they even did. There was no running. The giant would catch them. The fields were open and the Blades would give chase. They had to stand and fight.

"Hit the giant, then concentrate on the farmers," Hall yelled to the spellcasters.

He hoped they heard. The giant was still roaring, the sound incredibly loud and deafening.

Shards of splinters shot out, quickly covering the distance. They slammed into the giant's shoulder. There was barely a drop in the Health of the massive creature. It didn't even turn to look. A black shaft of energy hit the giant, splashing against its body. More Health dropped and the creature did turn. It wasn't hurt, just annoyed. Sabine followed up the *Shadow Bolt* with *Hexbolt*. Purple energy spread across the giant's body but didn't seem to slow it.

Pike swooped in, blasting the giant with lightning. The dragonhawk didn't try to slash the giant. The hide would have been too tough for Pike's talons, and he didn't want to get close enough for the surprisingly fast giant to grab him.

Activating *Leap*, Hall jumped into the air.

He had fought giants before, thinking back to the last raid with his original Guild before the Glitch when they had been fighting the frost giants, called Jotunn. Giants were big, strong, and fast. But their size could work against them. Get inside their reach and they were pretty helpless. But Hall had another favorite tactic.

Landing on the giant's massive shoulder, Hall grabbed a lock of green hair. Fighting to keep his balance as the giant moved, Hall stabbed sideways with his spear. The weapon's tip struck the giant just above the eye, the creature roaring in pain. The *Splinter* effect was activated and a small shard lodged in the wound. A decent chunk of Health dropped away.

Hall leapt off the shoulder before the giant's large hand could grab him. Its free hand cupped the side of its face as the unwounded eye angrily searched the yard for the one that had attacked it. Spotting Hall, the giant tried to move to attack but roared in pain as an axe sliced into one of its legs and a hammer slammed into the other.

Hall knew they had to take the giant out quickly. Very quickly. The other Blades would react and reinforce the massive creature. And they had to take out the giant and the Blades before the farmers arrived. Those numbers would just be too great.

Jackoby spun quickly, intercepting an attacking Blade. Roxhard was slower. The other Blade's dagger sliced down the Dwarf's side, causing him to stumble and fall as he tried to swing his axe. The wild swipe pushed the Blade away but left Roxhard vulnerable.

The giant saw him down on the ground and raised a massive foot.

"Rox," Hall shouted. He went to activate *Leap* knowing it would be too late.

The massive foot slammed down but stopped. Jackoby had caught the foot, not strong enough to stop it, but enough to slow the giant down. Roxhard struggled to move out of the way. Hall leapt into the air, not trying to land on the giant's shoulder but landing right in front of the creature. He could see Roxhard just get out of the shadow caused by the foot, the veins in Jackoby's lightly furred arms standing out as the Firbolg struggled to hold up the foot. The giant was leaning forward, pushing with more force. Hall took it all in quickly, deciding on the best use of his *Attack of Opportunity*.

He stabbed up with his spear, the ironwood tip catching the giant where leg met waist. The creature roared in pain, trying to stop its momentum and get away from the spear. It leaned backward and Jackoby lifted the foot. The giant stumbled. Hall bent down and grabbed Roxhard, helping the Dwarf to get out of the way.

Stabbing out with the spear, he pushed the two Silver

Blades away. Neither saw Caryn behind them. Her two swords dripping blood, she slashed across the back of both Blades. They grunted in pain, trying to turn but too slow. Caryn caught one, a blade through the stomach, while Jackoby's hammer found the head of the other.

Hall pushed Roxhard toward Caryn and turned to face the giant. It had regained its footing, blood dripping down its leg to the ground. The creature was enraged, one eye closed and covered in blood as it looked for Hall. The good eye focused on the Skirmisher, seeing the hated spear. The giant got a step and stopped as Pike hovered in front of its face.

With a screech, Pike let out a bolt of lightning into the forest giant's face.

The giant roared as smoke drifted up into the sky. Its bark-like skin was blackened, blistering. Crossbow bolts slammed into its chest, fired from across the river. Caryn darted in, twin blades slicing across the back of one leg. The giant, one hand holding its face, tried to lift its leg, but Jackoby's hammer slammed into the knee. Already weakened because of Caryn's cut and with the knee shattering, the giant fell backward and into the barn.

Wood splintered and cracked, a terrible sound as the massive giant fell against the structure. The posts and beams held, supporting the giant. Hall leapt into the air, the giant close enough that he could use *Leaping Stab*. He landed on the creature's shoulder and stabbed out with the spear. The tip slammed into the giant's good eye with a squishing and popping sound. The giant tried to cry out but couldn't as the tip found the creature's brain.

It fell silent and lay still.

SLAIN: *Oak Crag Hold Giant*
+100 Experience

Skill Gain!
Polearms Rank Two +.2

Congratulations!
You have achieved Polearms Rank Two, Skill Level 15. You have gained +100 Experience and +1 to Agility.

Hall barely paid the notifications any attention. He landed on the ground, staring at the battlefield. There were no more Silver Blades or Farmers left, and he could see Ulysses and two Door Knockers, the only survivors, looking for a way to cross the river. He glanced at Roxhard, seeing the Dwarf standing, thanking Jackoby. The Firbolg just grunted. Caryn was breathing hard but held her blades ready, eyes darting around. He leaned against his spear, using it to hold himself up. His Energy bar was pretty depleted and he saw it rising slowly.

Where had the giant come from? he wondered. *And how did the Silver Blades hide the thing in the barn?* He looked up at it, the head drooping.

Sounds from around the side of the barn pulled his attention back to the fight. He had almost forgotten about the farmers. Leigh and Sabine were busy throwing spell after spell, trying to keep the Blades reinforcements from arriving.

Grabbing the spear, taking a deep breath, Hall ran toward the fighting. He heard the others behind him. Turning the corner, he saw Angus charging around the walls, which meant the farmers were close.

Four men, waiting for a gap in the casting, jumped a low stone wall. They charged forward, smart enough to spread out. Both of the casters stepped backward, gripping their staffs, waiting for their Energy to recharge. Angus intercepted one, the small cow's horns goring the farmer in the chest, the force of the impact sending the man flying to crash into the stone wall.

Hall's *Leap* landed him just behind another farmer. Spinning, he stabbed out with the spear and caught the unarmored farmer in the back. The tip burst through and the man stopped running. The remaining two didn't see what happened to their comrades; they just kept charging to attack Leigh and Sabine. Only to be blocked by Jackoby and Caryn.

The fighting didn't last long.

SLAIN: *Durnpoole Farmhand*
+10 Experience

Skill Gain!
Polearms Rank Two +.1

"Is that all of them?" he asked, quickly looking around the fields.

"I think so," Leigh said, leaning on her staff.

"That was fun," Sabine growled, also using her staff for support.

The women looked tired and drained. They hadn't gotten into a physical fight, but that much magic use was still tiring. Which was also something new to this version of the game. Before, no matter how many times a caster drained their Energy pool, they weren't physically tired. Both Leigh and Sabine looked like they could sleep for three days.

Hall knew how they felt. He hadn't been wounded in the fighting, but all that jumping around and combat had taken a toll. He just wanted to lay down and sleep. But they weren't at that point yet. There was still business to deal with.

He walked back around to the front of the barn. The giant's body had slipped a little lower, deep furrows in the ground where its weight had caused its feet to slip and dig up the ground. Hall ignored that body as well as the others and headed to the dock.

Taking the steps down, holding onto the railing, he carefully stepped over the bodies. He could hear Ulysses and the Door Knockers splashing through the river, finding a place to ford. Ignoring them, he stepped onto the small riverboat. Flat-bottomed, a rudder, and single sail, it was not large. Four crates were set into the empty hull. Four feet square, two or three feet high, made of dark wood slats nailed together.

That seems like a pretty small haul to have this much protection, Hall thought as he set his spear down within easy reach. He pulled out his dagger and used the blade to pry the cover off a crate. He tossed it onto the dock and looked inside.

THE NEW BLOOD I
Disrupt a Silver Blades Operation 1/1
Question a Silver Blades Guildmember 0/1

PART THREE
THE CUDGEL

CHAPTER THIRTY-ONE

"W<small>HAT THE CRAP</small>?" H<small>ALL SAID OUT LOUD AS HE LOOKED AT</small> the contents in the crate.

It was not what he had been expecting.

Gold, jewels, weapons, illegal goods like wine or hides. Paintings even. But what he was seeing was a crate full of ledger books. Dozens of them. Leather bound, finely crafted with gold thread stitching. He picked one up and looked it over, opening it to find empty pages.

Setting the book back in the crate, which wasn't even full, he quickly opened the other three. Those held things he had assumed would be in the crates. One was filled with bottles of wine, neatly packed with hay for protection. He didn't bother looking to see where the bottles were from. The third and fourth were piled full of hides. Dire Wolf, Crag Cat, Kiot, Alcest and others.

"Well, ain't that interesting," Ulysses said from the dock.

The small man was dripping wet, leaving a puddle at his feet. He glanced at the first crate, barely sparing the others a glance.

"What's the point of those?" Hall asked.

"Ain't got a clue," Ulysses replied with a shrug. "Ya leave one alive to ask?"

Stepping out of the boat, the small Door Knocker following, Hall walked back into the yard. The others had moved the bodies and searched them, collecting the gear in a neat pile off to the side. Roxhard was pulling himself up the giant's body, reaching for a pouch attached to the large creature's belt. It looked like Leigh had healed him. The Dwarf was moving a little stiffly but was moving. Off to the side, Leigh crouched near a black-clad figure, Caryn and Jackoby standing over them with weapons ready.

"Looks like we did," Hall said to Ulysses and quickly walked over.

Leigh looked up at him and smiled.

"He's stable," she said, stepping away.

Skill Gain!
Identify Rank One +.1
Silver Blade Cutthroat (White)

The Silver Blade was maskless. He was still dressed in his black clothing but the mask had been thrown aside. The sleeves and cloth shirt were ripped to shreds, dried blood across his chest. One hand clutched at the wound, the other holding him up. He had a blank look on his face. Black hair, blue eyes, he looked young.

Hall crouched down in front of the Silver Blade, who didn't notice. He did notice Hall snapping fingers in front of his face. Eyes focused on Hall. There was anger there, but fear as well.

"What's your name?" Hall asked.

The Blade ignored him.

With a sigh, Hall moved to the side and pointed at the giant. The fear in the Blade's eyes grew, the anger running away.

"Yeah," Hall said looking at the giant. "Wasn't that hard. We barely worked up a sweat. Same with the Hobs. That's what? Five or six of them we've taken out?"

Hall didn't wait for an answer, just leaned in closer to the Silver Blade. He needed the Blade to be afraid of him, of them. That was the only way they'd get any information from the prisoner.

"Easy kills," Hall continued with a shrug. "We had been told that you Silver Blades were formidable. Haven't seen that yet. But it is interesting that you have Hobs working for you, let alone that guy," he said with a wave to the giant. "Where'd you find him?"

The Silver Blade looked at the corpse of the giant, licking his lips nervously in thought. He shifted his position and winced as pain cut across his chest. He still refused to talk.

Hall stared at him for a minute, waiting. The Blade looked past him, not at the giant, but out toward the forest. With a shrug, Hall stood up, the motion causing the Blade to look at him.

"Well if you won't talk, we'll just keep going until we find one of you that does," Hall said. "But that means we don't need you anymore."

He raised his spear in both hands, tip aimed at the Blade. It took a moment for the young man to realize what Hall meant, and his eyes widened in fear at the sight of the iron-wood tip.

"You can't," he said, barely getting the words out.

"If we don't, the Door Knockers will," Hall said without lowering the spear. "And they won't be quick. We're doing you a favor."

He started to lower the spear and both of the Blade's arms reached up, the young man turning his head away from the tip.

"Wait," he said quickly, spitting the word out. "I'll talk."

Hall didn't lower the spear, holding the tip a foot away

from the Blade. The man turned back to look at it, eyes hopeful. Hall stared at him down the length of the shaft.

"So, start talking," he said.

———

"I was recruited out of Land's Edge Port," the young Blade said. He looked down at the ground, not making eye contact with any of them.

Ulysses had sent the remaining Door Knockers to watch the fields while the rest listened to the Silver Blades story. Hall wanted to search the barn and the farmhouse, but they had the kid talking and needed to keep him talking.

"They gots a long reach," Ulysses muttered, not happily.

It did worry Hall as well. If the Silver Blades reached as far as Land's Edge Port, just how far was their influence? It extended beyond Silver Peak Keep, which was very worrying.

"At first, it was just helping with some smuggling. Offloading in the southern mountains, carrying it north, that kind of thing."

Hall exchanged glances with Leigh and Roxhard. Could the smugglers they had killed in the forest outside River's Side have been Silver Blades?

"Moved me here not that long ago..." the Blade said and trailed off.

"And?" Hall prompted.

"What?" the kid asked. "I don't know anything."

Ulysses stepped forward, sword in hand. The small man had a hard look on his face, a glint in his eye that scared the Silver Blade when he looked up. The captive could feel Ulysses stare, the power and rage of it. The Blade held up his hands.

"Where did the giant come from?" Hall asked, pushing his hand out in front of Ulysses. The thief glared at Hall but didn't move forward. The bad cop to Hall's good cop. *Did they even know what that was on Hankarth?* he mused.

The Silver Blade pointed toward the forest across the river.

"Further south past Durnpoole Wood," he said, gesturing vaguely in that direction. "They snuck him up here a couple days ago for muscle."

"How is it that a thieves Guild can hire Hobs and Giants?" Sabine asked.

"I don't know," the kid answered. "That's the Cudgel's doing."

Hall leaned forward, searching the kid's face.

"Have you ever met the Cudgel?"

"No," the kid said a little too quickly.

Hall lifted the spear from where he had set it down, bringing the tip in close to the kid's face. He didn't say a word, the intent clear. The Blade looked at the spear, glancing around at the others. Leigh and Roxhard turned away, not comfortable, but the hardened looks from everyone else convinced the kid.

"I've seen him but I don't know who he is," the kid said. "He wears a mask. He's rich, though. A noble, I think."

"How du ya know that?" Ulysses asked.

The Silver Blade chuckled and stopped at the glares from the people watching him.

"Nobles, they talk different," the kid said. "Walk different, wear clothes different. The Cudgel didn't wear any of that fancy finery that nobles do. He wore black like we all do, but you could tell it was uncomfortable on him. Not his normal clothes. And the way he talked. All proper like. He's a noble."

There was no reason to doubt the kid, and to Hall, it made some sense. For the Silver Blades to be a new organization and already have crossroads into Land's Edge Port and be able to hire Hob mercenaries and somehow entice a giant to serve as muscle, they needed money. A lot of money. Not the kind they would have on their own. Not yet. They had major financial backing from somewhere, and only rich nobles had that kind of gold to throw around.

The question was which noble, from what city, and why?

"Where do we find the Cudgel?" Hall asked.

The Silver Blade stopped talking, realizing he was going too far. His eyes darted to the barn though, Hall catching the quick movement. Hall didn't respond, didn't show that he had noticed.

QUEST COMPLETE!

THE NEW BLOOD I
Disrupt a Silver Blades Operation 1/1
Question a Silver Blades Guildmember 1/1
Rewards: +50 Door Knocker Reputation
+50 PeakGuards Reputation
+50 Alliance Reputation with Sergeant Brient
+50 Experience

You are now Known to the PeakGuard. You are now Known to the Door Knockers. You are now Known to Sergeant Brient of the PeakGuard.

Sitting back on his heels, Hall studied the Silver Blade. There was no immediate prompt for the next step in the quest chain, which meant there was more to get out of the Silver Blade.

"What is with the books?" he asked, catching the Blade by surprise. The thief had expected another question and took a moment to recover.

"What books?"

"In the crate," Hall said, wondering if the Silver Blade did know about the ledger books.

"I don't know anything about books," the kid said quickly, forcefully, trying to make sure Hall believed him.

"What about the other stuff?"

"The furs and Highborn wine?" the kid asked and Hall nodded. "Trying to get them past customs in Essec so don't have to pay taxes. That was where I came in on Cumberland," he said and showed some pride. "Helped get 'em through the wilds and to the merchants in Spirehold."

Interesting, Hall thought. He had assumed the smuggled goods were staying on Cumberland, but they would be worth more in the capital of Spirehold. It seemed like the long way to go about it. Ship the goods from Edin to southern Cumberland, carry them overland to near Land's Edge Port, and reload them to fly to the island of Essec. Why not just fly directly from Edin to Essec? He pushed those thoughts away. It didn't matter. Not to him. If the Cudgel, and Dyson for that matter, thought they got more profit doing it that way, who was he to argue?

You have discovered that the Silver Blades are smuggling in a crate of ledgers for an
    unknown purpose. Sergeant Brient would be interested in learning more about the ledgers but even more interested in seeing whatever plan the Blades had disrupted.

THE NEW BLOOD II
Learn what the Silver Blade's plan to do with the ledgers 0/1
Rewards: +50 Door Knocker reputation
+50 PeakGuard reputation
+50 Alliance
Reputation with Sergeant Brient
+20 Experience

ACCEPT QUEST?

He accepted the quest and looked back at the Silver Blade.

"How do you get the goods into the city?" he asked and then smiled. "The tunnel, right?"

The Silver Blade's eyes widened in surprise, shocked that Hall knew about that. His eyes again darted to the barn, the action obvious, and now everyone's eyes looked that way.

"How did you..." the kid stammered and stopped as Hall raised his hand.

"Doesn't matter," Hall said. "Now tell us about the tunnel. Especially where it comes out and if there are any guards."

———

Hall spread the parchment that was his map on the ground in front of the Silver Blade. He held down the ends that threatened to curl up. Before pulling the physical representation of his World Map out of his pouch, he had opened the translucent one that hung in front of his face. He had played with the zoom and layout until he had a picture of Silver Peak Keep. It was large and in scale, copied exactly when the physical map came out.

The Silver Blade was tracing a line from where the Durnpoole Farm was located alongside the river and almost midway between Peakdock and the plateau. He took a sip of the cup of water that Leigh had given him, running the finger into the city. He leaned down, studying the buildings that were shown in detail, at least the ones that Hall had seen himself. The rest was missing, the kid's finger stopping right at that missing area.

"Can I?" he asked and pointed at his own pouch.

Hall nodded, as they all gripped their weapons tighter and watched every move the Silver Blade made. He pulled out a smaller piece of parchment, his map. He laid it down next to

Halls, his showing the entire city of Silver Peak Keep in great detail, even some areas that Hall knew were off-limits to anyone not of noble birth or part of the city guard.

"Here," he said and pointed at a large building in the Nobles Quarter.

Hall almost started laughing. Pretty close to where it had begun.

He studied the Blade's map and then touched his own map. A small pin appeared on the parchment, or the image of one.

Skill Gain!

Cartography Rank Two +.1

"How did you do that?" the kid asked, again surprised. "Only Cartographers can..." his voice trailed off and he looked at Hall in awe.

"Ain't ya full o' surprises," Ulysses remarked with a chuckle.

Hall grimaced, knowing that Berim would soon know that he was a Cartographer. He didn't think it was that important, but he hadn't told anyone and hated people learning things about him that he didn't tell them himself. And Cartographers seemed so rare, and mysterious, that he really wanted to learn more before it became common knowledge.

He had not been able to learn much about this Cartographer's Guild he had heard about. Only knew that it existed and an unGuilded Cartographer was rare. He expected that he would soon need to visit them before they visited him.

And if Guilds were anything like the unions back in the real world, they wouldn't like it if someone non-Guild was operating in their territory.

A problem for another day, he knew as he rolled up the map and put it back in his pouch.

"Thank you," he told the Silver Blade as he stood up.

The captive's eyes darted all over the place, extremely

nervous now. Hall turned away and could feel the Blade's eyes following him, trying to grab him.

"What happens to me?" the Blade asked.

Hall stopped and waited a couple seconds before turning, making it look like he was deep in thought. He stared at the Blade, expressionless. The kid's eyes were pleading, hopeful. Ulysses was looking almost predatory, waiting for a chance.

"You live," Hall said and the Blade visibly relaxed, sagging to the ground. Ulysses grumbled. "For now," Hall added, drawing all eyes. "If your information of what is in the tunnel and on the other end is right, then you live. If it's not..." Hall trailed off, eyes hard and staring at the Blade, making sure he understood.

The Blade nodded. Hall turned and walked away, heading for the farmhouse.

"We'll keep him nice an' cozy," Ulysses said, looking down at the Blade.

"No," Hall replied, stopping and staring at Ulysses. "They can keep him tied up here," Hall said and pointed at the other two Door Knockers. "You are coming with us."

"Hells I am," Ulysses growled, taking a step toward Hall.

Hall turned, walking back to stand in front of Ulysses. He was a foot or more taller, looking down at the smaller man. What Ulysses lacked in height he made up in girth. The man was a solid block of muscle and weight. Hall knew Ulysses might be a Level, maybe two, higher as well. But at the moment, Hall did not care. He was tired of being used, being pushed and prodded by others. It was time to take control back.

"You. Are. Coming. With. Us," Hall said, emphasis on each word. Ulysses started to say something but Hall held up a hand. "Shut up," he said calmly, his lack of anger or inflection having more of an effect. "Don't say anything. You're coming. No argument."

The two men stared at each other. The two Door Knockers, sensing the tension, took steps back and put hands over weapons. Hall's companions spread out, hands hovering over their own weapons or raised to start casting spells.

The stare down went on for a minute, neither budging.

Finally, Ulysses smiled and shrugged.

"Sure," he said as if the contest of wills had never happened and he was always going to go along. "What else I gots ta do?"

Hall remained staring at the thief for another minute or so before turning. Without a word, he headed into the farmhouse.

"Tunnels there, ain't it?" Ulysses said, pointing at the barn.

Hall ignored him.

———

He wasn't sure why he felt the need to search the farmhouse, but he did, so Hall led his companions into the building. They spread out, each taking a room and floor. It was two stories, wooden planks laid horizontally on posts, steep shingle roof. Three rooms on the first level with the stairs up. A living room, dining room, and kitchen. Upstairs were three bedrooms.

It didn't take long to search.

Hall was upstairs in what looked to be the master bedroom, combing through a drawer of clothes when he heard Sabine call his name.

"I found something," she said from one of the other upstairs rooms.

The one she was in had been converted to an office. A writing desk, shelves, and a couple chairs. The closet was empty as were the desk drawers. But on top, where Sabine was pointing, were two identical ledger books. They looked the same as the ones from the crate.

Both were opened. Each page of the one on the left was

filled with small and neat handwriting. Top to bottom, margin to margin. Columns of numbers with notations. The book to the right was only half-filled. A single column.

Hall bent down, looking at the books closer.

The unfinished on the right was a copy. The letters and numbers were identical to the left, the handwriting nearly identical. It was close, but Hall could tell the difference.

"Get Ulysses," he said.

The thief walked in a minute later, grumbling but stopped when he saw what Hall was looking at. Motioning for Hall to move aside, Ulysses studied the two books. He ran a finger down a column on the left book, stopping halfway down. He looked to the right book, finger pointing at the last line. His eyes jumped from one to the other.

"Well, damn," he finally said, leaning back. "That explains ta ledgers in ta crate."

"What's it mean?" Roxhard asked.

The others had all gathered in the room, the only one with anything of interest, while Hall and Ulysses had studied the ledgers. The thief shot Roxhard an annoyed glare before rolling his eyes.

"Ter forging ta book," he muttered. "Ta other ledgers are practice ta get the writing right."

QUEST COMPLETE!

You have discovered that shipment of ledgers are being used to forge an existing ledger book.

THE NEW BLOOD II

Learn what the Silver Blade's plan to do with the ledgers 1/1
Rewards: +50 Door Knocker reputation
+50 PeakGuard reputation
+50 Alliance
Reputation with Sergeant Brient

+20 Experience

Hall partly closed the original book, looking at the cover. It was unmarked, no name or initials or mark to indicate who owned it. The color, stitching, and design were identical to the ones he had found in the crate.

"Who uses a book like this?" Hall asked, looking at Ulysses.

The thief started to shrug but noticed Hall's glare. He sighed.

"Silver Peak Keep's Councilor of Coin," Ulysses answered.

He flipped through the pages of the ledger, looking at the columns of numbers and the dates.

"That answers how ta Councilor doesn't know this is missing," he muttered. "It's an old book."

"Why are they forging an old ledger?" Roxhard asked.

Ulysses looked at the Dwarf and chuckled, rolling his eyes.

"It's for practice," the thief chuckled. "Not that hard ta figure out."

Roxhard looked down at the ground, what little was visible of his cheeks reddening in embarrassment. Hall shot Ulysses a harsh glare, which the thief ignored.

"The Councilor would most likely not miss an old ledger," Leigh told Roxhard, laying a hand on his shoulder.

"Which is true," Hall said as he looked down at the book in thought. "But Roxhard might be onto something. The only reason to forge the ledgers is to fix the numbers. Either make it look like there is more or make it look like there is less. Might make sense to alter some of the older books as well. Really make a mess of it when they go to check if the forgery of the latest is discovered."

"But what is the point?" Caryn asked. "What are the Blades up to?"

"Only one way to find out," Hall replied, turning to leave the room. He left the ledger on the table.

"At least we've shortened the suspect list for The Cudgel's identity," Sabine said as they started walking down the stairs.

"The Councilor of Coin?" Roxhard asked.

"No," Sabine replied shortly, annoyed. Hall figured she was rolling her eyes. "That makes no sense. The Cudgel will be someone that has access to the Councilor of Coins or wherever the ledgers are kept. There can't be that many people."

Hall stepped down to the first level and glanced up the stairwell. Roxhard was still at the top, waiting, and again looked embarrassed. Hall sighed, it was so hard to remember that Roxhard was really just a kid, a teenager.

"Doesn't really help us that much," Hall said. "The Cudgel doesn't need to have direct access him or herself. It can be just someone highly placed in the Silver Blades."

Roxhard brightened a bit but Hall got an annoyed glance from Sabine.

He sighed. Dealing with the egos and personalities of Players had always been his least favorite part of raiding. Living in Sky Realms Online didn't seem to be changing that.

"But it does give us a starting point," he said to try to mollify Sabine.

You have discovered that the Silver Blades plan to forge account ledgers belonging to the Silver Peak Keep Councilor of Coin. Sergeant Brient needs to know this information.

THE NEW BLOOD III

Inform Sergeant Brient of the Silver Blades forgery plan 0/1
Rewards: +50 Door Knocker reputation
+50 PeakGuard reputation
+75 Alliance
Reputation with Sergeant Brient
+25 Experience

ACCEPT QUEST?

THE NEW BLOOD III (ELITE) (OPTIONAL)
Stop the Silver Blade's plans for the forged ledgers 0/1
Rewards: +75 Door Knocker reputation
+75 PeakGuard reputation
+100 Alliance Reputation with Sergeant Brient
+50 Experience
Unknown Reward x2

ACCEPT QUEST?

Hall stared at the quest prompts, looking to the others to see if they had received them. All nodded, including Caryn, which Hall found a little strange. Ulysses did not, seeing the blank look on their eyes but recognizing it. This was the second time Hall had received an optional and Elite quest. The first had led to Roxhard and him destroying a camp of raiding goblins and had rewarded Hall with Pike. For him, it was an easy decision on which quest to take. The part about the two unknown rewards was interesting and helped tipped the decision in the Elite quests favor.

"Elite?" he asked.

Roxhard and Leigh nodded. Sabine looked off over their heads, thinking, before finally nodding. Hall had explained about the Elite and optional quests to her soon after she had joined them. Jackoby didn't bother responding, the Firbolg as noncommittal as usual. He didn't care until it came to fighting, and then he was committed to seeing the combat through.

"I got it too," Caryn said a little sheepishly. Her eyes darted from one to the other, ignoring Ulysses.

Hall looked at the Duelist. She was aligned with the Door Knockers, or had been. What was she now? She had fought beside them, bled with them. Seemed she could be trusted but how far? Was she really loyal to Berim and the Door Knockers or did she truly want to be rid of them? It was hard to tell. She was a Player, though. He couldn't just abandon her. He thought about the Bodin Player they had met after disembarking in Auld. Davit? He thought that was the name. That one had been trouble. Caryn didn't seem the same. She seemed nice, slightly naive and innocent.

Making a decision, realizing he was doing it without checking with the others first, he nodded to Caryn.

"You're with us," he said and saw the gratitude in her eyes. Roxhard and Leigh smiled, the Druid reaching out and clasping Caryn's shoulder. Sabine didn't look happy, not looking at either him or Caryn. It was hard to tell with her, Hall knew. The Witch seemed to be easily aggravated and annoyed. And she was getting worse every day. "Elite it is then."

CHAPTER THIRTY-TWO

THE CENTER OF THE BARN WAS WIDE OPEN, A TWO-STORY SPACE. The dirt had been churned up showing where the giant had been sitting and rapidly standing up to join the fight. Stalls lined both sides of the large space, a second story above the stalls. Built of traditional post and beam, the barn showed signs of heavy use. The stalls were empty, piles of moldy hay in the corners. Dust was everywhere except where it looked like the giant had leaned against the posts.

To enter the barn, they had to squeeze past the dead giant, crouching low and moving under it, trying to avoid the dried blood. Pike squawked, irritated that he had to walk in as there wasn't enough space to ride on Hall's shoulder or Angus' back. The talons stepped in the blood, leaving a thin trail. Once inside, Pike hopped over to a corner and started trying to clean the blood off his talons.

They spread out, looking through the stalls. Hall stood in the middle of the open space, eyes scanning the ground looking for the trap door. The Silver Blade, now tied up inside the house and under guard, had said it was a large hatch in the middle of the barn floor. Walking to the middle, he scuffed his foot along the ground, moving some of the loose dirt aside.

He listened to his footsteps, the thud of boots on hard-packed dirt was replaced with the sound of boots on wood. Smiling, he bent down and started pushing aside more of the dirt and found the edge of the hatch.

"Got it," he said and stood up.

He started moving to the side, kicking the dirt out of the way to reveal more of the hatch. He got to the corner and started up the side until he got to the other corner. A minute later he had the entire hatch revealed. Hinges were on the end opposite the barn door. Big and heavy looking, the door was solid when he stomped on it. Six-foot square.

Crouching down, he felt around for a hole or a handle, something to open the hatch with. There was nothing and the seam between hatch and floor was tight. The Silver Blades, or whoever had built the hatch and tunnel, had put wood another foot or so out from the edge, giving a solid surface to line up against. He tried to pry it up enough to get a finger under but couldn't. Jamming his dagger into the seam, he tried and managed to get it up a half inch but not enough.

The hatch was heavy.

Standing up and stepping aside, he motioned for Jackoby to take his place. The Firbolg grumbled but did so, setting his shield and hammer down on the ground. Crouching, he used his dagger to lift the hatch up enough to fit a finger underneath.

"Dwarf," Jackoby called, grunting as he tried to lift the hatch enough to get the rest of his fingers under.

Roxhard rushed over, fitting his slightly thinner fingers under and lifting. Together, Dwarf and Firbolg managed to pick up the heavy hatch. Each moved to a side and worked the hatch up, letting it fall to the dirt floor with a loud thud. Dust kicked up as the hatch hit, and they coughed.

Waving his hand through the air to clear the dust, Hall looked down into the dark hole now revealed. Wood planking lined the wall, holding back the earth. A ladder had been set into one side, leading down into the dark. The floor was lost in shadow. There didn't seem to be anything moving, no lights. He could see brackets on the walls for torches, but none were there.

"Be right back," Hall said and activated *Leap*.

———

He landed at the bottom in a crouch, spear pointing up, eyes searching the dark. He had used the class ability instead of climbing down for the surprise of the move. Climbing the ladder, he would have been easy pickings for anyone waiting in the dark. Now he was down in seconds and ready to defend.

Or attack.

His eyes shifted as his racial ability of *Limited Night Vision* activated, using the ambient light from the opening above. Before him, in a direction that would head straight to Silver Peak Keep, was an opening in the wooden walls. Arched, he could see timbers set into the hard-packed dirt walls at intervals to support the ceiling. About eight-feet tall, six wide, the tunnel ran off into the darkness past where his vision could see.

He listened, eyes searching the dark.

"Clear," he said a minute later, not taking his eyes off the tunnel.

Standing, he moved into the entrance, out of the way. Sabine was the first down, followed by Caryn and Ulysses. He grimaced as Angus' annoyed moos echoed through the shaft and into the tunnel as the cow was lowered by rope. Jackoby and Roxhard were above, slowly lowering the cow as Leigh descended the ladder, gently petting at Angus.

Once down, the cow gave a last indignant moo and settled

down at Leigh's feet. Jackoby and Roxhard came down the ladder quickly, followed by Pike, who flew down and settled on Angus' back. They all looked down the dark opening.

"That looks inviting," Sabine muttered.

"Torches," Hall said.

"Gots better," Ulysses replied with a chuckle.

He reached into the pouch belted to his side, his hand disappearing into the magical hole that was the inside. Hall turned away, not wanting to look at the strange distortion where the larger hand entered the smaller opening. He had seen it when he placed or removed items in his own pouch, and it disturbed him every time.

"Here they be," Ulysses said with a smile as he pulled out a lantern. Setting it on the floor, he reached into the pouch and pulled out another one.

Each lantern, made of a thin and dark metal, was about eight inches tall and four inches wide. Shutters covered the sides and a small ring on top served as the handle. Hall recognized them as Thief Lanterns. The shutters would allow a very limited amount of light to shine through, the amount able to be controlled by the holder of the lantern. Ulysses handed one to Hall, who shook his head, pointing at Sabine.

"Roxhard is in the rear," Hall said. "Ulysses is in the lead with Caryn behind, looking for traps."

"The Blade said there were no traps," Ulysses pointed out.

"You believe him?" Hall asked and the thief laughed before moving to the front of the group. "Jackoby behind them with Angus. I'm next, Leigh and Sabine to follow. Keep some space between you."

Ulysses took a couple steps, and Hall heard the small thief fiddling with the lantern. He saw a bright beam lance out, thin but focused. The thief looked back at Caryn and held up five fingers. Without waiting for a response, he started walking.

Caryn waited for him to get five feet ahead and started to follow.

They moved slowly, Ulysses shining he lantern back and forth across the floor, up into the ceiling and along the walls. The captive Silver Blade had said there were no traps, but they were not taking chances. That was why Hall had put Ulysses and Caryn first. He hated not being the one in front, putting others at risk, but he was glad to have two people with Trap Detection skills.

As he stepped into the tunnel, the dark closing in, he glanced at Roxhard. The Dwarf looked fine, weapon held in both hands, but Hall wasn't sure. The last couple hours hadn't done anything to help Roxhard's self-esteem and being a four-teen-year-old kid, he didn't have much to begin with. Hall was starting to think that having Jackoby along wasn't helping. One Warden was all that a party had typically had.

They currently had two, and Jackoby was a higher level.

Was Roxhard starting to feel useless? Unwanted?

Hall knew he would have to talk to Roxhard about it soon and wondered if putting Roxhard in the back had been the right decision. He had done it because he didn't trust Jackoby and wanted someone he could rely on in the rear. He thought of it as a boost for Roxhard, giving him an important job. Would the kid see it that way?

He sighed, focusing on the current issue. Roxhard would have to wait.

––––––––

The light from Ulysses' lantern, as well as the one that Sabine had behind him, was enough for Hall's *Limited Night Vision* to still function. Not that he saw anything. Roughly dug walls, a floor that was worn smooth, arched ceiling and thick wooden posts. All of it done in shades of black and gray.

They moved as silently as possible, shifting more than walking as their feet slid across the ground. The footsteps seemed to echo down the long tunnel. At one post, Hall paused and ran his hand over it, noticing an odd dark spot. Fingers hit metal and he felt a steel ring. A torch bracket, and like the opening from the barn, there was no torch.

At one point, the floor started to slope down. Not a major change in pitch, but enough to be noticeable. The ground started to soften, becoming like mud. Putting a hand against the wall, Hall could feel moisture. He wondered how close to the river they currently were.

Without clear reference points, it was hard to tell how far they had traveled. Hall thought the sloping had continued for a couple hundred feet before leveling out for a couple hundred more. It started sloping back up, taking twice as long.

He mentally thought about his map and could barely see the translucent window in front of his vision. It was too dark to make out details, and he doubted the meager light from the lanterns would help. He closed the map and continued walking.

With Roxhard watching behind them, the Dwarf's *Dark Vision* perfect to see into the darkness of the tunnel, and Ulysses and Caryn checking for traps ahead, Hall didn't have much to occupy himself with during the walk. It was long and boring. He could at least see shapes and thought it must be extra hard on Leigh and Sabine who could see nothing except what was shown in the thin light of the lantern.

Nothing else to do, Hall started thinking about the tunnel itself.

There was no way that it had only taken months to build. To make a tunnel this long, this wide and tall, it had to have taken years. Especially without anyone discovering the construction. Where had all the dirt gone? How had it been removed in the first place? Could this have been dug by magic of some kind?

Some Druid spells might have been able to manage it. But it still would have taken a year at least, not months. The dirt had to go somewhere. Could it have always existed?

Sergeant Brient and Berim had said the Guild war had only been ongoing for a month, maybe a little more. There was no way the Silver Blades had dug this in a month. That hinted at some very long-term planning from the Cudgel or very intimate knowledge of the history of Silver Peak Keep.

The Cudgel must have started the Silver Blades years ago and had been planning for the Guild war since. They were better prepared than Hall had been led to believe. They were better prepared than anyone had thought. This was not a group just trying to make a power play and take over the Door Knocker's operations. There was a bigger plan at work.

The idea was scary.

And Hall had no idea what it all meant. There was so much he was missing where the Silver Blades were concerned.

So far, the captive Blade's information about the tunnel had been accurate, but Hall expected there to be a surprise or two. Or three. Traps or something else.

The first surprise came in the form of a pinprick of light further ahead. Instantly, Ulysses shuttered his lantern, Sabine a little slower. They all fell quiet and watched the small dot of light, expecting to see it moving closer and to hear shouts of alarm.

There was nothing.

Moving even slower they crept forward, this time with no light.

The thin dot of light could have meant they were nearing the end, but Hall didn't think they had gone that far. Not yet. So, what had it been? A guard? Unlikely. There was no need for guards midway down the tunnel.

Without any light, Hall saw nothing but darkness. No shadows, just black. But as they walked, getting closer to where he assumed the pinprick of light had been, he started to see shades again. Not much definition but enough. There was more light ahead.

Not a bright spot, but more of a glow, like daylight leaking around a curtain. It was diffused, barely noticeable. None of the others reacted to seeing it, but Hall knew there must be light. Otherwise, his racial vision would not work. And he was glad it did.

The tunnel was different just ahead. An arch similar to the one they had entered by. He couldn't tell for sure, but he thought there was wood planking around the arch. Another shaft? Stretching forward with the spear, able to tell the difference in their shapes, Hall tapped both Ulysses and Caryn on the shoulders. To their credit, they turned quickly and didn't cry out. Neither could see his hand motions so he just walked forward until he was right next to them.

Hands on shoulders, he squeezed, one then the other. A signal to wait. Hall crept forward, a single step at a time. He reached out a hand and touched wood. The walls of another shaft.

Leaning against it, he listened. There was a faint movement on the other side. Breathing and the shuffling of feet. Someone sitting or standing, moving impatiently.

Their light had been seen and whoever was on the other side of the wood wall knew their light had been seen as well. It was a waiting game. The ambushers were waiting on Hall's group to get to them, and Hall's group had no idea there was anything ahead. Hall assumed there were lights, lanterns probably just inside the shaft ready to be unshuttered and shined into his companions' eyes. There was no way of knowing how many were on the other side.

Couldn't be many, not remaining that silent.

Could they hear his breathing? Probably. So, they knew he was there, waiting on them as they were waiting on him. Was there time to get Roxhard up to the wall where the Dwarf's *Dark Vision* would help? He turned to head back down the line of companions in the dark but stopped when he heard a footstep shift on the other side.

The hairs on the back of his head stood up, and he felt as if someone was staring at his back. He felt exposed. His *Evade* skill was excellent at helping him avoid attacks, thanks to his high Agility, but there was no protection or evading attacks from the blindside. Protection, the ability to defend from an attack and not take damage, was based on armor and Agility, but when attacked from behind, it was only the armor that was factored in.

It had always been that way, in the original game and most likely in the new. Game mechanics designed to make it so lower-level monsters were still dangerous when in numbers. Even a high-level character could be killed by a horde of goblins. No one could evade attacks from multiple attackers at once.

Hall paused, listening harder. There it was again, a foot sliding across dirt.

He moved to the side, too late, feeling a blade cutting along his back, cutting into his overly repaired leather armor. Grunting in pain, he stumbled a couple steps away, seeing the shadowed shape of an arm and blade sticking out through the opening.

"Lantern," he yelled.

His spear dropped from his hand as he reached to draw his sword. The cut across his back flared as the skin stretched, and he felt the blood running down his side. He turned his head away as he heard Ulysses or Sabine, but probably the thief, playing with the lantern. Light flared as the shutters were opened.

Bright, more so because of the total darkness.

Hall heard grunts of annoyance and pain from behind him, glancing toward the opening and seeing that arm and blade start to disappear. Quickly, sword in hand, Hall swiped at it. Somehow, he connected, the enemy's blade dropping to the ground with a loud echoing clatter, the owner screaming in pain.

There was a rushing and a large blur that momentarily blocked out the light. This was followed by grunting and the sound of something hitting a wall hard. Jackoby had used *Battle Rush* and ran through the opening. Carefully moving, trying not to strain his wounded back, Hall leaned against the wall and looked into the shaft, trying not to block the light.

Jackoby was in the middle of the space, about ten or more feet in diameter, hammer swinging. A shadowed form lay crumpled against the far wall, another opening across from the first. Two figures, dressed all in black, were facing off against the Firbolg. Only the wild swinging of the hammer was keeping the two at bay.

The light got brighter, showing more detail of the shaft, as Ulysses stepped closer. More light was added as Sabine opened her lantern. Hall stepped into the shaft, the noise catching the attention of one of the black-clad attackers. The man swung his long and thin blade, Hall catching it on his sword. The shock of the impact traveled through the hilt and into his arm. He could feel it as his back tensed, the wound flaring again.

He kicked out, catching the Blade in the knee. The man's leg buckled, stumbling back, and Hall stabbed out with his short sword, the tip entering the Blade's chest. The thief fell to the ground.

SLAIN: *Silver Blade Cutthroat*
+25 Experience

Skill Gain!
Light Armor Rank Two +.1
Small Blades Rank Two +.1

Turning, Hall took a step to the side, watching as Jackoby's large hammer connected with the remaining thief. There was a loud thud, a cracking of bone, and the Silver Blade dropped to the ground in a heap. The third man, the one Hall had wounded and been wounded by, moaned from the wall. He was trying to get up but a quick thrust from Hall ended his life.

SLAIN: Silver Blade Cutthroat
+10 Experience

Hall stepped to the other opening, looking down its length, the light from the lanterns allowing his racial ability to see the shadows. There was nothing that he could make out, just a long and straight tunnel similar to the one they had come up. The others all crowded into the shaft, Jackoby and Roxhard moving the bodies of the Blades and searching them.

There was a ladder against the wall, and looking up, Hall could see the outline of another hatch. This one didn't fit as tight, and there was light leaking in around the edges. Not much but it had been just enough for Hall's *Limited Night Vision* to work. For which, he was thankful. If he hadn't been able to see just a little bit, the ambush could have gone much different.

"Thanks," he said as he felt Leigh's hands touching his back. There was a flare of blue light, and he felt warmth spreading through his body as the skin knit itself back together.

"What's up there?" Roxhard asked.

Hall mentally opened his map. The icon that indicated their progress was more than halfway toward the plateau and Silver Peak Keep. He tried picturing what had been in the land above. Farms, farms, and more farms. The more he thought about it, the more it made sense for the Silver Blades to have a third means of entering and exiting the tunnel that was halfway through its length. There was a long way to go in the dark underground without being able to get out.

There didn't seem to be any more Silver Blades. Or they were waiting up top.

Hall didn't want to poke his head, or anyone else's either, out of the hatch to find out but knew they had to. There was no way they could leave potential enemies behind them that could sneak up on them in the dark. Sighing, Hall sheathed his sword and retrieved his spear.

"Get ready," Hall said and motioned to the hatch with the spear.

He climbed the ladder, keeping an eye on the hatch, trying to be quiet. Near the top, he adjusted his grip on the spear, holding it butt end up. Slowly, he lifted it until could feel the resistance of the hatch against the spear. He started to apply more force, pushing up with the spear. The hatch was heavy, and he struggled to lift it one-handed.

If he climbed higher, he could use more force, but Hall did not want to risk exposing himself more than he already was.

The heavy hatch lifted an inch, then two. Hall could hear nothing. The light didn't change, daylight that was probably coming in from a window. No shadows crossing the light, no noise of someone breathing or shuffling. He pushed harder on the spear, and the hatch opened some more, creaking.

Hall paused, cursing. The hinges had creaked. Not much, the sound just starting before he had stopped. He waited, listening.

"Is someone there?" a voice asked, tired and cracked, female. "Please help us."

That caught Hall by surprise. He almost let the spear move, dropping the hatch, but managed to keep it open. He pushed and opened it wider.

"Hello?" the voice came again. "There are no Silver Blades. It's just us." The voice coughed.

The sound was coming from behind the hatch, from where the cover would open. Besides being female, it sounded young and weak. There was a banging of something hitting wood. Then a shaking that sounded like a door being pushed against, the handle played with.

"Please."

Hall glanced down into the shaft. The others were looking up at him, confused. He wondered if they could even hear the voice down there. It was quiet and he could barely hear it. Curiosity won out and Hall climbed the ladder the rest of the way. He pushed the hatch up enough so he could squeeze out, holding it up awkwardly.

He found himself in another barn. Not as large and without stalls. One large open space with a second story in the back half. Under the second story was a small room with a single door. Looking down the hatch, Hall motioned to his companions, telling them to wait. He slowly shut the hatch and stood up.

Cautiously, silently, he walked to the door. His eyes roamed the barn, looking for hidden Blades but there were not many places to hide. Aside from the room and the second story, there was nowhere. One giant and empty space.

Set in the middle of the back wall, the room was only about ten by ten feet square. No windows, wood planking for walls and just the door.

"Hello?" the voice said again.

It was louder as Hall was closer, the person probably trying to shout to get the sound through the door. But it was still a weak and tired sound. Speaking sounded like a struggle.

Studying the door, Hall saw the wooden bar set across the door which held it shut. Heavy and thick, laying over two iron clasps. The voice came from inside, and whoever it was pushed on the door again. The bar shook, the door pushing against it, but not enough to slip the clasps.

"I don't think they heard me," the voice said, moving away from the door, disappointed.

"You tried," another voice said, weaker and quieter. "It was probably just the Blades."

Hall stared at the door and the crossbar. The two, maybe more, inside the small room seemed to be prisoners of the Silver Blades. But were they people that Hall wanted to let out? If this had been the original Sky Realms Online, he wouldn't have hesitated. But even though it was still a game, he was trapped here and the choices could have dire consequences. They still didn't know if death was permanent or if they would respawn.

A cough came from behind the door. Harsh and hard, painful to listen to.

"Ssshhh," the first voice said, trying to be comforting. "It's okay. They have to let us out soon. We can get you help then."

Cursing, figuring he would regret it, Hall lifted the crossbar. Throwing it to the side, he opened the door and stopped, staring into the room in shock and surprise.

CHAPTER THIRTY-THREE

THE SMALL ROOM WAS DARK, THE ONLY LIGHT COMING IN FROM the open door. But it was enough for Hall to see and he wished he hadn't. The floor was dirt, scraps of moldy hay littered it, a stained and overflowing chamber pot in the corner. An unpleasant smell wafted out of the room. Human excrement and sweat, mold and fear.

Huddled against the back wall were two women. One older and one younger.

The older was crumbled in a pile, tired eyes staring at Hall from behind limp graying hair. She was wearing a thin dress, more rag than clothes. Her body was shaking, from cold and sickness. Though she looked right at him, the woman barely moved.

"Who are you?" the younger asked, and Hall recognized the voice as the one that had been calling for him.

She was much younger than the other but looked just like her. A daughter. Blonde hair, blue eyes. Thin from hunger. Her clothing was a little better, pants and a wool shirt. Worker's clothes. Farmer's clothes. She crouched next to her mother, arms around her. Her eyes stared at Hall with fear and hope. Standing up, she stood protectively over the other.

Hall ignored her question and ran back to the hatch. He pulled it open, letting it crash to the floor. The sound was loud, startling everyone. He heard the two women jump and cry out, saw his companions at the bottom of the shaft squinting against the sudden light.

"Leigh," he called down. "There are two hurt women up here. Ulysses, get up here." He stepped away from the hatch and stopped, turning back. "Rox, I need you to stay down there with your *Dark Vision*. Caryn, you come up to stand guard at the door."

He walked back to the woman, stopping a foot or so away from the opening. He leaned his spear against the wall, arms held out away from his side. He could hear the others coming up the ladder. The young woman had taken a couple steps toward the door, the older forcing herself to stand up. Leigh got to the top of the ladder and gasped. She ran past him and into the small room.

Ulysses came to a stop next to Hall, looking at the women.

"Bastards," he growled.

———

"They came a couple weeks ago, I think," the young woman, she had said her name was Hitchly, told them.

She sat on the ground, arms around her knees, looking up at Hall and Ulysses. Next to her, the older woman lay on the ground sleeping. Leigh had done all she could with her *Nature's Touch* spell. The magic was more for physical wounds than sickness, but it had managed to restore some of the woman's Health and Vitality. Leigh was busy mashing down some of their *Greenroot* supply and mixing it with water in hopes that would help. The older woman's name was Dinah and she was

Hitchly's mother. Dinah appeared to be in her late forties, her black hair mostly gray and with dark eyes. Hitchly was mid-twenties.

"That's our land," Hitchly continued and waved her hand out the barn door. Caryn stood there now, looking out into the fields and making sure no Silver Blades appeared. "The tunnel had been right under us, and we never knew. Not until they wanted that built." She pointed at the open hatch. "Took our lands. Locked up Ma and me. Killed..." she started and stopped. She roughly wiped tears away from her eyes with the sleeve of her filthy shirt. "He put up a good fight. Da used to be a guard before he met Ma and settled down on the farm. Killed one of them, he did," Hitchly said, looking up at Hall with fierce pride burning in her eyes. "Took two of 'em to put him down." Her eyes dropped again and she fell silent, head against her arms.

Hall didn't push her to continue. The young woman had been through a lot. He couldn't imagine what the Blades had done to her or why. She probably didn't know either. He thought to say something but wasn't sure what. To his surprise, it was Ulysses that spoke up.

"This shouldn'a happened ta ya," he said, his rough voice gentle. "Ya gots caught up in a war. Not ya fault. But ta ones that did this ta ya, that took ya Da, they will pay, believe me."

Hitchly looked up at him and nodded, her face dropping again.

Hall motioned for Ulysses to step away. The thief followed him to the doors.

"Why did the Silver Blades..." Hall started to ask and stopped, not able to put it to words.

"Keep 'em alive?" Ulysses supplied and Hall nodded. "Not sure. I can't think o' ta value in it," he finished with a shrug. His eyes kept darting to the two women, sympathetic.

"You seem especially angry about it," Hall said.

"Anyone would," Ulysses growled. "I may be a thief but there be some lines even I won't cross. Just tells me how depraved these Blades are."

Hall bit back a laugh. Ulysses and the Door Knockers were thieves. They killed and stole for their own profit. He found it odd that Ulysses was upset about the Blades kidnapping the two women.

"The Door Knockers have never kidnapped anyone?" he asked.

Ulysses turned to look up at him, angry.

"O' course we have," the thief snapped. "But ya don't keep 'em locked up like that," he growled and pointed at the room in the back of the barn. "Ya treat 'em well. Ya want 'em ta survive. Ya don't treat 'em like animals."

Hall nodded, understanding. He was surprised he under-stood what the difference was. Even thieves, it appeared, had somewhat of a moral code.

"Hall," Leigh yelled from the rear of the barn, motioning for him to come over there.

He walked quickly over, Ulysses behind him. He thought that Dinah, or Hitchly, had gotten worse but he found Dinah still asleep. It was Hitchly, though; she was still sitting with her arms around her legs, but she was talking again.

"Tell them what you told me," Leigh prompted her.

Hitchly started talking. Quiet, hard to hear.

"We don't own the land," she said. "Da rented it so when the Silver Blades first appeared, we thought them to be from the landlord. We weren't behind on rent, the land had been producing the quota, so didn't know why they had come. Thugs, the lot of them. Big and strong. No reason for them to be here. 'He said the land is ours now,' one of them said. The landlord. He gave the land to the Blades. Da protested and that's when it happened."

Hitchly fell silent again.

Ulysses crouched down in front of the young woman, just looking at her until she lifted her head to look at him with haunted eyes.

"Who owns ta land?" he asked.

"Lord Cronet," Hitchly said. "The thugs told us that Lord Cronet said the lands were theirs."

Ulysses watched her for a couple more seconds before standing up. He glanced out the open barn doors and then at the open hatch. Then he cursed, loudly and long. Curse after curse strung together. He finally stopped with a sigh.

"What?" Hall asked, knowing the thief had learned something important.

"We know who ta Cudgel be now," Ulysses replied and he sounded worried.

––––––––

THE BLADE'S CUDGEL I
Learn the identity of The Cudgel 1/1
Learn the location of The Cudgel 0/1
Reward: +100 Door Knocker Reputation
+75 PeakGuard Experience
+50 Experience

"What are you talking about?" Hall asked.

Ulysses had taken a couple steps back, turning to face the open doors.

"We need ta leave," he said. "Now. Pack up 'n leave ta city."

He was almost at the door when Hall reached him, grabbing the smaller man by the shoulder. Hall spun him around, and Ulysses looked like he would have stabbed Hall if he had a blade in hand.

"Who is this Cronet?" Hall asked, not backing down.

368 • TROY OSGOOD

Ulysses glared but settled down, sighing.

"The next ruler o' Silver Peak Keep," the thief said. "That be what this is about. Cronet is staging a bloodless takeover." He shrugged out of Hall's grasp but did not move closer to the door. The small thief looked defeated.

"But the fighting between the Door Knockers and Silver Blades will be bloody," Roxhard said from near the room in the back. "Won't it?" he asked and looked to the others.

"O' course it will," Ulysses replied. "Too damn bloody but the folk won't care. That be just thief 'gainst thief. And Cronet will be there ta pick up ta pieces. Controlling who wins from ta shadows 'n putting 'em down in ta light. He cares nuthing for running ta crime. It's just a means ta an end. A distraction."

Hall thought about it for a moment, putting the pieces together.

By using the Silver Blades, this Cronet would have a way to undermine the current ruling authority of the city. The war between the Door Knockers, who had an uneasy but long-standing truce with the Guard, and the Silver Blades would spill out into the streets. They would make sure of that and the Blades wouldn't care. It seemed they were recruited from elsewhere, so what did they care about the citizens of Silver Peak Keep? And once the Blades had control, they could wreck whatever chaos they wanted. And the ledgers. The faked ledgers would undermine the Councilor of Coin and what the city actually had for funds.

First, the people would feel threatened by the Blades and that the PeakGuard would not be able to protect them. Then, they would lose all belief in the rulership of the city as the records were shown to be falsified or wrong. The final step would be to lose faith in the ruler of Silver Peak Keep, Chancellor Valorem. The leader of the Keep was voted in by the Council, and Cronet would have things lined up so he would be next in line.

"Which seat does Cronet hold?" Hall asked.

Ulysses nodded, realizing that Hall was seeing the bigger picture now. The thief stared at Hall, waiting for him to put the last pieces together.

Hall worked through what he knew about Silver Peak Keep. The lore from the original game had not been extensive. There had never been a need for it. There was the Chancellor that was the final say in all matters, the ruler of the city, both the Keep and the Dock. He was assisted by the Council, each ruling over a different aspect of life in the city. Arms controlled the PeakGuard. Coin was in charge of the coffers and taxes.

"Not Coin or Arms," Hall said. Cronet was working to undermine both of those so it would not be the position he sat.

That left only one Council seat.

Trade.

"Yep," Ulysses said. "Cronet be ta Councilor o' Trade."

Hall looked back at the others. They had heard it all. Hitchly and her mother, Dinah, were both standing. They looked fearful, confused. He turned back to Ulysses.

"Cronet be a rough one from what I hear," the small thief explained. "Ruthless 'n cruel. Not well-liked by anyone. But he be a good merchant. That be how he gots ta be Councilor."

"He is a cruel man," Dinah said, coughing. Hitchly helped hold her mother up as the older woman continued to cough. She straightened a bit once the fit stopped. "The first month we were here, Cronet had a thug beat Hitchly's Da bloody because he was a day late on the rent. As long as the rent was paid and the quotas were met, things were okay, but be off a day or a pound..." Dinah trailed off, coughing again.

"Sounds 'bout right," Ulysses muttered. "Guy like that in charge o' ta city and no one will be happy."

"How does a man like that get elected?" Jackoby asked. Hall realized this must all be new to the Firbolg. Where he came from, politics like this did not happen.

"No other choice," Hall replied. "There will be no faith in Coin and Arms. And with Valorem failing in his duties, there will be no choice but to elect Cronet."

Ulysses nodded.

Hall thought about all that he had learned. It was a lot to take in but did it change anything? He had already committed to stopping the Cudgel, no matter who it was. Knowing that it was a powerful ruler of the city didn't affect that. And now he had another goal. Silver Peak Keep was Skara Brae's neighbor. He didn't want a man like Cronet in charge. How soon would it be before Cronet decided he wanted to expand his holdings beyond the Keep?

A man like Cronet would not stop with just a city. He would build a kingdom and in such a way that no one would dare to stand in his way or stop him. The worst kind of expansion, the kind that made sense. The kind that you would welcome until it was too late.

"Knowing who the Cudgel is doesn't change anything," Hall said. "He needs to be stopped."

Ulysses just nodded, over his initial bout of fear

"Just be making it harder," the thief said.

Hall was about to nod in agreement but stopped. Did it make it harder? Or was it easier now that they knew who the Cudgel was?

"No," he said after some thought. "It makes it easier. We now know where he lives."

QUEST COMPLETE!
You have discovered the identity and the location of the Silver Blade's leader, the man called The Cudgel.

THE BLADE'S CUDGEL I
Learn the identity of The Cudgel 1/1
Learn the location of The Cudgel 1/1

Reward: +100 Door Knocker Reputation
+75 PeakGuard Experience
+50 Experience

Knowing the identity of the Cudgel, you now have to defeat him to prevent the takeover of Silver Peak Keep. This will be easier said than done.

THE BLADE'S CUDGEL II

Defeat The Cudgel 0/1
Reward: +50 Door Knocker Reputation
+50 PeakGuard Experience
+50 Experience

ACCEPT QUEST?

CHAPTER THIRTY-FOUR

Hall watched as Hitchly and Dinah walked away from the farm and to the road that would lead them to Peakdock. He had sent them to see Sergeant Brient, the only person he knew they could trust. Everything that Hall and the others knew, Hitchly now knew and would tell Brient. Hall hoped the guardsmen would know what to do with the information.

Hall wasn't sure that he did. All he knew was that Cronet, the Cudgel, had to be put down.

He wanted to do more for the two women, the least of which was to escort them back to the Constable's office. But time was important now. Soon the Cudgel would wonder what was going on with the botched shipment from earlier and why none of his people at the Durnpoole Farm were reporting back. At that point, Hall was afraid the man would go into hiding.

The time to strike was now.

Which was why Hall and his companions had abandoned the tunnel and were making their way to the road, only north not south. They were heading back to Silver Peak Keep, the city on the plateau. He didn't have a plan, not yet, but hoped one would come to him once they were in the city.

"Why are we doing this?" Sabine asked.

She had been asking a variation of that question the whole time they had been in Silver Peak Keep. Hall understood that she wasn't happy with how they had gotten involved. She had essentially been kidnapped and they had been blackmailed into fighting the Guild war. And at the beginning, he had wondered the same thing. This wasn't their fight. He could have gotten the resources he needed elsewhere. That had just been an excuse.

He realized that he was treating the whole thing like he had before. A quest had appeared, he had accepted, and he had run the chain. As much as he had convinced himself that this new life was not a game, that it was real, he was still falling back to old gaming routines.

That had been at first. But as they had advanced through the quests, fought the battles and gotten more involved; Hall had come to realize that the reason why he was doing it was beyond the quests and their rewards. It was something that needed to be done. The Door Knockers were thieves, but they had lines they would not cross. They did not want the death of innocents. The Blades did not care who they hurt.

Seeing Hitchly and Dinah had sealed it for him.

What had been done to them was needlessly cruel. There was no reason for it. In either the act or keeping them alive. It was cruelty for cruelty's sake and done at the command of Cronet. That was not a man that should be in charge of a city the size of Silver Peak Keep. Hall did not want him as a neighbor and would be forever fearful of seeing Cronet's army on the ridge overlooking Skara Brae.

He didn't bother answering Sabine, just kept walking through the fields.

They left Hitchly's farm at an angle, making a straight line for the plateau that became jagged as they passed over the fields, working their way through crops and plowed land, climbing over rock walls. It was hard going, as darkness had settled in while they had been in the tunnel. Dark shapes appeared everywhere, lacking in detail.

Hall could feel the push of the corn stalks against him as he made his way through them. He could remember traveling through other fields in the game where the crops had been spaced out to allow passage, the physical weight barely registering. That was no longer the case. Those fields had been replaced with ones that were truer to reality.

Like the forest outside of Grayhold after the Glitch. It had started out like the original game, space between the trees, but quickly changed to a real forest with only a few feet between the trunks. Just one of the many things that had changed. But when had it occurred?

He couldn't remember seeing it happen; it just did. Everything seemed natural, the way it should be, and it was only when he forced himself to concentrate, to remember, that he noticed the difference.

Pike circled overhead, a dark spot in the dark and cloud-filled sky. Hall could see darker shadows further up, passing behind the gray clouds. Other islands blocking the stars. Between the islands and the clouds, barely any star or moonlight was reaching Edin and the fields around Silver Peak Keep. While it made travel harder, Hall was glad that it was night. There wouldn't be any farmers in the fields, fewer people to come across. Any of the people they encountered could be Silver Blades.

The Cudgel, Lord Cronet, had already shown he had no problem replacing the actual farmers with his hired thugs. And that was what they were. Thugs. Mercenaries.

They walked in silence, a long line with Hall leading and Roxhard once again in the rear. Firbolgs had a *Limited Night*

Vision, similar to the Half-Elves, so Jackoby had been sent to the middle of the line to provide aid and watch. Hall would have liked one of the Wardens closer in case he ran into any trouble, but they were the only ones besides him that could see in the dark at all. They needed to be in a position to help guide the others. With Pike flying overhead for a broader view, Hall kept them marching.

────────

It was a couple hours later when they hit the road that led into Silver Peak Keep. They could see the gates at the top of the plateau, two great doors set in the stone wall. Closed, with guards posted on the sides. No way in.

But they hadn't planned on entering the city that way.

Ulysses led them around the plateau's edge, keeping the slope to their right. Thirty minutes later, at a section of the plateau that was straight up and down, a sheer cliff, Ulysses stopped.

"Now ya will be forgettin' ya saw this, right?" the thief grumbled.

He walked over to the cliff and a collection of boulders. There was nothing special about them, looking like the dozens they had already passed, but Ulysses seemed to find what he was looking for as he started pushing them out of the way to reveal a small cave. Only a couple feet high and wide, they would need to crawl to enter.

Hall crouched in front of the opening, looking in. With his *Limited Night Vision*, he could see that the tunnel stretched only a couple feet before widening. He wasn't sure how much, but at least it did. The thief had just said that the Knockers "have a secret entrance past the walls" but would say no more. Hall could see why. This was an escape tunnel, not a smuggling tunnel. Angus and Jackoby would barely fit inside and might get stuck if it narrowed at all.

With a sigh, he sent a mental command to Pike, telling the dragonhawk to stay on the outskirts of the city and wait for a call. Hall wondered if they would end up anywhere that he could summon Pike or would he be without the dragonhawk for what came next?

Pushing thoughts of the future away, there was nothing he could do about it now, Hall got down on all fours and started crawling into the tunnel. He had to push the spear in ahead of him as he moved. His sword, sheathed at his side, kept bumping the walls. More than once, the tip of the javelin above his shoulder caught on the low dirt ceiling. He could feel bits of dirt sprinkle down onto his back. Crouching lower, he pushed on and made his way through the first part of the tunnel.

It did widen out but not enough for him to stand. Cursing, staying on all fours, he continued to crawl. He could hear the others entering behind him, Angus coming second. The cow mooed, complaining.

"Angus," Leigh scolded quietly. "Shush."

To his credit, Angus did quiet a bit. He kept up the mooing, but it was quieter.

Hall had never thought of himself as claustrophobic but as the tunnel narrowed, the walls and ceiling closing in, he fought down the panic. His breathing became ragged, finding it harder to catch a breath. Ahead was darkness, no ambient light to see anything by. He had to trust in Ulysses, which was hard. Bit by bit, he crawled, the floor starting to slope up.

Slide the spear forward, crawl along the shaft until he got to the tip and slide it forward again. Repeating the process over and over. The slope got steeper, the floor of the tunnel littered with loose rocks.

How long is this tunnel? he thought. His knees were aching, his shoulders hurting. He kept pushing, cursing with each shift of the spear. He could hear the others behind him. The scratching of Leigh and Sabine's staves against the floor. The screech of Jackoby's shield as it caught against the ceiling. The scrap of Roxhard's axe as he pushed it ahead of himself.

All echoed loud in the tight space.

Hall reached forward with his hand, expecting to touch the sloping floor of the tunnel, the loose rocks moving beneath his gloved fingers, but instead, he felt the floor even out. He had reached the end of the tunnel. Quickly, bolstered by being at the end, he pulled himself out into a larger room. One in which he could stand, and did so happily.

His knees cracked in protest, his body stiff and aching as he stretched out tired muscles. His back did not want to move, almost stuck in the bent-over position. He glanced at his Status and saw that he had lost a point of Vitality from the trek through the tunnel.

Angus' front half popped out of the tunnel and the small cow was having a hard time bending his body to get the rest out. Hall reached down and helped, pulling the cow out as the rear hooves scrambled against the floor. Small stones and dirt fell down the tunnel, the others coughing and crying out as they were hit with small rocks. The cow mooed happily and danced in a circle, stretching his legs. He shook, dust flying out of his fur causing Hall to cough.

He shoved against the cow, pushing the animal away from the tunnel set in the floor. Looking around, Hall saw that they were in a wide space with a low ceiling. A rectangle, the sides almost perfectly smooth and straight. Above him, faint light leaked through wooden floorboards, allowing him to use his *Limited Night Vision*.

They were in some kind of empty cellar.

Angus started to moo again, but Hall shushed the cow, who surprisingly obeyed. There was no movement above, no shadows visible through the floorboards, but Hall wasn't taking chances. They had already made too much noise and would make more still as the others exited the tunnel.

One by one they came out, each stretching and brushing off loose dirt and rocks. They spread out, each looking up at the thin light coming through the floorboards. The final one out was Ulysses.

"Forgot how tight it was in thar," the thief chuckled as he brushed himself off.

No one else said anything. In the dark, he couldn't see their glares of annoyance.

"Now what?" Hall asked.

While waiting for the others, he had examined the room and couldn't find a way out besides the tunnel.

"Typically, we donnut come in this way," Ulysses explained as he walked toward one of the end walls. "It be an escape tunnel, right?" He stopped in front of the dirt wall, looking up at the wood ceiling. "You, Hall, bring yer spear," he grunted.

Hall walked over to the thief, spear in hand. He stood there for a second, waiting. He knew that Ulysses couldn't see him, but the thief would be able to tell he was standing there. Hall was annoyed with the small man.

"Push up 'gainst ta end boards," Ulysses said after a bit with a small chuckle, which just made Hall more annoyed. "Hopefully, it be not locked."

Hall had rotated his spear, ready to push the butt end against the boards when he registered what Ulysses had said.

"Locked?" he exclaimed, ready to smack the thief with the spear.

"Weren't able ta warn ta Knockers in ta city that we was coming," Ulysses said and probably shrugged. Hall was even more annoyed that he had spent enough time with the thief to get a read on Ulysses mannerisms. He knew when the thief would shrug. "Shouldn't be. Standing orders be ta keep it unlocked since ta war started."

Silently cursing, Hall pushed his spear against the boards. He felt resistance at first, fearful it was locked, but then the first board popped up with a loud creaking. He stopped, waiting, listening as the sound seemed to echo and echo.

"Not locked," Ulysses chuckled.

Hall still wanted to smack Ulysses with the spear, but he concentrated on pushing the hatch open. It lifted up and Hall struggled to push it over. The spear and his reach were just not enough. He couldn't lift the spear high enough to flip the hatch.

"Jackoby," he called out.

The Firbolg walked over, handing Hall his hammer. Hall grunted as he took the weight, never realizing just how heavy the weapon was. Taking the spear, and using his longer reach and strength, Jackoby pushed up. They watched the hatch stand straight up, bright light coming from above. With one final push, the hatch fell over. Hall winced as the loud crash caused them all to jump, the floorboards shaking with the impact. They waited, listening, but it seemed nothing and no one had heard the hatch slamming into the floor.

Hall looked up at the opening. It was eight or nine feet above them. They could possibly have Jackoby lift them up through the opening but would have a hard time reaching down to pull the Firbolg up. He was about to start doing just that when he noticed Ulysses running his hands over the dirt wall. Revealed by the light coming from above, Hall could see indentations dug into the hard-packed wall. A ladder had been carved into it.

Smiling, glad something was going their way, he pulled a length of rope out of his pouch.

"Angus," Hall called out, stepping over to the cow. "Hold still."

The cow grumbled but let Hall tie the rope around him.

———

They found an empty room above, lit by small windows on the ends that let the daylight shine through, showing the street outside and walking feet barely visible. The cellar was as big as the carved-out space below, the ceiling and walls supported by posts and beams. A thin and railing-less stair was set along the opposite end wall. It led up to a solid-looking door.

"What's above?" Hall asked as he walked around the room.

Jackoby and Ulysses were the only ones up, except for Angus. They had just pulled the cow up, Angus mooing quietly to himself. Leigh was climbing the last of the dirt rungs, which was hard as there was nothing to wrap their fingers around. The ladder had been designed to go down, quickly, not climb up.

"A small shop and office," Ulysses replied. "Couple bedrooms on ta second story."

"Leigh," Hall said, waving Ulysses to go up the stairs first. "Have everyone wait down here. Don't close the hatch yet."

At the landing, Ulysses paused at the door, leaning against it. He reached out for the handle, listening through the thick wood. Reaching up, he tapped on the door and waited. Nothing happened so he tapped again. Still nothing.

With a shrug, Ulysses opened the door and stepped through.

Hall followed the thief into a dark room. It was small, another door directly across the few feet. It was a storage closet, small crates stacked to the side. Ulysses repeated his tapping procedure and opened the next door. The room beyond was bright, lots of daylight streaming through large windows. Hall could make out a street through the windows, people walking by. Stepping through the second door, he found himself in an office. A desk was against the wall, another door next to it, windows directly opposite with another door.

It was empty, some papers scattered over the desk with quill and inkwell. Signs that someone used it, or just for show from anyone looking in the window. The office was small but functional. Quickly, he moved to the windows, Ulysses alongside. They looked out onto a street, more buildings across and to the sides. People of all types; commoners, workers, and a few higher class; moved up and down, none of them paying any attention to the store and the two men looking out the windows. Hall didn't recognize the street.

"Know where ya are?" Ulysses asked with a chuckle.

Now knowing that he should recognize it, Hall studied the street in more detail.

He cursed, now fully recognizing the street. He and his companions had crossed it a couple days ago when Sergeant Brient had first sent them on the quest. They had walked past this shop while looking for a Silver Blade extortion operation.

It explained how Berim and the Door Knockers had known to expect them. They had been watched from this very shop.

They were in the Noble's Square.

Back where it had started.

"You said there were bedrooms above?" Hall asked.

———

There were two rooms on the small shop's second floor. The Door Knocker front was the office for shipping concerns, which meant it never got much visitor traffic but wouldn't raise any questions being in Nobles Square. A rich merchant with his own fleet would want his offices near his home and his people there at all hours. The second floor was a full apartment, with a bedroom and a small kitchen and living space.

Ulysses assured them it was safe, but Hall still had them pull watches. Two to a shift, including Ulysses. They took turns sleeping after eating a quick dinner. The windows gave an excellent view to the street below, and there was no back alley or access from the rear, which made keeping watch easier.

Hall, as was his habit, took first and last watch. He had pulled a chair from the table closer to the window was looking out onto the street. He had the second floor and Caryn was downstairs. The sun would be rising soon, the start of a new day, one he hoped would bring an end to this quest chain.

Pike was somewhere above, having settled on a nearby rooftop where the dragonhawk wouldn't be noticeable but could come to Hall's aid quickly.

Hall watched the citizens of Silver Peak Keep start their morning routine. It had started with just the nightly Peak-Guard patrol, the streets empty, and then slowly more and more people had appeared. First were the merchants, opening their shops, and then the servants of the rich. They came to buy wares their households would need for the day. Food mostly, but some clothing. Picking up orders their rich masters had commissioned.

As he watched the people go about their day, Hall tried to come up with a plan.

He was failing.

Knowing he was considered the leader, he knew they would look to him for a plan for confronting Cronet. The problem was that he had none. If this had followed the old Sky Realm Online rules, there would be quest prompts and markers to follow to where they were supposed to face Cronet. It would probably be classified as a dungeon, even if in the Councilors mansion, with lots of combat and traps as they made their way through the building followed by a final Boss fight. But he had no marker. Ulysses knew where Cronet's mansion was, but without a Wikipedia guide, they didn't know what they would face.

Or if Cronet would even be there.

If they had the time, Hall would have some Door Knockers stake out Cronet's mansion, warehouses, and other places of business. Establish a pattern, scout out the locations, and determine the best place to make their move. At least that was what he had learned from reading and watching many movies and books. It was something he had never needed to put into practice before, not in any games and especially not in Sky Realms Online. He knew they couldn't hit Cronet in public. Sergeant Brient had warned against it and without immediate and visible proof of his being the Cudgel, they would be the ones perceived as the attackers and wrongdoers.

There was one part of the plan he had down. Remove Cronet.

That was the easy part.

Where it would fall in the sequence and how it would happen, he didn't have any idea.

He opened up his Character Sheet, checking his status. At least he had fully recovered his Health and Vitality. Back at full strength, except his gear. All of his weapons and armor were in bad need of repairs. It was the best they were going to get.

Playing with the menus, just randomly cycling through them, he passed the time while looking out the window. What was he going to tell them? *There is no plan. Your fearless leader has no clue what he is doing.*

Which was true. He had been winging it from the beginning. Even after gaining lordship of Skara Brae, he was still just making it up as he went along. They had set out from the village, heading to Silver Peak Keep with a vague idea of getting supplies to rebuild the village. There was Duncant, the carpenter, but would that be enough? And Hall had fallen into him by pretty much accident. It had been a lucky break.

When Raiding in the game, pre-Glitch, leading the Guild or party hadn't been difficult. They knew the objective and the game pretty much guided them on where to go. The *how* came from the various Wikipedias. Even new content was solved fairly quickly just by the sheer mass of Players that threw themselves at it. That made leadership easy.

It was just a matter of keeping the various personalities of the Players under control. But now it was more. There were still the personalities of Players, and now free-thinking NPCs, to contend with along with no guidance from the game.

He had accepted being stuck in the game, but more and more it was starting to feel like not a game. Not just the physical elements but now the mental. No RPG had ever had a puzzle like what he was facing now. He required real training to figure it out.

Or did he?

They had managed fine so far. No real tactics, just brute force. Why not continue? It was working for them. No need to change.

He smiled as he closed his Sheet. Now he had his plan.

CHAPTER THIRTY-FIVE

THE WAREHOUSE WAS BURNING.

Even in the morning sun, the flames were bright and visible.

Smoke billowed out of the open doors and windows, thick and black as it drifted into the air. Clouds of it formed over the city. Flames could be seen within the wooden walls. Bright orange and red, flickering as they spread throughout the inside and along the floors. Crates could be seen burning, some already nothing but piles of ashes.

Everyone in Peakdock was out and watching. All activity had stopped on the docks themselves, all eyes turned to watch the flames. Bucket brigades were forming, throwing water onto the nearby buildings to keep them from catching. None bothered to try and save the burning warehouse.

No one had seen what had caused it. Or at least no one said anything.

Most knew who had set the blaze, and they thought it best to stay out of the Door Knocker's business. If the thieves Guild wanted to destroy a warehouse belonging to the Councilor of Trade, Lord Cronet, a wise man would just let it burn.

———

Hall watched the smoke and the burning warehouse from just outside the gate. He stood on the thin strip of land between the heavy stone wall and the edge of the plateau, watching the flames engulf the wooden building. Visible from even this far away, he was not alone. Dozens of citizens crowded the land in front of the wall to the sides of the gates. The PeakGuard at the gates had to push them away from the road to keep it clear. But it was only half-hearted as they too watched the fire.

Bets were made if other buildings would catch. Questions were asked about who owned the warehouse and how it had caught fire.

Hall was just amazed at how good a job the Door Knockers had done. When he had outlined the plan to Ulysses, the thief was only too eager to carry it out. Hall thought it was the sheer audacity that appealed to the small thief.

More smoke joined the sky over Peakdock. The new stack came from a series of homes in the middle of the town. Wooden homes, surrounded by others, were catching fire. One by one, the flames were not spreading but starting in each of the buildings. Two next to each other, another four streets over, a fifth even further away.

The people around him starting talking, more than before. They pointed, they yelled. And then someone from within Silver Peak Keep shouted.

"Fire."

The one word drew all attention. All heads turned to look into the gate, even the guards. People screamed, they yelled, they cursed. The sound of the city, always loud, took on a panicked pitch. More voices took up the cry.

Hall glanced up, seeing the small speck that was Pike circling high above. Connecting with the dragonhawk, he was given a good bird's-eye view of the city. He could see all the rooftops, the guards walking patrols along the tops of the walls, the people moving through the streets. And he could see the two thick plumes of smoke rising out of the city. One in a random street in the Trade District and another from a home in Nobles Square.

Cronet wanted a Guild war. Everything was pushing and moving toward that. Now that they knew the Cudgel was Cronet, the Door Knockers would be able to start attacking the Councilor's holdings. They had a name and they had targets. Cronet was going to get the war he wanted.

Just sooner than he planned and not on his terms.

Hall knew it wasn't what Brient would want. There was considerable risk to the citizens of the city, both the Keep and Peakdock. But it was the only way to flush out Cronet. If they waited on him to consolidate and launch the war on his terms and schedule, they would never be able to catch him. But to do it before he was ready, they could catch him unprepared and vulnerable.

Brient would just have to understand.

He could see more PeakGuards running down the street. Unlike the ones currently at the gate, dressed in leather and chain armor and carrying spears, the newcomers were dressed in heavier armor and carried shields, a couple with crossbows. They took up positions on either side of the gate, stepping out and directing the citizens back inside.

Hall followed the crowd, inching his way closer to where the commander of the newcomers was talking with one of the gate guards.

"Orders from above," the commander was informing the other. "We're reinforcing the gate. With all the chaos, the Guard is being sent out in force."

"Chaos?" the guard who had been at the gate asked, confused. "The fires?"

"And the rest," the other replied. "Almost a dozen citizens

have turned up dead or missing, including a couple of Hobs. And the Councilor of Coin found a strange delivery left for him this morning. A large crate. Inside were dozens of ledger books just like his official ones. It looked like someone had been forging city ledgers."

"What?" the first guard asked in shock. "How would they do that?"

"There was an actual ledger taken from the archives," the commander said.

Hall was pushed away from the gate by the press of people, unable to hear anymore.

QUEST COMPLETE!

You have managed to stop the Silver Blade's plans for the forged ledgers. Your methods for stopping the Blade's plans was unique and results in gaining new skills.

THE NEW BLOOD III (ELITE) (OPTIONAL)

Stop the Silver Blade's plans for the forged ledgers 1/1
Rewards: +75 Door Knocker reputation
+75 PeakGuard reputation
+100 Alliance Reputation with Sergeant Brient
+50 Experience
+10 Increased Perception Skill
+10 Strategy Skill

Skill Gain!

Increased Perception Rank Two +10.0
Strategy Rank Two +10.0

You have stopped the Silver Blade's plans to undermine the citizen's faith in the city's finances. Sergeant Brient would want you to eliminate the Silver Blade threat completely.

THE NEW BLOOD IV
Eliminate the Silver Blades Guild 0/1
Rewards: +100 Door Knocker reputation; +100 PeakGuard
reputation; +200 Alliance Reputation with Sergeant Brient; +100
Experience

ACCEPT QUEST?

Beyond the Cutthroats in the Silver Blades Guild, the Cudgel has
increased the Guild's ranks by hiring Hob mercenaries. Convince the
Hobs to void the contract with the Cudgel.

"HOB"LESS FORCES I
Slay Hob Mercenary 0/8
Rewards: +25 Door Knocker reputation; +25 PeakGuard reputation;
+50 Alliance Reputation with Sergeant Brient; +50 Experience

ACCEPT QUEST?

Hall saw the prompts flash across his vision, momentarily startling him. He hadn't expected to get quest prompts then, but it made sense. His plan had stopped the forged ledger threat. He quickly ran through the prompts, accepting the next step in the quest chain plus the new quest. He was about to dismiss the notifications when he reread the first. The Elite quest seemed like it had been easy to complete, and he wasn't sure why it had the Elite designation, but then he thought about it.

The quest task had been difficult to complete. It had been purposely vague. Stop the plans. Which could have been accomplished in a variety of ways, some of which could have gone very badly for Hall and his companions. The Elite difficulty came in completing the quest in a way that didn't harm him.

And the two unknown rewards. Never before had acquiring new skills been a quest reward. He tried to find information on the skills and what their benefits would be but there was nothing. *Increased Perception* seemed obvious but *Strategy*? That was another new skill with no hints as to what it did.

Questions for another time, he thought as he moved deeper into Silver Peak Keep. There was more that needed to be done, and he had to get into position quickly. He smiled.

So far, all was going according to plan.

The smile disappeared. He knew it wouldn't last.

Murphy's law would see to that.

————

"I don't like this," Leigh said, reaching down to scratch Angus behind the cow's ears.

"Hall was right," Sabine replied, indifferent. "It was going to happen sooner or later. Why not do it under conditions we control?"

Leigh nodded. She understood but that didn't make it easier.

The two women were in the Nobles Square at the central fountain, watching the citizens react to the chaos that was attacking Silver Peak Keep. Sabine sat on the edge of the fountain, her long legs crossed and pushed a loose strand of purple-streaked blonde hair out of the way.

She had to admit to herself that she was enjoying watching the chaos. Kind of. But only a little. She didn't want to see innocent people get hurt, but these were only NPCs. She glanced at Leigh standing next to her.

The Druid made her uncomfortable.

She knew Leigh was an NPC, a person made up of a computer program's algorithms and Artificial Intelligence. A series of coded impulses and responses. At least that was what an NPC was supposed to be. Leigh was not that. Sabine wasn't sure exactly what Leigh was.

Not a person. No matter how much she acted like one. Sabine could not bring herself to consider Leigh, or even Jackoby, as a real person. Not like herself. Or Hall and Roxhard. Or even the new girl, Caryn. Those were Players. Real people.

Even if now they were as computer-generated as the NPCs were. They had still started out as real people, and that made all the difference.

But it was hard to consider the NPCs as just computer programs. Everything about them, about Leigh, felt real. The way they acted, their responses, their reactions. There was nothing preprogrammed about them. It was AI that was light years ahead of where it had been before the Glitch. No way could it have developed that much in just two years.

The old Sky Realms Online NPCs had been advanced, but there had been limitations. They could still only act within a predetermined set of parameters. Those were beyond anything at the time. It was what had first drawn Sabine to the game, but they were still obviously NPCs. Even the Companion ones from Pre-Glitch. They still had a limited amount of reactions and responses they could follow.

Sabine could see what Hall found attractive and interesting about Leigh. The Druid, with her wild red hair and bright green eyes, was beautiful. And she was nice. So damn nice. The perfect girl next door. Even Sabine found herself attracted to Leigh. It was obvious that Hall was and that Roxhard had a kid's crush on Leigh. And it seemed Leigh was attracted to Hall.

She wasn't sure what she thought about that. At first, Sabine had thought she could form a bond with Hall, become a powerful couple. She did like him, and it wasn't like there were many options. But from the start, he was interested in

Leigh, so Sabine had pushed those thoughts away and just concentrated on playing the game.

But now there was Caryn. The Duelist was pretty and somewhat interesting. Naive but that would be hammered away with this new life. *Caryn wasn't too annoying*, Sabine thought, thinking of the woman and smiling. She could be fun. And would be joining them. It had only been a couple of weeks, a month or maybe more, but already Sabine knew how Hall's mind worked. She accepted him as the leader because the others did, and she knew he would invite Caryn to join their group and live in Skara Brae.

Which was something else that was bothering Sabine. She was jealous. She wanted a village. Not necessarily Skara Brae, not one as worn down and out of the way, but just a village. And Hall had claimed it already. If she had been with Hall, as his partner, the village would have basically been hers anyway, but now she was just one of the citizens.

A citizen of a run-down village in the middle of nowhere, weeks from any true civilization. A place so badly in need of attention that they had needed to come to Silver Peak Keep to find the means of fixing it up.

Which was her biggest annoyance. This damned city.

Being arrested by Brient and used as blackmail had angered her, which was the biggest part of why she enjoyed seeing the chaos in Silver Peak Keep. It served them right for using her. But it was her own stupidity that really caused her anger. She had let them capture her. Instead of fighting like she had first wanted, she had instead thought of how Hall would react. To both the arrest and her fighting. She had backed down and been humiliated.

They were working to fix that.

Finish off Cronet and they could leave this place and get back to what mattered.

But what was it? What mattered to her?

To Hall, it was his new town and Leigh, who just happened to be the new Custodian of the Grove next to the village. Roxhard would just follow Hall around like a puppy dog. The kid in a Dwarf's body had found a big brother in the Skirmisher. Jackoby was a non-factor. She didn't like the Firbolg and only cared about what he could do for her. Having a Firbolg Warden was a bonus, but he would care nothing for her. And she didn't see a way to change that. Caryn was too new. No way to gauge what the Duelist would want. Not yet.

So, what mattered to Sabine? What did she want out of this new life she was trapped in.

She didn't know. A village, with followers, seemed like a good goal. To level and get to this seemingly maximum Level of Twenty or Twenty-Five. Leigh hadn't been much help on that, but either way, that was a good goal to set.

To get to max level and have a village of her own.

That was what mattered to her.

And the sooner they got out of this city, the sooner that could happen.

"There," Leigh said, drawing Sabine's attention.

She had been staring off at nothing, just watching the citizens of Silver Peak Keep running around, lost in her thoughts. The Druid brought her focus back, and she looked to where Leigh was indicating. A tall man was making his way through the streets, the crowd being pushed aside by two armed Peak-Guards. Four other men followed, dressed in various pieces of leather armor and carrying drawn weapons.

"That's him?" she asked, being careful to not point.

"Fits the description," Leigh replied.

Gray hair, streaks of brown, that was cut short. Clean-shaven. The tall man was thin, dressed in expensive-looking clothing. Bright button-up shirt that shone like silk, wool pants, and a cape. Not a cloak, but a short cape. He wore a rapier belted to his waist, one that looked more ornamental than functional. Hard black eyes stared straight ahead, strong and square jaw set in anger.

Cornet, with the four men trailing, passed past them. Closer inspection showed they were dressed in mismatched armor. Leather and chain, a couple with iron pauldrons and greaves. They carried an assortment of weapons, swords and axes, a single shield and two crossbows. Bodyguards and mercenaries. Their eyes scanned the crowds, moving and watching, pausing briefly on Sabine and Leigh.

Sabine didn't know if it was them, the two women being dressed differently and attractive, that had caught the guards' attention or if it had been Angus. The cow sat next to Leigh, mooing quietly to himself. The sight of a Highland cow in the middle of Nobles Square should draw attention, it was so odd. Whichever it was, it didn't flag the guards' attention as they kept on walking.

They waited until the small group had turned down a street before leaving the fountain. They moved slowly, not in any hurry, knowing where Cronet was headed. Their part of the plan was to just follow and be ready for the next part.

Sabine let her thoughts wander again. She knew what she wanted and why she deserved it. But was that enough? Hall was earning respect, making friends and allies. He was showing that his way worked. Could that be a path she followed? Could she settle for less than what she thought she deserved?

And what had she done to deserve it in the first place?

Nothing yet.

There was no hurry, she told herself. She was surrounded by people that could be considered her friends, and she was moving down a path. Slowly but at least still moving. Glancing at Leigh, she realized that part of the reason the Druid made her uncomfortable was because Sabine was fighting the impulse to like her. There was nothing to dislike about Leigh, and Sabine knew it was only because Leigh was an NPC. She could be friends with Leigh, true friends, if she could just get over that fact.

Hall had. Roxhard had. Why couldn't she?

The question followed her as they followed Cronet.

———

Hall smiled as he saw the small procession walk down the street. Cronet, led by the two PeakGuards, stopped just outside the small shop. A jeweler. The front window had been smashed, the door kicked in. Smoke drifted out of the open window and into the air. Not a large fire, it had already burned itself out, just the smoke and smell left. Along with the blackened remains of wooden display cases.

Empty display cases.

The shop had been broken into. Not cleanly but openly. It was meant to send a message. The theft of the shop's entire inventory, done in a matter of minutes, was message enough. The extra insult of the small fire just added to the owner's anger. That owner was Cronet.

Councilor Cronet owned the jewelry store direct, not through others' names or means. It was his name on the deed. Which is why the Door Knockers had paid it special attention. Before, his name alone had kept it safe from theft, and no thief would ever take an entire store's inventory. There wasn't usually enough time and too much for one person.

But this job had not been done by just one person.

Hall didn't know how many Door Knockers there had been, at least six, but they had done a good job of cleaning the shop of every last gem and necklace. From where he stood in front of a bakery, a couple buildings down, along with dozens of others all watching the jewelers, Hall could see how angry Cronet was. The man was almost shaking with rage.

Cronet looked around, standing a couple inches taller than

the guards around him, eyes searching the gathered people as if he could spot the Door Knockers that had stolen from him. He turned and motioned the bodyguards to move and push their way through the thickening crowds. He didn't even dispatch someone to get the shop repaired, he just ignored it. Not even giving the shop a final glare, Cronet followed the two lead guards as they headed back toward the fountain in Nobles Square. As they passed, Hall stepped away from the bakery and into the street. He followed along behind.

Ahead, he could see Sabine and Leigh approaching. It was time to start the next phase.

Skill Gain!
Identify Rank One +.3

Mercenary Fighter (White)
Mercenary Fighter (White)
Mercenary Fighter (White)
Mercenary Fighter (White)
PeakGuard Soldier (White)
PeakGuard Soldier (White)
Councilor Cronet (Blue)

Hall activated *Leap*. He jumped up into the air, high, and came down hard. His spear caught one of the rear mercenaries in the back. The force of the impact pushed the fighter down and the man fell to the ground. He didn't get up. Using *Leap* again, Hall jumped up onto the rooftops to the side. There and gone so quickly the guards barely had time to react.

SLAIN: Mercenary Fighter
+25 Experience

Skill Gain!

Polearms Rank Two +.1

At the same time as the guard fell, Sabine struck. She raised her hands and shouted a word. Bolts of purple energy shot out, slamming into the two PeakGuards in front. Smaller bolts scattered and spread across their bodies, the *Hexbolt* preventing them from moving and preventing them from coming to Cronet's defense. They each took a small amount of damage.

Angus charged, the cow's horns slamming into one of the mercenaries. The man was sent flying back a couple of feet, landing hard. Turning quickly, the cow ran back to Leigh who had her hand raised and staff pointed. As a word was spoken, dozens of small splinters shot out from the staff.

Cronet ducked, the splinters hitting the shields of the guards, who had barely gotten them up in time. Wood struck wood, some lodging in the shields and others bouncing aside. A few got past, and the guards grunted in pain as the splinters pierced armor and entered skin.

Sabine and Leigh were already turning, running down the road before the last splinter struck. The mercenaries pulled in tight around Cronet, facing out and eyes scanning everywhere. The attack had been fast and vicious. Over as soon as it had happened.

The guards were left wondering what had happened. There was no follow-up, just the quick attacks. The ambushers could have kept attacking, possibly even killing all the guards before they could respond. But the attackers hadn't.

Which made the guards even more paranoid.

Leaving the dead mercenary and the two PeakGuards, who still suffered from the *Hexbolt*, behind the remaining guards rushed Cronet into an alley between shops.

———

Hall landed on the ground, jumping down from a two-story roof and onto the hard-packed dirt of the alley behind the homes. A quick glance around, making sure no one had seen him, he knocked on the door in a pattern, quickly opened the door and slipped into the Door Knocker safehouse. Roxhard and Jackoby, along with a couple Door Knockers, all looked up at his approach, lowering weapons.

"Did it work?" Roxhard asked.

He shrugged, not sure.

They waited, none approaching the windows. Time stretched and Hall got nervous. He started pacing back and forth. There came a knocking on the door, a pattern like he had done, and the door opened. He was right there as Sabine and Leigh entered, followed by Angus, closing the door behind them. He grabbed Sabine in a hug, surprising her. It was short and he pulled Leigh into another hug. This one was longer, tighter, and the surprised woman wrapped her arms around him. It lingered and both stepped back awkwardly. Angus mooed and pushed Hall out of the way.

"We took the long way around," Sabine explained. "Went through the Square and then some alleys before doubling back."

The next wait was even longer but no less intense. The small building was crowded, people spread out on the levels and rooms. Sabine was in the bedroom, trying to nap. Hall wished he could but he was too wired. This had been his plan. He had worried enough about sending Leigh, and Sabine, into danger but they had made it back. Caryn was the last to return. While her part was the easiest, involved the least risk, it was the most important.

Her report would tell him if the plan worked.

Half an hour later, she returned. The same pattern of knocks on the back door and the Duelist entered. She pushed her dark hair out of her face and smiled.

"The mercs practically pushed him back into his house," she said to Hall's unspoken question. "Hour or so later, a carriage came barreling out and went roaring off down the streets."

"Which way?" Hall asked.

"East," she replied and gave him a description of the carriage.

Hall smiled. It had worked.

CHAPTER THIRTY-SIX

PIKE SOARED THROUGH THE SKY ABOVE THE PLAINS. THE dragonhawk flew east, following the road that would lead to Auld. His sharp eyes, which somehow seemed even sharper now, scanned the land below him. Through the shared connection, Hall saw what Pike saw, the dragonhawk apparently benefitting from the *Increased Perception* skill.

The road ran straight through the grass of the plains surrounding the city. Hard-packed dirt, a brown line in the green. To the southeast, a large forest. To the northeast, the plains stretching as far as the dragonhawk's eyes could see. Directly north, the Thunder Growl Mountains and Silver Peak itself. All of it seen in detail. People, animals, and the lone carriage taking a smaller side road heading for the forest.

It fit the description Caryn had given. Four wheels, two smaller in the front and larger in the back. The sides painted red with gold tracings. Carved details in the corners. A high seat for the driver. Four horses, running fast. The only carriage on the road, any of the roads.

Hall had no idea where Cronet was running to but it was out of the city, which is what they needed. The plan had worked. Hall had realized that there was no way to fight the Councilor in the city. They would be the attackers, the bad guys, and would end up fighting the PeakGuard as well as the Silver Blades. If it even came to that. Cronet, smartly, would have played the victim.

In the end, he would have won.

The only way to fight him was out of the city. To do that, they had to flush him out. They had to panic him so he would flee the city to someplace the Door Knockers didn't know about, a place they had no influence, a secret base of operations. Somehow, to Hall's amazement, it had worked. He really hadn't expected it to.

Pike lost sight of the carriage as it disappeared under the thick canopy of trees. Swooping in lower, the dragonhawk was able to catch glimpses as the carriage sped down the thin and rough road. In and out of the trees, he followed it, until it came to a stop at a collection of buildings in the middle of the forest by a large pond. Spread out in a large clearing, the buildings were all one story and made of logs with shingle roofs. Men could be seen moving about, some carrying large axes. What Hall took to be a mill was built next to the pond where a river flowed through the forest into the body of water.

Together, Half-Elf and dragonhawk watched the carriage came to a halt. The horses were panting, tired from the frantic journey. The driver jumped down, and before he could open the door, six mercenaries jumped out. They were followed by Cronet. The man was angry, rushing across the clearing toward the largest of the buildings. The mercenaries started barking orders to the other men, spreading out as they did.

Through the eyes of Pike, Hall watched as over a dozen Hobs ran out of the large building. They were all armored, some pulling pieces on as they ran. The camp was chaotic in the activity, people running everywhere as if unsure where to go. Hobs shouted, mercenaries shouted, workers shouted.

Hall canceled the connection. It was time to go.

─────

They had immediately left the safehouse. Most of the Door Knockers had retreated into the tunnels to head to Peakdock and gather the troops. One Knocker followed, dressed as a citizen of Silver Peak Keep. Hall and his companions stood out more than the Knocker did, who looked natural, like he belonged.

Leaving the city by the east gate, they started running down the dirt road. A quick sprint to make up some distance and then a jog, finally turning to a walk. Hall didn't want to tire out; there was going to be intense fighting soon. But he didn't want to take a long time to get to the forest either. The more time they gave Cronet and the mercenaries, the more defenses could be put in place. The one advantage they had was that Cronet didn't know they were coming.

As they walked, Hall described where Cronet had stopped.

"That's the old Derish Mill," the Door Knocker had told them. "Didn't think anyone was still working it."

Once the location was confirmed, the Knocker left to join up with the Guild. It was his job to lead the Knockers to the Mill. It was Hall's job to keep Cronet occupied in the meantime.

Pulling up his mental map, Hall marked the location of Derish Mill on it. The area had been filled in, no longer clouded, as Pike's scouting had revealed it. On the map, he could see the pond and the clearing.

Skill Gain!
Cartography Rank Two +.1

With a direction fixed, they left the road and made their

way through the plains to the forest. The sun was starting to set as they approached the forest's edge. With a last look up at Pike circling above, Hall led them beneath the trees.

Thick and old, the trees towered above them. Branches spread out, blocking most of the sun, letting filtered beams hit the ground, which was covered in needles and leaves. They moved silently, spread out in the trees, keeping to cover as much as possible.

The forest was silent, very few creatures stirring. A slight rustling of a squirrel in the branches above, a bird chirping and taking wing. The loudest noise was Angus stomping over and snapping twigs and leaves. The small cow could not move gracefully.

It was an hour later, much darker beneath the trees, when Hall held his hand up. A signal for them to stop. The group was spread out, but the signal was passed, and they all stopped, crouching low.

Hall saw a shadowy figure moving through the trees ahead. Not looking their way, the figure was crouching at a small stream. It looked like the person was getting a drink as they stood up and seemed to wipe their hand across their face. They started walking again, forward, but not toward Hall and the others. He was walking past on an angle, a path that would take him away from them.

Close enough that Hall could make out the details, the man was not paying much attention. A bored Sentry. No one was expecting anyone to have tracked Cronet to the forest, so the guards were not on alert. The man was dressed in dark-colored leathers, a bow slung over his shoulder and a short sword belted at his waist.

Skill Gain!

Identify Rank One +.1

Silver Blade Sentry (White)

Hall was tempted to let the man pass by but didn't want a chance of the Sentry coming up behind them. And one less Silver Blade now was one less they would have to face later when the odds would be against them. He had been worried when he had seen, through Pike's eyes, the amount of Silver Blades at the lumber mill. That was a lot of enemies and they didn't know for sure when the Door Knocker reinforcements would arrive.

Or if.

He wasn't fully convinced that Berim and Ulysses would send help. The only course of action, besides stepping away which they could not do, was to proceed as if the Door Knockers were going to arrive in force.

The smart move was to eliminate every Silver Blade they came upon. Quickly and quietly.

Hall was tempted to do it himself but knew he had to remain focused on leading the group. He was starting to agree with Roxhard. They needed a name.

Raising his hand, Hall pointed to Caryn and then the Sentry. The Duelist, crouched behind a low tree, stepped away and moved slowly and quietly after the Sentry. Her shadowed form seemed to disappear in the forest without a sound, as her *Stealth* ability activated. Hall wondered how much higher hers was. He had put no effort into raising his, it seemed that Caryn had. He had been lamenting how the group needed someone with thief skills, and it looked like they had found her.

Giving Caryn a couple minutes, Hall stood up and motioned the rest to continue.

———

SLAIN: *Silver Blade Sentry*

+ 25 Experience

Skill Gain!
Small Blades Rank 2 +.1

Hall held the body and slowly lowered it to the ground. The Sentry had stopped kicking and fighting. The man had stiffened and tried to cry out as Hall's hand covered his mouth from behind. Before the Sentry could fight back, Hall's short sword had stabbed him from behind. With the base damage from the weapon added to the Critical Strike from the ambush attack into the Sentry's unprotected rear, the man didn't have a chance.

It was the third Sentry they had come across, the first that Hall had taken out himself. Caryn had gotten the first and Jackoby the second. None had been very effective Sentries. Checking the map, Hall saw that they were only a half-mile or so away from the Mill. He expected to run across more Sentries and was right.

Skill Gain!
Identify Rank One +.1

Silver Blade Sentry (White)

A Sentry had stepped out from behind a tree only twenty feet or so in front of them. Luckily, the man's back was turned. He was looking toward the Mill, grumbling to himself. Hall motioned for a halt and studied the surrounding land, trying to figure out the best way to the Sentry.

This was going to be the hard part. Taking the Sentries out while doing it quietly. One shout and it would be over. They were still a good distance from the Mill, but it was close enough and sound could travel. A barely heard shout would be just as bad as a louder and closer one.

The ground between him and the Sentry was covered in low bushes, no clear path. If he tried to *Leap*, he would enter the branches and make a lot of noise. It was hard to tell if other Sentries were near. He couldn't see them, but that didn't mean anything.

Hall decided to wait for the Sentry to move. They would have to run the risk of the man coming up behind him. Or hope the Door Knockers took him out.

It was a slow couple of minutes. Only five or so, but to Hall, it felt more like fifty. The Sentry walked off, heading away from the group. He took his time doing it. Once he was out of sight, Hall gave it another couple of minutes to be safe.

Hall pulled them closer together, not wanting them to be so spread out. Angus was quieter, figuring out how to move without making as much noise, but it made him slower. Hall had adjusted the pace to compensate for the cow. They would need him when the fighting started.

Slowly, they crept across the last half mile. Hall stole glances of the sun through gaps in the trees. He wanted to time it for just as the sun set beyond the horizon, hoping it would be when the majority of the Silver Blades were starting to eat dinner.

Finally, after what felt like an eternity, they got to the clearing that was the Mill. High grass and dirt paths spread out through the clearing, bordered by the pond on one side. One-story log buildings with low sloped shingled roofs. The rear of each building had no windows, the sides only one or two that were closed with shutters. All the doors faced the middle of the Mill where Cronet's carriage still sat.

Sentries stood in front of each building, a couple roaming the grounds. Most were Humans. He could see a couple of the Hobs, those clustered closer to the largest building in the middle. It was hard to get an accurate count as the Sentries kept moving, and some were blocked by the buildings, but Hall was able to count three Hobs and eight Sentries, which might have been a mix of the Sentry and Cutthroat. It looked like there were two Archers. No casters from what he could see, which didn't mean they weren't there.

Hall and his companions were seriously outnumbered.

He watched their movements, trying to see if there was a pattern they could exploit. The Sentries followed no set paths or timing, it was all random. Maybe they could pick the Silver Blades off a few at a time. Kill them quickly, retreat to the woods, get chased by a couple and take those out. Return and get some more. Hit and run tactics.

That could work, he thought as the ground started to shake.

Hall looked to the east, the far side of the Mill, and watched as the trees moved. They shifted and shook as if something was pushing them aside. Out of the trees stepped two large figures. Giants. Not as big as the one they had faced at the farm, but they were still giants.

Hall cursed.

CHAPTER THIRTY-SEVEN

Skill Gain!
Identify Rank One +.2

Oak Crag Hold Giant (Blue)
Oak Crag Hold Giant (Blue)

HALL WATCHED THE TWO GIANTS SIT DOWN JUST PAST THE border of the trees. The ground shook as their great bodies hit. Each held a tree trunk club and seemed to be ignoring the smaller people running around.

Their arrival changed Hall's tactics.

The plan had been to take out a small group of Silver Blades, lure the rest into the woods, and take that group out before coming back for more. The giants would be across the open space before Hall and the others were done with the first group of Blades. There would be no chance at separation. They'd end up fighting the entire Mill plus the two giants.

Not smart.

But what if they took out the giants first?

Staying low, he melted back into the forest and gathered

the others around him. He made a couple quick hand motions and realized the others didn't understand. With a sigh, he started walking and they followed. *We'll have to work on that and come up with some common ones*, he thought.

As they moved through the forest, keeping well back from the clearing, he realized that the motions he had been making were fairly complicated and carried a lot of meaning. Was that a result of this new *Strategy* skill he had acquired? There would be time to figure it out later. Right now, they had thieves to kill.

The walk to the other side of the Mill took almost an hour. Long and slow, constantly stopping to listen to the noises around them. Alert for any Sentries. They found one, and Caryn quickly dispatched the Blade. Hall stayed the closest to the open clearing that was the Mill, keeping it to his right and always in sight. He was able to guide them as it turned back toward the pond.

As they got closer to the two giants, they walked with more care. There was no telling how well the giants' ears were. Because they were bigger, that had to make hearing easier. Through the trees, Hall could see the back of the two giants. Dark shapes in the darkness about twenty feet away, blocking out the moon and starlight.

Pulling the others in close, he quickly whispered the plan.

Skill Gain!
Strategy Rank 2 +.1

Pointing at the Firbolg and Caryn, he motioned them to the right-hand giant. He positioned Roxhard near him at the left. Sabine and Leigh were stationed between the two groups, Angus in front of them. Satisfied that it was as good as it would get, Hall watched the Silver Blades, waiting for the perfect moment.

It seemed like the Blades were avoiding the giants. They never came closer than twenty feet. The Sentries in the area would walk toward the giants and turn, not even looking that direction. Hall studied the patterns, timing them. Toward the giants and away, momentarily lost to sight behind the nearest building.

One more rotation, toward the giants, away and behind the building. Hall tapped Roxhard on the shoulder, and the Dwarf Warden activated *Battle Rush*.

He burst from the forest, leaves and branches exploding out into the clearing. The Dwarf crossed the small distance and slammed into the back of the sitting giant. Because it was sitting, the giant did not get pushed forward or knocked down, but the impact did shake it. It leaned forward a tad, grunting in pain. Roxhard bounced but was ready for the impact.

Landing on his feet, he swung his axe in a heavy two-handed blow. The head cut into the giant's back, slicing a large gash. Hall saw its Health bar, the red dropping by at least a third. Taking a couple steps to clear the trees, he activated *Leap*.

As he soared high into the air, his arc bringing him down, he saw Jackoby rush out of the trees and slam into the other giant. The Firbolgs size and weight did cause the giant to slide forward a foot or so. Before Jackoby could even swing his hammer, Caryn had darted out and her two swords sliced thin lines of blood across the giant's back.

Hall landed on the tall humanoid's shoulder and stabbed down with his spear. His angle hadn't allowed him to land and stab into the eye like he had before, and the giant was recovering quickly. The point of his spear slammed into the giant's shoulder, and the weapon's special ability activated. A large shard of wood stuck in the wound, causing a bleeding-over-time effect. Leaping off, Hall landed on his feet behind Roxhard and facing the giant.

A second attack from the Dwarf, cut into the giant's arm as the creature tried to push itself up. It stumbled, falling back down hard, as a bolt of purple energy slammed into it. Crackling lightning flared around the giant's body, spreading out from the point of impact. Roots and grass grew around the giant's arms and legs, the creature trying to pull up to break the hold.

Roxhard kept attacking, each blow falling hard onto the giant's unprotected back. The plan was to keep the giant from moving, unable to turn and defend itself. Because of the flanking attacks, each would have increased damage, and if they could keep it up, they would wear the giant down quickly.

With another *Leap*, Hall landed on the giant's shoulder again, this time the right. Because he was so close, he managed to get a *Leaping Stab* attack along with the *Leap*'s Attack of Opportunity. The two attacks scored deep hits, taking a chunk of the creature's shoulder. It howled in pain, and Hall knew they had lost the element of surprise. Roxhard kept chopping as Hall leapt off again. His energy was depleted so Hall started stabbing the giant in the back, aiming for sensitive areas. The red of the giant's Health was quickly being lost.

The creature stopped struggling, blood leaking from its many wounds. It finally just stopped moving altogether. The giant sagged forward and gave one last breath.

Glancing to the other giant, Hall saw that it had more life left and was ripping the trapping roots and grass up. Soon it would be mobile again. Pointing Roxhard into the trees, Hall used *Leap* and landed on the giant's shoulder. He adjusted his angle so he came in almost level, the tip of his spear leading.

The spear slammed into the side of the giant's head, the ironwood material bending but not breaking. The special ability activated again, leaving a large splinter in the giant's skull. It screamed in intense pain, and Hall saw Silver Blades running toward them.

The fight had only been seconds, but it was taking too long.

One last blow from Jackoby, a great slam of the hammer, into the side of the giant where Caryn had been carving out pieces, and the creature gave a final roar before it collapsed to the side, falling with a crash. Hall jumped off and ran into the woods with the others as the Blades just got to the front of the giants.

SLAIN: *Oak Crag Hold Giant*
+15 Experience
SLAIN: *Oak Crag Hold Giant*
+10 Experience

Skill Gain!
Polearms Rank Two +.2

Turning, Hall saw the three Blades approaching cautiously. None were too eager to rush in and confront the strange group with unknown numbers and abilities that had just taken out two giants in a matter of seconds. He stood just outside the treeline, spear held in both hands, waiting.

Skill Gain!
Identify Rank One +.2

Silver Blade Cutthroat (White)
Silver Blade Sentry (White)
Silver Blade Sentry (White)

Hall held up one hand, waving it in a 'come on' motion. The three Blades looked at each other and stepped closer, away from the cover of the giants' bodies. More Blades could be seen in the distance along with a couple of the Hobs. It was going to get crowded soon. Hall still held his ground, not turning or running. He waited as the Blades crept closer.

Crouching down, activating *Leap*, he jumped into the air. Three heads watched him arc into the air, coming down right in front of the middle one. The spear jabbed out, catching the Blade in the stomach as the man tried to back away. He was too slow, and the ironwood tip cut through his leather jerkin and into flesh behind.

The other two Blades, thinking they had flanking attacks, raised their weapons but stopped. They could hear running feet pounding into the ground. Both flew backward, crashing into the dead giants, as Roxhard and Jackoby each slammed into one. The two Wardens each stepped forward quickly, weapons descending and ending the lives of the Blades.

Hall stabbed out with his spear again, changing the angle and catching the reeling Blade in the throat. The thief dropped to the ground, arms moving from one wound to the other in a futile attempt to stop the bleeding.

SLAIN: *Silver Blade Sentry*
+10 Experience

Skill Gain!
Polearms Rank Two +.1

"Now," Hall shouted to the two Wardens, and all three retreated under the cover of the trees. Shadows enveloped them, hiding them as they crouched down, all but disappearing.

Skill Gain!
Camouflage Rank One +.2

Hall knew the darkness was aiding him; otherwise, his low skill wouldn't have helped against the Blades, appearing from around the edge of the buildings, who now milled about at the treeline. They were unsure what to do. None wanted to rush into the forest in the dark.

"Torches," one yelled.

"Form a perimeter," another shouted.

Hall sighed. Of course there had to be a smart one in the group.

While some kept an eye on the forest's edge, others ran back to gather materials and torches. They would form a wall of eyes and objects to prevent Hall and the others from attacking out of the trees. Now that the Mill was on high alert, it would be next to impossible to sneak attack again. Remaining behind were two Hobs and three Silver Blades.

Hall tried not to move, watching the Sentries pace back and forth. The Hobs didn't move, eyes focused on where Hall and the others had disappeared into the woods. A couple others were racing back when noise and commotion came from the other side of the Mill.

Flames could be seen against the black of the night. An orange and red glow creeping around the edges of the buildings, the flames poking out above the rooftops. A building on the other side had caught fire.

"Door Knockers," came a shout, louder than the others.

Hall smiled. Ulysses had kept his word.

Attacks seemed to come from all sides, including the pond, sending the Mill into chaos.

The three Blades turned, distracted. The Hobs did not.

They did when a small and furry blur shot out of the trees and slammed into the Blade the furthest away. The Sentry was sent flying and landed hard. He tried to get up but the furry form ran into him again. What looked like horns gored into the

Sentry's chest. Stomping on the fallen body of the Blade, the furry form looked at the Hobs and mooed.

Purple bolts streaked out of the dark, slamming into the two Hobs and remaining two Silver Blades. Cascading energy wrapped around each as they tried to move but spasmed in pain. Shards of wood whistled through the air, striking one of the Hobs. It stumbled and fell to the ground, struggling to get up as the energy of the *Hexbolt* contracted muscles and shorted out nerves.

Trying to move, the two Silver Blades were pushed backward as each was hit by a running form. They landed in heaps, forcing themselves up as the purple energy dissipated.

"Mine went further," Roxhard said to Jackoby.

The Firbolg grunted and swung his hammer, the Blade ducking out of the way.

Roxhard started to swing high, the Blade moving low to avoid the attack, when Roxhard instead kicked out with a heavy boot. He caught the man in the stomach, all breath leaving the Blade, who doubled over giving Roxhard a nice target for the axe. The Blade dropped to the ground.

The Dwarf turned to say something to the Firbolg but Jackoby was already standing over the dead body of the Blade he had faced.

"One each," Roxhard said, holding up a stubby finger. "Shared kills don't count."

Even in the dark, it was easy to see Jackoby rolling his eyes.

Hall heard the Dwarf and just shook his head as he activated *Leap*. He was going to have to talk to Roxhard soon, but it would have to be later. He arced up into the air, stabbing down with the spear at one of the Hobs. Scoring a hit in the Hobs shoulder, causing the creature to spin aside, he landed and quickly stabbed out at the other Hob. The spear caught the Hob in the side, forcing it to step back and into the path of a Shadowbolt from Sabine. A bar of black energy slammed into the Hob's side, splashing against its leather armor, a wave of cold energy spreading out.

The Hob stumbled, reaching down to its numb side, leaving the other exposed. Hall had pulled his spear back and jabbed it forward again. The tip slid through the joint in the Hob's armor under its arm. Blood shot out, the Hob growling in pain. It fell to the ground, struggling to get up, and Hall adjusted his grip on the spear. He stabbed down and the Hob stopped moving.

A couple steps away, the other saw what had happened to its comrade and the two Silver Blades. It slipped as it tried to turn, to run away, but a thrown javelin caught it in the shoulder and forced it down to the ground. An axe swing from Roxhard finished it off. Hall pulled his javelin out of the corpse and replaced it in the holder on his back.

SLAIN: *Silver Blade Hob Enforcer*
+15 Experience
SLAIN: *Silver Blade Hob Enforcer*
+15 Experience

Skill Gain!
Polearms Rank Two +.2

"HOB"LESS FORCES I
Slay Hob Mercenaries 2/8

Hall took a moment to rest. There were no more enemies near, not at the moment. The others had all been drawn to other parts of the Mill. He could hear the sounds of fighting from everywhere. Grunts and screams of pain, metal on metal of weapons clashing, the cries of the wounded and dying. Flames still roared into the sky, visible above the other buildings, an orange glow around the edges. Hall thought it looked like more buildings were ablaze.

His companions all came out of the woods, and with a screech, Pike swooped down out of the night sky and settled on his shoulder. They were all tired, but so far not wounded.

"Let's finish this," Hall said and started walking to the center of the camp.

———

He almost dropped his spear as the Hob's weapon slammed against his arm. The flat of the blade against his wrist hurt, but Hall somehow kept a grip on the weapon. The Hob was in too close to use the spear so he held it in his left, drawing his short sword with his right. He managed to twist the Hob's weapon away, leaving the creature's chest unprotected. A quick jab with the sword and the Hob stepped back, releasing the pressure against Hall's arm.

Kicking out, Hall caught it in the knee. The creature buckled and fell, Hall's sword slicing across its throat.

SLAIN: *Silver Blade Hob Enforcer*
+10 Experience

Skill Gain!
Small Blades Rank Two +.1

"HOB"LESS FORCES I
Slay Hob Mercenaries 4/8

Hall glanced to the side and saw Roxhard standing over the body of another Hob. The mercenaries were crowded in front of the entrance to the largest building. Thirty feet long, thirty feet wide, with just the one door that was raised up a couple of steps and glass-filled windows along all walls, gable roof ends making the building seem larger. Behind them, Hall could feel the heat from the many fires, big and small, that spread throughout the Mill. The Door Knockers were still engaged with the Silver Blade forces, more from each group seemingly appearing out of nowhere. They just kept coming.

More Hobs stood in front of the building. Four of them, including what looked to be the leader. He was larger than the others, in better-crafted armor and holding a two-handed bastard sword. His eyes roamed from Hall to the others, studying them.

"HOB"LESS FORCES I
Slay Hob Mercenaries 6/8

Hall couldn't see the bodies, but the quest prompt told him that the others had killed two more. That left the five in front of them, arrayed in a half-circle around the stairs, the leader in the middle. Hall had a feeling there were more inside.

Slowly, his group advanced. The Hobs were outnumbered, six to five. More if counted Angus and Pike, who had flown above and was now sitting on the peak of the roof over the Hobs, causing them to look up nervously.

Stopping about ten feet away, Hall pointed his spear tip at the leader. The Hob growled and spat something in his own language. Hall couldn't speak it, but he understood it well enough. Smiling, spear still pointed, Hall made a motion with his free hand. The middle finger raised. He wasn't sure if the Hob would know what the gesture meant, but it understood the meaning.

With a roar, the Hob charged, two-handed sword raised over its shoulder. The other Hobs followed, leaving the steps and the door unprotected. Jackoby and Roxhard both rushed two of the Hobs, slamming into the creatures, axe clashing with sword and shield catching a down sweeping blade.

Hall sidestepped the Hob leader's attack, swinging out with his spear. The shaft slammed into the Hob's side, the mercenary stumbling. They both took a couple steps back, the Hob swinging his sword in quick and powerful slashes that made Hall step back each time. Hall activated *Leap* and jumped into the air, barely missed by a swing of the mighty blade.

The jump was a short one. *Leaping Stab* caught the Hob in the shoulder, the tip of the spear catching and pulling the Hob off balance. As Hall arced past, the spear tip ripped out, leaving a large gash in the Hob. Landing a couple feet behind the Hob, Hall spun and stabbed. The spear entered the Hob leader's back, tip ripping out the other side.

Still struggling against the spear embedded in his body, the leader tried to raise the heavy blade. Blood dripped from the wounds and he couldn't lift the sword. He growled at Hall, who held the spear in his left and now his sword in his right. Arms reached for him, but Hall batted them away, before slamming the tip of his sword into the Hob's throat.

SLAIN: *Silver Blade Hob Enforcer Commander*
+30 Experience

Skill Gain!
Polearms Rank Two +.1
Small Blades Rank Two +.1

Hall heard more bodies hit the ground, a light thud that was somehow audible over all the chaotic noise in the camp. Then came the sound of booted feet on steps, metal and leather hitting the wood. He turned, pulling his spear out of the Hob Commander, to see another half dozen Hobs run out of the building. They spread out, joining the other two of the original five that were still alive.

The Hobs looked down at their slain leader and the other bodies. The first two growled and muttered in their tongue, the newcomers listening intently. All eyes turned to Hall and his companions. The Hobs gripped their weapons tighter, taking a step forward.

A screech from Pike drew all attention. They all looked up, watching the shadowed form of the dragonhawk silhouetted against the star-filled sky. He was raised to his full height, wings outstretched and screech echoing through the night.

One of the Hobs stepped forward, after looking at the others. He held his weapon, a long sword, out to the side. His other hand was empty. He walked slowly, eyes locked on Hall.

QUEST COMPLETE!

You have eliminated enough of the Hobs and their leader that the remainder are fearful. They suspect they will not get paid, and with no clear leadership or guarantee of payment, do not want to face your powerful band.

"HOB"LESS FORCES I

Slay Hob Mercenary 8/8
Rewards: +25 Door Knocker reputation
+25 PeakGuard reputation
+50 Alliance Reputation with Sergeant Brient
+50 Experience

Now that the Hobs are leaving the Cudgel's service, the enemy ranks will even out and the Door Knockers will have an easier time against the Silver Blades. Berim will be pleased.

"HOB"LESS FORCES II

Report to Berim for a reward 0/1

Rewards: +100 Door Knocker reputation; +10 Gold; +50 Experience

ACCEPT QUEST?

The Hob, eyes still locked on Hall, motioned to the others behind it. As one, they turned and walked away. No rush, without looking back, the Hobs disappeared into the night. Fighting raged around them, but no one tried to stop them and they did not get involved. The last Hob, still facing Hall, backed away until twenty feet separated them. He turned and followed the others.

Hall shared looks with the rest of his companions. That was not how he had expected it to go, but he was not going to complain.

Sheathing his sword, Hall marched up the steps.

CHAPTER THIRTY-EIGHT

THE INTERIOR OF THE BUILDING WAS WIDE OPEN. NO POSTS AND empty of anything else. When the Mill had been operational, the building would have been a communal mess hall and meeting place, the doors to the kitchen area at the rear. Torches lined the wall to provide light, large iron rings with torches hanging from the high and sloped ceiling. The floor was made of heavy wood planking, the walls made of logs.

At the far end stood two men and a woman.

In the middle was Cronet, easily recognizable. He was dressed in leather armor and carried two long swords. The Councilor stood with barely contained rage. He gripped his weapons tight, anger in his eyes.

To the right was a large man, Human but the size of Jackoby. He had blond hair, shaved on the sides and spiked. Black tattoos covered his bare arms and across the shaved sides of his head. In one hand, he held a large sword, and in the other, a metal diamond-shaped shield. Chain shirt and metal-plated leather armor covered his chest and legs. A Storvgarde Warden. He stood there calmly, eyes studying the party.

The woman, on Cronet's left, was tall and thin. Long black

hair and pale skin. She wore a long black form-fitting dress of some shiny material, a leather belt around her waist with a wand tucked through it. There was no ornamentation along the dress, just black. She wore no earrings or rings and didn't carry any visible weapons. Laying across her shoulders was a long cat with an equally long tail that ended in a point. She looked at them like they were beneath her. When her eyes found Sabine, she sneered.

Skill Gain!
Identify Rank One +.3

Councilor Cronet (Orange)
Yorvgr The Warden (Blue)
Keyley The Black Witch (Blue)

"That's a Minx Cat," Sabine whispered, just loud enough that her companions would hear. "A familiar for the Witch. It'll make her attacks stronger."

Cronet and his bodyguards were higher level but outnumbered. If it had been three on three, Hall would have been more worried. The high levels would be negated by the numbers. It should be an even fight. A tough fight, but he thought they could still pull it off.

"Who are you?" Cronet asked. "Are you the ones that have been causing me so much grief?"

The man spoke calmly, getting his anger under control. He was trying to get control of the situation, and Hall had no desire to let him. He watched each of the three across from them and saw the Black Witch's fingers start to move. In one fluid and quick motion, he grabbed the javelin from over his shoulder and threw it at the Witch.

She hadn't been expecting the attack but was able to avoid it anyway. But that interrupted her spellcasting.

"Attack," Hall yelled.

Jackoby charged at Yorvgr, who also charged at the Firbolg. They met in the middle of the room, a tremendous slam. Shield against shield, the clang of metal was loud. The Firbolg was pushed back a couple of feet, the momentum of both Warden's *Battle Rushes* lost.

Activating his *Battle Rush*, Roxhard ran at Cronet. Booted feet slammed against the wooden planks as the Dwarf barreled at the Councilor. Roxhard got close, shoulder leading ready to slam into Cronet, but the man dodged. Roxhard crashed into the back wall, breaking through the wood planking.

Hall *Leapt* into the air, the high ceiling allowing him a high arc. The ceiling came fast and he came close to hitting but started the downward side of his leap, just missing hitting it. He set his spear, aiming for his target. Thrusting the spear forward, using *Leaping Stab*, Hall scored a hit on one of the two identical targets in front of him. Keyley had used the Witch Ability of *Shadow Self*, creating two of her.

She cried out, taking some damage as the spear stabbed through the image, which wavered slightly. Landing, Hall pulled the spear back and used his attack of opportunity. He struck again, aiming for the other image. It wavered, the spear piercing the illusionary figure. Keyley groaned. Neither attack had done anywhere near full damage.

Hall was about to take a couple steps back when the images of the Minx Cat on the Witch's shoulder blurred and disappeared. He felt claws scraping across his arm, drawing thin lines of blood as the cat appeared. It was attached to his arm, small claws dug in deep. The cat was a dark green, with purple stripes, bright yellow eyes. Large ears, ending in tufts, grew out of the small head. It hissed at him as he tried to shake it off.

MINX MAUL!

You have been struck by a Minx Maul attack! The claws of a Minx Cat

*contain a powerful toxin that weakens the blood and increases
damage from Shadow attacks.*

Shaking his head, Hall tried to push the long cat off. It struggled but he pried the beast off, the claws digging long cuts in his arm. He growled just as a black bar of energy slammed into his chest. Intense cold spread out from where the bar had struck, numbing cold. He fell to the ground, managing to hold onto his spear. He'd been hit by a *Shadowbolt* before, but this was so much worse, so much colder.

He looked at his status and saw his Health bar drop.

As he fell, Caryn jumped over him. She slashed out at the Witch, causing the black-dressed woman to step backward. One of Caryn's swords caught an attack by Cronet, and she twisted out of the way of the other attack until she brought her second sword in to block. The two Duelist traded blows, faster than Hall could follow.

He pushed up to his feet, seeing Roxhard stepping out of the hole he had made in the wall. Behind the Dwarf, Hall could see someone in the back room, cowering in the corner. Not attacking. Roxhard had ignored the person so it had to be a non-combatant. They'd worry about who after the fight was over.

Holding his spear in both hands, Hall stabbed out at Keyley, keeping an eye out for the cat. There were still two of the Witch, her cruel face sneering at him as she easily avoided the spear. Hall wasn't trying to attack but was working to keep her from casting a spell. He angled his body, moving to the side and rotating Keyley so she was exposed to Sabine and Leigh.

A swarm of splinters shot out toward Keyley, the Black Witch somehow seeing them. Dodging Hall's thrust, both images raised their hands and barked a single word. Darkness seemed to follow her hand, but only one, as she waved it in a large circle, Smokey blackness gathered, a mass of cloud. The splinters struck and disappeared as they hit her *Shadow Barrier*. Keyley's form blurred, shaking, as the two images slid together. Details focused and there was one Keyley the Black Witch staring at Hall with hate-filled eyes.

Glancing past her, Hall could see Cronet somehow fending off the attacks from both Caryn and Roxhard. The Councilor was fast. Incredibly fast. As a Duelist, quickness and speed of attack was his main offensive and defensive capabilities. Duelists were so fast they were hard to hit, evading attacks instead of taking damage. On the attack, they used that speed to move faster than the opponent could follow. When a Duelist attacked, it was sometimes called dancing because that was how it looked.

Cronet was dancing. Caryn, almost as fast, was a blur. She moved in patterns, swords swinging and striking, blocking and slicing, each movement shifting effortlessly into the next. Roxhard just swung with strength. Each swing of his axe, while not fast, had strength and power behind it. But somehow Cronet was faster and stronger. Where Caryn was grace, Cronet was form and function. There were no wasted movements. Every placement of sword or kick of leg was planned to be precisely where it needed to be. There was a beauty to his dance, but it lacked grace. It was effective. Somehow the thin long swords were able to deflect each of Roxhard's attacks, managing to score quick ones of his own.

Not deep wounds, just glancing cuts, but they would add up as the fight went on.

Hall felt more coldness along his shoulder. He had let himself get distracted, catching a *Shadowbolt* in his shoulder. He felt the muscles contract, stiffen, as he tried to move the arm. The numbness spread, more Health dropping.

Stupid, he thought, *concentrate on your opponent.*

He turned his spear lengthwise, fighting against the numbness in his shoulder, holding it across his body and pushing it out toward the Witch, who shifted her hand and moved the *Shadow Barrier* to block an attack from Sabine. Small blobs of energy streaked into the Barrier, disappearing in the black cloud. Drawing his sword, Hall took a couple steps closer to Keyley.

Swinging the sword, he aimed it along Keyley's chest. She stepped back, moving her hand across the sword's path and caught the blade in the long folds of her dress. She twisted and tried to yank it out of Hall's hand, but he was stronger and pulled it back, slicing a long line through the thin fabric. Quickly, Hall changed the angle of his swing and sliced back in the same path. He scored a hit on her arm, drawing a bloody gash.

Keyley shrieked in pain, and Hall gasped as the Minx Cat darted out of nowhere. It jumped up and its claws raked across his arm as the creature bounded back onto the Witch's shoulders.

Cursing, Hall sent his thoughts out to Pike. The dragonhawk screeched from outside the building.

Growling, the Witch drew her wand. Hall couldn't react in time as a ball of energy shout out and slammed into his chest. He was pushed back, landing hard, losing his grip on the spear. His chest felt like it was on fire. His shoulder was numb from cold while his chest was hot from the ball of light. Another globe struck him and more of his Health dropped. He was at fifty percent. Before Keyley could attack him, Pike streaked into the room. The dragonhawk let loose with a bolt of lightning which Keyley absorbed in the *Shadow Barrier*. The smoky cloud looked thinner, wispier.

Pike swooped out of the way as Keyley launched another globe of light from her wand. She threw another at Hall, who rolled out of the way.

Angry, the Witch stepped backward toward the wall. Her eyes darted around the room. Cronet still held his own against

Caryn and Roxhard but was beginning to tire. His attacks were no longer as smooth, a fraction slower. Near the other wall, Jackoby and Yorvgr exchanged blows. Hammer on shield, sword on shield. Leigh and Sabine stood in the middle, alternating between targets. Whichever of the three enemies presented an opening, the Druid and Witch would take it. It was hard for them, though. The group had Cronet and his cronies outnumbered, but two of their forces were hindered by the layout of the room.

But it was only a matter of time before Hall and his companions would get the advantage. It would happen soon. There was a chance one of his group would make a mistake and Cronet or his cronies could take advantage, but the chances were greater that one of the three would make the first mistake. And once they were down to two, the fight would end soon after.

Hall stood up just as Keyley got to the wall. Smiling evilly, the Black Witch ran her free hand through the blood dripping down her arm from Hall's attack. She held up her palm, covered in her own blood and slammed it against the wall. The blood flowed down the wooden planks and stopped, hitting a barrier.

He had to turn away as the wall erupted in a bright light. It flared and died down, still glowing but now a deep red. Hall watched as the Witch's blood flowed around into a circle and then flowed down the wall. Everywhere the blood went, defying gravity, it left behind shapes. Lines and swirls, borders of rings.

"Stop her," Sabine yelled, somehow her voice carrying over the sounds of fighting. "She's summoning."

Hall cursed, recognizing the symbol now. Summoning was a Magic Skill that Witches could learn. It allowed for the Witch to call on aid from any number of creatures. Low Skill, it summoned animals from the surrounding environments. Small rodents to larger wolves as the skill progressed. At the higher skill levels, the Witch could summon a demon from weak to stronger. But each summoning took some time to prepare. It appeared that Keyley had taken that time before they had attacked.

The warning came too late. The circle and runes of blood were completed. The glowing red flared, not as bright as before, and a bright black line of energy appeared in front of it. The line grew, longer and wider, until a door was floating in space. Five feet high, three feet across.

Time seemed to slow, the fighting stopped as all eyes turned to the black door. Hall held his breath, afraid of what would come out.

They saw the foot as it came out of the blackness.

CHAPTER THIRTY-NINE

THE FOOT ENDED IN A HOOF, BLACK WITH DARK BLUE FUR ON the leg above. Tall and thin, with a backward working knee. Rough fur covered the legs and waist as the body came out of the door. Light blue, bare-chested, covered in scars of all sizes, lean but muscular. A long tail ending in a point waved in the air. An arm appeared, wrist covered in the dark blue fur, ending in a five-fingered hand with long claw-like nails. A dark blue fur-covered shoulder came followed by the head. Yellow eyes glinted from the hairless head, thin black irises moved across the room. The mouth was open, revealing sharp teeth and long canines. Horns grew out of the temples, curling around to the back over the pointed ears. Thick and black-colored bone.

It stood fully out of the door, which shrank behind it. The red glow of the runes faded, disappearing as the door did. Keyley's blood stayed smeared to the wall, dried in the shape of the runes and rings.

The demon stretched, standing about five feet tall. Its eyes moved from person to person, a split tongue darting out and licking its lips in anticipation.

Skill Gain!
Identify Rank One +.1
Lesser Cobalt Koracki Demon (Orange)

Hall watched the demon, momentarily frozen in shock. The creature growled, speaking rapidly in a language that hurt to hear. Even though the demon had done nothing yet, the momentum in the room shifted. It still hadn't moved, and Hall could see a waviness to its features. The demon was not fully on this plane of existence.

Not yet.

The blurring stopped, all the details of the demon coming into focus.

But Hall had recovered from his shock.

His javelin soared through the air, slamming into the demon's shoulder. The creature growled, pulling the weapon out. Silver blood dripped to the floor, smoke rising from where it struck wood. A small amount of red disappeared from its Health bar. Holding the javelin in both hands, the demon bent the weapon. The wooden weapon snapped in half, small splinters flying into the air. The Koracki threw the ends, looking around for the one that had thrown in. Looking for the one it would attack first.

Hall didn't give it a chance.

He pulled one of the throwing knives from his bracer, launching the small weapon at the demon. The small blade struck the demon in the chest, exploding in a spark of lightning. The flare was brighter than Hall had expected. A Koracki Demon had lightning affinity so he hadn't expected the lightning damage from the throwing knife to do any damage. A Critical Strike must have hit as more silver blood dripped from the wound and smoke curled up from where the lightning had struck.

More red had dropped from the demon's Health bar. It had lost close to 10% of its Health in Hall's two attacks.

The Koracki seemed confused that lightning had done any damage to it. It looked down at the wound, touching it with one of the clawed hands. The head shot up, focusing on Hall, hate in the yellow eyes.

Hall activated *Leap* and jumped into the air. He drew his short sword while in the air. On the downward side of the arc, he stabbed out with the spear. The tip slammed into the Koracki's shoulder, the special attack activating and leaving a large splinter in the demon's shoulder. Pulling it out, Hall gashed the blue skin of the demon. Landing, he used the attack of opportunity and stabbed out with the spear, scoring a hit in the demon's chest. He pulled the spear back and sliced out with the sword, slashing a line of silver blood across the demon's arm.

The creature roared, a sound with power behind. Hall felt like he was hit by a gust of wind. He was pushed back, trying to maintain his footing. He slid back a couple of feet, using his spear to brace himself. The wind tore at him. He could feel it against his skin, cutting him like knives. His Health dropped as the wind cut into him.

Seeing that its sonic attack had hurt Hall, the Koracki smiled. It licked its sharp teeth and pounced on Hall, who barely got his spear up in time to block. Held across his body, the spear caught the leaping demon. Hall tried to hold his arm straight, the weight of the demon pushing him to the ground. He could feel his elbow wanting to bend, the demon's shorter arms trying to slash Hall's face and across his chest.

Hall managed to stab at the demon with the sword in his free arm. The angle was off, but he scored a light hit. Enough to make the demon move and Hall to push it to the side. He stood up quickly, jumping back to give him some space before the demon could attack again.

The Koracki crouched low, almost on all fours, as it watched Hall.

It wasn't paying attention to anything else. It didn't see the furry blur charging its way.

Angus slammed into the side of the crouched demon. The sound of breaking bone filled the room, the crack and the snap louder than the clash of metal on metal from the other fights. The demon rolled to the side and came up facing Angus.

Pointing its clawed fingers at the cow, it barked a word in the hideous language. Bolts of black lightning shot out from the fingers and struck Angus in five different spots. The crackling of energy wrapped around the cow, causing him to moo in pain. Angus spasmed as the energy snapped and cracked, burning the cow's fur. Smoke rose up as Angus dropped to the floor, mooing quietly.

Pike swooped in with an angry screech. The dragonhawk slashed across the Koracki's back, talons drawing lines of silver blood. The demon growled and swiped at Pike, barely missing. Turning back, Pike opened his beak and shot out a bolt of lightning. The attack hit the Koracki in the shoulder. Sparks erupted on the impact and smoke rose up from the wound, but the demon was barely injured.

Hall mentally shot Pike a command. For the first time ever, Pike argued. Hall could sense the dragonhawk was angry about the injury to Angus and wasn't listening. Pike's lightning was useless against the Koracki but not against others. Hall pushed hard at Pike, mentally telling him that he could help Angus more by attacking a different target.

The resistance faded and Pike spiraled to the top of the buildings where, with another screech, he dived down at Keyley. The Witch got her arms up in time to block Pike's attack, the sharp talons ripping her robe's sleeves to shreds.

Watching the bird attack the Witch, the Koracki took a step toward them. Hall threw another throwing knife, catching the

Koracki in the back and doing minimal damage. But it got the demon's attention. Turning, yellow eyes focused on Hall. Which is what he wanted.

He took a couple steps back, drawing the Koracki away from the others, getting the demon lined up just how he wanted.

Hall activated *Leap*. The Koracki's eyes followed the Skirmisher as he jumped into the air. The demon braced itself for Hall's attack.

Landing behind Yorvgr, Hall stabbed out with his spear. He caught the Warden in the back, earning a flanking and critical strike bonus. A large chunk of the Storvgardian's Health disappeared. Hall wished he had been able to use *Leaping Stab* but had been unable to when he switched targets and the angle of his jump.

"Take the demon," he yelled at Jackoby, whose last attack prevented Yorvgr from turning, which gave Hall another undefended hit.

The Koracki had turned when Hall jumped away from it, confused. It wasn't ready for Jackoby's *Battle Rush*. The large Firbolg slammed into the smaller demon. While it was supernaturally strong for its size, it was unprepared and hadn't braced itself. The demon was pushed backward, knocked off its feet, and rolled across the floor. Jackoby followed it, hammer raised to attack.

Hall was cursing himself for not thinking of this plan earlier. He had allowed Jackoby, their strongest Warden, to attack the other Warden. Caryn the Duelist had attacked the other Duelist. That wasn't a good match-up of Classes and Skills. Sky Realms Online had never had a real PvP aspect, but some had still occurred during quests and specific events as well as dueling. Hall had never been a fan or been that good, but he understood the basics of how some Classes stacked up against others.

Duelists and Skirmishers were good one-on-one against Wardens. Those Classes' Evade and Dodge abilities allowed them to avoid the Wardens strong attacks and slip past the defenses. By a good Warden, those advantages could be mitigated somewhat. But a Warden-on-Warden battle was always a long fight, the two just pounding on each other and getting nowhere.

Hall had thought that having Jackoby occupying Yorvgr was the smartest move. And it might have been if the demon hadn't been summoned. The Koracki changed everything. Now, speed mattered. They had to take down some of the opposition.

"Caryn," he shouted as he avoided the swing of Yorvgr's sword. "The Witch. Sabine and Leigh, the demon."

He stabbed with the spear, slipping past Yorvgr's shield and scoring a slicing hit across the Storvgardian's chest. The Warden managed to swing his shield and knock it away from his body. Hall was left exposed but ducked to the side as the huge sword sliced through where his head had been.

Drawing his short sword, he swung it at Yorvgr in one smooth motion. The blade sliced along the leather covering the Warden's leg. The larger man growled in pain and tried to slam his shield down onto Hall. Managing to avoid the shield, Hall grunted in pain as the Warden's sword sliced across his back. The pain and force of the swing dropped him to the floor.

His Health dropped, putting him just under fifty percent.

Pushing himself up, Hall sprung away from Yorvgr, giving himself some room to work in.

He wanted to see how the rest of the fighting was but knew he had to concentrate on Yorvgr. It was hard, but Hall knew he had to trust the others to know what to do. It was his job to occupy the Warden.

Not just occupy. He was going to end the Warden. His back hurt, the cut flaring as he tried to move. Yorvgr had around seventy-five percent Health remaining. Hall knew he couldn't let any more blows land. Leigh was occupied with assisting the others and wouldn't be able to heal.

Jabbing with his spear, keeping the huge man back, Hall reached down to the other pouch he kept on his belt. Found as loot from a smuggler's camp back on Cumberland, it was a leather carrying case for small potions. Lesser potions. He opened the clasp on the case, fumbling as he had only one hand at an awkward angle and couldn't spare any time to look down. Getting it open, he pulled out a potion and was glad he got it right on the first try.

Using his teeth to pull out the cork, spitting it to the side, Hall downed the Health potion in one gulp. The green liquid felt hot and thick like syrup, searing the insides of his throat. He didn't remember potions having a taste before, but it did now and it was horrible. Hall felt a cough, his body wanting to reject the thick and foul-tasting substance, but he forced it down.

The warmth spread throughout his body causing a tingling sensation, his nerves almost bursting. Hall watched his Health bar climb quickly, the gash along his back sealing up. Still tender and stiff, it was no longer a gaping wound. The heat and tingling left his body as rapidly as it had come, and he saw he was around sixty to sixty-five percent Health.

Not as much as he had wanted, but it would have to do.

He dived to the side as instinct cried out a warning. Yorvgr's great sword sliced down where Hall had been. Falling down, Hall thrust out with the spear and scored a hit in Yorvgr's unprotected thigh. The *Exceptional Breakridge Ironwood Spear* activated its *Splinter* ability and a large chunk of wood lodged in the wound, causing it to keep bleeding. Yorvgr's leg buckled from the pain, and the large man fell to the side. He used the shield to push himself up as Hall also stood up.

They stood facing each other, the Warden's Health down

past fifty percent and still dropping from the *Splinter's* bleeding effect. The Storvgardian growled, testing his weight on the leg. It wasn't good, but at that point, Yorvgr didn't care. He charged Hall, shield raised to block the spear and his sword swinging.

He was too close for Hall to use *Leap* or to avoid the charge by diving to the side. Even wounded, the Warden had shown himself to be quick. No matter which way Hall dove, the Warden would be able to follow with an attack.

Or would he, Hall thought as a reckless plan came to mind.

The timing would need to be perfect and luck would have to go his way.

He watched as Yorvgr charged, most of the Warden's weight on the uninjured leg. Closer and closer until the Warden was right on top of him. Hall dove to the side, the injured leg side. He rolled as he fell, dropping the spear and drawing his short sword. Yorvgr planted on the injured leg intending to pivot around and smash his shield into Hall's back. The weight caused the wound to flare and the muscles to spasm. Instead of pivoting smoothly, Yorvgr stumbled and seemed to wobble. His shield went wide as he tried to balance.

On his back, Hall pushed himself up, the point of his sword leading. He stabbed Yorvgr in the groin area, where there was just leather armor. The Warden screamed in pain, blood gushing out of the wound. The force of Hall's attack and the weakened leg caused Yorvgr to fall backward. He slammed against the floor, the planks shaking and buckling. The shield was knocked from his grasp.

Standing up, Hall stepped on the Warden's sword and adjusted his grip on his own weapon. Yorvgr's eyes were filled with pain and with hatred. The Warden struggled to free his weapon, trying to swing his other around to grab at Hall, but the Skirmisher was too fast. Down came the short sword, straight into Yorvgr's throat.

The Warden's hands twitched and fell still, blood flowing onto the ground.

———

Breathing heavy, thanking whatever Spirit watched out for foolhardy adventurers, Hall looked to the rest of the fighting. It had felt like hours, but the fight with Yorvgr had only lasted a few minutes. He moved from fight to fight, trying to determine the best place for him to attack.

Jackoby was sparring with the Koracki demon. Claws lashed out at the Firbolg's shield, which was holding up under the ferocious assault. The warhammer could barely hit the blue-skinned demon. Jackoby would push out with his shield, pulling it back quickly, and while the Koracki was a couple steps away, he would swing the hammer and score a glancing blow against the fast demon. Then the demon would be on him again.

Bolts of purple energy surrounded the demon, flaring when it tried to move. A black bar of light slammed against it as Sabine attacked when she could. Hall saw that Leigh had moved away from the Witch and was closer to the other fights, laying hands on Angus and others when able.

Caryn drove Keyley the Black Witch back against the wall, dodging wand attacks. The Witch's *Shadow Self* and *Shadow Barrier* were deflecting most of the attacks from Caryn as well as Pike, who Hall saw get struck by a *Shadow Bolt*. The black bar slammed into the dragonhawk, knocking him into a spiral and crashing against the wall where he dropped to the ground. Holding herself low, Leigh started moving toward Pike.

Against Cronet, Roxhard was barely managing. The Silver Blades' leader, the man known as the Cudgel, was taller than Roxhard. Faster and with a longer reach. His twin blades would get through the Dwarf's defenses. Two blades against Roxhard's one, the two-handed axe, was not a good match up.

A quick check of Health bars showed that Roxhard was the lowest. Sabine was full, but her Energy was low and not recharging quickly. Already she was switching to her wand, waiting for an opening somewhere in the chaotic fighting. Hall figured it was the second or third time she had done so, letting her Energy recharge. Jackoby was just over half while Leigh was full and Caryn around seventy-five percent.

The Koracki was near full Health as it seemed to have some kind of *Regeneration* ability. Keyley was hovering just over fifty percent and Cronet near full.

Drawing one of the throwing knives, he shifted away from the middle and a couple steps to the back wall. He watched, waiting for an opportunity. Finding it, he let the knife fly. The small blade slammed into the back shoulder of one of Keyley's images, lightning erupting on impact. Magic from the attack cut through the protection of the multiple images, and Keyley felt the full impact. The Witch growled in pain, her spells wavering and Caryn struck. She stabbed both her blades straight out, the points penetrating the *Shadow Barrier*. Each blade was aimed for one of the *Shadow Self*s. Each blade struck and the images wavered, drawing together into one.

Keyley clutched at her belly, blood leaking out between her fingers. She stared down at the wound in shock. Caryn dashed in, swords swinging, and the Black Witch dropped to the ground.

Cronet saw the Witch fall, his eyes going wild. He scanned the room, seeing only the demon remaining and his opponents all alive. He could see the Druid healing the ones that had been wounded. Growling, he increased the speed of his attacks on the Dwarf.

Roxhard stumbled back as the tall man's weapons became a blur. He felt one hit his shoulder, screeching off the metal pauldron, another blade scored a slashing hit across his unprotected arm. Biting back a cry, Roxhard took a step back.

Hall drew his remaining throwing knife, waiting for a chance to launch it at Cronet, but the man was moving too fast. He had never seen a Duelist dance that quick before. Both Cronet's Health and Energy bars were dropping quickly, draining, but his Vitality was filling up. It was some kind of Special Move, Hall realized. A Boss Ability. Roxhard fell back, stumbling and falling to the ground under the barrage.

Instead of pressing the attack, Cronet turned and ran. He kept his blades out, running as fast as possible for the entrance. There were still sounds of fighting coming from the Mill's yard, but Cronet thought his chances of slipping away better out there. He was almost to the door when Hall used *Leap*.

He arced high into the air, almost touching the ceiling, spear pointed down. The tip slammed into the back of Cronet, the momentum driving the man to the ground. Hall's force from the *Leap*, and the strength of the spear, cracked through the wooden planking, pinning Cronet. The man struggled, legs and arms kicking wildly until he finally just stopped moving.

With effort, and a cracking of the wood flooring more, Hall pulled his spear free. He checked it over, seeing no damage to the Ironwood. Making sure Cronet was truly dead, he turned back to the demon.

Only to see it suffering under multiple attacks. Pike was flying through the air, blasting it with lightning. Caryn was attacking from the creature's rear, swords slashing as now Jackoby was able to really start hitting with his hammer. Roxhard sat on the ground, Leigh's blue tattoos glowing as she laid her hands on his many wounds. Sabine fired globes of energy from her wand, each striking the demon.

The Koracki's Health was dropping fast.

Breathing hard, Hall walked toward it, spear held loosely and sword sheathed. The demon whirled in a circle, trying to attack everywhere at once. Under constant attack, it could not use any of the special abilities it possessed, only able to growl in futility. Health dropped quicker until it finally disappeared.

They all stepped back as smoke started to pour from the demon's eyes, nose, mouth, and ears. Thick and black, it swirled around the creature, faster and faster into a tornado. It engulfed the Koracki from head to toe, swirling madly and then started to constrict. The cloud shrank, bit by whirling bit. Smaller and smaller until it just disappeared and the demon was gone.

CHAPTER FORTY

HALL LEANED AGAINST HIS SPEAR, THE REST OF HIS COMPANIONS looking just as tired. The notification icon flashed at the edge of his vision, and Hall opened it.

SLAIN: Councilor Cronet
+20 Experience
SLAIN: Yorvgr the Warden
+20 Experience
SLAIN: Keyley the Black Witch
+10 Experience
SLAIN: Lesser Cobalt Koracki Demon
+15 Experience

Skill Gain!
Light Armor Rank Two +.1
Polearms Rank Two +.3
Small Blades Rank Two +.2
Strategy Rank Two +.2
Thrown Rank Two +.1

QUEST COMPLETE!

With the death of the Cudgel, the Silver Blades should be easy pickings for the Door Knockers and the PeakGuard, effectively eliminating the Guild.

THE NEW BLOOD IV

Eliminate the Silver Blades Guild 1/1
Rewards: +100 Door Knocker reputation
+100 PeakGuard reputation
+200 Alliance Reputation with Sergeant Brient
+100 Experience

Sergeant Brient will be interested in learning about the Silver Blades' loss of leadership.

THE NEW BLOOD V

Inform Sergeant Brient of The Cudgel's death 0/1
Rewards: +100 PeakGuard reputation
+100 Alliance Reputation with Sergeant Brient
+25 Experience

ACCEPT QUEST?

QUEST COMPLETE!

You have defeated the man known as the Cudgel.

THE BLADE'S CUDGEL II

Defeat The Cudgel 1/1
Reward: +50 Door Knocker Reputation
+50 PeakGuard Reputation
+50 Experience

The Cudgel has been killed and the Silver Blades Guild mostly eliminated and rendered easy prey, but Cronet's identity is not known and a Councilor has been killed. His identity as the Cudgel must be proven.

THE BLADE'S CUDGEL III
Discover proof of The Cudgel's identity 0/1
Reward: +50 Door Knocker Reputation
+50 PeakGuard Reputation
+100 Alliance Reputation with Sergeant Brient
+50 Experience

ACCEPT QUEST?

"That was fun," Sabine muttered as she leaned against the wall.

Hall just nodded as he joined them near the back wall. Leigh was next to Jackoby, healing the Firbolg as Pike settled on Hall's shoulders. He grunted at the added weight, which made the wound along his back flare, but he was glad Pike was fine. The dragonhawk's feathers looked rough, a couple seemed to be missing, but the bird was flying and squawking. A quick mental conversation told Hall that Pike was good and the feathers would grow back eventually, but in the meantime, Pike was upset at how ugly he would be. Hall bit back a laugh.

Making sure that everyone else was good, he turned to walk back to Cronet, intending to loot the body when he heard a noise from the back room. He turned, raising his spear. They all looked that way, wearily raising their own weapons. Hall cursed himself for not looking in the back, forgetting the person he had seen.

"There's a guy tied up back there," Roxhard said, looking a little embarrassed that he hadn't said anything

Sabine sighed, relaxing but rolling her eyes.

"Sorry," Roxhard said, eyes downcast.

"It's all good," Hall told him as he headed for the door to the back room. "Search the bodies, see if there's any coins or items of value," he told them.

———

Hall opened the door and stepped into the long room. It was thin, only about ten feet wide, but ran the entire length of the building. A storeroom of some kind. It was empty except for a small chest and a man sitting on the ground. Roxhard had been right, the man was tied and gagged. Pieces of wood and splinters lay everywhere, exploding in when Roxhard had gone through the wall. A Dwarf-sized hole was there, and Caryn was peeking in to make sure everything was good. Hall waved her away.

The man looked up at Hall a little fearfully. He was tall and thin, older with a full head of gray hair that was long, tied in a ponytail. He had very black eyes and a long-beaked nose. Clean-shaven, the hair was the only evidence of age. Dressed in fine clothes, the man pulled at the rope bindings.

Ignoring him for now, Hall looked at the chest. A foot-long, foot-wide, and foot-tall with a flat top. Made of a dark wood banded in iron. It had a single keylock on the front. Crouching down, the man squirming and muttering behind the gag, Hall examined the chest. He didn't get too close, not wanting to set off any potential traps. The chest had to contain items that Cronet had wanted to save, to protect. Whatever was inside would be valuable and trapped.

They had Caryn in the group now. It was time to put her thieving Skills to work.

He turned to face the man.

"Who are you?" he asked, reaching over and pulling the gag down.

The man coughed, taking some deep breaths and working spit back into his mouth. It was a minute or so before he could speak.

"My name is Timmin," he finally croaked, his voice hoarse from lack of use and the gag. "Who are you?" the man asked with some arrogance in his tone, as if he was speaking to a lesser.

Hall ignored the question.

"Why are you tied up?"

Timmin looked at Hall, tilting his head, and Hall knew the man was trying to come up with an angle or a story. Hall didn't give him the chance. Taking the tip of his spear, Hall lightly poked the man in his ribs. Not enough to draw blood, but enough to get Timmin's attention.

"The truth," Hall said.

With an exasperated sigh, Timmin pulled at his bonds. His annoyed glare told Hall that the man wanted the ropes cut before speaking. Hall shook his head and made a 'continue' motion with his hands. Timmin glared.

"Fine," he said with another sigh. "I am an administrator in the Councilor of Coin's office."

Hall smiled and chuckled.

"You're Cronet's forger, aren't you?" he asked and saw the surprise in Timmin's eyes.

The administrator's eyes moved back and forth quickly, not focusing on Hall as the man tried to talk his way out of it.

"I do not know what you are talking about," Timmin said, drawing out each word.

Hall sighed and stood up.

"Okay," he said and started to walk away.

He got five feet before Timmin yelled out.

"Stop," the thin man said with a drawn-out sigh. "Fine. Cronet was forcing me to forge the ledgers. I've worked with the Councilor of Coin for years and knew the shorthand used in the ledgers."

Timmin stopped talking and held up his hands.

"Caryn," Hall called out loudly before walking over to Timmin.

Drawing his dagger, Hall cut the bonds around the man and helped him to stand. Timmin stomped and lifted his legs, stretching his arms, working to get the circulation back.

"Thank you," he said, voice filled with arrogance.

Hall just shook his head, wondering if he should have kept Timmin tied up.

Caryn came in and Hall pointed at the chest. She crouched down and started looking it over, holding her fingers an inch or so above it.

"Might want to move back a bit," she said.

Hall did and grabbed at Timmin, who hadn't moved. He pulled the thin man back. Timmin shot him a glare, but Hall just pushed him further back. Timmin tripped over his own feet, almost falling before regaining his balance.

Ignoring the man's complaints, Hall watched as Caryn's hands moved quickly. She pulled a long wire out of her pouch and inserted it into the lock. With a couple twists and turns, she moved the wire around as her other hand ran along the edges of the chest. Hall couldn't follow everything that she did, but a minute later, she stood up and smiled.

"Done," she said and stepped back. "Even got a couple Skill gains."

She stood watching as Hall opened the lid. He stayed back at arm's length, not that he didn't trust Caryn, but just out of basic cautiousness. At the edge of his vision, Hall could see that Caryn had her fingers crossed.

The lid tipped over, the force shaking the small chest, causing it to rock a bit. Hall leaned forward, looking in, and smiled broadly. He reached down and pulled out a thick pouch. There was a loud clinking of metal on metal. Opening the drawstrings, Hall saw a large collection of coins and uncut jewels. There seemed to be a sizable amount of gold. Pulling the strings tight, he placed it in his pouch and began pulling out the other items.

There was not much in the strongbox. Cronet had to flee in a hurry so had only taken what he would need to restart his life elsewhere. Besides the pouch of coins, Hall saw small books that appeared to be journals and two more pouches of what he assumed to be more coins. Picking up a journal, he flipped through it quickly and let out a surprised whistle.

"What?" Caryn asked, the small woman coming close and looking around his arm at the book.

"Proof," Hall replied. "Proof that Cronet was the Cudgel. The idiot kept a journal."

QUEST COMPLETE!

You have found a journal penned in Cronet's own hand and containing his thoughts and plans for the Silver Blades and his ascension to the Generalship of Silver Peak Keep.

THE BLADE'S CUDGEL III

Discover proof of The Cudgel's identity 1/1
Reward: +50 Door Knocker Reputation
+50 PeakGuard Reputation
+100 Alliance Reputation with Sergeant Brient
+50 Experience

Sergeant Brient will be interested in the journals proving Cronet is the Cudgel as well as the other journals and what they may contain.

THE BLADE'S CUDGEL IV

Give the journals to Sergeant Brient 0/1
Reward: +25 Door Knocker Reputation

+75 PeakGuard Reputation
+50 Alliance Reputation with Sergeant Brient
+100 Experience

ACCEPT REQUEST?

Before replacing the journals in the box, Hall noticed a pile of folded papers at the bottom. Pulling them out, he opened them partway and was confused by what he saw. From what little he could see, it appeared to be plans for an airship. Interested, but knowing he didn't have time to review them now, he replaced the plans and the journals in the strongbox. Hall closed it and stuffed the chest into his pouch. There was a warping as the magic distorted the strongbox, twisting and shrinking it as he stuffed it into the pouch. Together, he and Caryn left the room. Timmin's eyes followed them, as if he was waiting for more. When neither said anything or even noticed him, the administrator followed.

———

They walked out into the main room to find a collection of weapons and armor on the floor along with a couple of coin purses, a leather belt, and the Black Witch's staff. The bodies were stripped almost naked, Keyley still in her satin robe, which had been practically ripped to shreds. Hall walked toward the pile but stopped, looking in the corner where Sabine was crouched down and staring at something.

Pike and Angus were hovering around her, the Witch kept leaning back and shooing at them. She made little kissing noises into the corner, holding out her hand.

Hall walked over and saw two glowing eyes in the shadows. The Minx Cat. It hissed at his approach, shrinking further back. Hall mentally told Pike to back away, the dragonhawk squawking but flapping up to land on Angus back. The cow made an annoyed moo and trotted back to Leigh.

The green cat, the purple stripes seeming to shift as its long form stretched, walked out to Sabine's outstretched hand. It sniffed at her, the whiskers brushing against the fingers. Sitting down, giving Sabine's fingers a lick, the cat started grooming itself.

Sabine stood up with a satisfied smile.

"Got your familiar?" Hall asked as he studied the cat. It ignored him.

"Yes," she replied, the happiest Hall had seen her.

"What's his name?"

"Salem," she answered quickly.

Hall started to walk away but stopped, turning back to look at the Witch. She had her arm outstretched and the Minx Cat had jumped onto it, crawling up to lay across her shoulders.

"What?" Sabine asked, looking at Hall, confused at the smile he had.

"Salem," he said with a chuckle. "The blond hair, the name." He paused and laughed. "Sabine. Sabrina. You named yourself after Sabrina the Teenage Witch?"

Sabine glared at him, stalking past as he continued to chuckle. Hall just shook his head, laughing. Sabine was so serious all the time, but to find out she was such a fan of the old cult show and had modeled her Sky Realms Online avatar after the character, it was too much and so out of character.

His chuckle vanished as Berim and Ulysses entered, their eyes scanning the entire room. They stopped on the stripped bodies, focusing on Cronet. Berim's eyes found Timmin and stopped, the thief smiling in recognition. The eyes looked predatory, like he had found his next meal. Glancing at Timmin, Hall saw the administrator take a step back, looking fearful.

"Our boys looted ta bodies outside," Ulysses grunted, looking at the pile of weapons and armor.

Both Jackoby and Roxhard took a visible step closer. The small thief laughed.

"Hope ya donnut mind," he added.

"I noticed the Hobs leaving the battle," Berim said, eyes still fixed on Timmin. "Good job there. We could have handled them but was nice to not need to."

QUEST COMPLETE!

Berim is glad that his Door Knockers did not need to waste time, energy, resources, or lives on the Hob Mercenaries.

"HOB"LESS FORCES II
Report to Berim for a reward 1/1
Rewards: +100 Door Knocker reputation
+10 Gold
+50 Experience

"This came off the leader you killed outside," Berim said and tossed a small coin purse at Hall, who caught it easily. "Was probably part of the payment. Seems only fair you get to have it."

Hall nodded and stuffed the purse into his pouch alongside the others.

Berim shifted his attention back to the administrator, who had moved up behind Hall, almost hiding.

"You work for the Councilor of Coin, do you not?" the dark-skinned thief asked, but it was more of a statement than question.

Timmin started to speak but stopped, trying to stand at his full height and normal arrogant bearing but kept melting under Berim's amused gaze.

"We're done here," Hall said, drawing everyone's attention.

His eyes were locked on Berim's, who appeared momentarily annoyed before the amusement returned.

"Not quite yet," the thief started.

Hall raised a hand before Berim could continue.

"We are done here," Hall said, more forceful, no hint of a question.

Ulysses stepped forward, hand hovering over his weapon's hilt. Berim studied Hall, measuring.

"Have a problem with that?" Hall asked, almost daring.

Berim's eyes flashed again. Anger. Before the normal amusement returned.

"Not at all," he replied and took a step toward Timmin.

"You're coming with us," Hall said, glancing over his shoulder at the administrator.

"Yes, sir," Timmin replied with a slight bow. "Of course, sir." His eyes never left Berim.

With the others, Hall gathered up the loot, glad that they had all emptied out their inventory earlier. Even with most of the slots open, they still barely had room for the gear. Hall was glad they didn't have to collect any from outside. He sighed at the thought of all the potential loot they had left behind across Silver Peak Keep and Peakdock. The last couple days had been so chaotic, there had barely been a chance to loot. He was sure that all of it had gone to the Door Knockers.

Hall noticed that neither Berim or Caryn said anything about her leaving with him and the others. The companions, along with their new Duelist, walked out the entrance, Berim's eyes following. Timmin kept looking over his shoulder nervously.

"I believe that my days as a forger are not over," he said fearfully.

"You said you were an administrator to the Councilor of Coins, correct?" Hall asked as the group walked across the yard. There were bodies everywhere. All dressed in black, it was hard to tell who was a Door Knocker and who was a Silver Blade. There didn't appear to be any prisoners, the ones left alive had to be all Door Knockers. A dozen of them stood around, searching bodies or keeping watch on the treeline. "Have you ever thought about administering a village?"

"A village, sir?" Timmin questioned and looked at Hall. His eyes widened in surprise. "What do you mean, milord?"

Hall paused, confused at being addressed that way. He realized that Timmin must have used *Identify* on him and seen the title that being Lord of Skara Brae gave him.

"It seems you might need to leave town," Hall pointed out.

"Yes, I think I might at that," Timmin replied with a last look back at the main building and Berim standing in the entrance. "A village, you say. Yes, that does sound interesting."

CHAPTER FORTY-ONE

HALL STOOD OUTSIDE THE CONSTABLE'S OFFICE. THE SUN WAS rising and he was tired. The others walked past, continuing to the Inn where they would gather their gear and look for an airship. Pike sat on his shoulder, talons digging in. Timmin stood nervously behind him.

"We can come back later," Timmin said. "I'm sure there is no one awake."

The hour was early but Hall didn't care. He wanted this business in Silver Peak Keep done with. They had walked through the night from the forest, the rising sun chasing them. Crossing the river, they had cut through the fields, passing between the two farms and over the tunnel. Hall wasn't sure if Brient, or some other Guard, was even in the office, but he intended to wait until the man showed up, if need be.

"Come on," he said and pulled Timmin after him.

They walked up the stairs and knocked on the door.

"Enter," a voice grumbled.

Walking in, Hall saw the same room as before, including Brient behind the desk. The Sergeant looked up, annoyed at first but mood quickly changing when he noticed Hall. His eyes flashed questions as they noticed Timmin hesitantly entering behind.

"Aren't you—" he began but Timmin interrupted with a sigh.

"Yes," the administrator said. "I work for the Councilor of Coin."

"This should be interesting," Brient said and leaned back in his chair.

Hall nodded and told him everything.

––––––––

Brient leaned forward, gloved fingers tapping on his desk.

"I was right," he finally said, after taking a couple minutes to digest everything Hall had said. "That was interesting."

QUEST COMPELTE!

You have informed Sergeant Brient that the Silver Blades have been destroyed, preventing the impending Guild War.

RIVALS IN THE DARK
Prevent the Guild war 1/1
Reward: +100 PeakGuard Reputation
+500 Alliance Reputation with Sergeant Brient,
+50 Experience
Crafting Guild Exemption Writ

You are now Friendly with Sergeant Brient

Brient handed Hall the Writ. A single piece of paper with the Constable's seal and signature on the bottom. Reading it quickly, Hall saw that it would allow any Guilded craftsman to work in Skara Brae and not have to pay the Guild tax for the duration of the project. Even with the unGuilded Duncant working for him, Hall knew that he would need the services of others from the city if he was to rebuild Skara Brae. This Writ would come in handy. He quickly placed it in his magical pouch.

"Thank you for stopping a Guild war," Brient said once more, leaning back. "Of course you did kind of start it with the fires, murders, and some fighting in the streets," he started and chuckled as Hall started to protest. "It stopped the fighting from spreading to the citizens. That's all I care about. And you're sure the Silver Blades won't return with the Cudgel dead?"

"Positive," Hall answered.

QUEST COMPELTE!

With the death of the Cudgel, the Silver Blades are no more and Sergeant Brient accepts your reassurances that the Guild will not return.

THE NEW BLOOD V

Inform Sergeant Brient of The Cudgel's death 1/1
Rewards: +100 PeakGuard reputation
+100 Alliance Reputation with Sergeant Brient
+25 Experience

"The Cudgel, Cronet, was not using the Silver Blades to take over the cities' criminal operations. He was using them as a means of becoming the General," Hall told Brient, reaching into his pouch and pulling out the strongbox.

He placed it on the Sergeant's desk with a thud.

"Right," Brient replied. "That makes sense, but without proof, it's hard to pin any of this on Cronet."

"My word is not enough?" Timmin asked, clearly shocked that anyone would doubt him.

"No, it is not," Brient answered eyes on Hall.

Flipping open the lid, making sure to keep it turned away from Brient, Hall pulled out the journals. He placed them on the desk and closed the lid. He could see that Timmin had seen the remaining items but wasn't saying anything to Brient about the purses or the plans.

Brient quickly flipped through the journals. One after the other.

"This will work," he said finally.

QUEST COMPLETE!

With the journals in hand, Brient has the proof he needs to show that Cronet was the Cudgel and behind the plan to usurp power in Silver Peak Keep.

THE BLADE'S CUDGEL IV

Give the journals to Sergeant Brient 1/1
Reward: +25 Door Knocker Reputation
+75 PeakGuard Reputation
+50 Alliance Reputation with Sergeant Brient
+100 Experience

*You have gained **LEVEL 5!***
You have gained +1 Attribute Point to spend.
You have accessed a new Class Ability: Leap Rank 2
See a Class Trainer to learn your new Ability.

Hall blinked in surprise as the level up notification flashed across his vision. He hadn't realized he had been so close. Brient was talking so Hall didn't bother bringing up his Character Sheet. It would have to wait.

"Thank you," Brient said and stood up, holding out his hand.

Hall shook it.

"You have done a great service to Silver Peak Keep," the

guard said, sincere. "And I apologize for how I roped you into this."

Hall had a sharp reply in mind but thought better of it. He understood the position that Brient had been in. Being black-mailed had not been the right way to do it, but Hall had received a lot of coin, some valuable experience, and a new companion as well as possibly someone to run Skara Brae. It had worked out.

"It's okay," Hall said instead of the first thought.

Brient nodded, thankful at Hall's reply. He turned to Timmin.

"As for you," he started but Timmin held out a hand.

"I am leaving Silver Peak Keep," the administrator said.

Brient glanced down at the journals and nodded.

"Probably for the best."

———

Three days later, the sun rose on Silver Peak Keep, the mountain shining bright.

Hall stood on the docks as supplies were loaded onto a medium-sized airship, Pike on his shoulder. The two-masted, two-engine ship bore Storvgarde colors and was named the *Frozen Blade*. The ship's captain, named Hrothgrav, was a large man. A Level Seven sailor. As loud and boisterous as the Captain, the crew seemed a tad on the chaotic side for Hall's liking. But it was the only ship that would sail up the mountainous coast, braving the rocs and shrikes, and land on a meadow in the middle of nowhere.

Hrothgrav took it as a challenge. He was looking forward to the risks, as well as the large amount of gold promised. Which Hall could supply. All counted, the companions had gained five hundred gold, three hundred silver, and four hundred copper. Most of which had gone to pay for passage on the *Frozen Blade* for a large amount of carpentry supplies, food-stuffs, clothing and bedding, various other items, six adventurers, a cow, a dragonhawk, a Bodin carpenter, and three Humans: an arrogant and constantly complaining administrator and two female farmers.

Hall had been surprised to find Hitchly and Dinah waiting for him at the Inn when he had returned from seeing Brient.

"There's nothing for us here," Hitchly had said. "Just bad memories."

He had tried to dissuade them as much as he wanted them to come live in Skara Brae. Experienced farmers would be a huge boon, but he wanted them to understand what they were signing up for. They understood, or so they said, and Hall had finally agreed. Which led to more gold being spent on farming tools and seeds.

Besides gaining the new villagers and supplies, Hall and the others had spent the last couple days selling off their loot as well as buying new gear to replace the items that had been badly damaged. There were no trainers in Silver Peak Keep, so Hall would have to wait until the next time he could find one to learn Leap Rank Two. He had taken advantage of the city's post office and sent out a couple of letters.

Most of the items they had recovered had been non-magical. Cronet's twin long blades had been an upgrade for Caryn, bearing a minor enchantment for damage, but the mark Hall had found on them had been a reason to keep them instead of selling. Where blade met hilt on each blade was a mark that he recognized. A point up triangle with a half-circle above, the straight line of circle's bottom midway through the triangle. It was the same mark that was on his own short sword.

Surprisingly, Berim and the Door Knockers had left them all alone. Hall had wanted to leave as soon as possible, and every day he thought that Timmin and possibly Caryn would be harassed. Or Berim would sabotage the ship to make them stay. But the thief did nothing.

Thinking of the thief brought back thoughts of Captain Hart and the *Twisted Gale*, the ship that had brought them to Edin from Cumberland. Hall knew Hart and his crew had experience loading and unloading from locations not set up with docks. He would have felt more comfortable with the smuggler's ship and crew. With the winds, uneven ground, and no dock at Breakridge Meadow, Hall wasn't sure how the *Frozen Blade* would fare. But then looking at Hrothgrav and his crew, Hall had a feeling they had done their fair share of loading and unloading in out of the way places.

The last of the supplies were being hauled aboard by the dock cranes. A load of wood planking ordered by Duncant. The small Bodin was at the rail, watching the planks being lifted into the air, hovering and shaking as the crane slowly moved them closer to the *Frozen Blade's* hatch. Two of Horthgrav's men were watching, directing the motions.

Hall picked up his traveling pack, slinging it over his other shoulder. Pike shifted as Hall started to walk away.

"Hold," a voice said with authority. One Hall recognized.

With a grimace and sigh, he turned around to see Sergeant Brient walking toward him. Hall was surprised. Brient was out of uniform and had a large traveling pack over his shoulder. He wore an unadorned mail shirt, leather leggings and sleeves. A sword was hanging from his waist, a dagger across from it. A small buckler shield was over his shoulder.

"Sergeant," Hall said in greeting, cautious. "We were just about to leave."

"Glad I caught you then," Brient said and paused. He now looked embarrassed, unsure of himself. "I...uhm..." he tried to continue but stopped.

"Sergeant?"

"Not any longer," Brient said with a sigh. "It seems

revealing Cronet as being behind an attempted overthrow stirred up a hornet's nest."

"You pissed someone off with those journals," Hall guessed.

Brient nodded. He turned and spat on the ground. "Politics," he cursed. "Turns out I was right about someone in the Guard higher-ups being on the Cudgel's payroll. He wasn't happy about losing his meal ticket." Brient paused and looked back at the wall of Silver Peak Keep and the shining mountain behind it. "All those years I worked for this place and this is what I get," he muttered bitterly.

Hall studied the former PeakGuard. He didn't know much about Brient's fighting ability, but the man was at least Level Five or Six and wouldn't have advanced to the rank of Sergeant if he didn't know how to hold a sword. But what Hall did know about was Brient's integrity and how he worked. Brient believed in the greater good, the greater justice, and didn't mind bending some rules to get there.

Just the kind of person Hall liked.

"I find myself in need of a Sheriff," Hall started. "It seems my little village has gotten a sudden influx of citizens. And being out in the wilds, they could also use some protection." He finished and smiled at Brient.

The former guard nodded.

"The further from this place, the better," Brient said and followed Hall onto the *Frozen Blade's* gangplank.

CHAPTER FORTY-TWO

"Hold the lines," Hrothgrav barked.

Sailors rushed across the ship as the winds buffeted it. Up, down, side to side. The heavy ship was rocked, the engines barely pushing it forward. They were near a hundred feet over the meadow, Skara Brae a collection of grass slopes and circular dirt road far below. The wind flew down out of the mountains from the north, the Frost Tip Peaks, and slammed into the southern range, the Thunder Growl Mountains. It tried to escape into the plains of Edin but hit the Breakridge, which pushed it up. Over and over the wind swirled, slamming against rock.

Hall hadn't remembered it being as bad down on the meadow itself. There had been wind, not gentle, but not like this. He held onto the railing, watching the land below. Small forms could be seen in the village itself, details hard to see this far up.

"Bring her down," Hrothgrav bellowed.

He stood at the ship's forecastle, next to the helmsman. His sailors ran back and forth, up the lines and across the deck. The helmsmen pulled a couple of the levers next to the great wheel. The engines strained, turning, and the ship's bow pointed downward. Not steeply but at enough of an angle that all aboard had to hold tight.

The wind seemed to push against the *Frozen Blade* but the engines powered it down, and soon it broke through the wind as if through a barrier. There was still wind, still fierce, but now similar to what Hall had expected. The ship settled, more like it had been on the four-day long voyage from Silver Peak Keep.

Hall released the railing, his knuckles white. On somewhat unsteady legs, he walked back toward Hrothgrav, who gave him a chilly look.

"Some warning would have been nice," the large Storvgardian captain growled.

"Had no idea," Hall said in apology.

Hrothgrav grunted.

"You need a dock," the Captain said.

Hall nodded and moved to the rail, Hrothgrav following. He looked down at the edge of the land, the meadow called Breakridge. It was rough, jagged, harsher than any other land's edge where a dock had been built. He glanced at Hrothgrav, skeptical. The big man nodded.

"Don't think can build a stable dock on that."

"What about the flat part of the cliff?" Hall asked and pointed to the north at the highest plateau on the mountains overlooking the meadow.

That mountain had two flat areas, the lower one where Leigh's Grove was, and a higher but smaller one. Hrothgrav shook his head.

"The winds," was all he said.

Hall moved to the back of the airship as he flew over the meadow. He leaned against the railing, looking down at the grass swaying in the wind.

"Suggestions?"

"Bring us down to fifty," Hrothgrav shouted before joining Hall at the railing.

The *Frozen Blade* shuddered, lurching as the engines shifted and started pushing it downward. The ship shook as the crew pulled the sails down.

"Here," Hrothgrav stated. He pointed down at the ground they hovered over, a sheltered niche behind the extending wall of the Thunder Growls. "Pretty protected from the wind. Land docks are rare, but most ships can land on them."

Hall thought about it and nodded. On the voyage up from Silver Peak Keep, he had come to the realization that Skara Brae would need a dock of some kind. The only way to get supplies to the village was by airship, at least until they were self-sustaining. It was too long a trek over dangerous land with no roads. The cost would be too high. Airship was the only way. Which meant a place for the ships to dock and unload.

"Anchors away," Hrothgrave yelled as he walked away.

Hall turned to watch as four sailors ran to the corners of the ship and the light ballista attached to the decking. There were no harpoons loaded. Instead, they set large iron anchors attached to lines tied to cleats on the side of the ship. The anchors had pointed tips with curved spikes just behind, meant to slam into the ground and get lodged in, unable to be pulled out. Once loaded, the sailors tilted the ballista down and pulled the triggers. Four loud blasts of air came from the ship, seconds apart, followed by sounds of rock and dirt erupting. The anchors dug in, the ship swaying in the wind, but being held pretty much in place.

The *Frozen Blade* tilted and lurched but only a couple of feet instead of twenty or more. The anchor lines pulled taut and snapped, but held.

Hall headed to the cabins to gather his stuff, wanting to get out of the way as Hrothgrav supervised the unloading.

———

"Welcome to Skara Brae," Hall said as he led the entire group, including Hrothgrav, toward the village. The airship hovered behind them, the engine noise loud. The rest of Hrothgrav's crew were finishing the unloading, stacking all the goods and materials on the meadow.

Not much of the village was visible from the meadow, just the tops of a few grass-covered roofs. And the Gnomes working on them.

"Are those Gnomes?" Duncant asked, his voice rising shrilly. "What are they doing? They'll ruin it all."

The small Bodin ran toward the homes, yelling and cursing. The Valedale Gnomes stopped working, looking at the strange man rushing at them. They appeared unconcerned with Duncant's wild shouting. They returned to their work as Duncant ran around the bottom of the slopes being ignored.

"Hopefully the Gnomes got some of the walls up," Sabine muttered reaching up to scratch Salem under the chin. The Minx Cat's purring was loud, almost in time with the *Frozen Blade's* engines.

———

Hall sat on a rooftop looking out over the dark sky of night beyond the edge of the meadow, stars and the dark shadows of islands. Behind and below, in the village, he could hear people talking and laughing. They were enjoying themselves, eating and drinking. The Gnomes had indeed restored some of the houses' front walls, cleaned out a couple, and made them somewhat livable. Everyone, including the newcomers, were essentially still rough camping but it was a start.

And things would only get better.

He would work out a delivery rotation with Hrothgrav, and

hopefully, the letters he had sent out would yield results. He had Timmin to help him with the village now, to get things up and running. Brient could start on some defenses. Hitchly and her mother could start farming. Leigh had the Grove to clean up. And there were other areas of the land surrounding Skara Brae to explore. As the *Frozen Blade* had flown in, Hall had noticed a dark spot on the island's cliff below the edge. A cave of some kind.

Pulling up his character sheet, Hall tried to decide where to place his newest Attribute Point. His Agility was looking good, much higher than anything else. He was afraid he was starting to get a little lopsided. As much as he wanted to put the Point into Strength or Wellness, he had a feeling that Charisma or Wisdom would be his best bet. Charisma was something he would need in the days and months ahead if he really wanted Skara Brae to become something.

The available Point disappeared and his Charisma total went from eleven to twelve. He didn't feel any different. *Probably not enough to make a huge difference,* he thought but every little bit would help. Looking over his Character Sheet, Hall was satisfied with his progress. He still had some work to do on the various Skills and to finally decide which ones to keep and which to raise. He was looking forward to exploring the new one, *Strategy*, more.

Closing the Character Sheet, Hall opened the village's Settlement Interface and was surprised at the changes.

Skara Brae Town Stats:
Lord: Hall
Status: Ruins
Morale: N/A

Government: N/A
Appointed Officials: Timmin, Administrator

Brient, Sheriff

Population: 11
Production: Carpentry Rank One - 0%
Farming Rank One - 0%

Faction: None
Allies:Gnomes of Valedale
Brownpaw of Fallen Green
Trade Partners: N/A
Enemies:N/A

Next to Carpentry and Farming under Production were more menus to open. Mentally clicking on Farming, he opened it up to see a listing that had just two names, Hitchly and Dinah. Alongside were Classes and Levels. Each had Farmer as a Class. Hitchly was Level Three and Dinah was Level Five. Next to each of their names was another menu. Opening that, he saw nothing. It was empty, a place for their known crafting patterns and knowledge to populate. Along the top of the main menu was a progress bar, currently at zero. Over it was written "Maximum Daily Output". Hall assumed the rest of the page would get filled in as crops were planted and livestock harvested. A quick look at Carpentry showed the same, just with Duncant's name and Carpenter Level Six. On each of the first menus was another progress bar, along the bottom. Over these was written "Production To Next Rank".

He was going to look deeper into the menus when he heard a noise, someone walking up the stairs from the village below.

"Hall," he heard Leigh's voice. A soft whisper carried on the wind.

"Here," he replied.

A moment later, she was sitting beside him on the roof, looking up at the night sky and the stars.

"Beautiful," she said.

"Yes," Hall replied, but he wasn't looking at the stars.

Leigh smiled and glanced at him shyly.

Hall looked into her eyes. She was an NPC, but so what? He was nothing but a computer program now. This life felt real. It was real. And so was she. He couldn't deny the attraction and knew she felt the same way.

Leaning in, Hall saw her moving closer as well. Their lips met. A deep kiss, a wonderful kiss. A perfect kiss.

Epilogue

"Good morn, Neighbor," the Bodin said as he walked by.

The voice wasn't that shrill, but to Davit it was shrill enough. All Bodin voices were. The NPC ones, anyway. His didn't sound that way. He hated the way it sounded. Hated being a Bodin. But at least his voice was somewhat like his own, just a little sharper.

Davit forced a smile as he waved at that Bodin and the many others he passed. The village, Crackleberry, was filled with them. As it should be. It was a Bodin village after all. Nestled in the Graystone Foothills, a small region on the southern edge of the island of Huntley. They lay in the eastern shadows of the Hardedge Mountains, home to the Dwarven city of Axestorm Hall. The Bodin barely saw their Dwarven neighbors, the two races rarely mixing.

Homes were built into the sides of the hills, some being two or three stories buried underground. Each had a good bit of wooden walls and roofs exposed. The fronts were decorated in wooden designs, planters, and vines. Stone walks led to each from the hard-packed dirt roads that meandered through the village of two hundred Bodin. There was no order. To Davit's eyes it was chaotic.

But it suited the Bodin.

The small race was attuned to the natural elements of the world. Perfect Shamans. Their homes and village reflected that alignment, at one with the natural world. Unlike human cities that seemed to force themselves upon the land, the Bodin village was part of it. Welcomed.

Like Davit had been.

He had been there for three days so far. His story was simple. A wandering adventurer just looking for a place to rest. It was close enough to the truth, even if it wasn't the truth. The villagers had accepted him quickly and easily. Adventurers were rare these days, they said. Used to be so many in and out of the village, exploring the mountains, but not anymore. They had asked questions at first, but he had pushed them off. They wanted to know his adventures. They wanted stories.

He had none to tell.

Could he tell them how he had killed numerous NPCs? How he wasn't one of them? How he was a human male from Earth and had become trapped in the game? How they were just computer programs and he was a true Player? Would they even accept that they were in a game? Would they know what an NPC even was? Would they accept that he was their better?

And he was. Davit knew this.

The villagers had accepted his standoffish nature easily. He was a hardened adventurer, after all. That kind of life couldn't help but weigh on a person. He had a haunted look and they responded. Still friendly, not keeping their distance, but not intruding on his privacy.

Ever since setting foot in Crackleberry, Davit had fought the urge to kill them. He could and would feel no remorse.

But he couldn't.

Not yet.

He was there for a specific reason. There was a job to do.

It had taken nearly two weeks of travel from Colds Ridge. No horse or wagon, just walking. There had been some random encounters, enough to work out his aggression. He had gotten bored and killing was just what he needed.

He had even leveled, gotten to Eight.

Progress was slow, not like before, not like Pre-Glitch. It was just one of the many things that he found annoying now. Pretty much everything was annoying. Especially being trapped in the body of a Bodin.

The women weren't that good looking, not to him. Not like Elves or Humans. But none of the women of those races would look at him. Even though he was a Player and their better. Even the NPCs in Colds Ridge, the town that Iron now controlled. He was one of the Players that controlled that town, one of those in Iron's inner circle. But that didn't matter to them.

Soon he would have to do something about that.

He passed by another Bodin who started to say a greeting but stopped, seeing the look on Davit's face. The other just kept on walking, concerned but not saying a word.

And what was up with that? Davit thought. Who says hello to everyone? All day. Everyday.

It was annoying.

Grumbling to himself, Davit walked toward the far edge of town and his task for the day.

———

Night had fallen. The moon was high, few stars dotted the sky, most of it in shadow from the many islands above. Huntley was low down, below so many others. It received sun during the day but was still cold most of the time. Home to mostly Storvgardians, it was a rough place for rough people. There were other islands below Huntley, places even colder.

Davit had no desire to travel there. Huntley was bad enough.

He quickly moved away from Crackleberry, deeper into the foothills, moving from shadow to shadow. He moved soundlessly, gaining in Stealth. He was close to gaining Rank Three. Any day now. Bush to bush, tree to tree, he made his way further from the annoying village.

It felt good leaving the place. He was glad to be rid of it, even if only for a couple of hours. A day at the most. He would return and finally be able to have his fun with the villagers.

An hour passed and he crested a larger hill, trees on either side. His eyes darted from shadow to shadow, looking but not seeing.

"You're late," a smooth voice said from the side and Davit jumped.

He cursed as the form of Cuthard materialized from the shadows. The Elf was tall, dressed in black. Level Nine, he had already gained Rank Three in *Stealth* and *Camouflage*. Davit cursed again, giving the much taller Elf a sharp look, before continuing on. Cuthard followed along behind, neither bothering to hide the sounds of their steps now.

Up and down a couple more hills and Davit saw the valley spread out below. A large fire burned in the center. Tents surrounded it, laid out in a ring pattern. Organized, in proper rows. As it should be, Davit thought as he walked down to the camp.

He heard snoring, laughing, other sounds coming from the tents. There were close to a hundred of the canvas tents. Each housing a soldier in the army. All Humans. All Storvgardians. All NPCs. Some of them turned and watched the tall Elf and short Bodin, standing out among the sea of Humans. But these

NPCs knew their place. They knew their betters when they saw them.

Ignoring the soldiers, Davit and Cuthard made their way through the camp, heading for the large figure in lost shadow before the fire. The flames rose high, ten feet in the air, logs laid in a pyramid, burning brightly. Iron stood facing the flames, shadows dancing across his large frame. Sitting on logs next to him, talking quietly, were Thellia and Corinth. The Half-Elf Skirmisher and Norn Shaman were always talking quietly. About what, Davit had no idea. The two women barely talked to him.

It had been two months since they had taken Colds Ridge. A month since their army had grown and Iron had become the leader of the Jorgunmund Clan, Storvgardian Barbarians that lived on the plains of Huntley near Colds Ridge. The large Warden had killed their Clan Chief at their village of Great Deer. That one act had gained them an army.

A small village, as the clan's village was smaller than Crackleberry and a Colds Ridge. That was all they had. For now. And it was a start.

Iron looked over his shoulder at Davit.

"Well?" he asked, his voice deep.

The army wouldn't grow with the destruction of Crackleberry. They would not bring many, if any at all, of the Bodin into their ranks. They wouldn't even leave a token force behind, or anyone in charge of the survivors. The destruction of Crackleberry was just to send a message to everyone living on Huntley.

It was a simple message.

Iron's Army was here.

ALSO IN THE SERIES

GRAYHOLD

YOU JUST READ: **SILVER PEAK**

UP NEXT: AXESTORM

About Troy Osgood

**LitRPG: the genre I always wanted to be writing in
but didn't know it until recently.**

I can't thank you enough for the reception *Grayhold* has gotten.
I've been amazed and humbled. Hopefully you enjoyed *Silver
Peak* just as much and look forward to the third book, *Axestorm*,
and all the others to come. And there are a lot. I hinted at my
plans for SRO and I'm waiting to see how well *Silver Peak* and
Axestorm are received before really committing to those plans,
but do I have plans. Lots and lots of plans.

And you might have thought you missed something with
the time jump that occurs between *Grayhold* and *Silver Peak* but
that story is yet to be told (it's coming). There will be another
jump between *Silver Peak* and *Axestorm* with that adventure yet
to be told. I plan on doing similar between all the main books.

By the time this comes out, *Axestorm* will be done and off to the editors. And the first Sky Realms Online spin-off will be launching either with the publishing of *Silver Peak* or sometime before *Hardedge*. Work-In-Progress chapters will be released on my Patreon page until such a time as it's ready for publication.

There is an endgame-goal for Sky Realms Online. Everything (including spin-offs by me) will be working towards that epic ending. It's a ways off but it will happen. Someday. A long time from now.

Join/follow the many ways to get ahold of me on Social Media. Facebook (facebook.com/ossywrites), my blog (www.ossywrites.com), Twitter (@troynos), Instagram (OssyWrites) and my newsletter (https://www.ossynews.com). That's the best way to get information on upcoming projects and when the Patreon launches (which you'll want to check out the book being shown there, it's a great spin-off in the overall SRO story).

You can find me in a lot of the litRPG related Facebook groups. I'm not shy, so drop a line and say hi. I'd appreciate it if say how much you love the book. Word of mouth is big in this genre. Please drop reviews on Amazon, Goodreads and Audible.

I'm a big craft beer fan and you can visit me on Untappd (troynos). I'm always looking for recommendations for beers and breweries.

Now for the thanks. I am still amazed at the job **Aethon Books** does with my work. I look at it and can't believe it's mine. **Steve Beaulieu** and **Rhett Bruno** are great to work with and do amazing stuff on their own. Have to thank Rhett and Steve for hooking me up with **Pavi Proczko**. His narration of the world and characters is amazing. Check out everything Aethon puts out. You won't be disappointed. My editor, **Holly Jennings**, did a great job catching my mistakes and helping wordsmith a couple parts.

How about that cover? Grayhold was beautiful but

Jackson Tjota knocked Silver Peak out of the park. Isn't that cover stunning?

And as always, without the love and support of my girls (**Kat**, **Heaven** and **Paisley**) none of this would be possible. Thank you girls. 3000 is too low, I love you to infinity.

Again, please leave a review on Amazon, Goodreads, and Audible. Reviews are the lifeblood for the indie/small press author.

See you in the next book,

Troy

Newsletter: https://www.ossynews.com

Don't forget to join LitRPG Addicts and come hang out with me!

I'm also very active and thankful for LitRPG Books and GameLit Society

To learn more about LitRPG, talk to authors including myself, and just have an awesome time, please join the LitRPG Group

FROM THE PUBLISHER

Thank you for reading *Silver Peak,* book two in Sky Realms Online.

We hope you enjoyed it as much as we enjoyed bringing it to you. We just wanted to take a moment to encourage you to review the book on Amazon and Goodreads. Every review helps further the author's reach and, ultimately, helps them continue writing fantastic books for us all to enjoy.

If you liked this book, check out the rest of our catalogue at www.aethonbooks.com. To sign up to receive a FREE collection from some of our best authors as well updates regarding all new releases, visit www.aethonbooks.com/sign-up.

SPECIAL THANKS TO:

ADAWIA E. ASAD
JENNY AVERY
BARDE PRESS
CALUM BEAULIEU
BEN
BECKY BEWERSDORF
BHAM
TANNER BLOTTER
ALFRED JOSEPH BOHNE IV
CHAD BOWDEN
ERREL BRAUDE
DAMIEN BROUSSARD
CATHERINE BULLINER
JUSTIN BURGESS
MATT BURNS
BERNIE CINKOSKE
MARTIN COOK
ALISTAIR DILWORTH
JAN DRAKE
BRET DULEY
RAY DUNN
ROB EDWARDS
RICHARD EYRES
MARK FERNANDEZ
CHARLES T FINCHER
SYLVIA FOIL
GAZELLE OF CAERBANNOG
DAVID GEARY
MICHEAL GREEN
BRIAN GRIFFIN

EDDIE HALLAHAN
JOSH HAYES
PAT HAYES
BILL HENDERSON
JEFF HOFFMAN
GODFREY HUEN
JOAN QUERALTÓ IBÁÑEZ
JONATHAN JOHNSON
MARCEL DE JONG
KABRINA
PETRI KANERVA
ROBERT KARALASH
VIKTOR KASPERSSON
TESLAN KIERINHAWK
ALEXANDER KIMBALL
JIM KOSMICKI
FRANKLIN KUZENSKI
MEENAZ LODHI
DAVID MACFARLANE
JAMIE MCFARLANE
HENRY MARIN
CRAIG MARTELLE
THOMAS MARTIN
ALAN D. MCDONALD
JAMES MCGLINCHEY
MICHAEL MCMURRAY
CHRISTIAN MEYER
SEBASTIAN MÜLLER
MARK NEWMAN
JULIAN NORTH

KYLE OATHOUT
LILY OMIDI
TROY OSGOOD
GEOFF PARKER
NICHOLAS (BUZ) PENNEY
JASON PENNOCK
THOMAS PETSCHAUER
JENNIFER PRIESTER
RHEL
JODY ROBERTS
JOHN BEAR ROSS
DONNA SANDERS
FABIAN SARAVIA
TERRY SCHOTT
SCOTT
ALLEN SIMMONS
KEVIN MICHAEL STEPHENS
MICHAEL J. SULLIVAN
PAUL SUMMERHAYES
JOHN TREADWELL
CHRISTOPHER J. VALIN
PHILIP VAN ITALLIE
JAAP VAN POELGEEST
FRANCK VAQUIER
VORTEX
DAVID WALTERS JR
MIKE A. WEBER
PAMELA WICKERT
JON WOODALL
BRUCE YOUNG

Printed in the USA
CPSIA information can be obtained
at www.ICGtesting.com
CBHW020842130424
6870CB00039B/278